The Believer's Game

The Believer's Game

BOOK TWO

HALCIE DAWN

Halcie Dawn
CARE ANNOUNCEMENT

Halcie Dawn's novels contain serious and complex content.

For a full list of Trigger Warnings and/or Content Warnings, please visit
https://www.halciedawn.com/my-books

For everyone who loves Crutch and Ella
I pray you love Holt and Merit too...
because this is just the beginning.

And

For everyone who loves Danny Kaye, Gene Kelly,
Clark Gable, James Dean, John Wayne,
Dean Martin, Cary Grant, and Elvis
This one's for you.

Author's Note

The Believer's Game is Book Two in *The Skeptic's Duet*.
This is not a standalone novel and you should first read...
The Skeptic's Playbook: The Skeptic's Duet Book One

The Hill Family Universe

The Skeptic's Duet is a standalone duet in a larger, interconnected parent series of duets and novels—*The Hill Family Universe*. While *The Skeptic's Duet* can be enjoyed by itself, the reader will experience a more immersive and pleasurable reading journey if *The Reality Duet* (*Escaping Our Reality* & *Finding Our Reality*) is read first. *The Skeptic's Duet* <u>will</u> contain spoilers about your favorite Hill Family characters and events from *The Reality Duet*.

Merit's Movie Playlist

White Christmas
(1954) Bing Crosby, Danny Kaye, Rosemary Clooney, Vera-Ellen

Singin' in the Rain
(1952) Gene Kelly, Donald O'Connor, Debbie Reynolds

The Wizard of Oz
(1939) Judy Garland, Jack Haley, Ray Bolger, Bert Lahr, Margaret Hamilton, Frank Morgan

Anchors Aweigh
(1945) Gene Kelly, Frank Sinatra, Kathryn Grayson

An Affair to Remember
(1957) Cary Grant, Deborah Kerr

Blue Hawaii
(1961) Elvis Presley, Joan Blackman, Nancy Walters, Jenny Maxwell

The Court Jester
(1955) Danny Kaye, Glynis Johns, Basil Rathbone, Angela Lansbury

An American in Paris
(1951) Gene Kelly, Leslie Caron, Oscar Levant, Georges Guétary

The Ghost and Mr. Chicken
(1966) Don Knotts, Joan Staley

Mary Poppins
(1964) Julie Andrews, Dick Van Dyke, David Tomlinson, Glynis Johns

The Apple Dumpling Gang
(1975) Don Knotts, Tim Conway, Bill Bixby, Susan Clark

Rear Window
(1954) James Stewart, Grace Kelly

Teacher's Pet
(1958) Clark Gable, Doris Day

Some Like It Hot
(1959) Marilyn Monroe, Tony Curtis, Jack Lemmon

Yours, Mine, and Ours
(1968) Lucille Ball, Henry Fonda

It's a Wonderful Life
(1946) James Stewart, Frank Capra, Donna Reed

Giant
(1956) Elizabeth Taylor, Rock Hudson, James Dean

Spencer's Mountain
(1963) Henry Fonda, Maureen O'Hara

The Parent Trap
(1961) Hayley Mills, Maureen O'Hara, Brian Keith

Pillow Talk
(1959) Rock Hudson, Doris Day

McLintock!

(1963) John Wayne, Maureen O'Hara, Patrick Wayne, Stefanie Powers

Honky Tonk

(1941) Clark Gable, Lana Turner

Double Indemnity

(1944) Fred MacMurray, Barbara Stanwyck, Edward G Robinson

Butch Cassidy and the Sundance Kid

(1969) Paul Newman, Robert Redford, Katharine Ross

Rio Bravo

(1959) John Wayne, Dean Martin, Ricky Nelson

The Man Who Shot Liberty Valance

(1962) James Stewart, John Wayne

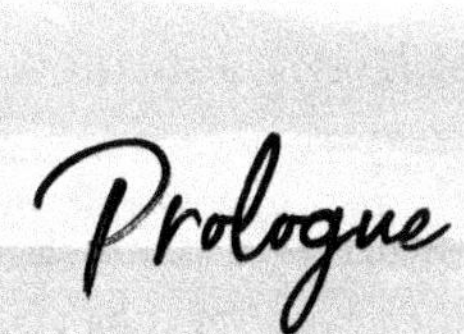

Prologue

Merit

Do you ever wish you could turn back time?

I do.

The question is... would I turn back time to before I even met Holt? What if I slipped out of the store for an errand before he came in to pick up those purple shoes? Then my heart wouldn't be breaking now.

Or... would I want to keep the love we shared—keep those months we had together safe and sound in a glass box, where I could watch them play on repeat over and over any time I wanted—and only turn back the last fifteen minutes? Because fifteen minutes ago, he loved me. Fifteen minutes ago, I wasn't a vindictive she-devil framing him for a horrific crime.

Well, to be honest, I'm *still* not a vindictive she-devil framing him for a horrific crime.

But he thinks I am.

Why? How?

I have no idea.

All I know is that after just one day with the attorneys and Marcum and Ella, I'm the bad guy.

I guess that means his mind is made up. Turning back the clock a measly fifteen minutes wouldn't make any sort of difference. The same accusations, the same anger, the same hate would have hit me no matter when I came home.

It's all my fault, really. I knew from the get go that I shouldn't date—and I said as much to him. And I *definitely* knew I shouldn't date someone so damn rich.

My worst fear has just been confirmed... Holt is so much worse than Edward ever was.

My tears stop falling somewhere on the walk down the marble hallway from the Big House to the Children's Wing. For the first one-hundred steps, I keep hoping that he will run up behind me, fall to his knees, and beg for forgiveness. Plead temporary insanity. Beg me to never leave him. Tell me that he loves me. That he will love me forever. That I'm his one and only. That he can't live without me.

Because you know what? I would forgive him.

I would forgive him in less time than it takes my heart to pump one single beat.

But I hit step one-hundred, and nothing happens. I actually stop walking for a second, hold my breath, and listen.

There are no hurried footsteps. No shouts telling me to wait, to stop. No...nothing.

Well, I'm sure there's *something*. There's probably a gaggle of frenzied and wild conversations among the pretentious-as-fuck lawyers, my now ex-asshole-boyfriend, and his douchebag family members. They're probably smoking congratulatory cigars and patting themselves on the back for finding the real criminal with such little effort.

I'm just glad I can't hear them from here. Because if I could? Let's just say I might do something that would turn me into a real criminal and not just the one they think I am.

My foot edges forward, ready to take step one-hundred-and-one. This step will change everything, the entire course of my life. After this step, there's no possibility of forgiveness. There's no redemption, no second chance. No second act.

I force myself to take a deep breath, and then I put one foot in front of the other, slowly picking up speed until I sprint the rest of the way to the Children's Wing. Racing to the closet, I grab every suitcase and duffel bag I own and fling them across the bed. I grab handfuls of clothes and toiletries, haphazardly tossing everything in. I drop all my jewelry in a Ziploc bag, taking extra care to wrap my diamond and ruby bracelet in layers and layers of paper towels to protect it. Wanting to keep that safe, I put it in my purse. When I realize I don't have any moving boxes for all of my old movies, I decide to steal Holt's laundry baskets. He already thinks I framed him for a sexual crime and attempted to steal millions of dollars, he can just add the three stupid, plastic clothes baskets to my tab.

I'm running around like a chicken with its head cut off. Sweat pours from my brow and trails between my breasts, soaking my bra. My heartbeat is erratic. So erratic I'm worried I may pass out. Trotting to the fridge, I grab a bottle of regular Coke and down it in just a few swallows, trying to stave off the inevitable fall of adrenaline. Of course, that just gives me gas bubbles in my stomach and makes me belch for the next five minutes straight.

I'm in such a hurry, I debate leaving my meager kitchen utensils and cooking supplies instead of packing them.

But I quickly change my mind.

Fuck that.

Holt just accused me of playing him as a long-con with Heidi. The last thing I'm gonna do is reward him with a free pizza cutter. I'm quickly running out of packing room, so I toss what I can on top of my clothes in the suitcases and bags. I'll be lucky if said pizza cutter doesn't slice my panties to bits.

Hauling what I can in my arms, I open the door so I can put the first load of stuff in my car. Of course, I'm not really surprised when I see two beefy security guards standing in front of my SUV. I've done nothing but smile and be nice to these guys since they started, and here they are trying to intimidate me.

I reckon Holt doesn't have the balls to do it himself.

"Ma'am," says the guy with brown hair, "we've been asked to document what you're taking with you. We need to confirm that nothing of value to Mr. Hill is leaving the premises."

Well, *I'm* leaving the premises.

And Holt used to think I was valuable. Does that count?

I shuffle my bags and hit the key fob to lift the tailgate of my SUV. "And how do you plan to do that? Do you know what belongs to *Mr. Hill* and what doesn't?"

"We've been asked to video record everything. Mr. Hill and his counsel will review it. If anything was taken without his permission, we…" he nods to the red-haired guy next to him, "would be tasked with retrieving it from you at a later date."

I can't help but roll my eyes. This weirdo even lowered his voice when delivering that threat. I may not be the sharpest knife in the drawer, but even I know that these private security guards have no jurisdiction to bust into my store and confiscate something they think may be stolen.

I could say no. I could completely ignore them. But what's the point? At this juncture of my day, Holt would probably call the cops if I refused, and I really don't feel like dealing with a mob of police swarming around me.

Been there, done that. Never want it again.

"Fine," I huff. He pulls out his cell phone and turns it on to record our interaction, but he makes no move to get out of my way. I sweep my hand in the air, pointing at my open tailgate. "You mind? I'd like to get the hell out of here."

Nodding, he finally steps to the side. I wrangle everything back into my arms. Something in my pink duffel bag keeps stabbing me in the shin. Could be a fork. Or a knife. Or tweezers. Or a clothes hanger. The possibilities are endless.

Red-haired guy clears his throat, drawing my attention. He at least has the decency to look empathetic. "Ma'am, I'm happy to help. Are there other bags I can grab for you?"

"Everything piled on the floor between the kitchen and living room comes with me."

Nodding, he heads inside. The dick with the camera lifts a brow at the luggage I just loaded. "I'll need to catalog what's in those."

Growling, I unzip everything and start rummaging through it all by hand, messing it up even further and praying I don't accidentally shiv myself with the metal kabob skewers that are playing hide-and-seek somewhere in these bags. "Here. You happy? If the famous Holt Hill needs to catalog my T-shirts and half-used shampoo bottles, be my guest."

I stand back, giving him free rein. Red-haired guy makes three trips in and out, carefully packing my items in the trunk and back seat. Of course, brown-haired guy comes right behind him and tosses everything around, trying to make sure the video has an eye on every single thing I'm taking with me. Closing the back seat door, he walks around to the tailgate, glancing in one last time. "This everything? Nothing in here belongs to Mr. Hill?"

I toss my head back and look up at the sky, slowly counting to five and begging Heaven and all the angels above for strength. Sighing deeply, I reach in the trunk area and start turning the clothes baskets upside down, dumping Blu-rays, DVDs, and all sorts of miscellaneous crap on top of my luggage. One by one, I heave the laundry baskets over my head and into the yard.

"There," turning back to my car, I point to the massive heap of my life, "all good now. I'm not taking anything that belongs to him. Not one damn thing." Slamming the door—well, as much as I can, I mean, it's an automatic shut—I fling my hand in their direction as I walk to the driver side. "Gentlemen, I'd say it's been a pleasure, but I think I've done enough lying for one day."

I'm opening my door when he throws one last jab my way. "And your purse? I need to check that as well."

"Seriously?" I thrust my face in his camera, probably giving nothing but a view of my snotty nose and red eyes. "Holt, you want back that pack of gum you bought me a few weeks ago? Tough shit, I already chewed it."

Brown-haired guy just purses his lips. Needless to say, he's not amused. "Ma'am, please..."

I shove my purse in his arms and slide behind the wheel. Peering straight ahead, not giving him the satisfaction of seeing how much this bothers me, I start the engine and grip the steering wheel so tightly my knuckles turn white. I wonder if I can peel my tires when I'm pulling out. How fast do you have to go for that to happen? I mean, the driveway's pretty long; I might be able to achieve it.

"What do we have here?"

His voice catches me off guard, and when I turn, I nearly fall out of the car when I see him holding my great-grandmother's bracelet.

And here I was thinking things couldn't get any worse.

"That's mine," I say, eagerly reaching for it. "Don't touch it."

He quickly pulls it from my grasp and dangles it in the air, like a master teasing a pet with a toy.

"Yours?" he questions, pinning me with a stare. "You think this is yours?"

"I know it's mine, you inconsiderate asshole. It belonged to my great-grandmother." I wiggle my fingers at him. "Now, give it back. I'm leaving."

He just smirks, like he caught me with my hand in the cookie jar. "If it's yours, then you won't have any problem with me confirming that with Mr. Hill."

I grind my teeth so hard my jaw hurts. "Check all you want. But call him." I point a finger in his face, "Because if you walk back into *that* house with *my* bracelet, I'll be the one calling the cops. And I'll march my butt right over there," I nod my head in the general direction of the street where we know paparazzi and reporters are camped out, "and tell them Holt's security team is stealing from me."

Mumbling something under his breath that doesn't sound too friendly, he glances over at red-haired guy. "Call Mr. Hill and confirm." He twists the bracelet back and forth. "Looks like diamonds and... I don't know... some kind of red stone."

And for the next three minutes, I have a staring contest with brown-haired guy and his cell phone camera. I should know because I count all one-hundred-and-eighty seconds in my head.

Eventually, red-haired guy comes back from wherever he wandered off to and simply says, "It's hers."

Scowling, he drops my bracelet back in the Ziploc bag, not even bothering to rewrap it in paper towels. As soon as my purse touches my fingers, I slam the door and pull out of the driveway as fast as I can.

No squealing tires, though.

And for some stupid reason, that makes me even sadder.

Fortunately, I'm able to hold my head high as I turn onto the street—just long enough for the photographers to get whatever picture they can. But as soon as I'm far enough away, as soon as the house I called home is little more than a tiny blip in my rearview mirror, I burst into tears.

I'm crying so hard I can barely see to drive. My sobs are so big and powerful, my lungs begin to ache. Sucking in deep, shaky breaths, I blink through my tears as I press the button on my SUV's Bluetooth to call Kyra.

She answers on the first ring.

"Close the shop early. I need you."

Her pause is quick. Only a millisecond. But in that millisecond, my best friend can hear my heart breaking. She can *feel* my pain, my sorrow. The end of my life as I know it.

And her words are like a salve to my throbbing head and pulverized heart. "Meet me at my apartment. I'm on my way."

Chapter 1

Merit

Ibump Kyra with my hip. "Thanks for letting me bum your couch for the past two months."

"How many times are you gonna thank me? It's a couch, not a suite at the Four Seasons." She watches as a mover carries one of the last boxes out of the store. "I still can't believe this is the end."

The end.

Yep. That's what this is.

I should feel worse than I do. But mostly, I'm just numb. I've grown accustomed to the numbness. I wear it like a weighted blanket, letting it drown me in heaviness and comfort. Because anything is better than those first few days, when I was basically catatonic.

So, yeah, I'll take the numbness over that any day of the week. At least with the numbness there's a dull buzzing humming around in my veins, giving me that druggy feeling of being half-awake, half-asleep. At a minimum, it allows me to function at a somewhat human-like level.

Which was needed. On more than one occasion.

You know, like when I was being hauled into the police department.

Turns out, confessing to a crime you didn't commit in front of a bunch of lawyers—and on videotape, no less—is not a smart idea. In fact, it's pretty fucking moronic.

It feels like I've been interviewed by every person with a badge this side of the Mason Dixon.

I thought for sure I was going to be arrested. Turns out, the wheels of justice move slowly when the police and prosecutors think they already have the right guy. I know Holt's legal team is pushing as hard as they can for more answers and more investigating, but I'm not sure they're getting very far.

The world still thinks Holt's guilty. And on top of that, other breaking and hot-topic news has come and gone, taking with it some of the limelight and pressure of deepening the police investigation. He's still a predominant focus of conversation, don't get me wrong; but he's gone from being splayed across every news show in the country in non-stop fashion to just a weekly follow-up story.

That is, except for the trolls who follow him, posting his whereabouts to social media on a daily basis, ensuring that he remains a pariah to all the fans who once sang his praises.

And he should be a pariah—worse than a pariah—if in fact, he were guilty.

But he's not.

Oh, he's guilty of many things...mainly being an epic asshole to me...but that doesn't mean he's guilty of the crime he was arrested for.

Despite my deep-seated hatred of him and contempt for what he did to me, I've never wavered from my belief in his innocence when it comes to Heidi.

Most people would say that makes me a fool. And I guess it does.

But the vitriol that's been cast his way still hurts my already-decomposed heart. People are just plain sick. There was even a ten-thousand-dollar bounty for someone to actually stab him in the scrotum and capture it on video.

I take a deep breath, refusing to drag any part of that into my last few minutes in the store. I'm lucky things worked out the way they did. I'm lucky I found a buyer for all of my inventory—he even wanted the shelving units and the computer system. I'm also very lucky my landlord let me break the lease. That part was definitely questionable when I was trying to pressure wash the painted dicks off the sidewalk.

And repair the broken window.

And clean the graffiti from the brick.

"So, you plan on moving back home after graduation in May?"

Kyra shrugs. "Well, I thought *this* was my home."

I frown. "Kyra..." My voice trails off, silently begging her to be strong. She knows I don't have any fight left. It's hard to keep a business afloat when you have absolutely no customers.

"But yeah, I guess I'll move back in with my parents until I figure out what's next. Toby's already looking for work positions up in my hometown," she says, talking about her boyfriend.

I snort. "I reckon there's a lot of that going around."

Digging in my purse, I pull out a small envelope and slide it in front of her.

"What's that?"

"Your paycheck." Being the best friend that she is, Kyra didn't even take a paycheck this last month. She knew the money was coming from my parents, and she refused to take it. "And before you say anything, it's not from my parents. It's from this," I say, nodding to the mover taking out the last box.

She shakes her head. "You need it. Add it to your pile for *him*."

I clear my throat, thinning my lips. "I have all I need. Don't you worry about that. I'm taking care of it before I leave town."

Kyra blows a raspberry. "What a shitty day. And you still have to see your douchebag ex-husband too?"

"Yep, but I'm focusing on the positive. I'll get the last of my stuff from Edward's attic, and then I'll never have to lay eyes on him again. I consider that a win in my book."

Kyra picks at a spot on her shirt. "What am I supposed to do without you?"

I wrap my arms around her. "Live your life and be happy. Put all this nastiness behind you." I kiss her cheek and look out the window. "Because that's exactly what I plan to do."

Sometimes, I wonder what it would feel like to punch someone.

More specifically, what it would feel like to punch my ex-husband.

He picks up on the fifth ring. "Edward, I've been waiting for thirty minutes. Are you nearly here?"

"No, I'm still on the golf course. We're behind a slow group." He rambles around, asking someone to bring him a putter. "Are you still wanting your stuff?"

What a stupid question.

I roll my eyes. "Of course, I want my stuff. That's why I'm here. You told me you would be back by now."

"Well, Merit, I have no control over the other people on the golf course."

"I want my stuff, Edward," I say, internally berating myself. I was a fool to keep some of my keepsakes in the attic after our divorce—my college diploma, photo albums, some antique china from my great-grandmother.

"Well, listen, Delaney should be on her way home from the gym. I already texted her and told her you need to get in the attic, okay."

Growling, I hang up on him and spend the next fifteen minutes tapping my hand against the steering wheel. When she doesn't show up, I text Edward, telling him that I'm going inside to get my stuff and that I'll lock up behind me. I really don't want to be here anymore. I have the world's worst errand to run after this, and this delay is doing nothing to calm my anxiety.

Walking around to the garage door, I enter the code on the keypad and wait for the door to lift, but nothing happens. I enter the code again. Still nothing happens. Abandoning that, I go to the front door and try that alarm keypad. The red light blinks at me, telling me I've entered the code wrong. I try again. Same thing. I pull out my phone and text Edward again, asking him if he changed the code to get into the house. Of course, he doesn't text back. The whole time I lived here, it was the date he passed the bar exam. I can only assume Delaney changed it.

With no other option, I flop down on the front steps and try not to flip my shit while waiting for Delaney. Ten minutes later, she finally pulls into the driveway. Refusing to walk to the driveway to meet her, I recline back on my elbows and watch her. She doesn't even look like she's worked out. There's no dewy glow. Her makeup and lipstick are still pristine. And her thousand-dollar, skintight outfit doesn't have the first sweat stain.

"Merit, good to see you." She places her sunglasses on top of her head.

"Uh-huh. Yeah."

"Edward told me you had some things you were needing to retrieve from the attic."

I nod.

She cocks her head and looks at me like I'm the most pitiful woman she's ever seen. "Leaving town, I heard."

I stand up and wipe the dirt from my butt. "I'm in a little bit of a hurry so if we can..." I say, twirling my finger in the air, nonverbally telling her to get the show on the road.

"Oh, absolutely." She shifts her custom handbag from one arm to the other. Leaning forward, she pauses over the keypad. "By the way, I received an alert on my phone that someone tried to disarm and enter." She cocks an eyebrow. "Was that you?"

I fold my hands in front of me, hoping my face isn't bright red. "Like I said, I'm in a hurry."

She grimaces with a fake smile. Turning her shoulder to block my view, she starts punching numbers. Entering the code, the keypad blinks green, and she opens the front door. The inside alarm chirps, letting her know all is clear.

But I don't follow her inside.

Because I can't move.

I'm frozen in place. It feels like I'm permanently glued to the concrete.

I'm paralyzed because her shoulders are skinny and petite. And I'm way taller than she is. I'm paralyzed because...turning her body didn't block shit.

1102.

She changed the alarm and entry code to 1102.

The date Holt found Mr. Hard Knock.

That has to be a coincidence, right?

Maybe her birthday is November 2nd? Maybe it's the last four digits of her Social Security number? The street number of her childhood home? The number of men she's had sex with?

A slow burn travels through my body, scalding my every nerve-ending. It feels like I've been dipped in acid. Like I'm being eaten alive.

Something tells me this is no coincidence. Something tells me there's more to the story.

So. Much. More.

"Merit!"

In a fog, I turn and look at her. Delaney rolls her eyes and sweeps her arm across the foyer. "I thought you were in a hurry?"

"Oh. Yeah." I force myself to put one foot in front of the other. My legs feel hot and heavy, like they're filled with lava and lead. My feet awkwardly plop forward, clunking across the foyer.

Shaking her head, she scoffs. She pretends to mumble under her breath, but it's still loud enough for me to hear. "Yep, Edward was right. Airhead." She puts her stuff on the small entry table and nods to the stairs. "You good? I'm assuming you remember where the attic is." Not waiting for my answer, she disappears around the corner. "You can let yourself out. I'm heading into the sauna." She's trying to point out the fact that Edward installed a sauna for her. Because it's definitely not something we had when I lived here.

I'm shaking uncontrollably. I have to grip the handrail to keep from falling. In record time, I gather my three boxes. Technically, I should make two trips, but I'm so damn nervous and anxious I just want to get out of the house. I lift my chin, trying to peer over the top box so I don't trip. I'm about to cross the threshold when something catches my eye.

A cell phone.

Delaney's cell phone.

I'm not exactly sure what possesses me to take it. But I do.

Then, I haul ass across town.

I don't even have to knock on the door before someone opens it. That's the benefit of living in a secluded area—you can always hear when someone's driving up.

My heart warms when I see Crutch holding Hardy. The baby opens an eye and then quickly decides he's too tired to stay awake. "Merit..."

"Hey, Crutch."

"It's good to see you." His tone is a mixture of surprise, relief, and trepidation. He looks out on the porch, making sure I'm alone. "What are you doing here?"

"I was hoping I could speak to Ella for a second. Do you think that would be okay?"

It must be because he shifts to the side, giving me access to his house. He disappears into the kitchen.

"Merit!"

My crumbled heart breaks a little bit more when I see Laura. I guess I didn't realize how much I missed Holt's family—especially the kids. She's sitting on the living room floor, using the coffee table as a desk. Papers and art supplies are scattered all around.

"Hey, Laura."

She looks down at her lap, debating getting up and giving me a hug, but she's covered in glitter and magazine clippings. "I wanna hug you, but I'm messy. I'm doing a project for school."

I shrug. "Well, a little glitter never hurt anyone."

Smiling, she jumps up and wraps her arms around me. For some reason, when Ella walks in, I can't help but feel a little guilty.

Crutch rubs the top of her head. "Little Girl, you wanna keep an eye on Hardy? He's in his swing in the kitchen."

Too wise for her age, her gaze darts to all three of us adults, appraising us with critical eyes. "You mean, you wanna talk about grown-up stuff and don't want me to hear, right?"

He just rolls his eyes and playfully slaps her on the bottom. "Get," he commands, nodding at the kitchen.

Giving me one last hug, she dramatically tiptoes out of the room.

It makes me wanna freakin' cry.

Ella reaches out. She's about to rub my shoulder when she changes her mind. Instead, her hand falls limply to her side. "Hi, Merit."

"Hey."

She looks me over. "You look good. Are you doing okay?"

I look down at the floor. How am I supposed to answer that? Does she actually want the truth? Or just a pleasantry? Playing it safe, I settle into formality. After all, it's my safe place. "I'm well. Thank you for asking."

She side glances at her husband. "You need to speak with me?"

I nod, looking down at the bulging manila envelope in my hand. My entire body trembles. I take a deep breath, trying to steady myself. "I was hoping you could give this to Holt." My voice cracks when I say his name.

"What is it?"

I nod, giving her permission to look inside. Her eyes widen, and she gasps.

Crutch looks over her shoulder. His handsome face studies mine. "Money?" he asks.

"I started saving the day I found out he paid off my loan. It's every penny I owe him. That includes the money I spent on his credit card for the Christmas inventory I bought."

"Where did you get this money?" Ella's curiosity is immediately piqued. I guess it's a valid question considering she's on Holt's defense team, and I *am* a prime suspect.

I snort. "Nothing illegal, if that's what you're thinking."

She frowns. "That's not what I was thinking."

"Well, I just wanted to drop it off before I left town."

"You're leaving town?" Crutch seems surprised. "For a few days?"

"Forever. I'm going home." I'm pissed when my voice cracks again on the word home. It's strange how our definition of that word can shift in the blink of an eye.

Neither of them says anything, so I can only assume I've shocked the words right out of them. I debate using their stunned demeanor to my advantage and sprinting out of the house, but I blurt out my next sentence, forcing myself to stay. "There's something else." I sigh, praying I don't sound like a lunatic. "I was at Edward's house today. I had to get some of my things from his attic."

"Okay..." Ella draws out her word, unsure where this story is going.

"Well, I couldn't get the door open. Apparently, Delaney changed the alarm code." I lick my lips. "She... she changed it to... 1102."

Ella's brow furrows. Crutch actually takes a step back and drags his hand across his jaw in thought.

"That's weird, right?" I look back and forth between the two of them. "Anyway," I reach in my right back pocket, "I thought you might wanna take a look at her phone."

Ella turns the phone over and looks at the screen. "Merit, did you steal Delaney's phone?"

Based on her reaction, I'm assuming stealing it would be really, really bad. "Uhhh... she let me borrow it," I say, tripping over my lie.

When Crutch whispers a curse, I ignore him. "She doesn't even have a passcode on it."

"Did you look in her phone?" Ella asks.

"No, I was afraid I'd get accused of planting evidence."

"Merit," Ella scolds.

I hold out my hands, refusing to get into a fight. "I just thought the whole thing was weird. I'm not sure why I took it," I say, coming clean. All of a sudden, I feel like a complete idiot. "But Crutch is a cop. He can return it for me. If she wants to press charges, I would understand."

Ella looks at her husband, nodding at him in their unspoken language. He walks down the hall, into his office. "Well, it's kind of ironic that we are talking about cell phones."

"Why is that ironic?"

Crutch returns and hands me a folded piece of paper. Nerves fire in my stomach. "What's this?"

Ella lifts her chin in the air, steeling herself. When I first met her, I thought that her attitude and mannerisms were just plain bitchy. Come to find out, she's one of the nicest and funniest women I've ever known. She just has a different persona for the uncomfortable situations in life—I guess we're kind of like long-lost soul sisters, if you think about it. "It's a subpoena. For your cell phone records. It was served to your cell phone provider on Friday. We're not required to tell you. But," her voice softens, "I... well, I'm not sure why I'm telling you."

A black shroud falls over me. Anger bounces around in my brain like a ping-pong ball. Skirting around the coffee table, I grab Laura's ink pen and write my username and password on the bottom of the legal document. "My passcode is four zeros." Grabbing my own cell phone from my other back pocket, I wrap the paper around it and give it to Ella. "Here's my username and password. I pretty much use the same ones on every single app on my phone." I chuckle cynically. "I know you're not supposed to, but..."

"You don't have to do that," Crutch says.

I wave him off and turn away. I'm just ready to get the hell out of here.

"I'll get your phone back to you as soon as possible. How can I get ahold of you?"

"Keep it. I'm changing my number."

Holt

Out of nervous habit, I scroll through my camera roll, torturing myself with images of Merit.

Smiling, laughing, happy Merit.

Sexy Merit.

My Merit.

"You ready for this?" Ridge asks. He catches a glance of my phone before I pocket it. "You talk to her yet?"

He knows the damn answer. He knows I would've told him if I had talked to her. "You know the answer to that."

He folds his arms across his chest. "You're such an idiot. What are you waiting for?"

He's right; I'm an idiot. I should've called her the day—months ago—when Crutch first tracked down her new cell phone number for me.

Fuck that, I should've burned up the roads and driven to the farm like a bat out of hell the second they cut off my ankle monitor.

But I didn't.

I nod to the people setting up the cameras and interview area on Crutch and Ella's patio. The TV people decided to use the pond as the background. We're just waiting on the sun to set behind the trees.

"You think that's magically gonna make it easier?" he asks.

And of course, I know the answer to that one...nope. Not one damn thing about talking to Merit will be easy, but maybe—just maybe—seeing this will help.

Just maybe.

It's been nearly five months since I've seen her.

One-hundred-and-forty-two days, if anyone is counting.

One-hundred-and-forty-two days since...

I accused her of setting me up.

I cast her out of my life.

I hugged her.

I kissed her.

Since I became the biggest asshole to ever walk the face of the Earth.

And I wouldn't be walking around at all if weren't for her. I'd be rotting in a jail cell.

Her lead about Delaney blew the case wide open. So much has happened in the two-and-a-half months since she gave Delaney's cell phone to Ella and Crutch. She saved my life.

She saved my life.

And I treated her like a piece of garbage.

Ridge grunts, waiting on my answer.

I shrug. "Ella said they're airing the interview Thursday night during primetime. It'll be one of the quickest turnarounds ever. I even saw an ad for it today. Maybe she'll watch it and..." I can't even finish my pathetic thought.

"And what?"

"Be a better person than me," I say with a sigh.

He claps me on the shoulder, falling on his best friend sword and trying to comfort me. "You're a good person, Holt. You were just under an extreme amount of stress, and your mind ran wild when those suggestions were thrown out there." He leans against the porch railing. "You have to look at the blessing behind it."

"There's a blessing to calling the love of my life a lying, criminal, gold-digger?"

"What happened between y'all made her leave town. She never would've gone to her ex-husband's house if she weren't leaving town. And if she never went to her ex-husband's house, she never would've seen that Delaney changed the alarm code to match yours."

I can't believe she left town.

She closed her store, left town, and I never even called her.

I feel like gutting myself with a fishing knife.

Ella eases out the front door, her gaze flickering back and forth between me and Ridge. "So, you ready for this?"

I snort. "I don't know. Am I?"

"You'll be fine. I picked Alaina because she's trustworthy. I've worked with her on several projects, and she's never been anything but professional. She tries to stay away from angles and just report on the truth. Her sister was a victim of violence. She really wants to bring justice to those who deserve it."

"I still don't understand how it's airing on so many channels at one time?" I say, turning my statement into a question.

"Her show airs on the true crime channel on cable TV. But that's just one of the channels owned by the same parent company. She worked out a deal for a simulcast. That's why it's playing on one of the Big 5 networks, at the same time. She's retaining all of the production rights, though. So, the true crime channel will be the only one showing re-runs of the interview."

"Re-runs. Yay," I deadpan. "There's nothing I'd like more than to keep reliving this nightmare for all eternity."

She smiles. "Each day is getting better. Just focus on that."

"You're right. I'm sorry for being ungrateful. I have to remember that I could be sitting in a cement cell." We watch as Crutch motions for us to come down to the patio. "Thanks for letting me do this here. I just couldn't stand the thought of the world seeing images of my home, my yard."

"Crutch's idea of doing it outside is perfect. With the backdrop of the pond, you could be anywhere," Ridge adds.

When I walk past Chloe, she gives me an encouraging wink.

When everything started winding down and the idea of a *Redemption Interview* came up, I put Ella in charge of it. This is her world, and I knew she would do right by me—just as she always does. It was her idea to introduce Chloe and Alaina Ontario. When going through Merit's phone, we saw Chloe's warning to her. Her warning to always say 'no comment' and ignore all reporters, even herself. It was a pretty-high class move. Fortunately, Chloe and Alaina hit it off, and Chloe was able to get out from under the pull of the tabloid scene.

Alaina Ontario, with her news anchor good-looks and gleaming white teeth, leans over and motions for me to sit down. "I'm sure I don't have to explain everything to you, Holt. You've probably given more interviews than me," she says with a chuckle.

True, but I've never been this damn nervous about one.

She turns to Crutch and Ella. "Thank you again for letting me use your home, Ella. We've always worked so well together, and I'm honored that you would think of me for this opportunity." She turns back to me, "Thank you, Holt, for giving me a chance to tell your story. To tell the truth. I want you to know that I will do right by you. You have my word."

I tug on my collar, hoping I'm not digging myself a deeper grave.

Because it feels like I'm already six feet under without Merit by my side.

The questions start easy enough. We talk about my childhood, my family, football. All things I could talk about for days. When the questions shift to my arrest, my jaw clenches. I try to take Ella's advice and take a deep breath before each answer, giving myself time to prepare and formulate a proper response. That's never something I had to do with my football interviews. The press asked a question; I answered. Boom. Boom. Boom. Simple and sweet. But those interviews didn't have as much riding on the line as this one does.

She wants me to talk about my days in jail. I do my best to describe my fear and terror without sounding like a complete pussy.

We talk about the allegations and my bail hearing and how the first attorney wanted me to plead guilty and take a deal.

She shuffles her notes with grace, putting on a perfect show for the camera. "It's fairly common knowledge that you have a very close relationship with your family and a very small circle of friends. Those closest to you became your biggest advocates after your arrest, declaring your innocence. Their unwavering faith must have given you some comfort?"

My gaze sweeps across Ella, Crutch, and Ridge. "I wouldn't have survived the last few months without them. Blessed doesn't even come close to describing it."

"And one of your biggest supporters has been your girlfriend, Merit."

Just hearing her name squeezes my heart with painful regret. "She's the most amazing woman I've ever met."

Alaina gives a breathy little chuckle. "I should say so. From what I understand, she took it upon herself to do a little sleuthing and cracked the case wide open."

"She did. I wouldn't be sitting here today if it weren't for her. She...she's given me my life back."

"So, one girlfriend helped turn the page of the investigation, and it flipped right on over to another girlfriend—an ex-girlfriend, actually. Tell me about Delaney Fitts."

My hands grip together, turning my knuckles white. Every time I talk about Delaney, I feel like cutting my tongue out. I rush the background story of our relationship and breakup, pausing only to answer the other questions that Alaina lobs along the way.

"So, we fast-forward to the end of last summer, and Delaney, who happens to be in a relationship with Merit's ex-husband, famed attorney Edward Ezzell, discovers that you and Merit are dating?"

I would never characterize Edward as *famed*, but still, I nod. "Yes, that's right."

"And Delaney does what? Hatches a plan to ruin your life?"

"Basically. Yes."

"Tell me about that."

"After I ended things with Delaney, she moved back here, back to Alabama. She briefly dated a Minor League baseball player who had hopes of making it to the majors. That pipedream ended when he was injured."

"And that baseball player was..." Alaina falls in sync with my story.

"Trenton Trevors. And he has a niece—Heidi Trevors."

"The very same Heidi Trevors who claimed the two of you had a sexual relationship? The same Heidi Trevors with whom you allegedly shared thousands of explicit text messages and phone calls?"

"Yes, the very same girl."

She lifts her chin and smirks. "Coincidence?"

"Nothing is a coincidence when Delaney is involved." I pause, waiting for her to nod, urging me to continue. "On occasion, Delaney would judge cheerleading competitions. One of those competitions occurred just shortly after Delaney discovered Merit and I were dating. Heidi was a spectator at the cheer competition, and when Delaney realized she attended the same high school where I taught and coached, she sought her out, under the guise of simply wanting to reconnect. You know, since they hadn't seen one another since Delaney's relationship with Trenton ended. Delaney immediately began enticing her to frame me. She groomed her. With money and friendship."

"And how did they frame you?"

I roll my shoulders, trying to stretch my tense muscles. I can't wait for this to be over. "It's what you would call a long-con, I guess. It started one night after a football game when Heidi claimed her car wouldn't start, and she asked me for a ride home. After receiving permission from Denise, Heidi's mother, I drove her home. Delaney knew that Merit was looking to hire some part-time help at the store she owned. On that drive, Heidi told me she had just lost her job. She cried and told me how badly she needed a job to save money for the future." I sigh, shifting my suit jacket. "Well, I felt like fate was smiling down on me when she said that. Merit thought she had someone lined up for the job, but that had just fallen through. Come to find out, Delaney even had a hand in that. She convinced the young woman's current employer to give her a raise in order to keep her from going to work for Merit."

Alaina drops her mouth in shock, even though she *isn't* shocked. This isn't news to her.

I simply clear my throat and continue. "Like a fool, I basically offered Heidi a job at Merit's store, right then and there. That's all it took."

"Meaning?"

"I did exactly what Delaney and Heidi and Denise all wanted. I paved a way for Heidi to be in our lives nearly every single day. Within hours of that car ride, they were already framing me as a sexual predator."

"Within hours?"

I nod. "Hours."

"What did they do?"

"They faked text messages and phone calls between Heidi and myself."

"Faked them how? Spoofing?"

She already knows the answer. She knows all the answers. But the world doesn't. Once it came out that I was innocent, the majority of news outlets didn't even cover the story anymore. They knew their ratings came from me being the bad guy. Not the good guy.

After all, you know what they say… bad news travels faster.

"No, nothing was spoofed. The sexually explicit text messages came from *my* physical phone. The hour-long phone conversations happened in real time."

"And you weren't involved in any of that—the messages, the phone calls, the secret meetings?"

A low grumble rolls in my chest, like thunder in the distance. "Absolutely not. I never sent one single text message to Heidi. I never called her. I never had any secret rendezvous with her. Nothing remotely sexual ever happened between the two of us." I cock my head. "And just to throw it out there, for the sickos who still have reservations about me... I never even had a sexual *thought* about Heidi. None. I have never had any inappropriate thought about a child—and never will."

She leans forward in her seat. Her diamond and gold bracelets jangle. "So, how did the messages end up on your phone?"

"Delaney broke into my house and sent them from my cell phone."

Alaina lifts her eyebrows like she's finding this out for the first time. "Really?"

"For years I used the same alarm code for my home—no matter where I lived. Delaney knew the code from the brief time she lived with me in North Carolina. When I purchased my home here, I changed the alarm code to match. Not only did the code work the alarm, but it also unlocked all the doors. It was a keyless entry system. Delaney snuck into my home nearly every single night for three months. She's the one who sent the text messages and made the phone calls in the middle of the night."

Alaina leans back in her chair, re-crossing her legs, staring at me in disbelief. I have to give it to her; she definitely knows how to work a camera. "You had no idea she was breaking into your home? Nearly every night? For three whole months?"

"I'm embarrassed to admit that at the time, my home was very light on security. Needless to say, that issue has been remedied. To the extreme." I lower my voice and eye the camera with a hard gaze, trying to convey that my house is locked up tighter than Fort Knox. I don't need any wackadoo fuckers out in TV land trying to recreate this sensational crime.

"Didn't you hear her? Walking into your room and grabbing your phone?"

I shake my head. "My phone was never beside me. I always slept with my phone outside of the bedroom, and I slept with the bedroom door closed. Plus, I'm a very hard sleeper. It comes with the territory when you're trying to sleep at a football camp next to a three-hundred-pound linebacker with a grass turf allergy."

"And Delaney knew all of that?" she asks. "That you slept without your phone in the room? And with the bedroom door closed?" She extends her hand in my direction, kickstarting my explanation with her own words. "You had those same habits during the time you and Delaney lived together?"

Just thinking about living with Delaney—willingly allowing her into my life, into my bedroom—makes me wanna carve those memories from my brain with a sharp hunting knife.

Fuck that. I deserve to feel the pain.

I should use a rusty, dull pair of fingernail clippers, instead.

I work to clear my throat. "Yes. Those habits started when I was growing up." I offer a small smile. "You know, back when your parents want to monitor your screen time."

Alaina gives a soft chuckle. "I know that all too well." Pressing her lips together, she works her lipstick for a second before sobering her face again. "And you didn't hear anything? No noises in the night?"

"There were a couple of times when something felt...off. Like if I woke up to use the restroom, I might've heard a little noise or something like that. But there was never anything to indicate someone was inside my home, walking around and framing me as a child predator, no."

"Didn't you see the messages or call history on your phone?"

"Before leaving, Delaney would delete all the messages on my end. She also erased the calls from my call history. I mean, I didn't even have Heidi's phone number as a saved contact."

She nods, gifting me and the camera with a wry grin. "It's a pretty fantastical story. It's hard for the average person to wrap their head around this."

"It's hard for me to wrap my head around it, Alaina."

"So, Delaney would send messages to Heidi in the middle of the night, and Heidi would respond back. They would do this for an hour—two hours—even?"

"Sometimes, it was Heidi texting back and sometimes it was her mother, Denise."

"So, Denise Trevors condoned this behavior? Condoned this toxic and criminal relationship between her daughter and Delaney Fitts?"

"Condoned it? She encouraged it. Denise and Heidi received nearly $75,000 from Delaney over those months."

"My goodness."

"Yeah. It wasn't even Delaney's money that she bribed them with. Delaney stole money from her father's account and Edward Ezzell's account."

"Speaking of Edward Ezzell, he and Delaney were residing together during this time. Didn't he realize that she was leaving his house for hours at a time during the middle of the night?"

I clear my throat, biting back a cynical chuckle. "From what I hear, he snores. Rather loudly. So, separate bedrooms were a part of their routine."

Once again, Alaina politely laughs, taking a brief pause, before steering the interview back on course. "So how was this discovered? How did you find out what they were doing to you?"

"A tip from Merit lead to a search warrant for Delaney's phone and a subpoena for all of her phone records. The proof was there. Just like there were thousands of text messages and phone calls between *me*," I say with air quotes, "and Heidi; there were thousands of text messages and phone calls between Delaney and Heidi. And Delaney and Denise. They talked about everything. How they were framing me. How Delaney wanted me to pay for breaking her heart. They discussed the money transfers Delaney made. They talked about anything and everything."

"How did the police not know this? Didn't they review all of Heidi's phone records when investigating you? Her cloud storage?"

"Yes, but Delaney gave burner phones to Heidi and Denise. She only contacted them—as herself—on those devices." I shrug, "Of course, she just wasn't smart enough to use a burner phone herself."

We spend a few more minutes talking about the ins-and-outs of the hoax. The hoax that nearly ruined my life. Well, partly ruined it…

Because Merit's not here. My world won't be right until she's back by my side.

And I have a feeling I'm going to have to work my ass off to make that happen. That is, if she'll even consider forgiving me.

Well, she has to consider it. I'm not taking no for an answer.

Because she's my lifeline to this universe. Without Merit, there's no sun or moon or stars. The galaxy is nothing more than a black void, filled with emptiness and despair.

She's my best friend, my partner, my wife.

She just doesn't know it, yet, of course. And she doesn't know it because I was a fucking shithead and derailed our picture-perfect future. If I'm being completely honest, I *more* than derailed it…I blasted that freight train with a nuclear bomb. Because I did the worst thing anyone could ever do—I accused her of lying and manipulating our relationship, when nothing but truth and love poured from her soul every single second of every single day.

So, I'll do whatever I have to do to earn her forgiveness and her trust.

Because I'm gonna grow old with that woman by my side.

I refuse to acknowledge any other outcome for our lives.

"And they've all pleaded guilty, correct?" Alaina's voice draws me out of my torrent of emotions.

"Heidi and Denise pleaded guilty, and they have been sentenced. Delaney pleaded no contest yesterday. She's scheduled to be sentenced sometime in July."

"How do you feel about that?"

"I'm very thankful there won't be a trial. Since the truth was discovered, everything has happened at breakneck speed, and I couldn't be more grateful to my team of attorneys, the DA's office, the local courts, and all of the officers working on the case."

"In talking to your attorneys and the DA, they all said you championed for Heidi's charges to be reduced to misdemeanors. She was sentenced to five years' probation and three-hundred hours of community service. She'll also live in a juvenile residence that specializes in therapy for traumatized youth until she reaches the age of nineteen. From what I understand, it's a state-of-the-art facility."

I nod, taking time to breathe and swallow. "Heidi fully cooperated with police when the information was found on Delaney's phone. She told them everything." I glance down at the ground, gathering my thoughts. "She was manipulated by her mother and Delaney. Don't get me wrong, I'm angry with her. I'm very angry. I don't know if I'll ever be able to forgive her. But she's seventeen years old. She's a kid who was exploited and preyed upon. She deserves to have a chance to heal her damaged life, her damaged way of thinking. She deserves to be happy one day. Going to prison won't allow her to do any of those things."

"And Denise was sentenced to three years in prison. She also has to register as a sex offender for her role in facilitating the text messages, which included nude photos of her daughter." Alaina softly sighs. "What are your thoughts on Delaney's punishment? I've heard she could be sentenced anywhere from five to twenty years."

I should feel some sort of sympathy. I dated the woman. Lived with her. Slept with her. But my sympathy for Delaney ran out a long time ago. A deep-seated desire for revenge claws at my heart. Dirty, nasty, painful revenge. I do my best to lock it inside and throw away the key. "I'll leave that to the courts. I'll have to trust their decision. I'm human. That inherit need for vengeance will grow and thrive like a malignancy if I let it. I can't let it. It's already taken enough of my life."

"It has. Hasn't it?" She pretends to look at her notes. "Let's talk about that a little bit. Your home was vandalized?"

I nod. "Before we added additional security measures, yes."

"What else?"

With every word, my heart beats a little louder, a little harder. "It wasn't just my house; it happened to all of my family." I look at the pond, watching as the reflection of the moon bounces off it. "Someone slit my mom's tires when she was at the grocery store." I take a breath. "My best friend is a firefighter. Someone wouldn't let him inside of their burning house to help put out a fire." My throat clenches. "My nephew got into a fight at school trying to defend my honor." I know Nate's not really my nephew, but in my heart he is. And that black eye fucking gutted me.

"Not to mention the money you've spent on attorneys' fees and your defense."

Oh, she has no fucking clue. It's astronomical.

When I don't answer, she adds to it. "And of course, there's Merit's store. Not only did she deal with vandalism, but the decline in customers actually forced her to shutter the doors, correct?"

Just hearing the words out loud...

It breaks me.

Shatters me.

Shreds me into little confetti pieces like a damn woodchipper.

I have put Merit through hell. Absolute hell.

I. Am. An. Asshole.

My whisper is a growl, low and thick. "Yes, that's right."

"We know she's been one of your biggest supporters. She's maintained your innocence to anyone who would listen." Alaina cocks her head in curiosity. "But we haven't seen her with you in several months. She's.... dropped out of sight. What's going on there?"

I knew this question was coming. Ella tried to prepare me for it. But there really isn't anyway to prepare for explaining that I'm a fool. A fool who let the love of his life walk away.

Well, in all honesty, a fool who kicked the love of his life out of the picture. Who cut her to the bone with his accusations and tone.

I answer slowly. "The stress of being falsely accused weighed heavily on me. I wish I could say I handled it with grace, with dignity.

But I didn't. Unfortunately, those I love the most bore the burden of my frustrations."

"So, you two are going through a...break, of sorts?"

"It's the first broken thing I plan on putting back together."

And if I can't put it back together again? If the pieces are too broken?

Well, I can't let myself think about that. Because my life isn't mine without Merit. Like I said, I refuse to acknowledge any other outcome for our lives—except for unbridled happiness.

"That's understandable. I can't imagine the level of despair you were fighting. But how has the distance affected your relationship? Specifically, have you been able to play an active role in her pregnancy and the preparations for the birth of your child?"

What the fuck?

Chapter 3

Holt

What. The. Fuck.

What. The. Fuck.

What. The. Actual. Fuck.

My vision tunnels. Flames of nausea eat away at my stomach. My brain liquifies to jelly. I open my mouth to speak but nothing comes out.

Fortunately, Ella scrambles in front of me, blocking the camera with her hand. "We need to take a break. Now."

I'm too stunned to even move. It's like I'm glued to the chair. Somehow Ridge gets me up and pushes me across the yard and into the house. Breaking free of his grasp, I race down the hallway and into the bathroom. I slam the door and grip the countertop, forcing myself to take some deep breaths.

I've never had a full-blown panic attack before.

Not before my multiple college National Championship games.

Not before my multiple Super Bowl appearances.

Not when I jumped off the cliff to catch Anna.

Not when I got arrested.

Not even when I was sitting in the damn jail cell.

But now? I feel like I'm dying. Like someone is squeezing my heart, just counting down the seconds until it implodes. My throat is swollen, and I can't even swallow. I toss my suit jacket on the floor and yank off my tie. I can't even undo the neck buttons of my shirt because my fingers are shaking so badly. Eventually, I just rip the small-ass buttons off. I'm too desperate for air to be patient. I splash cold water on my face and stare in the mirror.

It's a face I don't even recognize anymore. If I were at my own house, I would smash my fist into the glass just to hide myself.

Gone is the man I thought I was. Before Christmas, I was a decent guy. At least, that's what I told myself. I worked hard. I built a life. I loved my job. I loved my family. And most importantly, I loved Merit.

I was going to make her my wife. I was going to spend every day of my life making love to her. I was going to give her a son. Give *us* a son. A son who would one day be a sod farmer, keeping her family's business in the family.

Now look at me.

I'm a total pussy. A complete and total pussy.

I let my punk-ass attorney plant some ill-fitted, cockamamie theory in my head, and I tossed my woman out like she was nothing but some worthless piece of trash. It took what? Ten minutes from the time the idea hit my brain for me to run with it as the truth? Maybe less than that. I did the exact same thing to her that the entire world was doing to me—I rushed to judgment.

And I didn't lift one single finger to fight for her. Why? Because I was blinded by the thought that she betrayed me. Blinded by the thought that she just wanted my money—like every other woman before her. Blinded by the thought that she tricked me into loving her.

I didn't lift a finger when Dad told me someone spray-painted dicks all over the sidewalk in front of her store.

I didn't lift a finger when Raylee told me the windows had been broken.

I didn't lift a finger when Crutch told me she refused to have any further police presence.

I didn't lift a finger when Ridge noticed everything being moved out.

And I didn't lift a finger when Ella brought me a huge stack of cash and a pile of Delaney's phone records.

And after that? I was embarrassed. I was scared. And I've been scared every second since.

The old me would have gone to her then, right that very minute. Fallen to my knees and begged for forgiveness. Begged her to help me fight Delaney and punish her for nearly ruining our lives, nearly demolishing our perfect life together. The old me would have pulled out the engagement ring that matched her antique diamond and ruby bracelet. I would have slid it on her finger and pulled her into my arms. And together, we would've watched her favorite movie. The movie that we never got the chance to watch because the police showed up and arrested me.

But that was the old me.

This me?

This me is a scared little pussy, and I never did any of those things because I've been so terrified at the possibility that she'll never forgive me. The thought of not having Merit by my side is so devasting that I've been forcing myself to live in limbo for months on end because at least in limbo, I have hope. Hope that she'll forgive me and come rushing back into my arms.

Because even though I refuse to accept any other future besides one in which we are man and wife, that doesn't mean *it will actually happen that way.*

Fuck knows a future like that isn't one I deserve. So why would the Heavens grant it to me...

I've been terrified to face reality this whole time. And the reality is that she most likely will slam the door in my face and walk away without ever looking back.

And if she walks away, is she taking our child with her?

Is she really pregnant?

With our baby? With our son or daughter?

Did I shut Merit *and* our baby out of my life?

Did those ten minutes in January ruin our family before it even began.

I'm not sure how long I stay in the bathroom, but eventually there's a soft knock at the door. "You need to come out, man," Crutch says. "Lulu needs to talk to you."

Crutch and Ella. Ry and Lulu—the names only the two of them call each other.

I grasp onto one small glimmer of hope, barely shining in the distance, like a small piece of fool's gold on a mountain. *If they can make it after the shit they went through, there has to be a chance for me and Merit.*

I leave the bathroom and find everyone in the kitchen, standing around the island. Ridge lifts an eyebrow, taking in my disheveled appearance.

"It's true." Ella's words are simple and finite. I ask her to repeat them. "It's true. She's pregnant. The paparazzi finally decided to head south to her parents' house after months of not seeing her here. With you." She pins me with a glare, making me feel even shittier. "They have pictures. If they aren't plastered all over the Internet by now, they will be shortly."

I drag my hands through my hair. "I can't believe this is happening. What the fuck have I done?"

There's a tap on the kitchen doorframe. "Excuse me?" Alaina takes a cautionary step into the kitchen. Chloe peeks out from behind her shoulder.

"They have pictures, Chloe?" I ask.

Thinning her lips, she nods. "I talked to some of my old colleagues earlier today." She frowns. "I'm sorry, Holt. I thought you knew."

I turn to Alaina. "Please, you can't put this on air. I'm begging you."

Alaina's eyes widen. "Holt..."

"Please!"

"But it's the truth. There isn't anything false in what I'm saying or in the questions I'm asking. Merit is pregnant." Her face softens. "I really am sorry. We all assumed you knew."

I sit on the barstool and drop my face in my hands. "Please don't. Don't mention her pregnancy. If you say something, she'll think I knew. She'll think I gave you permission to talk about it. Merit's a very private person. She'd be devastated." Lifting my head, I pray she can see the sincerity in my eyes. "I screwed up. Bad. I have to get her back in my life. I love her. I love her with every fiber of my being, and if you ask me about her pregnancy in this interview... it'll be the nail in my coffin."

Alaina takes a deep breath. It feels like hours before she answers. "Okay. I won't mention her pregnancy. You have my word."

That's all I need to hear. I jump up, racing from the room, calling thank you behind me.

"Holt! Where are you going?" Ella asks, but I'm pretty sure she already knows the answer.

"What!" Alaina squeaks. "Where's he going?"

"You already have enough footage from tonight and the other day to put something great together." I glance over my shoulder as I race down the porch. "I'm going to get my girl."

I used to be smart.

Well, I'd like to think I was.

But I'm really beginning to question my intelligence. Because this? This may not be the smartest idea.

I pound on the front door, not giving myself a chance to devise a wiser plan. I'm pretty sure they already know someone's here. When you live in a rural area, the night sky is even darker, and most people wake up when headlights flash across the bedroom in the middle of the night.

My impatience is suffocating all of my sane thoughts, snuffing them out like dying embers in a fire. "Merit!" I pound the door again. "Merit! Open the door."

And then, the door opens.

To the very angry and sleep-deprived father of my knocked-up girlfriend. I mean, ex-girlfriend. Well, you know what I mean.

"What the hell do you think you're doing?" he barks. "Have you lost the two brain cells you have left? It's one in the freakin' morning."

"Is it true? Is she pregnant?"

Deke curses under his breath and drags a hand down his worried face. "I thought I saw those bastards taking pictures." There's a rumble low in his chest. "It's on the Internet? That's how you found out?"

I bypass that question, asking one of my own. "How could she not tell me?"

"Tell you?! You kicked her out of your house! You tossed her on the street!" His jaw tics with anger. "Even worse, Holt, you trampled her heart."

I lean against the doorframe, bracing myself. "I'm so sorry."

His eyes narrow. "I'm not the one you should be apologizing to."

"I know. Please, Deke. Please, let me talk to her. I've made the worst mistake of my life. I love her."

"You have a funny way of showing it."

It feels like I'm dying. "Please."

He sighs, shaking his head. "Go home, Holt. Before I call the law." Without looking back, he slams the door in my face.

Merit

He finally showed up.

Finally.

I peek around the staircase, hoping to catch a glimpse of him. And...also hoping I don't see a damn thing.

His voice is like a soothing balm to my aching body. I immediately curse myself for feeling this way.

I hold my breath, afraid I'll miss what they say. Of course, it's hard to miss Daddy's yelling.

My heart thunders in my chest. It pounds so hard my ribs actually hurt.

A minute later, he's in his truck, driving away.

Well, there you have it.

He finally showed up.

Finally.

But just for the baby.

Not for me.

Chapter 5

Holt

It may be a small town, but at least it has a Walmart and a small mom and pop motel. Of course, I didn't sleep at all, but at least I was able to change clothes and get a shower. I'm also thankful that I have a family filled with investigators. It only took one phone call to Crutch to find out where Merit is working now.

Stepping on the sidewalk, I glance up at the sign for the small insurance office. I lift my ballcap and tug it back down on my head. I'm glad it was in my truck. I guess it's kind of like my security blanket. As soon as I open the door, a bell dings.

"I'll be right with you."

Holy hell. *Her voice.*

I can't see her because people are blocking my view, but I can hear her. Her voice is like a soothing balm to my aching body.

I can't help but wonder if she ever feels the same.

Well, *felt* the same.

An older couple is standing in front of her desk, talking about the insurance for their new tractor. When she laughs, I nearly lose my shit. And it's not even a real laugh; it's her polite laugh.

It feels like an eternity before they walk away. She doesn't immediately look up, but instead finishes writing herself a note. She's sitting behind her desk, focusing on her penmanship. I take a small step in her direction, and she freezes.

Completely freezes. Right in the middle of writing a word.

She can feel me. She can sense me.

All the air is sucked out of the room, charging the distance between us with electricity.

I can't swallow.

She slowly lifts her head.

And there she is. My Merit. My beautiful and made-for-me Merit. Her redwood hair is perfectly styled, and her makeup is perfectly applied. She's completely breathtaking. I can't help but wonder if she's dressing up for work because she wants to, or because she has to. My perusal of her body is severed all too quickly, however, because the rest of it is hidden behind the bulky desk, shadowing and blocking views of anything below her breasts.

But that doesn't stop my own body from reacting to hers. In quick fashion, my asshole status is even further cemented when my dick jumps in my pants. I cup my hands in front of my crotch, trying to camouflage my erection, as my eyes travel across her face, soaking in the features I see every time I close my eyes. It doesn't matter if it's for a night's sleep or simply a half-second blink...she's there.

Despite her beauty, I can't help but notice her own hazel eyes.

They're dead.

Void of all spark. Void of all life and joy.

Do they look that way because she's been emotionally dead these past few months? Just like me?

Or do they look that way because I'm standing in front of her?

"What are you doing here?" she hisses.

"I'm here to see you."

"Why?"

Well, that's a loaded question. I go with the truth. "Because I love you."

"How dare you say that to me," she spits through clenched jaw.

"It's the truth. I don't lie to you. You know that."

She snorts in disgust. "Yeah, sure. You keep telling yourself that, Holt."

I sigh, reaching out to her. "I'm so fucking sorry, Merit."

Her back stiffens, and she looks over her shoulder at the hallway behind her. "Shhh! This is an office. You can't cuss in here. Are you trying to get me fired? I need this job. I already lost one job because of you, you know."

Shit. I'm acting like a damn buffoon. "Can we please go somewhere and talk?"

"No! It's the middle of the workday. I know you've got millions of dollars just chilling in the bank, but some of us have to work, and we can't just walk out in the middle of the day."

"Merit?" An older man walks around the corner and brightens when he sees me. "Well, hello, young fella. Something we can help you with? Do you have an insurance need?"

I stuff my hands in my pockets. "No, sir. I was just hoping to have a moment with Merit. It's personal."

He scowls and looks between the two of us. "Well, Merit knows she can't conduct personal business on my dime," he scolds her. "That's not what I'm paying her for."

How dare he speak to her like that. I shake my head and point at him. "Listen here—"

Merit jumps up, immediately interrupting me. "He was just leaving, Mr. Shore." She taps the large file folder that she's now holding in front of her stomach. The folder completely blocks my view. "I have those numbers you wanted to see."

He grumbles, perching his folded arms on his bulbous belly.

"Goodbye, Holt." She pins me with her stare. The dead void in her hazel eyes shifts, and she silently pleads with me, begging me to leave.

Lifting my hat, I settle it back on my head. Fine. I'll let her win this battle.

But after that?

It's war.

I'm waging a full-on war, and I'm not stopping until my family is back with me—my wife and my baby.

"I'll see you tonight, then, Merit." I toss her a wink and push out the door.

I walk across the yard, heading to the back of the barn, where I hear music playing. I parked my truck at the end of the long driveway, behind a tree, hidden from plain view. I guess I'm trying to be sneaky.

"Don't you know that sneaking onto a man's property is likely to get you shot?"

Well, I guess I'm not as sneaky as I thought.

Deke's leaning against the front porch railing wiping his dirty hands on an even dirtier rag. I nod in his direction. "Sir."

"What are you doing here again, Holt?"

"I have to talk to her. You had to have known I wasn't gonna give up that easy."

He stuffs the towel in his back pocket. "You did before. You gave up on her pretty damn easy, in my opinion."

I try to swallow some of my shame. As always, it chokes me. "I did. It was the worst mistake of my life."

"So, everything's different now that a baby is involved? You think you can just come in here and say 'I'm sorry' and she's gonna run back into your arms like nothing happened?"

I shake my head, agreeing with him. "I don't think it's gonna be easy, no. But I'm prepared to do whatever it takes to have her back in my life."

"How do you think she feels knowing that you only came back for the baby? You're only breaking her heart more."

"I had planned on fighting for her, even before I knew about the baby. I was... I was just giving it some time."

"Time? What the hell for?"

My words come out slowly. They sound even more pathetic when I say them out loud. "There's a big interview I did airing on TV on Thursday night. I was waiting for that."

He scoffs, sizing me up as the world's dumbest man. "You think she cares about what you tell some TV reporter?"

No. It's one of the many things I love about her.

The glass storm door opens, and Marie pokes her head out. "You might as well let him pass. You know this has to happen."

Deke frowns, mumbling something to her that I can't hear. She lifts her eyebrows but doesn't say anything back. Before shutting the door, she gives me a little nod. It's not exactly a confidence booster, but I'll take anything I can get at this point.

He pulls his bottom lip between his teeth and bobs his head at the barn, giving me permission to pass. I only take a few steps when he catches my attention. "I guess I should thank you."

"Sir?" I ask in confusion.

"You said you wanted to '*find her*'. And you did. The little girl I raised is back." He turns and walks around the side of the porch, laughing like he knows a secret. "You might not like what you're walking into."

The second I see her on the back deck of the barn, my heart skips a thousand beats. She's bent over a flowerpot, planting something. She's wearing a short white sundress and yellow and green striped rubber boots. Her ass is bouncing up and down, moving to the rhythm of the song playing through the speaker of her phone. I'm not sure what it is, but I can tell it's some kind of song from one of her old movies. I can see the outline of her panties through the fabric of her dress.

My heart dives into my stomach, and my dick threatens to spring to life.

Just then, she stands up and stretches her back. She's turning opposite of me so I'm out of her line of sight, but I can still see everything.

Everything.

The sun dress pulls against her beautiful, rounded stomach. I never thought a belly could be so damn sexy. The setting sun hits her in just the right way, and her dress becomes nearly see-through.

I can see the shape of her body. Every curve. Every delicious inch. A strand of hair escapes her messy bun and tickles her nose. She snorts and quickly brushes it away with the back of her hand, getting potting soil on her cheek in the process. She's glowing, flushed with color from the summer sun and spending her days outside.

No matter how hard I try, I can't draw my eyes away from her stomach. Away from our baby. The baby that we made.

She looks healthy. Happy.

"Mer," my voice croaks.

Well... she *did* look happy.

Her head snaps in my direction, and her eyes narrow in anger. "What are you doing here?"

I climb the stairs. "You know what I'm doing here. We need to talk."

She cocks a hand on her hip, drawing my gaze back to her belly. "Well, I don't really feel like talking to you right now. You nearly got me fired today. Haven't you done enough?"

I ignore that line of questioning and say what's immediately on my mind. "Holy hell, Merit. You're breathtaking. This..." my hand instinctively reaches out to her. "I mean, this is the picture I'm gonna have in my head when I'm lying on my death bed."

She scoffs. "And is that soon? Should I be preparing? Ordering flowers?"

I can read her face. She immediately feels bad about joking about my death. She opens her mouth to apologize but quickly decides against it, refusing to give in.

Holy shit. I love this woman.

I immediately jump in feet first. "I'm so fucking sorry."

She glances down at the floor, avoiding eye contact. "Yeah, you said that already." She slides her hands across her belly, shielding our child from me, and then grimaces when she realizes she just used her white dress as a towel to clean her dirty, soil-covered hands. Gaining her strength, she lifts her head and stares directly at me. "Thanks for that, by the way." Her voice drips with sarcasm, and

I'm not exactly sure if she's talking about her job or her now-messy clothes. "Didn't you hear me? You nearly got me fired today."

"Your boss seems like a total prick."

"Well, of course, he is. But that's beside the point. I need that job."

"Why?"

"Why?!" She rolls her eyes and points at her stomach. "I need health insurance, dumbass."

Merit Eliza Browning just called me a dumbass.

"I'll pay—"

She immediately cuts me off. "Holt Hill, I would choose your next words very carefully because you are about two seconds away from me giving you a colonoscopy with my garden shears."

Well, that doesn't sound pleasant.

I hold up my hands in defeat.

After a beat of silence, she finally looks at me.

I mean, she *really looks at me.*

Up until now, the hurt has clouded her vision, the pain I caused blinding her.

As it should.

But when she looks at me, it nearly makes me double over in relief.

There's still love in her. Love for me. Even though I don't deserve it; it's there. It's buried deep, under layers and layers of torment and disappointment. Despite her best efforts, her eyes roam over my body. And when her breath hitches in her chest, I nearly lose my mind with want.

But it's so much more than the physical. Yes, I want her. I want to hold her, kiss her, make love to her. But more than that, I want to give her my soul. I want to share my life with her. Forever. I want to marry her and grow old with her. I want to shelter her from the storms and carry her in the sun.

I have so many things to make amends for with her, and I'm praying she gives me the chance.

My voice is a whisper of gravel. "Why didn't you tell me?"

She sucks on her bottom lip. "I was gonna tell you."

I chuckle softly. "When? Our child's high school graduation?"

She rolls her eyes and grabs her phone. "Way before his high school graduation," she says. "I was just waiting until the legal documents were drawn up."

Time stops. My ears ring and my vision pinholes. "He?" I take another step closer to her. "Did you just say *he*?" When she doesn't answer, I press her. "Mer, are we having a boy?"

She can't hide the brightness of her smile, though she tries. "Yeah. I just found out last week."

We're having a boy.

A son.

Our son.

And I missed it. "Shit. I can't believe I missed it." All of a sudden, the other part of her sentence attacks my brain like a mad man with a machete. "Legal documents? What legal documents?"

She taps around on her phone screen and then passes it to me. I can't help but notice how she does her best to make sure our fingers don't touch. I scroll through the pages, skimming the legalese, barely able to focus on it because of the panic in my heart. "Custody papers?"

She shakes her head. "Don't say it like that. I would never keep you from your child. I know how important the kids are to you. After seeing you with them, I have no doubt you'll be a wonderful father."

My brow furrows as I read. "Anytime? It says you'll have primary custody, and I can have visitation as frequently as I want. Anytime at all?"

Her face serious, she just nods.

I lift an eyebrow at the next section in bold type. "No child support?"

She wraps an arm around our son, horror etched on her face. "I don't need your money," she spits. "I can provide for him." She looks out over the fields of growing green grass. Her eyes glisten with unshed tears. "I don't *want* your money."

Fuck. Her broken heart is killing me.

I set her phone back on the table. "Well, it's a moot point because I'm not signing that."

She jerks back to me, fear pouring over her like a waterfall. "What? You're gonna fight me? For custody? Holt, no, please."

"I would never fight you for custody of our child. It's a moot point because we're gonna be a family."

She cocks her head, lifting her eyebrows. "Holt..." she draws out my name, warning me not to continue.

"Like I told you earlier today, I love you. And that will never change."

Her hand rubs her sternum, like she's trying to smash whatever feelings may be coursing through her. "Don't say that."

"You know it's the truth, Merit. I don't lie to you." I take another step, trying to close the distance between us. "I'm in love with you. I never stopped. I never stopped loving you."

She stumbles backward, like my words physically assaulted her, like I'm brutally attacking her with every single syllable. Her leg knocks against the table, making her cell phone bounce, and she splays her hand in the air, fingers wide, nonverbally telling me to stop. Her whisper is laced with a flurry of warring emotions. Adoration and abhorrence. Softness and sharpness. Detachment and pain. "Take me out of the equation, Holt. You keep saying that you don't lie to me, but who the hell cares. Because it's yourself you've been lying to this whole time. You might not have stopped loving me, but you started despising me the second those attorneys painted a target on my back."

I open my mouth to defend my indefensible behavior, but she jams her hand back in front of me, begging me to keep quiet. "Stop. You're only making this harder on both of us. I've done my best to find some small modicum of peace with what you did to me. I've had to do that—as a *mother*. It's time for you to do the same. Because this," she wags her finger back and forth between the two of us, "is never happening again."

"Wanna. Fucking. Bet." My growl is harsher than I intend for it to be, but I can't help it. I'm gonna fight for her. To the fucking death, if need be. My ass is done standing on the sidelines like some kind of beaten-down and defeated, little wimp. "You better buckle up, baby, because this world already stole you from me once before. And like a fool, I let it. But that's over and done with. Get ready, because this is a battle you're never gonna win. Because I'm not stopping until you're in my life, in my arms, in my bed. I'll tear down fucking mountains and rip trees from their roots. I'll scorch this world from the top of Heaven to the bottom of Hell, if I have to. I'll do whatever needs to be done to put you back where you belong. And once I get ahold of you, I'm never letting you go. We belong together. In *our* home. In *our* life. I'll be damned if I leave this farm without you."

Her whole body is shaking. Her eyes are wide and innocent, filled with disbelief and yearning. A slow ember is starting to flame, knocking away some of the death I saw in them just a few hours ago. I erase the distance between us, stepping to the side a bit to avoid bumping into my son, nestled lovingly in her belly.

But I don't dare touch her. She deserves *more* than me just trying to manipulate her buried feelings with my kiss, with my touch.

She deserves more respect than that. God knows, she's earned it.

She's the strongest woman I know.

But I don't have to touch Merit to *feel* her.

"Don't touch me." Her whisper fans across my face. We're mere millimeters from one another.

"I don't have to touch you to feel you, Mer," I say honestly, conveying the thought that just raced through my head. "Our souls are connected. Our hearts beat in tandem." I turn my face, nuzzling against her hair, breathing in her scent of summer flowers and grass and sunshine. And of course, the scent of the potting soil still streaked across her cheekbone. "And you're wrong. I never despised you. I was mourning you. I let charlatans and thieves steal my faith in us. I was weak." I kiss the top of her head, softly and gently, with one small peck. "And in you, I find my strength."

Chapter 6

Merit

Lying in bed, I move my finger quicker, trying to chase the orgasm that my body is craving, needing.

I do everything I can think of, definitely giving it the old college try—finger on the outside, dildo on the inside. And I do everything I can think of *not* to picture *him*.

Him and his rippling muscles.

Him and his cute freckled nose.

Him and his sexy-as-hell, flexed forearms.

Him and his gorgeous blond curls.

Him and his insanely hot, tight stomach.

Him and his fuckable blue eyes.

Actors. Musicians. At one point, my mind even plays images of Crutch, Ridge, and Cullen, like a slideshow on a loop. Of course, that feels completely and totally wrong, so I have no choice but to yank my hand from my panties and give up.

For the past five months I've touched myself and thought of nothing but him. But now? Now, he's here. And he's messing with my fantasies—making them real, making me want things I can no longer have—and he's stomping on the ash of my charred heart.

I flip on my side and stare at the moon shining through my bedroom window.

I can't wait for Holt Hill to give up and leave me the hell alone.

Because he gave up on me once before. My still-broken heart is sure it will happen again.

"Why is his truck here?" I demand the second I walk through the kitchen. I fling my purse and lunch bag on the table.

Mom and Granny look at one another before Mom finally answers. "He's working."

"What?"

"He showed up as soon as you pulled out of the driveway this morning and asked your father if he could work with him today. That way, he'd be here the minute you came home."

I down a glass of water, trying to quench the fire of anger bubbling in my stomach.

Well, in all honesty, it could be acid reflux instead of anger. Pregnancy reflux is no joke. "And Daddy let him?"

Mom just shrugs. "Not like he gave your father a choice."

"Why on earth would your father turn away an able-bodied man offering free help?" Granny says. "I can guarantee you Deke's worked the skin off that boy's bones. Making that young buck hurt as much as he hurt you."

I bite back a smile. Good point.

I'm already walking up the stairs when Mom calls behind me. "What are you gonna do?"

"I'm gonna wash my face and get out of these dumb clothes. Then, I'm gonna get a front row seat to the torture. It's the least I can do to show Daddy my appreciation."

By the time I make it outside, the work in the fields is already finished, and I spot Daddy at the back of the barn sharpening the blades on a hand-held sod cutter. "Hey," I say, climbing the stairs, grabbing the underside of my stomach out of habit. My nonchalant attempt to glance around must not be too nonchalant.

Daddy jerks his head at the barn. "He's inside."

I shrug. "So."

Daddy just rolls his eyes because he knows I'm full of it.

I lower my voice to a whisper, "Why'd you let him stay here today? I told you I didn't wanna see him again."

He lifts an eyebrow and puts his tools on a side table. "Well, we both know that's a lie, isn't it?"

I'm not sure how to answer without lying again, so I don't.

"Did your mom say when supper will be ready?"

"No, sir."

"Well, I better get cleaned up." His stoic, fatherly expression breaks into a smile when he gets closer to me. "How's our boy today?"

I catch his contagious grin, softly giggling. "Active." Taking Daddy's hand, I lay it on top of my belly where there's been the most activity today, and we're rewarded with a small bump.

I have to say that feeling my baby move has been the most joyous thing about pregnancy. It's like my enormous love grows with every single kick and punch. And seeing the awe on my parents' face when it happens, and knowing that I'm giving them a grandson? It's beyond wonderful.

My heart catches in my throat the second Holt walks out of the barn and onto the deck. My mind instantly thinks back to last night, back to when I did everything I could not to picture him when I was touching myself. Of course, it's just my luck that he looks downright sinful today. He's wearing a Browning Sod Farm T-shirt, covered in dirt and filth. His legs are spattered with mud and grit, doing nothing but drawing attention to the muscular lines of his thighs and calves. His discount store tennis shoes are already torn, with the rubber toe flapping each time he takes a step. A bead of sweat escapes from underneath his ballcap and rolls down the side of his face.

The flare of desire pulsing between my thighs embarrasses me, instantly making me blush. He always said he could read my face. Can he read this? Does he know what I'm thinking? Does he know what I want?

Does he feel it too?

My embarrassment is of little consequence because he's not paying attention to my face. He's focused on my stomach. And Daddy's hand. He looks... sad. Envious, maybe?

Daddy pats my shoulder and walks away.

It takes a few beats before Holt lifts his eyes to mine. A soft smile tugs at the corner of his mouth. "Hi."

"Hey." For a brief moment, I revert back. Back to my old self. I fold my hands in front of me—as best I can—and look down at the ground. Remembering I'm not that girl anymore, I look up, capturing him with my gaze. "What are you doing here, Holt? Why'd you come back?"

"I told you last night, I'm not leaving here without you. I'm taking you home."

Home. He means the home he kicked me out of.

Before I can tell him that, he reaches up and shifts the ballcap on his head. His T-shirt catches against his sticky skin, and I can see the band of his boxer briefs. Normally, Holt does this on purpose. He knows I love it when he lifts his arms. I mean, I used to love it. There's something about that small movement. It's so graceful and predatory. Safe and dangerous. Kind and evil.

Except this time, he's not doing it on purpose. He's completely distracted. His eyes keep flickering up and down my body.

He's nervous.

And that's not usually something Holt Hill is.

"Are you... I mean, is..." he trips over his words. Sighing, he forges forward. "Is something happening?" He nods at my baby bump.

Our baby bump.

"I mean... is he okay? Your dad's hand was on your stomach, and I didn't know if something was wrong." His brow furrows in concern and curiosity.

As much as I want to ignore him and kick him off this land— punish him the way he punished me—I can't. We're tied together forever now. We're having a baby.

And fuck me for wanting to be the bigger person because of that.

"He's fine. He's just been kicking some today."

His mouth opens and then closes, wrestling with the words that want to come rushing out.

Shit.

I wish I could kick and scream. Sometimes, it totally sucks being civil with the devil for the sake of your child.

Well, maybe I'm being a little dramatic. I don't really think Holt's a devil. Not all the time, at least.

"Come here," I say, holding my hand out to him.

I start to shake in anticipation. And that makes me furious.

He grabs a towel from his back pocket and tries to clean the dirt. It's a losing battle. But it doesn't bother me. I grew up around this dirt. My son will grow up around this dirt.

When his fingers slide against mine, I nearly lose my shit. Calloused and powerful, they're just like I remember. His blue eyes lock with mine, freezing us in place. He sighs deeply and contently, my name a heated breath passing through his lips. "Mer."

My heart pounds faster in my chest, thundering like a train. Shaking my head, I break our trance, refusing to indulge every little flare of desire and longing that Holt stirs in my body. I guide his hand around my bulging belly, settling on top, where Daddy's hand was. His forearm grazes against my breast, which was not part of my plan. So, of course, I curse myself to holy hell when my nipple pebbles.

But Holt's more preoccupied with my stomach than with my boobs at this particular moment.

He stops breathing and bends closer, impatiently waiting for our son to kick.

He doesn't. Our son doesn't move.

Holt frowns.

Unable to bear his frown, and once again being the bigger person, I give him some advice. "He can hear you. That's what I read. I talk to him. I think he likes it, because sometimes, he'll start moving." I place my hand back on top of his and press down on my stomach.

Licking his lips, he nods. "Hey. Hi, son. It's me. Your dad." He clears his throat. All of a sudden, the tension drains from his body, and his shoulders slump. "God, help me, I'm so sorry, son. I'm sorry I wasn't here for you and your mom. I promise that'll never happen again. I love her, and I love you. And we're going to always be a family. Please...please forgive me."

The second the last word leaves his mouth, our son somersaults in my stomach. Over and over. It actually takes my breath away. He's never done that before. He's never moved like that.

"Oh, shit!" Holt's eyes fire with excitement, and his other hand flies to my stomach, desperate to feel every single movement. The joy on his face is devastatingly heartbreaking. I blink rapidly, praying that my tears threatening to spill over don't fall. Holt laughs loudly—free and unencumbered, filled with a levity that I haven't heard since before his arrest. And that makes our baby even more excited. He bounces against the bottom left side of my stomach. Without even thinking, I move Holt's hand lower so he can feel it. His thumb accidentally slips into the waistband of my shorts.

Everything stops.

I think the world actually stops spinning. It's just dangling there in the middle of the galaxy, a suspended ball of blue and green, waiting to see what we do next.

Love and passion and lightning flash across his face. I feel like I'm suffocating. Suffocating in the unbearable beauty of knowing that the three of us are a family. That we could go back to the way it was between us—if only I'd yield to my fate, accept his apology, and surrender to my true feelings.

If only I'd...

And then my cell phone dings with a text message.

I don't have to look to know who it is. It's Mom, letting me know supper is ready.

The moment is over now, ripped away and gone, like so many of our moments. I take a step back, giving distance. His hands fall to his side, and he looks down at them, like he can't believe what just happened.

"I... I need to go. Supper's on the table."

He drags his hand down his face. "Oh, okay. I was thinking maybe we could talk some more tonight?" He looks over his shoulder at the firepit to the right side of the barn. "Maybe we can sit by the fire? I don't mind waiting. I can wait on you to finish eating. I'll wait for however long it takes."

Well, I don't have to be a rocket scientist to know that declaration is about more than just me eating a casserole.

If given the chance, he'll break through every one of my defenses. So I shake my head. "I don't wanna talk tonight. This has been a little... much." Grabbing the handrail, I walk down the deck steps, making the poor decision to glance back at him. The pitiful look on his face mimics the one I've been walking around with for months. "Well, I guess you gotta eat too, huh? No sense in Mom's food going to waste."

I immediately wanna punch myself in the face for saying that out loud, for extending that invitation. Those words slipped out of my mouth all on their own.

Fuck this *'being the bigger person'* bullshit.

Chapter 7

Merit

Two days. Two nights.

Two days of him working with Daddy.

Two nights of us all eating supper together.

And two showers.

That's where he is now. Upstairs, showering. In my shower. The thought alone is so distracting I can't even focus on the John Wayne movie playing on the TV. And it's a good one too.

The sad truth is, I think I need to check myself into an insane asylum. Because at the heart of this entire screwed-up situation, there is only one reality: I'm still in love with him.

How can I still be in love with him? After what he did to me?

Don't get me wrong, I'm angry. Furious and hurt and devastated. But... the more time I spend with him, the more I remember how things used to be. Just a few short months ago, I was happy. Holt made me happier than Edward ever did. Of course, the major difference is I never actually loved Edward.

I had a life with Holt. I had my store. I had his family. I had friends.

I had *his love*.

And then, he threw it all away. He threw it all away—and I lost everything in the process; and yet, I'm still in love with him.

I'm totally pathetic.

Yep. I'm the pathetic, glutton-for-punishment, apparently-brain-dead moron still in love with Holt Hill.

The whole situation is unbelievably tragic, and what makes me even sadder is that no matter what happens—no matter what he does—we can never be a couple again.

Co-parents? Yes.

A loving couple? No.

A married couple? Building a life and growing old together? No.

And it's all because of him. And Delaney.

That bitch-ass Delaney.

Scowling, I take another big bite of my chocolate chip ice cream. The ice cream slides off my spoon and plops on my chest. I stare down at it, debating what to do. Well, it's my last bite, and I'm eating for two, so I guess there really is no debate. I scoop it up with my fingers and toss it in my mouth.

Unfortunately, that's right when Holt peeks around the corner. "Thanks for letting me use the shower again." He fails to hide his chuckle.

I quickly grab a napkin and try to clean myself.

Great. Just great.

Not only do I look like a big, old pig, but there's a piece of shirt fuzz stuck to the ice cream that I shoved in my mouth and now I have to swallow it.

Leaning against the doorframe, he studies me. "Feel like talking?"

Of course, I do. Because like we established, I'm totally pathetic. He offers me his hand but I ignore it, hopping up from the couch on my own. I mean, everyone is watching us. I don't need them getting the wrong idea.

It's raining tonight, so sitting by the firepit—like he wanted to do last night, before I shot him down—doesn't appear to be on the agenda. We settle in the side-by-side rocking chairs on the front porch instead. We chitchat about my incredibly boring job and my dick of a boss. He tells me what work he helped Daddy with today. I have to stifle my laugh when he runs through the list of back-breaking, bone-crushing work that Daddy has him doing. Some of it is so hard, we typically use the machinery for it. And yet, Daddy has Holt doing it by hand like we're living on the Ingalls Farm in Walnut Grove. He catches my eye, studying me for a moment. Gifting me with a sexy, little smirk, he shifts in his chair before glancing down.

Huh.

I wonder if he recognizes that Daddy is giving him the crap jobs on purpose. Surely, he knows what a manure spreader does. It's not like we actually expect him to spread the cow shit over every single acre by hand.

That shit—literal to the word—can have bacteria and parasites and pathogens harmful to your skin if you roll around in it for long enough.

"Hey, you're wearing gloves when you work with the fertilizers, right?"

When I catch him looking at his hand, I can't help but reach over and grab it.

"You're hurt." I lean closer to him, eyeing the roadmap of his hard labor—the rough patches here and there, dotted with a couple of puffy bumps, colored red and black.

He shakes his head. "It's nothing. Just a couple of blood blisters. And yes, I wear gloves when working with the fertilizer, but some of the other stuff is just easier without those getting in the way." He sighs a small, breathy chuckle. "I can definitely say farming is much harder on the body than football."

He turns his hand, caressing his calloused fingertips across my palm. My breath catches in my throat, and a flutter of excitement floods through my core.

It's a small gesture.

How can something so small feel so erotic and forbidden?

I pull my hand away.

Exhaling long and deep, Holt rocks back and forth, watching the night sky. "You haven't told me how far along you are. I mean, I know from Raylee and Ella that the normal time is forty weeks. That y'all count it at forty weeks while the rest of us just say nine months. Which I still don't understand because isn't that more like ten months?"

I ignore his second question and just answer his first one—because I'm not about to attempt to explain something as complicated as gestational calculations. "I'm a little over twenty-three weeks. My due date is October 3rd."

He nods. "So, it definitely happened that morning? That morning in the living room, right?"

Instantly, my defenses go up. I'm on high alert like a military man, waiting for a bomb to strike. "I didn't do this on purpose, to trap you, if that's what you're thinking. I took the morning-after pill, just like I told you I would. Bought it that morning and chased it with a bottle of chocolate milk. It's not like I planned this."

He stops rocking. "Mer, that's not what I was insinuating. I know this was an accident." A smile tugs at the corner of his mouth. "A wonderful-amazing-perfect accident." He chuckles. "In fact, from here on out, I vote that we never refer to our son as an accident again."

Instantly, I feel like a crushing weight has been lifted from my shoulders. A weight I didn't even realize was pounding me into the ground. And it's not just knowing that he believes I didn't do this to get to his money; it's the fact that he thinks this *accident* is wonderful and amazing. Because I do too. It's pretty damn spectacular.

"It's funny, you know?" There's no hiding the amusement in his voice.

My brow furrows. "What's funny? Our baby?"

He shakes his head. "Definitely not our baby. But you know that was my first time ever having sex without a condom. Very first time and bam...you get pregnant." He leans his head back and hums around a throaty whisper. "Pretty damn wild, huh?"

A slow burn sizzles in my body. "Are you serious? I was your first?" Well, that came out wrong. Obviously, I'm not his *first*. "I mean, you've never had sex with any other woman without a condom before? Never?"

Rubbing his hand across his lips, he tells me no.

That shouldn't make me feel special. That shouldn't be hot. That shouldn't turn me on. But it does. So, help me, it does. And I'm blaming these damn pregnancy hormones for having me all up in my feels right now—and not the fact that I haven't been with a man in one-hundred-and-forty-six days. Not that anyone is counting. And what's even fucking sadder is I probably wouldn't even be counting if I got knocked-up by any other guy. But this is Holt we're talking about. The man who buried himself so deep in my heart and soul that I never thought we could be separated. Never thought we could fracture.

That is until the seismic event known as Delaney Fitts ruptured our world.

Pathetic City. Population One.

I'm the mayor, chief of police, and citizen of the year.

When I don't comment on the fact that I'm the only woman who has ever felt the warmth and hardness of his bare cock inside of her body, he changes the subject. "You're small."

Well, that's an unexpected turn in conversation. "Huh?"

"Next week will be five months since I got you pregnant," he says with a sexy wink, made even sexier by the darkness of the stormy night, "but I remember Raylee and Ella being way bigger at five months. In the stomach, I mean." The teasing smile on his face falls as the possibilities flood his mind. "Are you okay? I know I asked yesterday, but the baby is healthy?"

"We're fine. We're both perfectly healthy." I shrug. "What can I say, I'm working on a farm every single evening and weekend. I guess the activity is keeping me slim. Well, as slim as I can be in my position."

"Are you sure?"

"Yeah, I'm sure."

"What about the doctor? Do you even have an OB/GYN in this town?"

"No, there's not one in town. I have to drive closer to the beach."

"What if he's a hack? You sure he's good? Are you positive you're okay?"

Rolling my eyes, I grab my phone and pull up the digital photo album I created for the ultrasound pictures. I dangle the phone in front of him. "He's not a hack. He even does ultrasounds at every appointment for no extra charge."

Well, 'no extra charge' might be overstating it. Daddy did give him six free pallets of Tifway 419 Bermuda. And that's not exactly cheap.

Holt's eyes widen, and he eagerly grabs the phone, intently studying picture after picture. "Holy hell, Mer. Look at this."

I bite back my smile, realizing I should have showed him these yesterday. "I know. I've seen them."

The rain starts falling harder, tapping against the roof like a drum. He cocks an eyebrow when he hands my phone back. "What are you craving?"

"Craving?"

"Well, with Anna, Raylee couldn't eat enough cheeseburgers. I swear she had five a week. With Ty, it was chips and cheese. You know, the kind from the Mexican restaurant."

I could lie and say I don't have any cravings, but he would just call me out for lying. "Fried rice. The kind you get at the Japanese restaurant. With the yum yum sauce."

He laughs. I ignore the way the sound makes my heart flutter. "Your town doesn't have an OB/GYN, but you have a Japanese steakhouse?"

"Yeah." I fold my hands over my stomach, wondering how much bigger I'm going to get. "I'm there so much he gives me a discount. Twenty-five percent off. He knows I hate spending money on eating out for lunch, but he knows the cravings are worse."

That makes him laugh even harder.

"I'm glad my addiction brings you so much joy, *sir*," I tease.

He's silent for an extra beat—an extra second longer than normal. And that one little second fills the air with an electric charge. A charge that makes my hair stand on end and gives me chill bumps. It fills me with coldness and warmth at the exact same time. It's strange how two completely opposite emotions can exist in the same space.

Loneliness and companionship.

Apathy and passion.

Hurt and healing.

Dislike and want.

His whisper is low and powerful. "I missed that. It's funny how the small stuff can bring you to your knees. Like what you just said. I missed you calling me, '*sir*'. You do it when you're mad or when you think I'm being too protective or when you're teasing me. And I missed how excited you would get every time I wanted to watch one of your old movies with you." He looks over at me. His gaze falls to my mouth, and he licks his lips. "And I missed your scrunched-up nose."

My body feels heavy and thick. "I don't scrunch my nose."

"Whatever you say, Mer."

I tell myself to shut up, not to say anything more, but my brain doesn't listen. "I missed your winks. You winked at me the very first time we met."

"That's it?" he asks.

"No. But I think that's all we should talk about," I answer honestly.

Why talk about the other stuff?

The way he always protected me. The way he brought me back out of my shell. The way he always supported my wants and dreams.

His kisses. His touch. The feel of his body on mine.

There's no need to talk about any of that. Because all those good memories coat my brain in a blanket of sunshine. But then the terrible truth of what he did spins around like a typhoon, wiping out all the good. He left me—alone and broke. *Alone and broken.* No home, no store, no safety.

No future husband.

And let's be real...that's where I thought our relationship was going.

He softly clears his throat. "Something is coming on TV tomorrow night. I'd really like for you to watch it."

"Your interview."

In true Holt fashion, he seems shocked that I know. "Deke told you about it?"

"Daddy didn't have to tell me. It's being advertised everywhere. I'd have to live in Siberia not to know about it."

He nods. "Will you watch it?"

I shrug. "If nothing better is on."

Chapter 8

Merit

Iglance at the clock, glad there's only five minutes left in the show. I've basically cried for two hours straight. My poor parents and Granny have had to listen to the TV through my snorts and hacks and sniffles.

This last sequence was obviously shot at a different time from the main part of the interview. Holt's not dressed in a suit, but in a T-shirt and gym shorts. He and Alaina are walking around the football field of the local university, and he's slowly working a football back and forth between his hands.

She asks him another question, using that calm, reporter voice. "So, do you place any blame on the authorities for what happened to you? I mean, it was a joint effort with multiple local, state, and federal agencies involved. That's a lot of people to get it wrong."

"No, I don't blame the police. They were working with the evidence they had at the time. I have several family members in law enforcement. The last thing they want to do is charge or convict an innocent man. They want to get it right. They want to bring the guilty parties to justice. We're all human. We all make mistakes," he says with a shrug.

"Besides the personal aspect of everything, what's been the most difficult part of all this?"

"Knowing that false accusations like these cast doubt on the truth. The survivors of sexual assault and domestic violence who come forward are warriors. They're fighters and champions. The same can be said of the families of the victims who have lost their lives to these crimes." He stops walking and looks into her eyes. "Statistics show that somewhere between two and eleven percent of accusations are false." He frowns. "I can't wrap my head around that. I mean, my cousin was a victim of a violent crime, including a sexual assault. She was murdered by her rapist. He wanted to keep her quiet. And to know that a small group of people take advantage of those horrors and report things that never happened? I can't even fathom it. The survivors of assault deserve more respect than that."

"I hear you're doing something about that." Like a true professional, Alaina gently steers the conversation. "When working out the details for this interview, you actually negotiated to receive a certain percentage of the ad revenue. Isn't that right?"

"Yes."

"And what are your plans for that money?" She softly giggles. "A bigger house? New cars?"

"We're in the process of establishing The Hill Family Charities. All the money from this interview will be diverted there. We've already designated two recipients. The money will be equally divided between two amazing organizations. One provides assistance to the survivors of sexual and domestic violence. The other provides resources to those who have been wrongly accused or convicted of crimes."

"That's wonderful. Really, it is. You're helping to provide a brighter future for those around you," Alaina says. "But what about you? What does your future hold? Do you catch yourself thinking about what *could have been*?"

"I can't focus on what could've happened. Yes, I could've been convicted. Yes, I could've spent years behind bars as an innocent man. But I've already spent too much time worrying about that. It cost me the most important thing in my life. Now, I've got to work on getting that back."

"Your girlfriend, Merit?" she asks, arching a perfectly waxed eyebrow.

He gives that *Holt* smile. The one that says he's hiding something, but it's all okay because he can still melt the panties right off you. "Alaina..."

She holds up a hand and softly laughs. "I know, I know. Boundaries for your loved ones."

The screen fades away to a newsroom set where Alaina gives her final remarks.

And finally... it's over.

I feel completely drained. Like someone pulled my plug and watched all my energy circle around and around before finally sliding down the sink.

How dare he?

How dare he make me feel sorry for him?

Make me understand him? Make me want to forgive him?

Make me love him again?

Not that I ever stopped.

It's not that easy. It can't be that easy. I *refuse* to make it that easy. He ruined me, he broke me. And here he is doing it all over again. I don't have the strength for this.

The truth is... I don't know if I'll ever have the strength again.

My family doesn't say anything when I leave the house, walking out to meet him by the firepit, where he's been pacing for the past two hours. The crackling flames cast his hard body in a haunting orange glow. He glances up, and I ignore how devastatingly handsome he is.

His brow furrows. "You've been crying."

All I do is nod.

"You watched it?"

What a stupid question.

"Of course, I watched it. We all did. I'm pretty sure every human on Earth with cable TV watched it."

His voice is soft and nervous. "What did you think of it? I mean, did it explain everything? I haven't seen it. I didn't even watch a rough cut of it."

"It explained everything." I take a deep breath. Unable to control myself, I cast my eyes downward, attempting to look at the ground. Of course, all I can see is my growing belly. "I really hope it helps you get your life back. Your career, your fans, your reputation. You deserve it."

He takes a step closer, erasing the distance between us. Unshed tears are forming in his eyes. "Fuck my reputation and everything else that goes along with it. None of that is important. All I want is you. I can't live without you. I don't give a shit about my career or my fans. I see that now. It's you. All I need is you." His hand presses against my stomach, and the baby immediately moves. "And our baby. We're a family."

I blink, trying to keep my own tears at bay, but it's completely useless. It's like trying to dam the Tennessee River with a sheet of typing paper. They spill onto my cheeks, burning my skin. A deep, dark anger curls around my damaged heart and suffocates it. "Fuck you." The curse feels foreign and vile on my tongue. "Fuck you, Holt. It's not that easy."

His hands slide up my arms, pulling me even closer to him.

My chest heaves in fragmented sobs. "You killed me. I was dead when you found me. And you resurrected me to life just to kill me again. You swallowed my love and then spit it back in my face. All I ever did was believe in you. I never questioned your innocence, not for one second. And one person—someone you don't even know— tossed out one simple theory during a brainstorming session, and you ran with it as truth."

My voice rises, and I'm yelling into the night. "I lost everything because of you. My store! You know how hard I worked for that, for that place to call my own. It was my heart and my soul, and I lost it because of you! And I'm not even talking about the lost income or the vandalism. I would've figured out a way to keep going if those were my only hurdles...but what was the point? When you tossed me out of your life, you kept part of me with you. The part that had fire and passion and a determination to persevere. You took away my will to fight. And you didn't even care! You never came to check on me. You never even called me." I wipe my face. "Kyra, my best friend, is half a country away from me now. She lost her job, too, you asshole!"

He shoves his body against mine, shadowing me with his massive frame. It's like he's trying to absorb my anger, soak it into his own body. He's so close I can see the freckles on his nose. "You're right. Nothing you're saying is wrong. I was a fucking coward. I should've never let you walk out that door. But...I did."

When he inhales, the sound rattles in his chest, like he's battling for oxygen. "I should've come to you, crawled to you, begged for forgiveness. I knew you had nothing to do with it. Even months later, when the attorneys and police were still trying to get a subpoena for your phone records, I knew. I knew you couldn't have had anything to do with it because you loved me just as much as I loved you. But I was scared shitless and kept my mouth shut. The more time that passed, the more excuses I made—even after you broke the case wide open. *'I'll let the trial get over and then I'll call her. I'll let the interview air and then I'll see her.'* They were all chicken-shit excuses because I was terrified of the possibility that you would hate me. I let my pride and embarrassment ruin your life and steal your store. I'll never forgive myself for that. But I promise you, Mer, I'll spend the rest of my life trying to make it up to you—to our son—if you just give me another chance. I love you."

I hate it when he says that. Why? Because I know it's still the truth.

He loves me.

Just like I love him.

His right hand slowly tracks a path over my shoulder and around to the back of my neck. Squeezing gently, he manipulates my head, giving himself better access to my emotion-filled and grief-stricken face. His lips graze my cheek. Chapped from spending the last few days in the sun, they feel like sandpaper against my skin. Rubbing his mouth back and forth, he dries my tears—licking the salt and softly kissing away the moisture. "Give me a chance to make us whole, baby."

He dips lower, and when his lips brush against my own, burning desire crashes over me like a tidal wave. Despite my inner protest, my mouth opens, and his hot breath fans into my body, begging for me to replenish his air with my own. And when his tongue gently teases me, I nearly collapse.

His whisper is filled with gravel and lava. "Tell me you love me, Merit. Tell me we're a family. Tell me you want me."

Reaching deep down into the pit of my soul, I muster all of my strength, all of my resolve. "I don't want you."

"Don't lie, Merit."

"Mmmm?"

"You might not forgive me. And that's okay. I don't deserve your forgiveness. But you still love me. It's written all over your face."

I stare into his eyes. It's too dark to see their striking blue color, but I know it's there.

"Tell me the truth."

I back away from his embrace. Instantly cold and empty, I wrap my hands around my stomach, holding our baby. "I want you to leave. Can't you see you're killing me all over again, Holt? Every time I lay eyes on you, it's a slow death. Over and over and over." I struggle to swallow. "Please leave. Give me some peace."

He shakes his head, ready to protest.

"Leave!" I scream. Louder than I've ever screamed before. "If you love me, listen to me! I can't be around you. I can't be next to you. I can't even look at you. Anger is festering in me like a cancer. I need time. Please... just give me time."

Folding his hands on top of his head, he walks around, pacing again and thinking. Eventually, he stops in front of me. His face is solemn. Determined. "Okay. I'll give you some space, some time to think. But I'm not leaving for long. I'll go home, pack a few things, and take care of some business. I'll drive back down on Sunday. And then? I'm. Not. Leaving." He punctuates each word, with a firm and swift delivery.

He takes a step forward, but he doesn't invade my personal space. "Because I meant what I said. Your place is with me. In *our* home. In *our* life. You're fucking mine, Merit. Your love is stamped on my DNA, branded into my bone marrow." His eyes dart around my face, absorbing me to memory. "I'm not stopping till I win this battle. I'll fight for our family... here, now, forever, and always. I'll fucking fight for *you*, Merit. Until my dying day."

Holt

I wipe down the kitchen counter. It's not like I can leave it messy; I have no idea how long I'll be gone. Could be days. Could be weeks. Could be months. But whenever I do come home, the last thing I want is rotten, crusty-ass food pieces stuck to everything. Mom and Raylee have been helping me clean over the past few months. This is a really big house for one person to clean. I used to have a group of retired ladies come in once a week to clean. Four of them. They would divide the house into sections and spend the better part of a day cleaning. I paid them well too. Really well. I mean, one of them used to be a special education teacher. I never wanted the bad karma of being a tightwad with them to come back on me.

But they quit.

They quit as soon as I was arrested in December.

Another one of them used to be my Sunday School leader when I was a kid. And she said she wouldn't scrub my toilets because she thought I was a pedophile.

My phone buzzes, alerting me that someone is at the front gate. Tossing the rag in the sink, I grab my phone and slide open the app from the lock screen. As soon as I do, the system automatically asks the person to identify themselves. When the video pops across my screen, my mouth drops open, and I can't even think straight.

To say I'm shocked is an understatement.

She scoots closer to the camera and yells into the microphone. "Merit Browning!"

I can't help but laugh. She's carrying my baby. I'm pretty sure I know her last name.

Buzzing her through, my heart pounds against my ribs. By the time I open the front door, she's already out of her car. Jogging to meet her, it's hard not to notice the scowl on her face. But even that can't take away from her beauty. I last saw her on Thursday night, and it's only Saturday, so I know it's probably improbable... but I swear her breasts have grown and her baby bump is sitting a little bit higher.

I can't fucking wait to get my hands on her and feel our baby move.

When her eyes roam across my bare chest, she blushes. My dick immediately responds, jumping in my shorts. I reach out to pull her into my arms, but she sidesteps me and folds her own arms across her chest. Sighing, I stuff my hands in my pockets. "Hey."

"Hey," she says as she looks down at the ground.

I'm not sure what to say or how to question her sudden appearance at my house—at *our* house. The last thing I want to do is scare her off.

After a few *really* long seconds, she looks up. Her voice is pouty and demanding. "I'm moving back into the Children's Wing. And you," she points a finger at me, "are gonna pay for my health insurance."

Holy hell.

She's moving back in. I'll pay for the entire state of Alabama's health insurance if that's what it takes to get her back here. "Yeah. Absolutely."

"And... and... I'll stay at least until the baby is six weeks old. I'll give you bonding time before we start the custody arrangement."

Over my dead body is she ever leaving my side again. Of course, I don't say that out loud. She already knows my feelings on the matter, and I know better than to rock this already-unstable boat. I'll take this win and build on it. I'll build the shit out of it—a damn skyscraper taller than the Empire State Building. "Perfect. Or even twelve weeks. That may be better."

She licks her lips and stutters around. "Well... I mean... we can discuss it, but don't push your freakin' luck."

It's impossible to hide my smile. I'm so damn happy. Despite myself, I can't help but lift a questioning eyebrow, praying I don't stick my foot in my mouth. "Mer, can I ask what changed?"

Her lips thin. "I lost my job."

"You lost your job?"

"Yep."

"Are you okay? What happened?" I ask.

Her eyes narrow in accusation. "You happened."

"What?"

"My boss found out who you were, and he called you a pedophile and a pervert." She swallows. "I corrected him. Using very colorful language." She shrugs. "And then he fired me."

My muscles tense with anger. "That guy's an asshole."

"Yeah, well, that asshole was my only source of income. The only jobs available down there are closer to the beach, and I would waste half my money on gas going back and forth, not to mention the time. Things at the farm are..." her voice trails off. "I mean, they already..." she sighs, unwilling to finish her thought. "Well, I just don't want my parents worrying about feeding me and paying my medical bills." Once again, her eyes trail slowly across my chest and down my stomach. With a quick flicker to my growing crotch, they dart back up to my face. "They shouldn't be burdened by the fact that their daughter chose to have unprotected sex." Her face reddens when she says the word sex. Granted, she could be blushing in anger because she quickly adds, "With a man who then believed an obvious lie, kicked her out of the house, and decimated her business."

Damn. It sounds worse every time she says it.

I am, without a doubt, the world's dumbest and shittiest man. Hell, I don't even deserve to be called a man.

"Mer, I—"

She quickly interrupts me, shifting the conversation. "Well, I'll just drive around and unpack. I guess I'll need the code for the gate and door. I assume you changed it?"

"Yeah. It's the day we met. Six digits."

She nibbles the bottom of her perfectly pink lip. "You mean it's Anna's birthday."

"Technically, her birthday is the day after. It was on Saturday. Remember, we had her party early on Friday night."

Her face falls into serious thought, and she stares at the ground once again. I use the distraction to my advantage and wrap my hand around her wrist. She immediately stops breathing. My body sizzles the second I touch her, heat filling my every nerve-ending, pulsing and buzzing through me like a charged current. That electricity that's always been there is still there.

And it always will be.

"Hey," I scrape my foot against the concrete and nudge my tennis shoe against her own, taking me back to the day when she first agreed to go on a date with me, when I brushed my bare foot against hers in the middle of the store. "Drive on around. I'll come through the house and meet you. Let's get you back where you belong."

Of course, she doesn't really belong in the Children's Wing; she belongs with me.

In *our* room. In *our* bed.

But there's time for that.

There's always that *push* and *pull* with Merit. Her need to push me away, protect her heart from damage. And her desire to pull me close, pour her lifeblood into my soul. The warring emotions were there before the arrest; and they're still there now—and even more prominent. I have to be smart. I realize there's an appropriate time and place for each of those actions. So, for right now, I'll let her push me away. I'll take the small wins and keep my eyes on the prize—the prize being the lifetime of happiness I'm gonna give to her and our son.

Her eyes lift, and she peeks at me from underneath her long, dark eyelashes. "I don't belong here, Holt. Don't mistake my necessity for need. Or even want." Yanking from my grasp and turning on her heels, she climbs into her SUV and drives back down the circular, guest driveway in front of the house.

She better enjoy the calm now, because there's gonna come a time when all I do is *pull*.

And I won't stop pulling until we're joined as one.

Just like the first time she moved in, it doesn't take very long. She brought even fewer clothes with her this time because according to her 'her ass is getting too big to wear anything that doesn't have industrial-strength elastic'.

I watch her as she's sitting on the floor arranging her array of old movies in the cabinet. She looks at the cover of every single one and smiles. She misses the shelf with one as she goes to put it in its place, and it slides out and hits her in the head. I can't help but laugh when she curses under her breath.

Standing up, I clap my hands. "All right, it's more than past time we eat. How about I go grab us some steaks and throw them on the grill?"

Her face immediately turns a pale shade of green, and her eyes roll back in her head. Her body shudders. And not the good kind of shudder.

"Uh-oh. No steaks?" I ask.

She shakes her head. "Your son doesn't like steak."

"Well, I'm gonna have to change that before he decides to take a girl out on a first date," I joke.

She wraps an arm around her stomach. "How about we worry about bottle feeding first, before you teach him about dropping two-hundred dollars on some steak dinner for a girl who doesn't even deserve it."

Laughing, I lift my ballcap and turn it around backward. "Whoa there, Momma. Someone's a little overprotective of him already, huh?"

She doesn't answer. Instead, she watches me. To be more exact, she watches the flex of my arms as I get my hat just right. When all the air drains from the room, she drags her gaze back to her movies. The one she's looking at is upside down.

I don't even think she realizes it.

She's so freakin' funny.

"Anyway, no steak," she says.

"Chicken fried rice from the Japanese steakhouse?" I ask.

Her multi-colored eyes light up, and it looks like she's about to start drooling.

Smiling, I nod. "I take that as a yes."

"Yes, please, if you wouldn't mind. I'll go to the grocery store tomorrow and get my own groceries."

Like hell she will.

I just ignore that comment because I don't want a fight. "I'll be back soon." Walking down the hall to the Big House, I can't believe how lucky my day has gotten.

Less than an hour later, I'm walking back through the door with more food than an army could eat. "Mer?" Rounding the corner to the living room, I find her fast asleep on the couch. The TV's softly playing some black and white movie, and a box of books is sitting on the floor in front of her. Stealing one from the top, I turn it over in my hand. It's got a picture of a pregnant woman on the front. It says it's some sort of guide from pregnancy all the way through the baby's first year.

Shit. I guess I need to read that.

Softly tucking a piece of hair behind Merit's ear, I try to wake her. "Mer? I've got the food. It's time to wake up. It's time to eat."

She answers me with a soft moan, weighed down by the heaviness of her dreams.

My God, she's beautiful.

Her arm protectively hugs her small baby bump. Even in her sleep, she's holding our child.

She's gonna be such a great mom.

Let's be real… a great wife, a great lover, a great partner.

A great everything. Forever.

If she'll forgive me, of course.

Fuck that. I mean, *when* she forgives me. Not *if*, but *when*.

I stroke her cheek. "Aren't you hungry?"

This time she doesn't even answer. She just softly snores. Tilting my head, I spend a few more minutes watching her. Eventually, I pull her into my arms and carry her into the bedroom. I should be given a medal for keeping her in the Children's Wing and not hauling her over to *our* bedroom in the Big House. But I want that decision to be hers. I want her to make it willingly and freely because she wants me just as much as I want her. Covering her with the blankets, I tuck her into bed.

Not wanting to leave—because what if she wakes up hungry—I store the food in the fridge and settle on the couch with my book about pregnancy.

Because I've got several months of catching up I need to tackle.

Chapter 10

Holt

I know I'm a hard sleeper.

Unfortunately, that didn't change. Even after everything that happened. Even after Delaney crawled around my house in the middle of the night like some freaky-ass vampire, it still didn't change.

But it's pretty hard to sleep when someone is constantly slamming a silverware drawer open and closed a couple of dozen feet away from your head.

Blinking against the sun, I drag my hand across my face and stretch out, wallowing into the couch. After a second, I sit up and lean back against the pillows. "And hello to you too." My voice is low and thick with sleep.

Merit stares at me from behind the kitchen island. She's got a plate of leftover fried rice in front of her, and her cheeks are stuffed like a chipmunk. I have to wait on her to chew and swallow.

She circles her fork around in the air. "This is completely unacceptable, Holt."

I cock an eyebrow, pretending I don't know what she's talking about. "Seriously? You know that Japanese steakhouse has won awards, right?"

She dramatically rolls her eyes. "I'm not talking about the food, and you know it." She drags her fork through the yum yum sauce and licks it. "You can't be sleeping on the couch. I said *I* was moving into the Children's Wing. Not you."

"It didn't feel right to leave you on your first night back. What if you woke up hungry? I wanted to be here to heat the food up for you."

"I know how to work a microwave."

"I'm sure you do. I just wished you would've used it last night." I lean forward, balancing my forearms on my knees. "You didn't eat at all yesterday after you got here. That can't be good—for you or the baby. Maybe that's why your stomach's small." I pick up the book from the coffee table and shake it. "This says you should be bigger."

She spoons another forkful in her mouth. "Those things are just a guide. They're not the Bible. I'm big enough. The doctor says everything is perfect." She looks down and pats her stomach. "He has plenty of room to move around." A smile tugs against her beautiful face.

I push off the couch and cross the room. "Is that what's happening? Is he moving now?"

"Yeah," she says softly.

I tip my head at her belly. "May I?"

She studies me, looking deeply into my eyes. I probably look like crap after sleeping on the couch all night long, but I can't help the swell of my dick when her pupils dilate.

I pick up her can of caffeine-free diet soda and swish it around my mouth, hoping to kill the stench of morning breath before I invade her personal space. She pretends to scowl. I'm sure she thinks I don't know when she's pretending.

But we all know I can read her face.

Fanning both of my hands across her firm and taut bump, I frown when I don't immediately feel anything. "What's wrong, buddy? You stop moving? You playing a trick on your old man?"

Nothing.

"Aren't you glad Mommy moved back home to Daddy?" I can't help but laugh when he immediately starts kicking and flipping. "See? He knows you made a smart decision," I say with a wink.

She spins away and busies herself with putting her dishes in the dishwasher. "The jury's still out."

Leaning against the countertop, I sigh, praying one day our lives can get back on track. I'll stop at nothing to make that happen. "I need to find a doctor."

Her eyes widen with worry, and a wild strand of hair falls from her ponytail. "What's wrong? Are you sick?"

She's so freakin' funny.

"Let me rephrase that. I need to find *you* a new doctor. We need a baby doctor. I know you liked the other one, but I can't imagine you wanna drive all the way down there for appointments. And what about when you go into labor?"

"I can find my own doctor." She grabs a wet hand towel and wipes at the crumbs on the countertop, her motions slowing as she thinks. Her voice drops an octave, showcasing the unease coursing through her like a flashing neon sign. "Unless you want me to use someone specific since you're paying for my insurance?"

"I wouldn't dictate that, and you know it. It's just..." I pause, shrugging. "I want the best for you. I want my family to be safe and healthy. I want *you* to be safe and healthy."

She nibbles on the side of her lip.

"Anyway, Raylee said she'd get us the information for her doctor. Ella used the same one. They both say he's great." I drag my hand through my hair. "We can get it today; they're coming over."

She folds her arms across her chest. Her cleavage plumps, straining against her tank top. Talk about distracting. "Excuse me?"

"Once things...settled down...the kids wanted to come back. I couldn't wait to see them again. They've been coming over on Sunday afternoons to swim."

Her jaw tics. "I've got some errands to run. I'll head out before they get here."

"They were hoping to see you. I called them last night when I went to get the food. I had to tell them I was staying in town. Last I talked to them, I told them I was leaving, at the ass-crack of dawn today, to be with you and had no idea when I would be back home." I cock my head, trying to gauge her reaction. "Everyone's really excited to see you."

She shakes her head and blinks against glassy eyes. "I don't wanna see them."

"Mer." I reach for her, but she shuffles away. "Why?" I ask.

"Because I didn't just lose you, I lost them too." She swallows. "They left me, just like you did."

She's right. They did.

Because I forced them to choose. And they chose me. Even though, they knew I was wrong.

So fucking wrong.

Chapter 11

Merit

I'm about to pull out of the driveway when Holt comes jogging out the door.

Of the Children's Wing.

Maybe I should buy a lock for the interior door that joins the Children's Wing to the Big House. A lock with only one key.

He definitely wouldn't like that. Not one bit.

Just like he didn't like the fact that I didn't come home last night until after ten. I waited until I knew everyone would be gone. I meant what I said; I'm not ready to see them.

I thought they loved me. Just like he did.

He knocks on my window. Of course, he would have to be shirtless. With small beads of sweat rolling down the tanned lines of his chest and stomach. His blond waves are damp with perspiration, and he lifts his arms, dragging his hands through his hair. The movement ripples the muscles across the ridges of his ribs.

Asshole.

He knows I love it when he does that.

Growling, I lower my window.

"Where are you going?" he asks.

"Out."

He sweeps his hand through the air. "Care to elaborate?"

"I'm going to look for a job. *Sir*."

"A job?" His brows furrow in confusion like he doesn't even know what the word means.

"Yeah, you know that thing you do to make money. To pay bills, to buy stuff."

He grunts. "Why are you looking for a job?"

"I have bills to pay, Holt. I have groceries to buy." I tap my fingers against the steering wheel. "I need to save money. Raising a child can't be cheap."

He props his arms against the frame of my SUV and leans in. He smells like soap and sweat. "Neither of you will ever want for anything. You know that."

"I told you I don't want your money. I won't take it." I look away, refusing to drown in his good looks. "Paying for my insurance is one thing. That's just me making a responsible decision for the health of our child. But when it comes to supporting him? To buying his food and clothes and putting a roof over his head? I can do it. With my own money."

His jaw tenses, but he doesn't fight me. "What are you thinking? Do you know where you're gonna look?"

"I'm not sure. I mean, I have the retail experience, of course. I worked at the law firm too. I guess I just need to see who's hiring."

He nods, not saying anything.

"Anyway, I'll stop by the grocery store on my way home and get my own groceries. You don't need to worry about bringing stuff over to my fridge anymore." I couldn't shop yesterday because I knew I would be out late avoiding the Hill Family. They've already hurt me enough; I didn't wanna add clabbered milk and spoiled bacon to the list of grievances I have with them.

He cocks an eyebrow. "So now, bottled water, caffeine-free Coke, and yogurt is too much? I can't even do that?"

"Holt," I warn.

He pushes away from the SUV, nodding. "It's okay. I understand."

The sad look on his face shouldn't upset me, but it does. It shouldn't hurt my heart, but it does. And for some inexplicable reason, I throw him a bone. "I saw the doctor's information you left on the countertop. I'll call him today and make an appointment."

And of course, the smile on his face shouldn't make me happy, but it does. "That's great. I started on your insurance paperwork already. Even if it's not in place by the time of your first appointment, I'll just pay in cash. Get it for as soon as you can, okay?"

"All right."

"Do... do you think it would be okay for me to go with you?"

I guess I could say no. But I did vow not to keep Holt away from his child. "Sure. That would be okay."

"Perfect," he says with a smile. One of those perfect Holt Hill smiles...

I raise the window but not before his words float in to haunt me. "Be careful. I love you."

My eyes are red and scratchy and nearly swollen shut. Glancing at the clock lit on my dashboard, I can't believe I've been sitting here for nearly three hours.

Staring at my store.

Well, what used to be my store.

It's obviously been rented to someone because there's no sign advertising it as available. Not only that, it looks like the men's clothing store next door has shut down too.

It still blows my mind that it's gone.

My store, not the men's clothing store.

Something I worked so hard for... just gone. Like it never existed. Well, except for the *Run and Jump and Twirl* sign still attached to the storefront roof. You wouldn't believe what it was going to cost to have it removed so I just left it.

Let the new people deal with it.

I sigh so deeply it hurts my ribs. And my heart. With one lasting glance, I start the car and head to the grocery store. After getting home, I unload everything and make a quick sandwich before snuggling on the couch with an Elvis movie. I'm fighting a losing battle with my yawns when I hear the hallway door open.

It makes me angry that even his casual walk sounds sexy.

I pull my blanket up to my neck, trying to hide my body. I'm wearing a skintight tank top with no bra and shorts that used to be loose.

Now they're not.

I feel his eyes on me, staring at me from the corner of the room. "Do I need to start jamming the door with a chair?" I ask.

A whisper of a laugh rumbles low in his chest. "Do you want to?"

Bastard knows the real answer to that. So, I ignore him.

He walks around. Instead of sitting on the loveseat opposite from me, he squeezes onto the couch, forcing me to fold my legs up so my feet aren't in his lap. "How'd the job hunt go today?"

I shrug. "I'm still looking." I applied at a dry cleaner, a gas station, three attorney offices, a tanning salon, and an insurance company. I'm willing to do anything until something better-suited for me comes along. I'm a hard worker, and a job's a job.

"I was giving that some thought," he says, slightly drawing the words out to pique my curiosity.

I study his profile. The side lamp paints him in a soft, ethereal glow. His facial hair is a little longer than normal, and the freckles on his nose are darker, bronzed against the sunburn of his cheeks.

I turn away. "I'm not mooching off you, Holt."

"I wasn't gonna suggest it. You made it pretty clear how you feel."

I shift, trying to ease the discomfort that's been plaguing my lower back today. "So?"

"How about you work for me?" He quickly shakes his head the second my mouth falls open to protest. "I don't mean *me*. I mean the new charity. I need someone to help me get The Hill Family Charities off the ground and running. Mom and Raylee and Ella have been helping in their spare time; but let's face it, none of them have that much spare time."

He spreads his arm across the back of the couch. His muscles loom over me, making my tongue thick in my mouth. "It wouldn't be forever. The plan is to hire a full-time employee and a couple of part-time workers once everything is up and running. In addition, we'll have an attorney on retainer—one with non-profit experience. I'm interviewing lawyers for it now." He smiles. "I'd love to think it could be successful and grow. Grow into something that makes a difference. More employees, more people, more organizations to help. But that's all down the road. Right now, I just need someone to handle the basic work while we're getting everything set up. With all the experience you had at the law firm and the store, it should come easy to you. What do you say?"

I furrow my brow in thought. "You're serious?"

"Yeah. Why wouldn't I be?"

"You wanna hire me?"

He smiles. "Hell, yes. You're the hardest worker I know."

"And you're gonna pay me for this?"

"I did some internet sleuthing and talked to a couple of contacts I have with small charities I worked with through the NFL. All the salary numbers are pretty much in line with one another. You'd be compensated fair and square. I'd pay your taxes. Plus, no health insurance would be deducted from your salary. I'm paying that separately, just like we agreed on."

I nibble on the inside of my cheek, wincing when I accidentally bite too hard. "How long are we talking?"

"At least through the birth. Oh, and paid maternity leave."

I stare at the TV, watching the bright Technicolor flashes color the screen. "Remember, I'll be moving out. After the baby comes and you have time to bond. I'll leave. I can't stay here."

He doesn't answer.

I sit higher on the couch. "Holt, you know I can't stay here, right? I need you to say you understand. Tell me—" My protest is cut off by a sharp tinge of pain in my lower back. I grimace, clenching my teeth through the muscle spasm from hell.

His eyes grow wide, and his hand snakes over the blanket, gripping my thigh. "What's wrong?! Are you okay?" His frenzied voice is almost comical.

I take a few deep breaths and pat his hand. "It's nothing. My back's just sore today. I had a spasm."

"Shit. Really? Does it happen a lot?"

I snort. "You're asking a pregnant woman if her back hurts often? You sure you got a college degree?"

He rolls his eyes. "Haha, smart-ass. You know what I mean."

I shrug. "Just depends on the day. It's better than the first four months. I threw up constantly. I mean, like anywhere and everywhere. Trash cans, the sink, the fields at home. I even threw up in my purse once because I was in the middle of Walmart and couldn't make it to the bathroom."

"But you're feeling better now?"

"My stomach's better, yeah."

Holt gives me that look. That look that says he can read my mind.

"But other things hurt instead?" he asks.

I really don't want to complain. The truth is I love being pregnant. Feeling my baby move inside of me? I can't imagine anything closer to Heaven on Earth. It's...miraculous. I give him a reassuring smile. "Don't worry. I'm fine."

He knows I'm placating him.

Letting me win this battle, he shifts the conversation. "Scoot over," he nods in his own direction. "I'll rub your back."

"Excuse me?"

"I'll give you a back massage."

"You... wanna put your hands on me?" My heart quickens. I don't know why the words from my mouth sound so breathless and intense.

He chuckles, gifting me with his panty-dropping smile. His blue eyes brighten in good humor. "You don't have to make it sound so scandalous. Contrary to what you may think, I can give a backrub in a completely non-sexual way."

He winks.

When I don't move, he reaches underneath my blanket. Grabbing my thighs, he yanks me closer. I ignore the scorching fire burning across my body with his touch. I completely disregard the pool of desire filling my core. He effortlessly shifts me into a seated position and spins me so my back is facing him. Without warning, his hands set to work, immediately burrowing into my tense muscles. Euphoria instantly floods me. Lobbing my head to the side, a moan tumbles from my lips.

"That good, huh?"

It really is.

He takes his time. Working my neck first, he slides the thin straps of my tank top down my shoulders. His fingertips trace the beads of my spine. His knuckles grind against the tight muscles of my low back.

It's hypnotizing. So very hypnotizing.

I'm not sure how long we stay like this...minutes, hours, days.

All I know is that I'm floppy like a wet noodle and completely refusing to even acknowledge the pulsing vibrations humming through my clit.

Nope. I'm keeping that monster locked tightly in the closet.

"So..." his whisper is low and gravelly. It sounds like he's struggling to even get the words out. "Does that feel better?"

"So much—" My sentence is cut short.

I've got that feeling.

Not the clit feeling, but that tickly, tingly feeling in the back of your throat that quickly shifts to the nose.

Oh no. This can't be happening.

"What's wrong?" Holt asks.

My head shakes back and forth, and my body shivers. "S... sn... sneeze." Right then, it happens. My nose explodes.

Really, it's no different than the sneeze I've had my entire life. No different than any normal sneeze from any normal Joe Blow off the street.

Except for one thing.

Now, I pee myself.

Ever since I got pregnant, I pee on myself. Like *all* over myself.

And it just happened.

I just peed my pants in front of the famous Holt Hill.

Now don't get me wrong, we used to live together. Like, in the same room *together*. So, we've seen each other pee. But always on a toilet. Never in our pants.

"Fuck me."

Holt's hands fall from my back. "What's the matter?" He can tell by the tone in my voice that the *fuck me* wasn't a plea muttered in sexual desire.

"I can't believe that just happened," I mumble.

"What? What just happened?"

I bury my face in my hands, not saying anything.

"Mer?" He leans around my shoulder. His breath smells like mint. "What's up?" He tugs on my hands. "Tell me."

I pull against him, fighting to keep my red face hidden. "I just peed."

"Huh?"

Giving up, I slap my hands on my knees and scooch around to face him. "When I sneezed, I peed. Like really peed. Not just a dribble."

For a split second he stares at me. And then he bursts out laughing. "You peed your pants?"

"Yes." I glare at him. "It's not funny," I say with a pout.

"Oh, come on, it's pretty damn funny." He bumps against me. "Let me see."

"How can you think this is funny? My bodily functions aren't even mine anymore."

He licks his bite-worthy lips, and before I know what's happening, he gently kisses my neck. Right in that wonderful spot under the corner of my jaw, where his breath tickles my ear and sends a chill down my spine. "I think it's funny because it is. Pee and poop are always funny. Shit like that happens to everyone. Literally, in my case. I had to leave the second Super Bowl game I played in during the third quarter because I shit my pants. Luckily, our pants were black that year. The announcers saw the way I was running and thought I pulled a groin muscle. They were astonished when I ran back onto the field ten minutes later. I missed a whole series."

My eyes widen. "Seriously?"

"Seriously. Now, let me see."

Groaning, I stand up and point my ass in his face. Feeling around with my hand, it's just a pile of soaked panties and pajama shorts. There's even a wet spot on his couch.

Fortunately, his laugh is now contagious, and I can't help but laugh at myself.

"When did this start?" he says, wiping at a rogue dribble running down my inner thigh.

"The minute you put a baby inside of me."

Wrong words.

I didn't mean for those words to carry such an impact. To have so much heat behind them, so much lust.

But they do.

And he knows it.

He stops breathing, and all the air is immediately sucked out of the room. Once again, that seems to be happening a lot lately. At this rate, I'm gonna need to buy oxygen masks to survive being near him for the next few months.

His eyes widen, and the muscles in his forearms twitch. My eyes instinctively dart to the bulge in his shorts.

I want nothing more than to fall against him. Kiss him. Hold him. Feel his body slide into mine.

Stumbling forward, I try to gain my composure. "I... I need to go change."

His arm reaches for me, but for once, thankfully, I'm quicker than him. And that's for the best. Because I'm not sure I'm strong enough to withstand the pull I have toward him right now. Holt's a magnetic field, and I'm beyond terrified I'm about to get trapped in its drag.

Chapter 12

Holt

I'm blessed.

I get that.

I don't take getting out of jail and having my name cleared lightly.

But right now? Right now, I'm seriously considering fucking everything up *again* and possibly landing my ass in jail *again*.

Because I'm about two damn minutes away from plowing my fist into the face of the guy who's obviously hitting on my woman.

My pregnant woman.

My future wife.

I take one last glance in the rearview mirror before climbing out and slamming the truck door. My jaw clenches as I cross the parking lot, making my way to one of the sidewalk tables in front of the coffeehouse. Not to mention, I'm already in a bad mood because she's not at her favorite coffeehouse—the one three doors down from her store. We're meeting at one that's near the middle of the university campus and crawling with preppy little college kids, ready to spend Daddy's money on overpriced drinks. I mean, last I checked, this coffee shop charges a whole two dollars more per smoothie than the other coffee shop. And it's a smaller cup. And it doesn't taste anywhere near as good.

Merit's willing to spend extra money on her weekly smoothie; that just goes to show me how hard she's still trying to avoid dealing with the loss of her store.

Hopefully, she won't have to deal with that loss for too much longer.

When she found out I had errands to run in town, she asked if I wanted to meet her here to go over some business with the Foundation. Merit has taken to her new position with The Hill Family Charities like a fish in water. She'd make a wonderful permanent employee; but alas, that would kind of defeat the purpose of the errands I was just running.

As soon as my sneaker steps over the curb, the guy's laugh assaults me, pounding against my brain like a tom-tom drum on steroids.

"That's so funny." He leans across the table, getting too damn close to her. "Has anyone ever told you that you're a great storyteller?"

Merit cocks her head, studying him with a small—but cautious—smile and just shrugs.

The summer sun is setting behind her, flaming her redwood hair in more red than brown. And the purple shirt she's wearing pulls tighter across her large breasts than it did last summer when I first saw her wearing it. She has her chair situated very close to the table, so close her stomach is hidden by the tabletop and her open laptop. That's the only reason I haven't ripped this guy's throat out—I'm giving him the benefit of the doubt, assuming he must not know she's pregnant.

With my son.

Her cheeks are tinged pink from the sun, and there's a very good possibility that a majority of the male population would cash in their 401(k)s just to kiss her lips right now—the way they glisten is so damn mouthwatering.

And considering today was a no-makeup day for Merit, I know the only thing on them is plain old Vaseline. Simple, effective, and cheap.

The douche leans even closer, grazing his hand against hers as it hovers over her mouse. "Well, if no one has told you that, surely they've told you how gorgeous you are."

What. The. Hell.

Merit looks into his eyes, considering if she should answer his question, even though it's rhetorical and nothing but a shameless flirtation. Don't get me wrong, what he's saying is the honest truth, but it's still him trying to get a piece of tail.

And I think what hurts me even more is the fact that Merit is enjoying this conversation. I can read it on her face. She likes this shitbag fawning all over her. I bet if he asked her out, she'd actually consider it.

Yeah, well, over my dead body.

And then it happens.

He does it.

He commits the carnal sin.

"Meeting a beautiful woman, here, just randomly? That feels like kismet, don't you think? I'd like to get to know you better," he says. "Would you like to go out sometime? Any day, any time. You pick."

I watch in slow motion as her mouth opens to accept another man's invitation for a date.

In one second flat, I dart from the shadows of the building and descend on their table like I'm the fucking Grim Reaper. "She's already got a man. She doesn't need another one." My voice doesn't even sound like it belongs to me. It's low and strangled.

They immediately turn to me, startled by the intrusion. Merit's jaw drops, and her eyes dart around, trying to calculate how long I've been listening to their little lovefest. He narrows his eyes, sizing up the competition before turning back to Merit. "You're married?" he asks.

Her eyes balloon, and she shakes her head. Her gaze keeps flickering to mine. "No, absolutely not. I mean...we're not together. We aren't even dating."

I hate those words. They just keep reminding me what a foolish asshole I am.

Not wanting to drag this out—because I selfishly want Merit for myself, plus I'm terrified that she was actually considering a date with this guy—I bluntly say the words that need to be said. "We're having a baby together." I pin him with a stare. "She's having *my* baby."

He sits back in his chair, completely shocked. "You're pregnant?"

Merit's face turns beet red, making her look like she just ran a marathon in the Sahara. She pushes back from the table, the wrought iron chair scraping against the concrete sidewalk. Once she's far enough out, she just nods toward her stomach and smooths her hands down the front of her shirt, accentuating her baby bump.

The guy blinks, absorbing the picture in front of him. After a moment, he takes a deep breath. "But you guys aren't together? You're available?"

Oh. Hell. No.

This better not be going where I think it's going.

He doesn't even give Merit a chance to answer, to nod, to send out a smoke signal; he just dives right back in where he left off. "What about the date? I'd still like to go out with you. I mean, once you pop, you won't have the kid with you all the time, right? We can still kick it when it's with him," he says foolishly, pointing his finger at me to indicate I am 'him'.

Okay.

There's so much wrong with this situation, it's almost comical.

One: Taint LeDouche referred to the miracle of my future wife giving birth as her 'popping'.

Two: Weasel Dickweed used the term 'kicking it' like we're in middle school.

And three: Pencil Cock Peckerhead called my son an 'it'.

Guess, my thoughts of the Grim Reaper were warranted.

Before I can make more poor choices and choke the life from this assclown, Merit saves the day by being Merit. Her hands fly across the table, and she knocks his expensive iced coffee drink into his lap. "Whoops," she says, none too convincingly.

He flies up from his seat, vigorously wiping the brown liquid from his khaki shorts. "What the hell?"

"Please don't ever refer to my son as 'it'." She possessively wraps her hands around her stomach before tilting her head and looking at him with utter pity. "And 'kicking it'? Seriously, what are you, twelve?"

Growling under his breath, he just turns and walks away, leaving his plastic cup and straw scattered on the ground. We both watch in stunned silence as he crosses the parking lot, hops on an orange Vespa with black flames running down the side, and putters away.

Which would be totally fine if we were in Italy. Or, I'd even grant some leeway at the beach—any beach in America. But we're in the middle of Alabama.

And it's orange with black flames.

C'mon, let's be real, dude.

"Umm. Was that a Vespa?" Merit's voice flitters through the quiet.

"Yes. Yes, it was."

She purses her lips into a pout. "Not really a storming-off-in-a-mad-angry-dash kind of vehicle, huh?"

All I have to do is side glance at her, and we both burst out laughing. We laugh so hard I get a stitch in my side. Eventually settling down, I grab his discarded cup, toss it in the trash, and sit in the now vacant chair across from Merit.

Sighing deeply, she turns back to her laptop, acting like she can ignore the fact that she nearly agreed to go on a date with a guy while carrying my baby. Nearly agreed to go on a date with a guy when she belongs to me. She's making me feel like a damn caveman with jealousy and abandonment issues.

Which I realize is totally uncalled for—if I'm looking at things from a purely objective stance—because my conscience frequently reminds me that I'm the one who ruined our lives.

But I'm not objective. I'm not impartial. I'm not neutral. I'm not fucking Switzerland in this situation. I'm the shot heard around the world.

And I'll do nothing short of beg, borrow, and steal to get us back on track.

Because I love her. I can't live without her.

"So, I'd like to discuss the future plans for the Foundation and our timelines for everything." She flips through her notebook, flashing pages and pages of her to-do list. "I've spent the last couple of days researching, and this to-do list is ginormous."

"Mer, aren't we gonna talk about what just happened?"

She lifts an eyebrow. "You mean do I wanna talk about you being a butthole and trying to insert yourself into my dating life? That's a hard no."

I can't even think straight. My rage and indignation are palpable. "Your dating life? What's that supposed to mean?"

She fiddles with the straw in the near-empty smoothie cup, swirling the pink froth, around and around. "Okay, so I don't *currently have* a dating life. Or a desire to have one. That guy just sat down right before you got here and started flirting. But the fact remains...we aren't together, Holt. At some point in the future, I'll wanna be with someone again. You shouldn't have any say in when that happens or with whom that happens. I mean, unless you see something that could be a threat to our child."

"A threat to our child?" I toss my hand behind me, jerking to the parking lot where the orange Vespa sat a few minutes ago. "You don't think a guy like that is a threat to our child? To *my son*." I work my jaw back and forth, soaking in the sharp pain of my teeth grinding against each other. "Every man in this world who isn't *me* is a fucking threat to my son. To my girl."

I don't give her time to react, time to retreat. I reach across the small table and grab her. Wrapping my fingers around her forearm, I flip her hand toward me and trace the pale blue-green lines of the veins in her wrist. She sucks a sharp breath into her lungs. And holds it.

My finger slowly meanders its way down her palm, and to her left ring finger. Where the diamond and ruby engagement ring should be. You know, if I weren't such a pathetic piece of shit.

Leaning forward, I plant a soft, gentle kiss on her golden skin. I can even feel the small, pounding beat of her heartbeat through the pulse point in her wrist. The comforting rhythm against my lips might very well be the best thing I've ever felt. "Mine," I say, stating the simple truth.

After a moment, she rips her hand away and folds it in her lap. Blinking rapidly, her eyes dart from object to object, refusing to settle on anything for longer than a second, as she struggles to keep her tears from falling. "But I'm not yours, Holt. You locked me out of your heart. Out of your home and out of your life. You buried the key under six feet of dirt. And just because you've dug it up, doesn't mean I wanna take it back. That door may not be something I ever wanna unlock."

I toss my hat on the table and run my hands through my hair, wishing I could rip the strands out handful by handful—anything to numb the pain I'm feeling. Her face tells me she's still in love with me, but here she is telling me in her own words that she wants to see other people. Hell, she was about to agree to go on a date with that horrible stranger. All to what? Prove a point? Prove that she's moved on?

I guess she's come a long way from the woman in the shoe store who refused to go on a date with anyone.

Refused to go on a date with me.

I wish I knew the right way to beg for forgiveness. I wish I knew what to say and what to do. It seems like every move I make is the wrong one. I'm hitting wall after wall, battering my already bruised heart and soul.

And what about her heart and soul? I'm the one who bruised it. Not some wall. Not some strange man at a coffee shop. Not Delaney. Not Heidi.

Me.

And I need to keep owning up to that.

I had no idea that one human body could experience so many different emotions at one time.

The consequences of my decisions—of my actions—have trapped me in a perpetual state of tug-of-war. I'm constantly battling all of my urges...

The urge to grovel and beg for redemption.

The urge to scream and yell and make her realize that we belong together.

The urge to fight like hell for my woman, for my son, for my family.

The urge to hold her, kiss her, make love to her. Show her with my body what my mouth can't seem to find the right words to say.

"You wanna date other people? You wanna be with someone who isn't me?" When she doesn't say anything, I forge forward. "Because I can't even fathom being with anyone else. And I acted the way I just did because it rips my heart out of my chest to even think of you being with someone. Having another man's hands on you? Having another man kiss you, touch you, laugh with you, comfort you? It blinds me with rage and pain and...self-pity. Because I love you, Merit. Completely and undeniably."

I sit back in my seat and watch as an older couple walk into the store, hand in hand. "I am so sorry for messing everything up. I'm so sorry for accusing you of something you didn't do, for failing to follow through in my belief of you. I swear it will never, ever happen again. If you just give me a chance."

I'm not even shocked when a few silent tears start to slide down my cheeks. I guess I should be surprised, but I'm not. I'm man enough to admit I'm a complete and total pussy when it comes to the thought of losing Merit, of losing the life I know we should have together. I quickly wipe my face, hoping she doesn't think less of me. Or worse, hoping that she doesn't think I'm putting on a show for sympathy. "I'm too fucking terrified to even think of living my life without you. The thought of you never forgiving me, never saying you love me, it guts me. I..." I drag my finger back and forth across my lips in thought, "I don't exist without you."

Her gaze meets mine, and I watch as two of her own tears slide down her cheeks. Just like me, she quickly wipes them away. Taking a moment to read her face, relief courses through me when I see the love there. The love she has for me. And it's not just the love of being connected to someone through a child; it's the burning, body-consuming, soul-engulfing love we shared before our world came crashing down.

I lower my voice to a whisper. "Mer, you were actually thinking about saying yes to a date with him. Why?"

"Because of the way he looked at me. He looked at me like I was honest and truthful. Like I was innocent." She stares at the table, and I hear her foot tapping against the concrete. Tap. Tap. Tap. "I'll never forget the way you looked at me. That day? When you accused me of framing you? Accused me of wanting your money, accused me of being like Delaney—like every other woman before me? You hated me, Holt. You looked at me with hate in your heart."

Remembering she's not the same Merit as before, she lifts her head, facing me head-on. With a steady voice she tosses my own words back at me. "How am I supposed to kiss you, touch you, laugh with you, comfort you...after seeing that look in your eyes?"

Chapter 13

Merit

He wouldn't take no for an answer.

Well, in all honesty, I might not have fought *too* hard to say no. But come on, what woman doesn't love a surprise? Just because I'm still mad at him, should I be forced to forgo all fun? What if the surprise is chicken fried rice? Or blueberry pancakes? And for some odd reason, I start thinking really hard about Cinnamon Toast Crunch cereal. That would be good right about now too.

Grunting to cover the growl of my stomach, I flop my head back on the headrest. "It's been long enough. Tell me where we're going. Tell me what the surprise is."

Grinning, he licks his lips and dips his eyes to my bump. "Did your stomach just growl?" I must make a face because he starts chuckling. "And did you try to cover it up by grunting?"

Scowling, I reach for the radio and turn it up, drowning out his sexy little laugh.

He calmly reaches over and turns it back down. "Just give it a few more minutes. It's not like I have you blindfolded. I'm sure you'll figure out where we're going soon enough." He taps his fingers against the steering wheel. "And yes, there will be plenty of food."

He thinks he's so smart. He thinks he knows me so well, doesn't he?

"Yes," he says simply.

My brow furrows in confusion. "Yes, what? What are you talking about?"

"Yes, I do know you. I know everything about you." Gifting me his signature wink, he turns the radio volume back up, letting me stew in my own thoughts about how much I *love* and *hate* the fact that he can read me like a book.

Ten minutes later, I know exactly where we are.

Movie night. At City Hall Park.

When I don't make a move to undo my seat belt, he reaches over and squeezes my knee. My breath catches in my throat, ballooning and choking me, and I have to physically demand that my body ignore how right his hot and calloused hand feels against my skin. "Do you remember the movie that was playing the very first time I came into the store, the very first time I met you?"

My eyes travel up his hand, mapping the veins that decorate his forearm. "You mean the night you were on a date with Bunny?" I quip.

Instead of responding to that comment, he just rolls his eyes and leans closer. "*Singin' in the Rain*. Do you remember that?"

"You said you had never seen it all the way through. I always meant to make you watch it, but...we ran out of time," I say honestly.

His fingers dig into my skin, making dimples in my leg muscles. "Now, we have all the time in the world, the rest of our lives."

He can't say stuff like that.

It's not wise, and it's definitely not kind to my heart.

I shift my leg, forcing his hand to drop away.

He quickly disguises the hurt in his eyes, recovering with a smile. "But why wait? We have tonight."

Despite my best efforts, excitement blooms in my chest. "They're playing *Singin' in the Rain* on the big screen?"

"Yep."

Suddenly, my excitement drops into the pit of my stomach, like the free fall of a rollercoaster. "Wait. Did you do this?" I ask him. "Did you pay for them to play this movie?"

The thought of him paying to have the movie played for me cheapens the moment, cheapens the small possibility that one day—in the very distant future—our lives may intertwine with love and forgiveness. I know I shouldn't even be thinking about such things, but for some strange reason, I can't help but want this to be fate.

To be a sign that maybe one day—just some day—we might become each other's *everything* again.

Call me a prude, but I don't wanna be his movie whore.

Instead of answering, he climbs out of the truck and jogs over to my side. Opening the door, he leans in and unfastens my seat belt. My body tingles from his touch. When his arm grazes my breast, my traitorous body responds, with my nipples immediately peaking. Wordlessly, he flicks the button on the glove compartment, and it bounces open between my legs. He hands me a piece of paper. It's a printed flyer for the movies scheduled this summer.

"When you left the coffee shop the other night, I went inside to use the restroom and leave a tip for the workers." His lip twitches, begging to smile, thinking back to the fiasco with my unwanted suitor. "I mean, we did leave dried, sweetened coffee all over their sidewalk. I figured ants would be there the next day."

I hope that guy's shorts are stained forever. If I had a plate of spaghetti to go along with it, it really would have been funny.

"The flyers were stacked next to the bathroom." He points to today's date and the movie listed. "I couldn't believe it when I saw it. Like you said before, they almost always play cartoons." Gripping the doorframe of the truck, I watch the flex of his muscles as he shrugs. "I don't know, it just felt like... fate. I keep hoping the universe will show you that we're meant to be together. That'll it'll show you how truly sorry I am."

Shock.

I wish I could answer him, throw out some smartass comment, but I'm too shocked to even speak.

"I love you, Merit."

Through no choice of my own, a soft, slow mantra starts chanting in my soul. It beats steady and firm, harmonizing with my spirit, anchoring itself to my subconscious.

Forgive him. Forgive him. Forgive him.

Forgive *yourself.*

I swallow against the rhinoceros-size lump in my throat. "Holt, I—"

And the moment is cut short by a scream. "Coach! I mean, Holt!" The little boy looks up at his dad, who is apparently chastising him for using Holt's first name. He quickly corrects himself. "I mean, Mr. Hill! Hi!"

And there's just another thing Delaney did.

She got Holt fired. He's not a coach anymore. What do you call a coach who is no longer a coach?

Planting a wide grin on his face, Holt spends the next fifteen minutes taking pictures, signing autographs, and handing out shiny pennies—not to just this little boy, but the twenty other people who soon join the circle. Not wanting to waddle my fat ass around everybody, I just hang out of the truck sideways, swinging my feet against the running boards, and watching and enjoying the interactions. I even take a few pictures for him and grab a fresh stack of pennies from the middle console when he runs out.

When the crowd filters away, he turns his full attention back to me. "What were you gonna say?" he asks. "You know, before this..." he waves his hand in the general direction of the dispersing crowd.

"Oh, I—"

Once again, cut off. "Excuse me?" The little girl slides up next to us, almost wedging herself between the two of us. "May I have your autograph?"

Holt looks down, studying her black ringlets and cocoa-colored skin. She's wearing a hot pink sundress, hot pink ruffled socks, and bright green tennis shoes. Green and pink bracelets are stacked on both of her wrists. She's one of the cutest little girls I have ever seen in my entire life. If I had to guess, she'd be about ten or eleven. "Sure, sweetheart. Do you have something for me to sign?"

She pouts her pink lips, smiles softly, and then gently pats his arm, like she's about to deliver horrible news. "Not you. Her," she says, turning her face to mine.

What did she just say?

"Huh?" I stab my finger against my breastbone. "Me?"

She nods so hard she looks like a bobblehead doll. "Yes, ma'am." She holds out a hand, gifting me with a torn piece of yellow legal pad and blue ink pen. "I wanna be just like you when I grow up."

My eyes dart to Holt, wondering if he finds this exchange as weird as I do. Something's got to be wrong with her; she has to be mistaken. Because I'm just *me*. Why in the world would this child wanna be like me?

But my confusion finds no answers with the famous Holt Hill. Because it's pretty clear to see that he agrees with the little girl. The look of pride on his face blows me away. He's looking at me like I'm a precious jewel that's just been discovered for the very first time.

Like I'm the very first diamond to ever be mined from the earth.

New, foreign, priceless, and fucking gorgeous.

It completely flusters me. I guess if he's not coming to my rescue, I have no choice but to navigate these waters myself.

"Ummm, well, hi."

She smiles widely. "Hi."

"Do you know who I am, sweetie?"

Her brow furrows. "Of course, you're Merit Browning."

"And you want my autograph?"

"Yep."

I think back through my memories, trying my best to place her. "Did you used to shop in my children's shoe store? It was called *Run and Jump and Twirl*. Have you been there before?"

"No, ma'am. My Mommy and Daddy usually buy everything from Amazon." She leans forward with a secret. "Even our toilet paper."

Holt's laugh splices the air between us.

I'm still completely lost. "Have we met before?" I can't believe I'm asking a child these questions. I probably sound like a lunatic.

"I don't think so." Her face scrunches in thought. "Wait, did you go to Dawson's birthday party at the skating rink?"

As much as I love children, I try to avoid crashing random birthday parties. "No, not me."

She shakes her head. "Yeah, I didn't think so. Don't worry, it wasn't much fun anyway. Scarlet sprained her ankle, so we all had to stop skating early because she's such a big baby and cried because everyone was having fun without her."

Well, this conversation is going off the rails. Time to get back on track. "Did you say you wanna be like me when you grow up?"

She bounces on her toes. "Absolutely! You totally solved a crime! You know, like Nancy Drew or Veronica Mars or Shelby Woo. You found the bad guy," she shrugs a shoulder, "well, bad girl, I guess, and kept your boyfriend out of jail." She turns and pins Holt with a stare, non-discreetly letting him know that she knows he was in jail, and in her humble opinion, I saved the day.

He turns to me, his lighthearted good humor from the toilet paper comment fading into something more serious, more sincere. "She's a hero. She's *my* hero," he says.

"And mine too," the little girl adds, shoving the paper and pen back in my face.

With a shaky hand, I grab it. "What's your name?"

"Vanessa."

"Vanessa," I roll the letters off my tongue as I write her name.

Now, what the hell am I supposed to write? *Good Luck? Be safe? Have fun? Don't do drugs?* Eventually, I settle on *It's nice to meet you. Remember, anything is possible.* Before I can question my own logic and start overanalyzing myself—because *is* 'anything possible'—I quickly sign my name. I don't have a Hollywood-type signature, so I just sign it like I'm signing a check.

Vanessa gingerly handles the paper and studies the words in fascinated awe. It's like I just gifted her with a rare artifact. Like I pulled Excalibur from the Stone and traveled across time to give it to her.

Nerves flicker in my stomach, making me feel hot and sweaty. I'm not sure what else to do. "Ummm." I reach behind me into the console. "Would you like one of his pennies?" I ask, nodding from the penny in my hand to Holt.

Vanessa glances at him, sizing him up, trying to determine if he's worthy enough to be granted the privilege of her carrying around his loose change. Giving a nod, she holds out her hand again, quickly pocketing the copper penny I drop on her palm. "Why not?"

Holt's eyebrows dart into his hairline, and he dramatically clears his throat. "Tough critic."

"Well, I better get back to my mom," Vanessa says, pointing to a woman milling around the sidewalk, filming our encounter on her cell phone.

Holt and I wave hello. She politely waves back and mouths a 'thank you' to us.

"It was a pleasure meeting you, Vanessa. I hope you enjoy the movie tonight," I say.

"You too. Bye!" And with that, my unexpected admirer skips away to join her family.

I sink back in the truck, wincing when the bony part of my ankle hits against the running board in a funny way, shooting pain across my leg and foot. "Ohhhhh. Ouch!"

Holt leans against the doorframe again, drawing my attention to the firm lines of his body. Grabbing my foot, he rubs my ankle, trying to ease the pain. A slight breeze blows, wafting his scent around me. Minty gum and a woodsy-cedar-deodorant smell. Back when we shared a bathroom, his deodorant came in a black container that had a picture of the woods on it. It had some super manly name. Like Ax-Throwing Lumberjack or some bullcrap. I can't help but wonder if he still uses the same one.

When his fingertips trail up my leg, massaging my calf, I pull away.

"Thanks," I mumble. I guess I should thank him, huh? The pain in my ankle is gone. Although, now I do have a pain in my crotch.

Eager to change the subject, I sigh deeply. "So, that was weird, right?"

"Me massaging your leg was weird?" he teases, adding his sexy little wink for good measure.

I wish I could say I was immune to his charm, but I'm not. "Haha," I playfully add before explaining what doesn't need an explanation, "the little girl, the autograph."

"Why was that weird?" He blinks twice before continuing. I know, because I count them. "You *are* my hero, Mer. Every little girl should wanna be like you when they grow up."

I shake my head. "I did what anyone would do. I just told someone what I saw. The real work came from everyone else—Crutch, Marcum, Ella, all those other people."

He tugs the ballcap from his head, puts it on the roof of the truck, and drags his fingers through his blond waves. Gripping the roof, he moves even closer to me, sliding his body between my legs, invading my space, depleting my oxygen and my will to be strong— my will to still be angry with him.

"Stop. Stop diminishing yourself and what you did. There's a very real possibility I would be sitting behind bars right now, and possibly for years and years to come, if it weren't for you." His hand cups my cheek, scalding me with heat, piercing me with tenderness. "You are my *everything*, Merit. I will love you forever. And I will beg for your forgiveness forever, if that's how long it takes." His other hand splays across my stomach, and our son instantly starts to move. "Every night I pray that he grows up to be just like you. And I pray that one day he finds someone he loves just as much as I love you. Someone he'd slay dragons for. And who would do the exact same for him."

My heart flutters, pumping those painful, familiar words through my body.

Forgive him. Forgive him. Forgive him.

And because I can be stubborn as a damn mule when I wanna be, I plaster on a fake smile and say, "We better go. We're gonna miss the start of the movie, and you know how I feel about that."

Merit

Ibalance the plate of chicken casserole in my hand, having a heart attack when the piece of buttered sourdough bread bumps against the doorframe, nearly knocking the china out of my hand.

Well, that wouldn't have been good.

My ass is getting too big to be wallowing around on the floor cleaning up casserole, creamed corn, and green beans.

Grunting in frustration, I shut the door to the gym.

Where the heck is he?

I've searched the entire Big House from top to bottom, and he's nowhere to be found.

Granted, I know we aren't together, and I know he's not required to tell me where he's going or where he's been… but, I mean, I'm having his baby. Doesn't that gift me with a little bit of latitude? A certain number of inalienable rights? If he's out on a date, don't I deserve to know?

If he's humping some cheap hoe he met at the grocery store, don't I have the right to object?

I take a deep breath, trying to calm myself.

He's not humping a hoe.

He's been gone nearly all day. Just like the past three days, before now. So, he's not having a sex marathon for days on end—with a random lady he picked up in the produce section—unless he's pumping erectile medicine though an IV. I mean, he *is* the great Holt Hill.

But no man is that great.

Not for four days straight.

Really, I should be given a major award for not asking him where he's been, for keeping my curiosity bottled up deep inside my chest. He's come over to the Children's Wing the past few nights, and I've refused to acknowledge the fact that he's not been around during the day. Personally, I think it's a testament to my strength. My resolve.

My resolve for what, though?

My resolve for pretending that I'm not still in love with him?

My resolve for pretending that I could move into the Children's Wing and not be affected by his nearness, his closeness?

Because it's so hard. Fucking epically hard, if I'm telling the truth.

Because sometimes he smiles at me, and for a brief moment— one absolutely perfect minute—I forget what's happened. I forget that he threw me away. I forget that he slithered out of my life, leaving me broken and shattered and traumatized.

And if he only knew how traumatized I really was...

It wasn't just his memories that buried me, but Delaney's and Heidi's too.

Buried alive, and fighting and clawing my way to the surface. Fucking battling for every breath I had to take.

For one-hundred-and-forty-two days.

Well, technically, I guess one-hundred-and-forty-three days since he didn't start banging on my parents' door until after midnight.

Weakened from my thoughts, I set the plate down on the mudroom cabinet tucked in the corner of the hallway. Sitting on the plush bench, I look down, counting the number of worn sneakers and football cleats. There's even two footballs, caked with dried mud, resting on the floor. I rub my fingertips through the dirt and spread it around on my fingertips. At the farm, we have a commercial washer and drier in the garage, just to wash our filthy work clothes.

Sod farming is dirty business.

That's not the kind of mess you want to track through your house—multiple times a day.

Huh, the garage.

I didn't check the garage. What if Holt's in there.

Hopping to my feet, I open the door caddy-corner from me—the last door on the left—and look around.

Nope. Nothing.

And just to rub the insult in my face, his absence is confirmed by his missing truck. The only vehicle in the massive garage is his old, slightly dented truck from years ago. Right then, the walls start to rumble, and the metal garage door starts to lift. Promptly crapping my pants, I squeak in surprise and shimmy the door shut so I have only one eye peeking out.

I know he has good vision, but surely, he can't make out one little eye from across this big of a distance. Especially with the setting sun pounding in my direction.

The garage door finishes rising, and I'm shocked to see Ridge's truck idling in the driveway and not Holt's. My eyes dart between the two of them as they sit in the car, talking. I haven't seen Ridge in a long, long time, and the shadowed sight of him, from yards away, brings tears to my eyes. My severed attachment to Holt's family and friends is just another trauma I had to fight back from.

I went from having all these people around me to being alone. Well, I mean, I still had my parents and Granny. But it's not the same. And I'd never admit this to Granny, but hanging out with Ridge is more fun—*was* more fun—than watching *I Dream of Jeannie* reruns with Granny.

After a couple of minutes, Holt halfway climbs out of the truck. His movements seem a little off-kilter. Like, maybe, he has a catch in his back or something. Half of his body is still twisted inside when he says his goodbye. "Thanks for everything, brother."

Sucking in a sharp breath, I immediately latch my peep-hole door, grab the plate of food from the mudroom cabinet, and race down the hallway, shuffling on my tiptoes, trying to be as quiet as possible so he won't hear me. All of a sudden, the sourdough bread flies off the plate, bounces against a huge, framed photograph of a football field, and lands on the floor. I'm about to turn and get it when I hear him open and close the door. His grunt echoes down the marble hallway, blaring like a bullhorn in my ears. Giving one last glance at the bread, I see it landed right against the wall and is leaning on the baseboard.

Maybe he won't even see it.

Sprinting as fast as my growing son will allow, I bolt into the kitchen. I quietly set a place at the kitchen island, flinging the plate, a napkin, and some silverware in front of a barstool. Then, I hop up on the seat next to it and slap my phone in front of my face, trying to appear bored as hell...even though my heart is thundering in my chest like a locomotive.

One millisecond later, he rounds the corner into the kitchen.

I don't look up.

Instead, I pretend to yawn.

"Hey."

Sweet mercy. His voice. It's like he's trying to fuck my eardrums.

"Hi." I have to swallow to even get the word out.

"What's up?"

I nonchalantly nod to the plate of food. "I cooked too much supper. I didn't want it to go to waste. I wasn't sure if you'd eaten yet or not."

"You been waiting long?" he asks.

I tap around on my phone, pretending to send some very important email or text message. Somehow, I end up on the App Store, downloading an app for a talking animated cat. "Yeah, it's been a while. I guess I lost track of time. I've been busy."

"Uhhh... Mer?"

"Yeah?" I respond, holding the button to delete the cat. I really hope I didn't just pay $4.99 for this thing.

"Is this yours?"

Begrudgingly, I lift my face.

Damn it. Sure enough, he's holding the sourdough in his hand.

But my embarrassment for this little charade—you know, the charade of me acting like I don't care about him or his whereabouts—dies the instant I see what's in his other hand.

Or more accurately, what's *on his other shoulder.*

An arm brace.

"Holt!" I fling my phone across the granite and jump from my seat. It takes me a second to round the corner of the island to get to him. He's already walking in my direction, and as soon as I'm within arms' reach, he grabs at me, lovingly folding me against his side—the side not encumbered by his left arm snuggly dangling in the arm brace. The crusty edge of the toasted bread scrapes against my shirt and shakes crumbs all over me and the floor.

"Shit," he says, with a chuckle. Twisting just a smidge, he tosses the bread across the kitchen, and it bounces into the kitchen sink.

I shift in his one-sided embrace, checking out his injury. There's a large bandage peeking out of the collar of his shirt. Lifting my eyes, I trail my fingers down his cheeks, bobbing my head left and right, searching his face for damage.

There is none.

His face is perfect.

Just like always.

He gifts me with his signature, sexy little wink. His whisper slows my rapidly beating heart, placing it back in a steady pattern. "See any damage, Mer?"

I peer into his eyes. "No. You're perfect."

His forehead lowers to mine, and he sighs. "We both know that's not true."

What the hell is happening?

Clearing my throat, trying to capture my unbridled actions and emotions, I step from his grasp.

As always, running away from the shadow of his body leaves me feeling emotionally hungover—spent and frazzled.

I drag my eyes down his body. He's grimy and grubby, covered in dried sweat and dirt. His hair is matted and tangled with little black particles catching in the blond waves. What the heck is that? I inch closer, erasing the distance I gained just a moment ago, and squint my eyes. Is that... asphalt?

Holt shit. He had a wreck.

I could've lost him.

I just got him back, and I could've lost him.

"You had a wreck?" I wish I could hide the unsteadiness of my voice. But I can't.

He shakes his head, wincing slightly with the motion. "No, I didn't have a wreck."

"What happened then? What's wrong with your shoulder and arm? What's in your hair?"

He nods to the barstool, nonverbally telling me he needs to sit down. Like a sad little puppy I follow, sitting beside him. He pushes the plate of food out of the way. "In my hair? That would be asphalt."

"Asphalt? But you weren't in a wreck?" Horror rushes through every part of my body, turning my blood to stone. Life doesn't pump through me; it stops. "What the fuck? You got run over? Someone hit you and ran you over?"

His boisterous laugh catches me off guard.

And then it makes me angry.

So angry that when he grabs my hand and kisses my wrist, I should pull away.

But I don't.

Kissing me again, he rubs his nose back and forth across my skin, smelling me. "How come you always smell so good? I wanna drown in your flavor."

Ummm...

What...

Coming to my senses, I snatch my hand back and tuck it underneath my thighs. I completely ignore his comment. "Why do you have asphalt in your hair? And what happened to your shoulder?"

"It's shingles. I have pieces of asphalt shingles in my hair."

I furrow my brow. "What?"

He takes a deep breath. "You haven't asked me where I've been going this week."

I shake my head, wondering if he knows how much his unexplained absence has affected my psyche.

"That surprised me. I thought you would be wondering where I was... too curious not to ask me." He smirks, charming and innocent, and it makes me think about what he must've been like as a little boy. Wondering if our little boy will be the same. "To tell you the truth, I was dying for you to ask me."

"Why didn't you just tell me, then? Tell me where you've been going, what you've been doing?"

He shrugs with his one good shoulder. The movement must still hurt because he grimaces. "I guess I was worried you wouldn't care what the hell I was doing."

I search his face, looking for the lie.

But he's not lying.

He's being truthful, being vulnerable. And not for the first time since his return to my life, showing me the man underneath the swagger. The man, who's worried our relationship may not end where he wants it to end—with me in his arms, in his bed, in his heart.

And him in mine.

"Where have you been going? Tell me what happened, Holt," I gently urge.

"Habitat for Humanity."

"Habitat for Humanity?" I repeat the statement back as a question.

"Ever since my name was cleared, I've been volunteering with them. Working to build houses. The last few days, I was on a job site."

He's been working to build houses? For the needy? In a thousand-degree heat?

No wonder his cheeks are sunburnt.

"You've been volunteering? Why?" I'm not surprised that he's volunteering per se; Holt has a giving heart. I'm just curious as to his thoughts behind it.

He attempts to shrug again. He's not exactly successful at it. "I'm not working. Once the threat of losing my life to a jail cell went away, I felt guilty for just wasting my days moping around. I mean, the police and prosecutors and everybody were still in the throes of finalizing the deals and investigations against Delaney, Heidi, and Denise, but I knew I was in the clear." He stabs me with his penetrating gaze. With a cautious hand—his good hand—he slides his fingers across my thigh. "I was drowning in my guilt over the way I treated you, the baseless accusations I hurled your way. All I did was sit around thinking of ways to apologize and agonizing over the idea that you may never want me in your life again."

I should move my leg.

I don't.

"I had to do something with my mind, with my time. I needed... a way to find purpose again. I needed something to give me a sense of worth. Because let's just say," he licks his lips and squeezes my thigh even tighter, "I wasn't in the best headspace." Sighing, he eventually moves his hand, shifting it back to the countertop and fiddling with his napkin. "I tried to volunteer with three different charities before I found Habitat for Humanity." He softly clears his throat. "Those three turned me down. They didn't wanna be associated with me. So, when Habitat said yes, I jumped at the chance to work with them."

"Is that part of the reason you decided to create your own charity, your own foundation to help others? Because you were turned down so many times?"

His head bobbles up and down. "Yeah. I guess so."

"So, what happened? How'd this happen?" I ask, with a nod to his jacked-up shoulder.

I can't help it; I instinctively lean closer to him. Like he's a magnet drawing my heart to his, drawing my soul to his. Drawing me into his orbit, forming our own universe.

He gives me that look of trepidation, the one that says he would prefer to lie but can't—because he's talking to me.

The woman he promised to never lie to again.

"Today was roofing day. I was working on the ground to finish the banister railing on the steps. There were a couple of other volunteers working on painting the inside. One of those was Tracey. I've worked with her several times. She's in her seventies. Her husband died last year, and she started volunteering because she was lonely. She's an amazing artist. Used to teach art at one of the elementary schools." He looks at me, making sure I'm following along. "She paints these murals in the houses. Like, if the Habitat family has kids, she'll paint a mural of something he or she likes in the bedroom. In this house, she's painting a wall of flowers."

He moves from his napkin to his fork and starts spinning it around. "She came outside to pick some flowers from the bushes. She wanted... inspiration," he says with a soft chuckle. "She was heading back inside. I was walking back from the trailer at the same time with some extra wood. I heard one of the roofers hollering. And when I looked up, I saw that a bundle of shingles was about to slide off the roof.

"It was headed straight for her. She was so engrossed with the pile of flowers in her hands, she didn't even know anything was wrong." A little growl rumbles in his chest, vibrating the air between us. "These things weigh sixty, seventy, eighty pounds," he says. He abandons the fork and drags his fingers across his lips and chin. "I couldn't let that hit her. Hell, it could've split her head wide open." His voice lowers to a whisper. "It could've killed her."

My heart is lodged in my throat, making it difficult to swallow. Making it difficult to speak. Hell, making it difficult to think. "It could've killed *you*."

He spins on his barstool. Hooking his foot around the leg of my own barstool, he slides me closer. So close, he has to straddle his legs to make room for me. His fingers reach out, grabbing a lock of my hair and twisting it back and forth. His blue eyes find mine, searching my thoughts, my feelings.

It could've killed him. And then I would be all alone again. *We* would be all alone... me and our son.

How does he expect me to absorb all this information? How can I comprehend all these actions that say he's a good and honorable man? How am I expected to understand that he would risk his life for this random woman, yet he would throw me to the curb based on nothing more than groundless accusations.

What made me different?

What made me expendable?

He said we didn't lie to each other. He said he could read my face, read my mind.

Obviously, he couldn't *read* shit. Because he told me I was his life. His reason for living and breathing. And then he shut the door in my face.

"I'm sorry," he says simply, breaking my train of thought.

"For nearly getting yourself killed?"

"For not giving my life for you like I should've."

I suck a much-needed breath through my teeth. The trapped air cools my overheated lungs.

His thumb grazes my cheekbone, sending fire into my skin. "You're the most important person in my life, Merit. You have been since the day I set foot in your store. And I let fear steal that truth from me. I let the anxiety rip you from my heart." His hand slides around my neck, gently massaging the base of my scalp. "I made you dispensable. Which is a lie." He licks his lips, and my watered eyes are drawn to the dirt smeared across his brow. "You're my only necessity in the world."

I'm not exactly sure how long I let him hold me in his semi-embrace. But long enough that when he makes a move to inch closer to my lips, his injured muscles spasm, and he winces.

Dropping his good hand, he leans back, trying to stretch his neck to relieve some of the pain.

My heart slowly beats in my chest, thumping a constant rhythm. Not frenzied. Not frantic.

Stable and undeviating.

And each pump releases a small stream of forgiveness into my blood.

"What happened? I'm assuming you pushed her out of the way… and what? The bundle hit you?"

He nods.

Shit.

Mere centimeters from his head. A few mere centimeters, and I might've been looking at him in the morgue instead of this kitchen.

He glances down, his eyes clouding with sadness. "I sprained her ankle." He turns back to stare at me. "When I knocked her out of the way, she fell on the porch steps and twisted her ankle."

My troubled concern and wild imagination flare, bursting to life with visions of one horrible scenario after the other. "Sprained her ankle?! What about you, Holt! You still haven't told me what's wrong. Your arm could be hanging on by a thread and filled with gangrene for all I know."

He lifts an amused brow. "I'm not filled with gangrene."

I flop my hands in the air, trying to mime the ridiculousness of my lack of knowledge.

"The singles hit my shoulder, obviously. I went down…boom. Like a ton of bricks." He pounds the table to emphasize the boom. "We were in Ridge's zone, but I knew he wouldn't show up. He's not working as a paramedic this shift. But he's the best, and I wanted the best for Tracey. I called him, and he drove out separately. He got Tracey's ankle stabilized and sent her in the ambulance to the ER—just to make sure nothing else was wrong with the ankle that he couldn't see. Then, he drove me in his truck to the hospital."

I shake my head in disbelief. There the two of them are again, taking a leisurely drive around while Holt is injured and broken. What the hell is wrong with those two?

I fold my arms across my chest and grunt my displeasure.

Grinning, he ignores my temper and keeps talking. "I'm gonna be fine. The bundle was open on one corner so the exposed shingles took a layer of skin off—kinda like road rash. Other than that, it's just bruising and some pulled muscles. No damage to the rotator cuff or anything like that. I've only gotta wear this contraption," he nods to the brace, "for about a week. Besides, I've been hit a hell of a lot harder on the field."

"Okay." Finally, I heave a sigh of relief, exhaling the worry and dread I've been holding inside. "What can I do to help? What do you need?"

He looks at the food, and I swear, he starts drooling. "Well, I'm really hoping the offer for these leftovers is still valid. I'm withering away to nothing over here."

Leaning forward, I bring the plate back in front of him and grab a fresh napkin from the holder in the middle of the island. There's no way he can wipe his mouth with the other one, he mutilated it. "Yep. The offer is still valid."

He starts eating, moaning his appreciation around a mouthful of casserole. "Mer, it's great. Thank you."

I blush. Like a little girl.

Getting up, I fix him a glass of water and set it next to his plate. "And after this?" I ask.

He immediately drinks half of it. "Obviously, I need a shower. I have sweat and dirt and hospital funk in places that haven't seen it in years. And obviously bits of shingle in my hair."

Oh, shit. He's gonna ask me to help him shower.

Naked.

Wet and slippery and soapy.

"Uhhh...I don't think that's a good idea, Holt." And I'm fairly certain I blush again. Because it feels like a thousand fire ants are biting my face.

His light-hearted chuckle is low and raspy and seductive as hell. "I'm pretty sure I can handle that part by myself," he says.

Well, damn it all to hell. Why am I a little disappointed? I blame my swinging and far-flung emotions on my pregnancy hormones.

"But I could use your help changing the bandage." He reaches down and pulls out a small plastic baggie from the leg pocket of his cargo shorts. It's got some waterproof bandages in it and some antibiotic salve.

"Yeah, okay. I can do that."

We make small talk while he eats, with me only leaving his side to get him some over-the-counter ibuprofen from the downstairs medicine cabinet to take with his food. Once he's done eating, he gingerly takes off his arm brace, and I help him with his shirt. I do my best to ignore the feel of his skin underneath my fingertips.

Although, it's hard to ignore his hitched breath and the jumping of his dick in his shorts.

And when I peel back the soft bandage that's currently covering his damaged shoulder, I can't stop the tears from rolling down my face. It doesn't look good...but it could've been worse. I don't think anything will scar. Like he said, it has more of a carpet burn or road burn look than anything else.

But it's on his beautiful skin. It doesn't belong there. What belongs there are little moles and sun freckles and drops of sweat.

Dutifully, I apply the ointment and doctor the area with his hospital-issued waterproof bandage.

And then, I kiss it.

I want to kiss away the thought of nearly losing him.

I want to kiss away the hurt.

If only kisses worked on *all* the hurt.

Things would be so much easier that way.

But things aren't that easy.

And when his face turns, brushing his lips against my jaw, and his fingers clench against my body, kneading into the curve of my hips...I steel my back, straighten my shoulders, and walk away.

And I pretend his words don't echo across the marble, chasing me all the way into the Children's Wing. "I love you, Merit."

Chapter 15

Holt

It's been a great couple of weeks.

Of course, it would be even greater if she would just move over to the Big House again. Into *our* room. Into *our* bed.

But she still hasn't fully forgiven me. And who the hell can blame her? Certainly not me.

It's Friday night and I'm supposed to be headed to the bar to meet the guys, but I can't go until I see her. So, patiently I wait, counting down the seconds until I hear her feet padding down the hallway.

Well, I'm *hoping* I hear her feet padding down the hallway.

She may not have forgiven me yet, but she's definitely testing the waters. For the past couple of nights, she's actually come looking for me, slowly treading her way through the house with a plate of leftover food in her hands, claiming she cooked too much supper for just herself—just like the night after I hurt my shoulder. I'm not exactly sure what the hell happened before I got home that night, or why there was a stick of bread in the hallway, but words couldn't describe how excited I was to see her sitting at the kitchen island, pretending to ignore me. And then last night, I even convinced her to sit on the couch with me and watch some TV. She agreed, even though it wasn't an old movie, but a sports documentary. And because she's

Merit, and she's always curious, she actually asked me a couple of questions about things she didn't understand.

All of a sudden, my cell phone rings, blaring the sound through the Bluetooth speakers in the gym. Hopping off the weight machine, I glance at the caller ID, surprised when I see the name of my old head coach. I've been pretty selective about who I give my new cell number to, but he has it. I mean, Alaina even interviewed him for the TV special to get background on my time in the NFL. He's been really supportive.

Twenty minutes later, we're finishing up our conversation when I see Merit's head peek around the corner of the doorframe. As always, she looks so damn good it nearly splits my heart in half. Her hair is piled in a messy bun, and she's wearing an old T-shirt, advertising *Run and Jump and Twirl*. It must be a men's shirt. Despite the tightness across her stomach, it falls off her shoulder, showcasing the strap of her purple bra. Not to mention, it's black. I've never seen a black T-shirt for her store before. They're always bright, girly colors. It falls down to the top of her thighs, making it look like she doesn't have any shorts on. Even though I know she does, a man can still hope, right?

She pretends to step back, pretends to give me privacy, but really, she's dying to know who I'm talking to. I curl my fingers, begging her to come closer. I'm not sure what she cooked tonight, but it smells freakin' delicious. My stomach immediately growls.

"Promise me you'll at least think about it, son. Let me know if you change your mind?" Coach's gruff voice booms on the other side of the phone.

"Yes, sir. I will." Hanging up, I toss my cell on the towel next to me and cock an eyebrow in her direction. "Leftovers?" I ask, not even hiding the giddiness in my voice. She has to know it makes me happy to see her. Just the same way I've been finding excuse after excuse to keep working on some of the charity stuff with her even though she has it all under control.

She dips the plate in front of my face. "I didn't feel like cooking tonight. I had a craving." Every square inch of the grilled chicken, steak, fried rice, and vegetables is drowned in yum yum sauce.

Just the way my son has been wanting it.

I smile. "You should've told me. I could've taken you out. We could've made it a date night."

She ignores that and just nods her head at the door. "Come on. You better eat before it gets cold."

Wiping the sweat from my brow, I grab my water bottle and phone and follow her down the hall to the kitchen. "You already ate?"

"Of course. You think I want you to see how much of this I can actually eat? They basically had to load it in my car with a forklift." Laughing at herself, she rewards me with her signature snort. Damn, how I missed that snort. She grabs me a fork and a napkin and settles next to me at the kitchen island. I count my bites, waiting to see how long it will take her to ask the question.

It takes two.

"So, who was that?"

"Hmm?"

"On the phone. It sounded serious."

I wipe my mouth. "Well, I guess it kinda was. It was my old coach."

"What did he want?" She leans forward, and her knee accidentally grazes mine.

"He wants me to be the new quarterback coach for my old team." I watch her face, waiting for her reaction. "In the NFL."

Her eyes widen like silver dollars, and the swirls of bright yellow and green darken. "In North Carolina," she says, her voice squeaking. "He wants you to move back to North Carolina?"

I take another bite. "Yeah."

"What did you tell him?"

"I told him no."

Her words flow out on an exhale, "You told him no?"

"I did."

"Why?"

"Because of you."

She stops breathing and just blinks. After a few seconds, she asks, "Because of me?"

"I won't pick up and move our family. There's no way I'd take you that far away from your mom and dad and grandma. Not to mention, I've gotten used to being back here with my parents. Raylee, the kids, Ridge. I mean, everyone is here. This is our home." I'm relieved when she doesn't call me out for assuming I could actually *pick up and make her move somewhere.*

"That's it?"

"Well, that's the main reason. But there's other things too. I never wanna fall back into the trap of missing out on the fun of the game. I think that would happen if I went back to the NFL. Not to mention, I like teaching the kids."

She looks down and rubs a possessive hand across her stomach. "I heard the school called and offered you your job back."

I don't bother asking how she knows. It's probably out on the Internet somewhere. "They did."

"And?"

I take a drink of water, washing my food down, and balance my elbows on the granite countertop. "I don't know if I can go back to that school." I shake my head. "They fired me. Everyone thought I was some sick pedophile who preyed on their children. The teachers, the students. The things they said I did..." my voice trails off. Just thinking about it makes me want to throw up.

"Not everyone thought you were guilty."

"I know that. But I don't wanna walk down the halls and feel like I'm dragging a thousand-pound chain filled with nothing but a painful history. Like some fucked-up Ebenezer Scrooge."

"It was Jacob Marley."

My brow furrows. "Huh?"

"It wasn't Ebenezer Scrooge who dragged the chains; it was Jacob Marley."

I wipe my hand across my mouth, chuckling. "Jacob Marley, then."

She nibbles on her bottom lip, and when she finally pops it free from her teeth, the pink, swollen skin pales to white for a nanosecond before flushing with color again.

Talk. About. Distracting.

I lift the ballcap from my head and spin it around backward, trying to pull my mind out of... well, you know. "There's more offers on the table."

"Really? From?"

"Well, I got a call from West River just the other day. They offered me the position of head coach and athletic director."

The high school I did work at is technically zoned for the county. West River is one of four high schools zoned in the city. Like my school—or my old school, I mean—it's known for high test scores, superb fine arts, and a kick-ass football team. Their last coach left at the end of the school year for a larger school district. He was a huge dick, but he definitely gave my team a run for its money. Not to mention, it's the school where Nate is going to be attending this year. He's starting ninth grade, and he's zoned for West River. Nate's one hell of a ball player. He's got *it*. The *it* that could take him all the way.

"You would do that to your team? To your boys? Up and leave them like that? You know most of the team supported you, right?" She sits up straight and stabs me with a scowl. "I mean, Carson spent weekend after weekend organizing and working car washes to raise money for your defense. Did you know that?"

Of course, I knew it. And that's why Carson will never have to worry about his future. Not as long as I'm around. It's why he got a late acceptance letter to the Georgia Institute of Technology for their aeronautical engineering program. It's why he's the first ever recipient of the Brighter Paths Renewable Grant. Funded by an anonymous donor, of course.

One guess who the donor is...

It's not like I did anything shady.

I mean, Carson has made all A's ever since sixth grade. He was valedictorian. He did great on his ACT, and he was even president of his class. He got in of his own accord, he just wasn't going to actually go because of the cost.

Now, he doesn't have to worry about that.

"Holt, did you hear me?" Merit pushes against my shoulder—fortunately, it's fully healed from my run-in with the shingles.

I nod.

"So, you're giving up on them? Just like that?" The look of disgust on her face is overwhelming. "I guess we found your modus operandi, huh?" Her irritated breath sputters from her lungs in short, shallow bursts. "Why do you keep trying to fight for us, then? If it's that easy, why not give up on us?"

Shock and anger clench my stomach in a death grip. She moves to hop off the barstool, but our son makes her movements more cumbersome than normal. I shift my legs, blocking her. My voice lowers, delivering a truth that is not up for debate. "I'm never giving up on us. Ever. I'm yours, and you're mine."

We're so close.

Mere inches away. I could touch her with my tongue.

Her head falls, and she studies the floor. Her emotions flood around us, turning the air into a tactile, living, breathing organism—anger, hurt, betrayal, frustration.

Love. Desire. Want. Need.

"Move, Holt."

I don't obey her command.

Steeling herself, she stares at me head-on. "What do you want me to say, Holt?"

Of course, I tell her the truth. "I want you to say you want me back. I want you to say you love me too. I wanna raise our son. And give him brothers and sisters and a life of happiness that we never even dreamed possible." I lick my lips, wishing she would fall against me. "I want your body on mine."

Her lip trembles. "Well, we don't always get what we want. If we did, you never would've thrown me away."

Pushing against my leg—and I have no choice but to let her—she walks away.

It's still early.

But I couldn't stay at the bar anymore, knowing she was here. *Home.*

If she's at home, I should be too.

I lean against the bedroom doorframe and study the curve of her body in the moonlight—her shoulders, her back, her hips. What I wouldn't give to slip underneath the covers and pull her tight little ass into the crescent of my own body. Wrap my arms around her stomach and hold her—and our child—until the morning light.

Her sleepy whisper catches me off guard. "How long do you plan on watching me sleep? It's kinda creepy." She rolls over, catching me.

I can't help but chuckle. "Can I get by with a couple of hours before I seem like a freak?"

"No. Freaky status happened the second you opened the door to my side of the house in the middle of the night."

I shrug. "It's not the middle of the night. It's only nine-thirty."

"Seriously?" She snuggles the comforter up to her chin. "I didn't even check the clock before going to bed. Sometimes I just get so darn tired."

I cock an eyebrow, even though she can't see it. "Was it still light outside when you went to bed?"

"Uh...I'd like to reserve the right to keep that answer to myself. People in Alaska have to sleep when it's light outside."

"I didn't know Alabama and Alaska were so closely related?"

She snorts, giggling as she thinks about a joke in her own head before saying it. "I guess someone didn't pay attention in geography class." She waves a flippant hand in my direction. "Jocks. Sheeesh."

Throwing her a bone, I laugh at her joke.

"So, tomorrow's the Fourth of July," I say, stating the obvious.

Merit flops over on her back and stares at the ceiling. "I know."

"So, that means today is July 3rd. Nate's Birthday."

"I know."

I click my tongue. "He's fifteen. That's a pretty big one."

"I know."

"I called him on my way to the bar. Someone sent him a really nice gift. A hand-sewn leather wallet with his initials on it." I tilt my head to the side. "Any idea who may have done such a thing?"

She wiggles her feet underneath the blankets.

"Mer?"

"I don't know."

I roll my eyes. "Even though I can't see your face right now, I still know you're lying." I push off the jamb and take a step closer to the bed. "He loves it. He got his permit today; so needless to say, the wallet is already being put to use." I study the rise and fall of her rounded stomach as she breathes. "It was a really thoughtful gift."

She doesn't say anything.

"Everyone's coming over tomorrow for the holiday. We're gonna celebrate his birthday too. Just like normal."

She wipes at her eye. "I'll be gone before they get here."

"I don't want you *gone*; I want you here. Everyone wants to see you. Please stay."

Her whisper is strained, and it breaks my damn heart. "I can't."

"Then, I'll cancel," I say simply.

She turns back on her side, watching me. "What? No. You can't cancel."

"I can and I will. Because I'm not spending the holiday without you. You and our son, you're the only ones who matter." I take another step closer. "We're a family."

"You can't cancel," she says again. "The kids will be devastated."

"They'll understand. I'll call and explain it to them."

"Kids don't understand that kind of thing."

"Trust me, they know the word *asshole*. And that's all I have to tell them—is that everything is messed up because I was a complete and total asshole."

She's quiet, taking a moment to think about my declaration.

When I step next to the bed, I expect her to roll over, but she doesn't. And when I reach down and stroke the side of her cheek, I expect her to flinch, but she doesn't.

She's so damn strong.

Little by little, she's thawing her heart for me.

No matter how painful it must be.

And trust me, I know it is.

I'm the villain in our story. I'm the evil monster hiding in the woods. And yet, she's still opening the door. She's peeking outside and daring me to come in.

Her eyes search my face, absorbing every detail she can see through the ribbons of moonlight dancing between the blinds. I love it when she looks at me. She always looks at me like she's trying to memorize me, trying to count every freckle, trying to remember every laugh line.

"I'll stay."

"What?" My hand trails down her neck, and my fingers tangle with hers. It sends a fire through my body. "Are you serious?"

"What you said is right. We're a family. No matter what happens, we're having a child together. I meant what I said, I will never take you away from your son. And the same thing applies to your parents, your sister. They deserve to be a part of our child's life." She swallows loudly. "I want our child to be surrounded by love. Not anger, not bitterness." She slides her hand away from mine. "I guess we'll have to learn the best way to co-parent. We might as well start now."

Co-parent, my ass. Merit's going to be my wife. I'm never leaving her side. Not until the Good Lord calls me home. And even then, I'll be waiting to spend eternity with her.

And I can promise you one thing, this is a battle I'm gonna win.

Chapter 16

Merit

I'm not sure if I'm ready for this. But, ready or not, here they come. *They*. Meaning all of them.

The entire family. Even Nate's parents are coming today.

I stare at myself in the mirror, wondering why I bothered with makeup. It's not like I have anyone to impress. Plus, it's a thousand degrees outside. It's going to melt off my face like butter on a pancake.

Huh. A blueberry pancake would taste really good right about—

"Hey."

Holt knocks on the open door, making me jump a mile.

He's not wearing a shirt. So, of course, that's super damn distracting. His tanned skin is tinged pink, and his muscles glisten with sweat. His blue swim trunks match the deep color of his eyes. And when he lifts his arm and flips his baseball cap around backward, I nearly lady jizz in my shorts.

But it's the soft, loving smile on his face that really does something to me. It warms me, thawing me from the inside-out.

"You look beautiful. I love it when you wear green. It makes your eyes look different."

I tug at the hem of my sleeveless green maternity top. Ruffles cascade down the body of it, hiding some of the width of my stomach. I don't have many pregnancy clothes. Mom found this shirt for me on the clearance rack at the discount outlets near the beach. Clearing my throat, I pull my ponytail tighter, making sure the hair is off my neck.

"I just wanted to check on you. The ribs are on the smoker, and everybody is swimming, hanging out." I watch in the mirror's reflection as he sucks his bottom lip between his teeth. "Are you ready?"

I glance back at myself. I'm definitely second-guessing my decision to wear makeup. Am I really trying to make myself look good for Holt? For him and his family? Even though my fuchsia lipstick looks fantastic with this top, I can't shake the feeling that I'm giving in, that I'm breaking. Grabbing a tissue, I haphazardly wipe my lipstick away. I toss the pink mess in the trash can and spin on my heels. "I'm always ready, *sir*."

Unfortunately, my confidence doesn't last very long. By the time, I step onto the back patio, I'm a nervous wreck. This is way worse than the first time I met everyone. Way, way worse. When Holt grabs my hand, wrapping his fingers around mine, I know I should push him away.

But I can't.

The pathetic truth is... I want his touch.

I need his strength.

I wish that wasn't the case, but it is. Knowing what I need, Holt gives my hand a firm squeeze.

And just like the first time, all heads pivot in my direction, cementing me to the ground like a deer in the headlights. The summer sun beats down on my head, making my scalp sizzle like bacon.

Bacon...that would pair nicely with those blueberry pancakes.

Teresa's gasp draws my attention, and she immediately races over to us. "Oh, Merit!" Her eyes fill with tears. Unashamed by her emotions, they spill down onto her cheeks, and she doesn't even bother to wipe them away. "Oh, sweetheart, it's so good to see you."

Without warning, she throws her arms around me, wrapping me in a hug. She holds me tightly, like she's afraid I'm going to run away. For a split second, I think about it too. Running might make things easier.

But then I take a deep breath. And I smell her.

That wonderful, comforting *mom* scent weakens my knees. It's like a mix of light perfume and sunscreen and cookie dough.

Before I even know what's happening, I'm hugging her back. My face falls against the side of her neck, and I can't stop the flow of my own tears. And when she starts to rub my back in small circles and whisper words of encouragement in my ear, I really lose my shit.

I'm not sure how long we stand there, cradling and comforting each other, but it has to be for a while. I know that because I hear a few of the other women sniffling.

Well, this is just great.

My big plans to flaunt around the party, proving how great I'm doing without all of them in my life is failing. Epically.

Eventually, she pulls away, giggling through a happy sob. "Oh, sweetie, I'm sorry. I ruined your makeup."

Smiling, Holt hands me a small towel. "It's okay. She didn't really wanna wear makeup today anyway. She hates it when it sweats off," he says with a charming wink.

Of course, he's right.

She shakes her head, scanning me from head to toe. "You're even more beautiful than the last time I saw you. If that's even possible." She nods at my stomach, her hand excitedly hovering in the air. "I... I..." she stutters over her words and forces her hand back to her side.

It doesn't take a rocket scientist to know she's dying to touch me.

Handing the makeup-covered towel back to Holt, I reach down and grab her hand, splaying it across my stomach. Her eyes widen in delight. I guide her hand, pressing her firmly against me so she can feel any movement through my shirt. But nothing happens.

I glance up at Holt. "Holt?" That's all I have to say. He knows what I want.

He slides beside me, getting closer than he technically needs to. One calloused hand covers mine and Teresa's. His other hand circles around the top of my stomach. He bends forward, pointing his mouth at my round belly. "What's this? You getting shy on us now, son? It's a party. You can nap later."

Sure enough, our son picks that exact moment to turn flip after flip, making Teresa squeal in excitement. Holt and I can't help but laugh. And when he kisses my temple, I should push him away.

But I don't.

The next thirty minutes are filled with sentiment and intensity. It's nothing short of what I've come to expect from the extended Hill Family...well, I mean, what I expected of them before they turned their backs on me.

They bombard me with heartfelt congratulations on my pregnancy and fill the air with raucous laughter and hyper chatter, with everyone talking on top of one another, layering their conversations like a seven-layer taco dip. Which, by the way, I can't currently eat because of acid reflux issues.

And despite the residual anger still festering in my soul, I'd be lying if I said I wasn't thrilled to see everyone here.

Ray and Teresa.

Dana and Jeff.

Marcum and Nancy.

Raylee and Will.

Ella and Crutch.

Ridge.

Cullen.

Anna, Ty, Laura, Hardy, and Nate.

Even Nate's parents—Brent and Stephanie.

When things settle for a moment, Raylee gently nudges my arm. "Here," she says, holding out a large tote bag. "Holt said you didn't have many maternity clothes. I brought you some of my old ones. I'm definitely never gonna need them again. I know you're taller than me, but most of them should work. There's even a swimsuit in there."

I look down at the bag like it has a snake in it. "A bathing suit?"

"Yeah, don't you wanna swim?"

Yes, I do.

But... I don't exactly look the way I used to. I'm not sure if I'm ready for Holt to see me in Lycra.

She slides her sunglasses on top of her head. "Look, it's been months. I'm dying to talk to you. Why don't you go change, and we'll fix some loungers. The guys are all here to watch the kids, which means we can finally relax and get a tan." She nods her head in Ella's direction, where she's spreading a towel across one of the loungers. "Hurry up."

Nodding, I clutch the bulging bag and head back inside. I'm not even to the threshold before Holt sees me and jogs over, immediately hoisting the bag on his own shoulder.

"I can get it." My protest falls on deaf ears.

"Where are you going?" His blue eyes dart back and forth across my face. "You're not leaving, are you?"

I shake my head, tears threatening to swell at the kindness and familiarity that I've missed so damn much. "No. Raylee gave me some of her maternity clothes. I'm just going to put them up."

"I'll do it for you." He closes the sliding glass door behind us and starts walking across the living room.

I tug on his arm, ignoring how the sweat and heat from his body make my mouth dry and how my hands glide across his bulging bicep with ease. "No, I'll get it."

He cocks an eyebrow. "What's up?"

"Nothing's up. What do you mean, *what's up?*"

His jaw twitches. "Don't lie, Merit."

"Mmmm?"

He takes a step closer, bathing me in his scent of sun and soap and chlorine. "Something's up. You're thinking about something. It's written all over your face."

I look down at the floor, counting the swirls in the marble.

"Tell me the truth," he urges.

Lifting my chin, I peer into his eyes. "It's nothing. I was just thinking about changing. Raylee said she brought me a swimsuit, and I wanted to try it on to make sure it looks okay."

His forehead wrinkles, not understanding. "But you already have bathing suits here. You left them. I saw them in the swim closet outside."

"You think this," I pat my stomach, "will fit in *those*? Think again."

The lightbulb finally goes off, and his eyes glisten. "Ahh, a pregnancy bathing suit." He slowly nods. "I was wondering why you hadn't been swimming. You love swimming." Oblivious, he keeps on walking. "Come on, I'll go ahead and carry this for you. It's heavy."

Sweet mercy, he's driving me crazy. I need some time to be neurotic and self-conscious, and he's not giving it to me.

It's not like we're together. So, why am I worried if he finds me attractive.

Just because I still love him, doesn't mean I *want* him. In fact, I don't know if I ever see myself wanting him. To want him I have to forgive him. And didn't he do something completely unforgiveable?

So... why do I want *him* to want *me*?

It's completely irrational.

For all I know, he's humped a different woman every single week since I left.

But in my thawing heart, I know that he'd never do that to me. I just refuse to acknowledge it.

After changing, I stand in front of the bathroom mirror, spinning and turning. I pick at the material riding up my ass. I guess in the grand scheme of things, it could be worse. It's a simple red suit with a front zipper. My stomach might not be as big as people think it should be, but my breasts are totally making up the difference. They're overly plump and swollen. If I bend my head in just the right direction, I bet I could even lick my own nipple. I look at my legs. A couple of small, little stretch marks on my upper thighs are new. Pink and purple in hue, they weren't there a couple of weeks ago.

I'm just waiting for them to start popping up on my belly.

"Mer, you coming?"

I rub my temples. "What are you still doing out there?"

"Waiting on you. What are you still doing *in there*?"

Well, I guess there's no point in hiding anymore. Unless I want to put on my clothes and scrap the whole idea. But it's the Fourth of July, and the temperature is hotter than Hades. I think I've more than earned myself a swim.

Taking a deep breath, I open the door and step out into the bedroom. Holt is laid back on the bed, tossing a small pillow in the air like a football. He glances over at me, and the pillow bounces off his face. He jumps up from the bed, and even after all this time, it's still surprising to me just how quickly he can move.

"Merit…"

I watch in fascinated hunger as his eyes dilate. His naked chest shudders with a ragged breath. His mouth falls open, and a barely audible sigh escapes, fluttering out of him on angel's wings. My traitorous body instantly responds to him. Equal parts of relief and desire course through me, making me feel drunk and fuzzy. It's like I'm snuggled in front of a fireplace after waking up from a long nap on a cold winter's day.

"Holt." It's the only thing I can say.

Crossing the distance between us, he firmly grips my hip. With his free hand, he gently strokes my cheek. "You're so damn beautiful." His chuckle is low and feral, the timbre of it vibrating in my heart. "Can you stay pregnant forever?"

"I don't think that's how it works," I answer.

My heart beats faster. I really want to kiss him.

Right now, I'd give a million dollars to kiss him.

I'd beg, borrow, and steal. From John Dillinger. From Bugsy Siegel. From Al Capone. From Lucky Luciano.

Yeah, I might've been watching a gangster movie while getting ready this morning.

Does Holt feel the same? About doing anything to be with me, I mean. Not about liking gangster movies.

His eyes grow heavy, and he slowly leans in.

And before I lose all of my willpower, hop up on the bed, and tug my swimsuit to the side, exposing myself to him...I step away, breaking from his hold and stumbling toward the door. "I... we... should go." I stutter over my words, barely making sense. Grabbing an old T-shirt from the top of the dresser to use as a cover-up, I speed walk down the hallway, disappearing into the Big House.

It can't be this easy, can it? The two of us going back to the way things were?

No. It can't.

Forgiveness is never this easy.

"So, when's your due date again?" Ella asks.

We're drying off in the sun, watching all the kids swim around in the pool. Even Hardy's in on the action. Crutch is pushing him around in a float while he splashes his small little fists up and down in the water. I cock my head, watching them. It's a beautiful sight, for sure. Not to mention, Crutch is a complete beast—brawny and impossibly sexy.

I'll say it again, it should be illegal for this many good-looking people to congregate in one location. It's not fair to the rest of us average-looking humans.

I reach for my bottle of water. "October 3rd."

"October 3rd," Raylee repeats. "So, based on the timing, you got pregnant..." Her syllables are slow, and her voice tapers off.

"The day before Holt threw me out," I say bluntly.

Raylee looks away, a frown on her pretty face. Ella's shoulders stiffen—the way they do when she meets someone for the first time. It only takes me a second to feel like a complete bitch. They've been trying hard all day to get back into the routine of our friendship. They've been kind and nurturing and attentive.

It's almost funny.

When I called Kyra first thing this morning to tell her about this little holiday party, she told me she'd drive down here and kick anyone's ass who wasn't nice to me. I keep picturing her sending threatening text messages to everyone. Maybe that's why they're being so nice to me.

I offer a little smile, trying to soften my attitude. "It was definitely a shock. It's the only time we didn't use protection." I think back on what Holt said. I try to cover my laugh but snort instead. "Your brother said it's the only time he's ever been with a woman without protection. So, now he thinks he has some kind of super-human sperm."

They both laugh. "He would think that, wouldn't he."

"How'd you handle the news? Of the pregnancy?" Ella asks.

I sigh, toying with the lid of my water bottle. "Truthfully? At first, I was devastated. I mean, my life was in shambles. He had broken up with me. My store was failing. And I was consumed with fear that he'd be sent to prison for a crime he didn't commit." I swallow. "A crime he thought I had a part in." I shake my head trying to clear my thoughts of the muddy shit from a few months ago. "Anyway," I press my hand against my stomach, trying to convince my son to stop kicking my ribs, "it didn't take me long to be overjoyed. Overwhelmed, for sure. But definitely overjoyed. It's amazing how you can love someone this way. I mean, this baby isn't even breathing air yet, and I love him with the deepest parts of my soul. It's a love you can't even describe."

Ella smiles brightly, dissolving yet another icicle clinging to the shell of my heart. "And it only gets better."

"I'm ready for it." I lift my eyebrows. "I know it'll be hard, but I'm ready." I lean my head back, soaking my face in the warm sun. "I'll tell you one thing, I never thought I'd be pregnant and unwed.

My old-school grandfather would have a conniption fit if he were still with us."

"You don't have to be unwed. Holt would marry you in a heartbeat," Raylee says.

My head jerks up. "Excuse me?"

"He's completely and totally in love with you. That never stopped." She cocks her head to the side. "You can't tell me he hasn't told you how he feels."

Oh, he has. In fact, he tells me multiple times a day. Despite my protests.

He's never mentioned marriage specifically, though. He just says he loves me and that we're a family and that he never wants me to leave.

But once again, it can't be that easy.

Sure, I love him.

But I refuse to be hurt again. He annihilated me. He pulverized my heart into a pile of dust. He took my happy life and crushed my dreams.

I will never let that happen to me again. Ever.

I do think he loves me. I can see it on his face. I can hear the truth in his words.

But there's that small, little nagging voice in the back of my mind that warns me. It warns me that maybe he only *thinks* he loves me because of the baby.

"I mean, look at him," she nods in his direction. He's over in the grass, tossing the football back and forth between Ridge and Nate. "He keeps looking over here, just checking to see if you're okay. He wouldn't even let you carry your own food plate to the table, for Pete's sake."

Well, that's because I dropped my first plate of food inside the kitchen. Everybody else was already outside eating, and I slipped on some water. Holt caught me before I went down, but my ribs and corn on the cob and salad splattered all over the kitchen floor. Holt cleaned it all up, fixed me a fresh plate, and carried it outside to the table for me.

"I think you might be a little too optimistic about our future, Raylee. I mean, we're not together. We're not even dating." I turn to her. "I lost my job and needed health insurance. That's the only reason I'm here."

Ella pins me with her knowing stare. "You may be telling yourself that's the only reason, but you know that's not the truth. Take my advice, fighting the truth only delays your happiness. And after everything you both have been through, you deserve to be happy. Together." She rubs the back of her neck. It's a habit of hers. "We were terrible to you, Merit. We all know it. But Holt was confused and terrified. He was overwhelmed with fear, and that fear made him do the unthinkable. We couldn't abandon him. We just had to hang in there and pray that he would find his way back to you. I know that forgiveness doesn't come easy, nor should it, but we really hope that one day you can forgive us. All of us. Because we have all grieved the loss of friendship in the name of family."

We sit in silence for a long time, watching the kids play in the pool. Anna and Laura are trying to teach Ty how to play Marco Polo. Eventually, Raylee takes a long swig of her beer and folds her arms above her head, draping them over the top of the lounger. "Well, you may not be together, but at least you get to use him to satisfy your needs. When I was pregnant with Anna, it was before Will owned the bar. He was still working at the finance company, and he was doing some big deal out of town. He was gone for three whole months. I was dying. My insides nearly shriveled up."

What. "Huh?"

She nods, like I should understand what she's talking about. "Your *needs*," she says, wiggling her eyebrows.

"What needs?" I ask.

The two of them share a knowing look. Ella bites back her laugh.

"What?" I demand.

"You're six months pregnant," Ella says.

I'm not sure if she's asking me a question or making a statement. "Yeah." I slowly enunciate every letter.

Raylee covers her mouth, snickering. Ella clears her throat, softly smiling. "So, aren't you horny all the time?"

I nearly die of shock. That is not a question I was expecting from
Ella Crutchfield.

Raylee starts laughing even harder. "You don't even have to answer. Your face says it all!"

Of course, their humor is contagious, and I immediately start
giggling like a silly schoolgirl. "Well, yeah." I fumble over my words
like a drunk climbing a ladder. "But I haven't...I mean, he hasn't...I
mean, we haven't...well, you know. We haven't done that. Again. Not
since this," I say patting my belly.

Raylee's eyes bulge, and she sincerely looks offended. "You
mean you haven't had sex since January?"

I shake my head.

"Shit. How are you surviving?" She studies me intently. "A vi-
brator?"

My cheeks pink. And it's not because of the blistering sun. "Well,
it's not actually that," I pause, trying to grasp the right words, "high
tech."

She nearly goes cross-eyed. "An old-fashioned dildo?"

I nod. Just once.

"Seriously!" She's basically yelling. "That's so..."

"Much work," Ella says, finishing her sentence.

For a split second, we're all quiet. But it only takes that split
second, and then we're all laughing so hard I think I'm about to pee
my pants.

Cullen interrupts us. He's carrying a fresh water for me and Ella
and a fresh beer for Raylee. "Something funny, ladies?"

Raylee smacks her lips together. "C, if I told you, you'd never
look at us the same."

His eyes bounce around the three of us, a look of panic on his
face. He turns and walks away without saying another word.

Chapter 17

Holt

We finally had an appointment with the doctor today.

It should've been a lot sooner, but Merit refused to throw my name around to get a quicker appointment. Trust me, I hate that bullshit. I'm not one to wave my dick in the air because my name is Holt Hill, but this is my kid we're talking about. I probably would've made an exception to my dick-waving rule if it meant I could've seen this picture—live and in person—sooner.

This new ultrasound.

This awesome, amazing, wonderful picture of my son.

My son. Growing in Merit's body.

Is there anything in this world more miraculous?

The answer is no. Hell no.

Her sweet voice draws my attention. "You're gonna wear a hole in that picture if you keep touching it."

I check it one more time and then slide it back into the folder from the doctor's office. "Good thing we got it on our cell phones too. Did you text a copy to your parents?"

She steps into the elevator. "Of course. What about you?"

"Group text," I say with a wink, making her giggle.

The elevator door is about to shut when a petite woman in a short skirt joins us, pulling a roller bag behind her. She's holding a tablet and a bunch of papers in one arm. A small name tag is positioned across her large chest, and expensive sunglasses are perched on top of her head. I'm guessing she's a pharmaceutical sales rep.

"Ground floor?" I ask.

She glances up and stares at me. It takes her all of two seconds to decide she likes what she sees. "Yes, please." She stands a little taller and draws a slow breath of air.

I take a step back, positioning myself halfway between her and Merit, eager to see how this is going to play out.

She nods at Merit's stomach. "Congratulations. You and your husband must be very excited." Her predator eyes dart back and forth between the two of us.

"Oh." Merit is caught by genuine surprise. Just another reason I love her. She glances at me before slowly answering the stranger's question. "We're not married." Her eyes fall to the floor, and she folds her hands in front of her, reverting back to the Old Merit. "We're not even together."

The way she says it not only breaks my damn heart in two, but makes me completely furious. I want to hold her in my arms *and* yell at her—all at the same time.

We are together.

Always. Forever.

Happy enough with the answer she receives, the stranger—whose name tag says Felicity—turns back to me, completely ignoring Merit. "That was a nice rain we had last night. Finally cooled things off a little bit. Wouldn't you agree? I've only lived here for six months, but it's without a doubt hotter than the seventh layer of Hell." She pops her head to the side and dramatically licks her lips. "You look familiar. Have we run into each other before? At the country club, maybe?"

Highly doubtful.

I don't exactly frequent the country club.

I give a little smirk, playing along. "Mmm, not that I know of. I'm not really a cigars and golf type of guy."

She chuckles and slowly undresses me with her eyes. "No, you aren't, are you?" Her eyes narrow, and she purses her lips. "I'm guessing...beer and football. Am I right?"

Is it really a guess? She just described nearly every single adult man in the state of Alabama.

I lift my baseball cap and turn it around backward. "Guilty," I say with a sly look.

Her eyes widen in delight and her cheeks flush.

Merit's nose immediately scrunches, and she looks like she's about to vomit. It's the best thing I've seen in days. Well, aside from our new ultrasound picture. I lift my chin in her direction. "What's wrong, Mer? Something smell bad?"

Felicity looks around the elevator and discreetly sniffs the air. "I don't smell anything."

Merit's face doesn't budge.

"Mer?" I ask again, loving the telltale look of jealousy etched across her features.

The elevator dings, and the doors slide open. Merit makes a bee-line for the hospital lobby. Before she slinks out, she nods at our elevator enemy, Felicity. "Yeah. I think *she* farted." She power-walks away, leaving us standing in the elevator.

Holy hell. I nearly die.

That was so unexpected. Merit is so freakin' funny.

Felicity scoffs and chokes on her words. "What? No, I didn't. I swear."

I hold open the elevator door, ushering her out. "I wouldn't worry about it. The pregnancy hormones make my wife very sensitive to smells."

Her face hardens. "Your wife? She said the two of you weren't together."

I shrug nonchalantly. "She did? Huh. I guess she must've forgotten."

Grumbling, she stomps away, dragging the suitcase behind her. "Fucking southern rednecks."

I meet up with Merit outside. She's leaning against the truck, pretending to be interested in something on her phone. I lean next to her, not saying anything. The suspense is killing Merit. I can taste it in the air. She's too curious *not* to ask what happened.

"So... she was pretty. Did you ask her out? It's pretty clear that's what she wanted you to do."

"Why would I ask her out? I'm not on the market. I'm not available. I'm in love with you."

Her phone falls limply to her side. "If you love me, then why did you flirt with her?"

I can't help but smile. "Because I wanted to see that little scrunched-up nose on your beautiful face."

Her head snaps to mine. "What?! I do not make that face."

I roll my eyes. "You most certainly do." I push off the truck and crowd her space. My lips drag across the side of her forehead. Being this close to her nearly breaks me. I can feel my heartbeat in the pit of my stomach. "And I missed seeing it. Just like I missed you."

If I bend a little lower, I can take her mouth.

Just. A. Little. Lower.

Abruptly, she clears her throat and gently shoves against me. When I don't move, she lifts her eyes and blinks. "Holt," she warns.

Reluctantly, I back away, giving her room. Taking a deep breath, she spins away and hovers her hand on the door handle, waiting for me to unlock it. When I bend past her and pull the door open, I don't shy away from the fact that my massive erection jabs her in the back. And she may not realize it, but she doesn't exactly shy away either. Because her back arches, and she rubs her ass against me.

Driving home, I keep glancing over at her. There's a softness to her that wasn't there earlier. Her features are relaxed, and she looks... content. "You look happy."

She nods. "I am."

I bite back a smile. "Well, me too. I'm just curious if there's anything making you extra happy right at this second."

She fiddles with a button on her shirt. "I'm just relieved." Her head falls back on the headrest. "I get nervous before every single appointment. You just never know what the doctor may say, what the ultrasound may show. It's terrifying to think something bad may happen."

She's right.

Just the thought of something bad happening to her or our son makes me feel like I'm trapped under a thousand-pound weight, suffocating. I can't imagine anything worse. I'd rather spend the rest of my life rotting in a jail cell as an innocent man than even think of anything bad happening to them.

It's hard to believe that six months ago I actually threw Merit out of my life. Hard to imagine that I even entertained the asinine idea that she could do something so vile and evil.

I am the world's biggest dickhead.

I reach over and squeeze her forearm. "Nothing bad is gonna happen." Before she can move away, I lift her hand and kiss her wrist. It's something I never did with frequency before the arrest, but find myself doing all the time now. If this is all she'll grant me, I'll fucking take it. I'll lap it up like a starving dog. "I'm sorry you had to go to all those appointments by yourself. That couldn't have been easy."

"It was nerve-racking and exciting, all at the same time." Her face falls a little bit. "And heartbreaking. I wish you could've been there." She shrugs, snorting on a sarcastic chuckle. "But it's hard to go to something you don't even know about." She swallows loudly. "I'm really sorry I didn't tell you sooner."

My jaw tenses thinking about the way I acted. "I didn't deserve to know sooner. I was a shithead. The only one who should be sorry is me."

And it's true.

I was shocked when I first found out—angry, even, that Merit kept her pregnancy hidden from me. But now? It's clear to me, Merit did what she did to protect our child and to protect her heart. I can't blame her for that.

In fact, she's the strongest person I know.

We spend the next few minutes driving in silence. I slow down when the Japanese steakhouse comes into view. "Are you hungry? Do you wanna stop and eat?"

She shakes her head. "We can't. Nate is coming over to help with the Foundation website. Remember?"

"That's right," I say, checking the clock.

"He's so smart with all of that technology. I told him the Foundation would pay him, but he keeps refusing. We're really lucky; you should see what some of those web designers charge." She side glances at me. "You think he's gonna do something with computers? For his job, I mean. When he grows up?"

"Not sure. He's one hell of a ball player."

"Like the famous Holt Hill," she says, teasing me.

I scoff, tapping my fingers against the steering wheel. "The *famous Holt Hill* was accused of domestic violence, broke his neck, blew out his knee, was arrested for sexually assaulting a seventeen-year-old child, and nearly lost the love of his life because of his own stupidity." I tilt my head. "Let's hope Nate turns out nothing like him."

"But he also won multiple National Championships in college, played in three Super Bowls—including the two he won—saved his niece's life, coached a high school team to a state win, and..." she looks down, studying her hands, "knows when to say he's sorry."

"Hey, maybe he's not that bad after all," I say with a playful wink as I turn into our driveway.

Chapter 18

Holt

"Are you sure you don't wanna come out? Just for a little bit?" Her eyebrow lifts. "Uhhh, to the bar? The bar that'll be swarming with young, thin, beautiful women?" She shuffles in her chair. "No, thanks."

I roll my eyes, reading between the lines of what she isn't saying. "It's just five pounds. The doctor said you looked great." My eyes travel down to the cleavage peeking from the top of her shirt. "And I have to agree."

Her cheeks flush the cutest shade of pink. "I'm carrying your child. You'd say anything to keep me calm and happy."

I lean back in my chair and fold my hands behind my head. I love the way her eyes automatically trail to my body. Like I'm a magnet she can't pull away from. "You're right; I would say anything to make you happy. But that doesn't mean it isn't true. Can't you read my face?"

Her eyes dance, sparking flashes of green, brown, and yellow. "Maybe," she says with a flirtatious grin.

Holy hell. Playful Merit is freakin' awesome. "C'mon," I urge. "Just for a drink or two. You have that huge non-alcoholic menu to choose from."

She looks around the large dining table at the scatter of papers and notebooks. Marcum and Nate just left, and we officially have the website up and running. There's a few small tweaks he and Merit want to make, but it's nothing that can't be done later. She shakes her head. "I wanna get this cleaned up for the weekend." She shuts the lid to her laptop. "Besides, I'm not really in the mood to see all those skinny sluts hitting on you, Ridge, and Cullen."

I choke on a laugh. "How do you know they're sluts?" I fake a scowl and narrow my eyes. "And why do you care who hits on Ridge and Cullen?"

She pretends to ignore me.

"Hey," I reach out and grab her hand before she can hide it underneath the table, *"you're mine.* Don't forget it."

Her gaze locks with my own, and she immediately stops breathing. Pins and needles travel the length of my arm.

I don't think I'll ever get used to touching her.

It's erotic. It's powerful.

The thought of touching her fuels my days and nights.

Loving her gives me a reason to get out of bed every morning. And the possibility of feeling her soft and scorching skin underneath my fingertips? Well, that's just icing on the cake.

Suddenly, she slides her hand away, leaving me empty. It's a fucking terrible feeling. I clear my throat and shake the fog from my brain. "Anyway, Ridge may be off the market soon. He started dating someone. They've been out a couple of times. Supposedly, he's thinking of introducing her to the family."

Her eyes grow comically wide. "Seriously? Oh man, what's Laura gonna say to that?"

"Who knows. But I'm thinking about selling tickets and popcorn for the first time they meet."

I made it three hours this time.

That's way better than I thought it would be. Truth be told, I was ready to come home after the first hour, but Cullen actually needed

Ridge and me to hop behind the bar for a little bit to help out. Both Will and the normal Friday night bartender came down with a stomach virus, so we had to jump in and help C until the other workers could come in. As per the usual, a really great band was playing, so the bar was packed out.

As soon as I open the door to the Children's Wing, I hear one of Merit's old movies playing in the living room. Ever since she came back, I've been trying to get her to watch her movies in the theater room, but she refuses. She still claims that's *my side* of the house.

Eager to see her, I nearly walk past her open bedroom door when a slight, yet familiar, noise catches my attention. A whimper. A whimper I've heard a hundred times—albeit nowhere near as loud as I'm used to—and a whimper I've been dreaming about for the past six months.

It's one of the things I think about late at night when my hand is wrapped tightly around my cock.

Turning around, I take a silent step.

My heart immediately thunders in my chest, pounding so hard it feels like my ribcage is bruising. She's lying back on the bed with her feet propped on the mattress and her knees in the air. Her hair is fanned around her—brown and black and red—like a forest set on fire by the sunrise. Her flimsy cotton nightgown is gathered around her pelvis, and her hand is between her legs, slowly pumping some sort of sex toy in and out. The bathroom light is on, casting her in a warm glow, allowing me to see her every move.

I've never been so thankful for electricity.

I watch in awe as her bare crotch flushes red, a tempered blush pouring across her flesh. But I'm utterly devastated because things aren't as they should be. Her pussy lips aren't swollen and thick; they aren't pulsing with need. Her cunt isn't glistening with the sheen of her moisture; it's not dripping and weeping. And although her hand is blocking my view of her clit, I can guarantee you that little bud is tucked away in the shadows, just begging for the sun so it can blossom. When my baby is ready for me, that clit is like a ripe cherry. Plump and juicy. And ready to be eaten.

Good thing I know how to remedy all those problems. Every single last one of them.

Not only that... I can solve them over and over and over again.

I'm instantly hard. So damn hard I literally think I'm about to explode. She whimpers again. And it's not her satisfied whimper. It's her *I'm about to get mad because I wanna come right now* whimper.

Here I come, baby. Your solution to this travesty.

"Mer." My voice is cut from gravel, like someone tried to strangle the life from me.

Gasping, she yanks her hand from between her legs and loses grip on the slippery, rubber toy. It flies across the room. She scrambles to a seated position, and we both stare at the hot pink dildo in the corner. It landed perfectly on top of her multi-colored tennis shoes. Even from the doorway, I can see her white streaks of desire coating it—desire nowhere near as thick and gorgeous as it usually is.

When it's covering my cock.

And let's be real. Technically, it only blanketed my raw and bare cock once. *One time.* One single, lonely time. A time when I wasn't in the best headspace, needless to say. So, I didn't fucking appreciate it the way I should've.

I. Want. It. Again.

It's impossible to think about anything but being inside of her.

Her eyes balloon, and she jumps up from the bed, tugging her nightgown around her naked bottom. "Wh...what are you doing home so soon?" When I don't answer, she flitters closer to me, studying the floor with every step. Eventually, she shakes her head and lifts her chin, staring straight at me. She cocks a hand on her luscious hip. "Just so you know, there's nothing wrong with what I was just doing. Most women have a very active sexual appetite during pregnancy. It's healthy and normal and nothing to be ashamed of." She points a finger at her chest, drawing my eyes to her peaked nipples. "I'm not ashamed."

"No?" I ask. I'm barely able to form a cohesive thought.

She frowns. "No. There..." she stumbles over her words again, "there's nothing wrong with it."

I tug the ballcap from my head and drop it to the floor. "There's something very wrong with it."

Her eyes dart back and forth. Her face is too easy to read. She's completely confused and is now wondering if she did something to hurt the baby. "There is?"

I erase the distance between us, skimming my body—ever so lightly—against hers. So close I can smell her cucumber-scented lotion. So close I can touch her if she'd let me. "It's supposed to be *me*. My body—my cock—pushing into you, making you scream. Not some piece of plastic." My fingers tangle at her side, squeezing with a punishing grip. "It's supposed to be me making love to you, Merit." I lick the shell of her ear, making her shiver. "Fucking you. Every. Single. Day."

She doesn't say anything. She doesn't have to.

The smell of her arousal floods the air.

I bet that pussy is crying now. And I wanna wipe its tears.

With my tongue.

I can feel the swell of her body. The hard caress of her nipples as they scratch against my T-shirt. The soft sway of her hips against mine, as she teases the bulge in my shorts. The air in the room pulsates. It's like a damn sonic boom against my eardrums.

"You want me inside of you."

"No. It's not a good idea, Holt."

"Don't lie, Merit."

"Mmmm?" Her noncommittal response sounds more like a passionate moan.

"You want me inside of you. It's written all over your face."

Her eyes flutter closed, and she takes a deep breath. The movement draws my attention to the delicate lines of her collarbone.

"Tell me the truth."

Her lips move. Her answer skirts across my face on angel's wings. "Yes, I want you inside of me."

I nearly collapse in relief. Months and months of tension drain from my body in no more time than it takes me to blink.

I need her. Now.

But... I also want to take my time with her. Savor this first time back together.

My fingers find their way under her gown. I drag them across the heated skin of her bare thigh, and when my thumb grazes her clit—that sweet, round cherry—her knees buckle. She doesn't have to worry about falling, though. Because I'm not letting her go. My free arm is holding her tightly, refusing to give her even an inch of freedom. I'm lifting her up. Her tiptoes barely touch the floor.

I pushed her away. Pushed her out of my life.

I'll be damned if I ever let her go again.

And sure enough, now she's wet. Soaking wet and ready for me. "Fuck me. There's my girl." My fingers slide into her. Her head lobs against my shoulder, hiding her eyes with wild strands of her redwood hair. Words of passionate adoration tumble from my lips. "You're so wet, baby. Tight and wet and perfect. My hands have ached for you. I want your cum dripping from my fingertips down to my elbows."

I work inside of her, teasing all the spots I know she loves. If it feels this good for me now, I can only imagine what it'll be like in a few short minutes when it's my cock inside of her instead of my calloused fingers. Her panted breathing quickens, and I can tell she's close. So damn close. She softly bites down on my skin, licking and tasting me. It's fucking erotic. And it makes me pump into her even quicker. Even harder.

And when she comes all over my hand and screams my name into the darkness of our house, I nearly lose my shit.

Carefully releasing her to stand on her own two feet, I drag my hand from between her legs and lick my fingers clean before kissing the holy hell out of her.

Sweet. Fucking. Mercy.

This kiss.

Her lips, her tongue, her teeth.

I think it's even better than the first time we kissed.

Why?

Because now I know what life is like without her. It's something I never want to experience again. She makes life worth living.

Merit is my everything.

Our son is my everything.

Our family is my everything.

I kiss her until she eventually pulls away from me, gasping for air. She giggles and her signature snort is music to my ears. "Are you trying to suffocate me, *sir*?"

I whisper against her neck, teasing her now with my own teeth. Her body shudders beneath my touch. "You know I hate it when you call me *sir*."

She smiles. Softly. Wickedly. "Don't lie, Holt Hill. You fucking love it."

Hell, yeah, I do.

Leaning back, I tug my shirt off. Her eyes devour me, leaving nothing but little shards of bone in their wake. And when she reaches out and traces the contours of my abdomen, I nearly combust. Her fingers scorch a path across my body, landing on my belt. Taking her lead, I undo my cargo shorts and kick them to the side. Her eyes dart down, hungrily eyeing the massive erection nearly ripping my boxer briefs in two. There's even a wet spot right on the crotch from my pre-cum.

Like I'm some pathetic teenager who can't even keep it in his pants.

"I need to see you, to see the stomach growing our baby," I beg. I grab the hem of her nightgown and pull it over her head.

And for the first time, I'm seeing her pregnant body. *All* of her pregnant body.

You wanna know how I know God is real? Because I'm watching the woman I love grow our child in her belly.

Right. In. Front. Of. My. Eyes.

Minute. By. Minute.

She's fucking gorgeous. That extra five pounds she was so concerned with has just added to her beauty. Her breasts are heavier than they used to be. Rounder. Swollen. Her nipples larger and darker. Her hips are wider and decorated with a few faint purple and pink stretch marks that weren't there before. And, most importantly, the skin of her stomach is stretched tight over our growing boy. Firm and taut.

I want to look at her and touch her and taste her all at the same time.

I want it all.

She bites her lip. "I'm different." I can't help but notice the tone of apology in her voice.

"Better," I say. "I'd like to think we're both better. Better than we were. Stronger. Ready to face forever together."

Her brow furrows. "This...this doesn't change anything, Holt. It's...it's just sex. We're not getting back together."

I can tell she doesn't believe those words. Not for one second. But instead of calling her out, I let her win the battle. Instead of chastising her, I kiss her, taking the opportunity to drag my hands across every inch of her skin, giving myself time to just relish the way she feels. The way she reacts to my touch. The way she haunts my soul with her every action.

Whimpering. Moaning. Shaking.

I've never been more ready for the screaming.

I push my underwear to the ground, grab her bare ass, and haul her into my arms. Instinctively, her ankles lock around my waist, and I carry her to the bed. The anticipation of making love to her again has sweat dripping from my body. I crawl over her.

"Wait," she half-heartedly shoves against my chest. "What about protection? Do you have a condom?"

My thumb traces around her wider-than-normal belly-button. "Uh, Mer, I don't think you quite understand how condoms and pregnancy prevention work."

She doesn't even crack a smile. "I'm not talking about pregnancy. I'm talking about protection from other *stuff*. I mean, it's been a long time. I wanna be safe."

"Is that your way of asking me if I've had sex with someone else?"

"It's fine. I mean, we broke up. You're allowed to have sex with whomever you want."

Well, that's a boldface lie. It's written all over her face in disgust.

"Merit, I haven't been with anyone else. The thought never even crossed my mind. Because that would be cheating. I love you. And only you. I will never, ever cheat on you."

She opens her mouth, ready to tell me that we aren't a couple.

I really don't wanna hear that again, so I drown her protest with a kiss. I play with her nipple, noting the texture is different than it used to be. And when her legs fall open, I position myself at her entrance. She's slick and primed and perfect. I glide into her, forcing myself to take it one slow and delicious inch at a time.

Holy. Fucking. Hell.

My memories of Merit don't do this justice.

Because my love and admiration for her have grown tenfold since the last time we were together, this is *more*.

So much more. This is...love and honor and passion and devotion and...life.

This. Is. Fucking. Life.

This. Is. Us. Creating. Life.

Her back arches, and she moans.

My cock is literally sending sparks of pleasure through every single cell of my body. I can feel every millimeter of her hot and heavenly pussy clenching around my dick.

Okay, it's official. I'm never using a condom again. And why should I? This woman is gonna be my wife. My forever. The mother of my children. My other half. My better half. We are going to make a gaggle of children if I have any say in it, or at least die trying.

I frame my elbows around her face and nudge her nose with mine. "Open your eyes, Mer. Look at me."

Her heated breath fogs between us, wetting my neck. "I love you, Merit. I'm sorry, baby. I'm sorry for hurting you." I lower down, taking care not to squash my son, and gently kiss her lips. I trail my tongue across her jaw and down her cleavage, relishing in the salty taste of her sweaty skin, in the feel of her swollen breasts. "I'll search the dark, find all the broken pieces, and put them back together again. I'll make us whole. I promise, baby, we'll be stronger than we ever were. We'll never break again." I kiss her. Softly, sweetly. "*I'll* never break us again."

And when one lone tear slides down her face, I lick that too. "Let me show you I love you."

I pull all the way out and plunge into her again and again and again.

But not fast.

No. Hell no.

Then, this would be over way too quickly.

And I want it to last forever.

Slowly, we make love. Until my mind and my body are about to implode and evaporate into nothingness.

Eventually, she's clawing at my back, digging her nails into my skin, forcing me to stay inside of her, forcing me to give her what she wants, what she needs.

Together, we chase and find our orgasms. Our screams echo against each other, battling for domination.

She drains me. Completely and totally.

And yet, I've never been more fulfilled. And so damn thankful.

Chapter 19

Merit

Walking back down the marble corridor to the Children's Wing, I shuffle the cold milk jug in my hand.

I can't believe he slept over last night. Last night was Night Seven. Seven nights in a row of having wild and passionate and wonderfully crazy sex with Holt.

And if I'm telling the truth, it's not just been the nights.

There's been some pretty spectacular midday romps in there too.

But I've kicked him out of my bed every single night. Until last night. Afterward, we lay there talking, and, well, I guess I fell asleep. Because the next thing I know, I'm waking up with his sleeping body tangled with mine. Needless to say, Holt still looks as delicious asleep as he does awake. And he still sleeps with a possessive arm wrapped around my body—specifically around my swollen belly, like he's unwilling to let me go—even in his dreams.

My heart skipped a beat having him next to me again.

Just like old times.

And then, I reprimanded myself for feeling that way and decided to focus on blueberry pancakes instead.

But I was out of milk. Hence, me raiding his fridge in the Big House. Seeing as how I had his massive cock inside my mouth last night, I figured he'd be more than happy to share some of his milk with me.

Of course, I'd still be happy to give him a blow job, even without the offer of free condiments. He makes this deep growl in the back of his throat when I'm going down on him. It's so freakin' sexy. And he plays with my hair, softly massaging my scalp. It sends shivers down my spine. Every single time.

I'm about to cross the threshold into the apartment when something catches my eye on the side table next to the door.

His cell phone.

Just sitting there.

Like it did a thousand times before. Before our lives imploded.

Unable to stop myself, I grab it. The lock screen lights up with a running list of sports and news notifications. It looks like he has a couple of texts from last night too, from Ridge and Teresa. I enter what used to be his passcode and it buzzes, telling me I've chosen wrong. I try the new security code for the house—the day we met—and it immediately opens.

I'm not sure how I feel about that.

I know the passcode to his phone again.

I could do anything I want right now. Text people. Email people. Call people.

And accusations of that very same thing ruined my life just a few short months ago. Accusations that tossed me to the ground and stomped me to death, leaving me lifeless and bleeding.

In my bedroom, he's still sleeping, with blankets piled around him, and spiky, sexy bedhead. "Holt. Holt, wake up."

Of course, he doesn't move.

I take another step closer to the bed and tap his back with the cold milk jug. "Wake up!" I scream as loud as I can.

Fortunately, that does the trick. He doesn't jerk awake like most people would, though. Instead, he shifts around, yawning and stretching, like he doesn't have a care in the world. Pursing my lips, I look up at the ceiling, refusing to watch the rippling movement of his muscles. Rolling over, he squints. The morning sunlight makes the freckles on his nose shine. "Hey." His voice is coated in sleep and sex.

I ignore the way it makes me feel. "What is this?" I say nodding at my hand.

His eyebrow lifts. "Milk," he says with a cute little smirk.

I roll my eyes. He knows I was nodding at my other hand. "Not that. This," I say, lifting the cell phone in the air.

"My cell phone. You need to make a call, Mer? I'll let you borrow it," he teases with his signature wink.

"Why did you leave it outside the bedroom? After everything that happened? How can you still do that?"

He sits up, dangling one leg off the side of the bed. The sheet is dangerously close to showing me his full naked body. Sighing, he drags a hand across his face, scratching his facial hair. "Because she took enough from us. I refuse to give her anymore. I refuse to let her win."

I look down at it. Something so simple. Yet, it caused so much heartache. "Her sentencing is Monday."

"Yeah, I know."

"Are you going to it?"

"Of course, I am. I want you there too. I want you by my side." He looks into my eyes, waiting for a response. "Will you go with me?"

I stare out the window, watching Crutch usher my parents up the steps of the courthouse, past the throngs of reporters and spectators. Just like he did with me about an hour ago. I had Crutch on one side, and Ridge on the other, blocking me from the prying eyes and flashing cameras.

Holt, trying to divert their attention, paused for a couple of questions. Then, he snuck over to the side where several Peewee football teams were standing and flashing homemade signs of support. He took pictures with every single kid and passed out bright, shiny pennies.

Teresa squeezes my shoulder, watching as my parents disappear from view. "I'm really glad they could come. They'd do anything to support you. They're wonderful people."

I blink, studying her kind and sincere eyes. "They're here to support him," I say, flashing my gaze to Holt. "No matter what's happened between us, they know he's innocent. They've known it since day one." I glance down at my growing stomach. "And no matter what happens from here on out, he'll be a part of our lives. Forever. It's important we show a united front." I try to swallow, but my throat feels incredibly dry for some reason. I guess it's the diplomatic bullshit I'm trying to spew forth. "Besides, I'm not even speaking today."

She smiles. "That doesn't mean you don't need support too, sweetie. This didn't just happen to him. It happened to all of us."

Yeah, don't I know it.

I look around the small family room connected to the courtroom. Everyone is here. And I mean everyone. Not the little kids, of course; although, Nate is here. He's old enough to understand. Hell, he even got a black eye over it. All of us were affected by Holt's arrest, terrorized by the allegations. I think we could all give victim impact statements, but only Ray, Raylee, and Holt have said they want to.

Relief courses through me when my parents finally make it into the room. I didn't realize just how much I missed them over the past several weeks. I guess I got used to living back at home. Wiping tears from her eyes, Mom flutters her hand across the wispy fabric of my oversized, navy-blue cardigan. "Show me. Let me see how much you've grown." Blushing in embarrassment, I open the lightweight sweater, flashing her the tight fabric of the off-white sundress I'm wearing. It's sleeveless and comes to above the knees. The linen shift is supposed to be a little baggy. Yeah, not so much. About two more weeks, and I won't even be able to pull it down past my boobs.

"You're bigger."

I roll my eyes. "Thanks, Mom. Confidence booster."

She laughs. "That belly's growing a human. What do you expect? Besides, you're still way smaller than I was. You need more red meat."

Just the thought of steak makes me nauseous.

The door opens, and a court deputy leans in, whispering to Crutch. He nods. "We'll be right there." His hand reaches out, instantly connecting with Ella's. They have an unspoken body language that's beautiful. Intense and completely beautiful. "It's time," he announces. He looks over at Holt. "You'll walk in last."

Holt doesn't waste any time. He crosses the room and wraps a possessive arm around my waist. "Okay," he says, looking down into my eyes, "we're ready."

Under normal circumstances, I'd quickly remind him that we aren't together anymore, but this is hardly a normal circumstance. And if I'm being completely honest, I think I need his touch. I need the silent power his body pours into mine. Without it, I might not even have the strength to put one foot in front of the other.

Wordlessly, we all file into the courtroom. I hate the quiet. It reminds me of a funeral.

The courtroom is packed, filled with people. The faint clicks of the cameras chafe against my eardrum, like nails on a chalkboard. The judge held a lottery for the press, only allowing five reporters inside. Well, five reporters we didn't approve of, plus Chloe. When her credentials weren't pulled in the lottery, we requested she be present as our personal press representative. After everything that's happened, she's proven herself to be a stand-up journalist.

I fold my hands in front of me and count the tiles on the floor, refusing to look at anyone. Holt guides me down the aisle with his hand on the small of my back. We stand, waiting for the judge to come in. My hair falls in my face, bothering me, but I refuse to move my hands from their steadfast position.

I can do this. I can do this. I can do this.

I repeat my mantra, trying to pump myself up.

Just pretend I'm back in court, watching Edward at one of his trials. If I could make it through those, surely, I can make it through this.

Surprising me, Holt reaches out and gently tucks the loose hair behind my ear. He leans down and whispers. "Look up, Mer. She doesn't have any power over you. None of these people do."

Steeling myself with a deep breath, I follow his advice, looking up. I don't have to search for Delaney. Even if I didn't know where the convicted sit, I'd still spot her right away.

Because she's staring at me.

Staring at us.

Staring at my covered and hidden baby bump.

Jail hasn't been particularly kind to her. She's gained weight, and her once flawless complexion is marked with a small bit of acne and ruddiness.

Huh. I guess the five-hundred-dollar night cream really does work.

Her hair is tied back in a bun, and she's wearing a black blouse and gray slacks. No expensive jewelry. No designer clothes. No movie-star makeup.

Not to mention, she doesn't seem particularly happy to see me.

Well, right back at ya, bitch.

Fortunately, our staring contest ends when the judge enters and immediately starts the proceedings. Throughout the hearing, Holt's hand never leaves my leg. His calloused fingertips indent my tanned skin with a death grip. It's quite possible I'll have a bruise afterward, but I would never shoo him away. Not during this.

We need each other.

The only person who speaks on Delaney's behalf is her ex-boyfriend, Heidi's uncle, Trenton Trevors. Not even her parents are here. I mean, she's completely ruined her father's career. Before all of this, I heard he was considering making the move from state politics to the national level. Edward's not here either. He had to agree with the prosecution's decision to also charge her for the theft of his money, lest he seem complacent with the plan to frame Holt. He and the other partners have been trying to save the sinking law firm. Needless to say, it's taken quite the hit to its reputation.

When it's time for the victim impact statements, Ray goes first, followed by Raylee. Of course, there's not a dry eye in the house when Raylee reads a letter written by Anna. Fortunately, tissue boxes are scattered along the pews.

Then, it's time for Holt.

To the naked eye, he's not nervous. How could he be? He's been exonerated. He's getting his justice. This must be a piece of cake. A breeze compared to playing in the highest-watched Super Bowl. Ever.

But I can tell he's nervous.

His graceful movements are a split second delayed. His firm and sure voice can only be found after clearing his throat.

"I always wondered what made me so lucky. It's actually one of my earliest memories. I went to bed every night with a full belly, in a warm bed, surrounded by a family. A great family. And then, I picked up a football. I played a game and found my place in the world." He smiles, softly chuckling. "I'd say that's pretty lucky. Not too many people can earn a living just from playing a really fun game."

He looks around the courtroom, absorbing the sea of faces. "Even the tragedies in my life had a flip side to them. The disappearance of my cousin brought my family closer together. It gave my other cousin a wonderful husband and son. The tornado that destroyed everything around us when I was in high school gave my best friend a life purpose, saving those around him as a firefighter. Even my injury was lucky. I was able to live my life, watching my beautiful nieces and nephews grow up beside me. I landed a job coaching high school ball and found my second calling." He looks over at me. The intensity of his stare nearly cuts off my circulation. "Most importantly, my injury kept me in my hometown, where I met the love of my life one Friday night at a children's shoe store."

He takes a deep breath and turns on Delaney. "And then you took all that away. You stole my luck. You kidnapped my happiness. You slaughtered my security." She pretends to pick at a piece of lint on her shirt, doing her best to ignore him. "I'm embarrassed to admit that I didn't even think about you when I was arrested. Not once. I didn't think about you when I was sitting in the jail cell. When I was locking my nieces and nephews out of my house because I was too scared for them to be seen with me. When I was turning on my family. When I was ruining the life and career of the woman I love. When I was burning my world to the ground because I was crippled by the shame of the horrible things I was accused of."

He shakes his head back and forth. "And I should have thought about you. In fact, you should've been the very first thing I thought of. Why?" He grips the podium with both hands. "Because I know you, Delaney."

That gets her attention.

He cocks an eyebrow in amusement. "I know how you operate. Deep down, I knew it even before I asked you out on our first date in high school. I could see the manipulation churning behind your eyes. I could see the evil of your heart. I could see the toxicity of your soul."

And that? That definitely gets her attention.

"Yet, I asked you out anyway. I ignored the warning signs. And those couple of dates? Well, let's just say getting tackled by a three-hundred-pound lineman was more fun."

A couple of spectators laugh. Even the judge hides a smile behind his hand.

"And then I made the mistake of opening my door to you in North Carolina. You stole from me, threatened me, and tried to derail my career. More importantly, you made me a complete skeptic. I started to think I'd never find my other half. The person I was meant to spend the rest of my life with. My reason for waking up each day. But despite your best efforts, it finally happened. It happened. And I was lucky again. You saw that. And you decided to take it all away."

His face hardens into true grit and determination. His words are coated in danger and rawness. "Well, I'm here to take it all back, Delaney."

Tears spring to the corners of my eyes. I fight to swallow.

"I'm taking back everything you stole from me. I'm taking back my life. I'm taking back my happiness. I'm taking back my freedom."

He slowly folds the piece of paper he's been reading from and lazily puts it in his pocket. His nerves are gone. His masculine grace is back. In full force.

Completely sexy.

He's the undeniable Holt Hill.

He locks eyes with mine. Our baby rumbles in my stomach, kicking and turning somersaults. Before walking back to his seat, he hits the courtroom with his last declaration.

"And most importantly, I'm taking back my family."

Chapter 20

Holt

The judge shuffles through some papers. "All right, ladies and gentlemen, I believe that's the last of our victim impact statements. It falls upon the duty of the court now to—"

"Wait!" Merit jumps up from beside me.

I wasn't expecting her to move. I wasn't prepared. My hand falls from her leg and slaps against the wooden court bench. Quickly recovering, I jump up and wrap an arm around the small of her back. I can't help but notice she's sweating. Her flowy sweater thing is sticking to her. "Mer, what's wrong," I whisper.

Worry eats at me. What if something is wrong with her? With the baby?

"Miss Browning?" The judge looks back down at the folder in front of him. "I was told you didn't wish to speak. Has that changed?"

She stutters, "Is... is it too late?"

"In my courtroom, it's never too late, Miss Browning." He waves his hand at the podium. "You may approach."

For a moment, Merit looks like she may turn and run. Or, at the very least, throw up everywhere. I lean close to her. "Mer, you don't have to do this."

Her eyes are filled with colors of green and yellow today. Swirling and shifting like a kaleidoscope. "Yeah, I do," she says matter-of-factly. She puts one shaky foot in front of the other.

My heart swells. She's the damn strongest woman I know.

The judge lifts an eyebrow. "Mr. Hill, you may return to your seat."

I shake my head. "All due respect, Your Honor, but I'm not leaving her side."

The court deputy takes a step in my direction, ready to enforce whatever the judge may demand. After a beat, and with a nearly imperceptible nod, he orders the bailiff back.

I'm glad. Going to jail for contempt is not high on my to-do list today.

Merit folds her hands in front of her and looks down. She studies the courthouse name engraved on the wooden podium and nervously shifts from one foot to the other.

And we wait.

The courtroom is completely quiet.

Too quiet.

I can even hear myself breathe. It sounds like a freakin' freight train.

I'm about to turn Merit around when she starts talking. "I couldn't sleep." Her head snaps up, and she stares at Delaney. "When I found out the truth, I couldn't sleep. I got out of bed every single hour. I would walk the entire house, making sure no one had broken in. I was home with my parents, with my grandmother. She heard me one night and came to check on me. It didn't even cross my mind that it could be anyone else but you. All I could think about was you." She scoffs in disbelief. "I nearly stabbed my granny with a kitchen knife."

Holy shit.

I had no idea.

Her hands grip the podium, turning her knuckles white. "And once I started sleeping through the night again, I had nightmares. About Holt. In prison. Nightmares about him being beaten to death. Threatened. Tortured." She looks over at me. Her eyes glisten with unshed tears.

My heart is literally ripping out of my chest right now.

Clearing her throat, she straightens her shoulders, powering through the details of her trauma. "I lost my job. My livelihood. My ability to provide for myself." Her breath echoes through the microphone attached to the podium, shaky and hollow. "Every single day my store was vandalized. My employees were harassed." She pauses, gathering her thoughts. "That store was my joy. Pure, unfiltered, passionate joy. And no one would even set foot inside. My sense of worth was trampled. I went from being a productive business owner to being a pariah." Her brow furrows. "People actually thought I was some kind of pimp, hiring Heidi so Holt could have 'easy access' to her," she says with air quotes. "It's sickening."

She sniffles, wiping her nose with her hand. "And what about Heidi?" she asks. Fury and rage circle around her like a fog. "That poor girl. How could you do that to a child? Objectify her? Lie to her? Sexualize her? Turn her into a criminal? Because of you she's gonna have to fight to prove she's not the person you tried to turn her into. She'll never be able to stop fighting. She'll never be able to forget. Ever."

She waits for a minute, trying to see if anything registers with Delaney. But alas, Delaney just sits there, stone-faced and solemn. Like a porcelain doll that's fallen from the shelf and is staring at the ceiling.

"Before you ruined my life, I was happy."

Unable to stop myself, I slide my hand over hers, trying to give her my strength.

Of course, she doesn't need it right now. Because she's My Merit. And she's completely badass.

"*We* were happy," she says forcefully. "And you took that away. Why? Because he wanted me instead of you? Because you thought I had the life you were meant to live?"

She waits for an answer that never comes.

"We're having a baby. A son. Our child will never know a life where his father wasn't accused of a horrible crime. It's part of our history now. On the Internet, on the television, in the magazines. Anytime someone talks about his father, this will be mentioned. You've tainted his father's legacy."

She nibbles on her lip.

"I... I think I hate you. I've never actually hated anyone before. Not the girl who tripped me on purpose during the field day race. Not the boy who copied my English paper in college and claimed it as his own. Not my ex-husband. And not even you when I caught you having an affair with my ex-husband. But then you did this, you did this to Holt. I've never met anyone better than him."

Her jaw twitches with anger. "I do hate you, Delaney."

She shrugs her shoulders and snorts with a small, cynical laugh. "What am I supposed to do with that? How am I supposed to live with that anger?" Her brow furrows, and she stutters again. "I... I don't know if I can forgive you. And I'm really scared about what kind of person that makes me. I'm scared you've ruined me."

Finally, she looks back down, and her body starts to shake as she whispers, "I don't wanna be ruined."

She doesn't seem surprised to see me.

I lean against the corner wall of the Children's Wing living room. Her eyes immediately roam my body. I didn't bother putting a shirt on. It's easy to see she's pleased with that decision. Her eyes widen, and her cheeks blush. Her body instantly responds to mine, and I catch her rubbing her thighs together before she can cover herself with a blanket. Instead of saying anything, I give her a devilish wink.

She rolls her eyes. "You do realize my parents are asleep in that bedroom right there," she says with a point.

I can't help but laugh. "You're the one whose mind is in the gutter. I, myself, am more than capable of controlling my urges for seventy-two hours."

"And just how do you know where my mind is?"

"Mer," I say with a tease, "don't forget you wear your emotions all over your face."

"Oh yeah, and what does this emotion say, *sir*?" She flips me the bird.

Playing dirty, I lift my arms and drape them behind my head. She still loves it when I do that. "I'm not good with sign language. Maybe you can show me."

She tugs the blanket closer to her, giggling and snorting.

Trying to calm the raging hard-on that's about to grow in my shorts, I nod to the TV. "What's this one?"

"*The Man Who Shot Liberty Valance.*"

"It's good?"

She looks at me like I've just asked her if fried rice from the Japanese steakhouse is good. Shaking her head, she turns back to the movie, pretending to ignore me.

"Let's go talk."

She eyes the bedroom door where Deke and Marie are fast asleep. "Holt, that's not a good idea."

Now it's my time to roll my eyes. "That's not a euphemism, Mer. I'm serious. I need to talk to you about something." I hold out of my hand, urging her off the couch.

Of course, she's wearing one of her simple cotton nightgowns. Sexy and thin and perfect against her growing body. She's washed off the makeup she wore to court, and her hair hangs wild and free around her face. Tossing the blanket to the side, her hand slips in mine, and she skirts around the coffee table.

Well, she attempts to skirt around the coffee table. With a loud thud, she rams the side of her foot into the table leg, stubbing her toe. She gasps and doubles over. "Ahhhhh. Motherfucker," she whisper-yells.

I jump over the side of the couch. "Are you okay?" I push her hair back, trying to get a better look at her face. It's grimaced in pain. She's trying to be quiet because of her parents, but she really wants to scream. Before she has a chance to fight back, I scoop her into my arms and carry her out of the Children's Wing. I'm nearly into the Big House's living room before she fully has her breath back.

"Holt, put me down. I'm too heavy. You'll hurt your back."

That's the funniest thing I've heard in a very long time. I shift my hand, intentionally tickling the soft skin of her ass cheek. She squirms in my arms, giggling. "Stop."

I head outside by the pool and gently set her on her feet. Bending down, I check the damage. Her pinky toe is pink and a little swollen. "Can you move it? Do you think it's broken."

She wiggles her toes. "I don't think so. I think it's just bruised. It hurt like a son-of-a-gun, though." She frowns, looking at her feet. "My ankles have been swelling really bad. I look like a marshmallow puff."

I stand up and splay my hands across her stomach. "You have never, nor will you ever, look like a marshmallow puff. You're gorgeous." I press harder with my hands. "Isn't that right, son? Isn't Momma pretty." Instantly responding to my voice, he rolls around.

A peaceful grin falls on Merit's face.

The same smile she always gets when he moves.

"I love you," I say, looking into her eyes.

Her smile falters, and she leans back, breaking our connection and turning serious—the way she always does when I take our playful banter a step further. "What did you need to talk about?"

"Well, I needed to tell you that I love you," I say honestly. "And I just wanted to make sure you're good, that everything from today sank in."

Ten years.

That's what Delaney got.

Ten years in prison with no early parole, followed by ten years of probation. And she has to register as a sex offender.

That covers all charges. Framing me, breaking into my house, distributing pornography of a minor, wire fraud, and so much more.

She walks to the edge of the pool. "I'm not sure how I feel." Sitting on the top step, she dangles her feet in the water. "I guess I should feel like justice was served, but I just keep wishing that none of it had ever happened."

"I wish that too. But then we might not have him," I say with a nod at her belly.

She looks down at her stomach, smiling. "Yeah, I've thought the same thing."

"You were great in court today—your statement. Why didn't you tell me any of that? About the nightmares and everything?"

She studies the water, watching the waves ripple away from her feet. "You weren't exactly on my speed dial at that time. In fact, I couldn't have called you even if I wanted to." Her voice hardens a little bit. "The police had my cell phone."

"I was such an asshole, Merit."

She looks over at the waterfall, watching as it tumbles into the swimming pool. After a moment, her face softens, and she decides to grant me more grace than I'll ever deserve. "You were in a horrible situation. I can't even imagine what you were going through. Knowing that you may spend years in prison for a crime you didn't commit?" She sighs. "Things could've been a lot worse for both of us. I guess we should just be grateful the truth came out."

"Because of you," I say. "You led us to the truth."

She shrugs. "Y'all would've gotten there. You and Ella and Crutch and Marcum." Her lips twitch with a smile. "Eventually."

It makes me laugh. "Ella's always looking for good help. Forensics? Investigations? Just saying, in case you're considering a career change."

Her smile falls. "What career? I have a pity job—helping with the Foundation."

"First of all, that's not a pity job. I have no idea how you've been able to do everything you've done so quickly. We're already helping people. Every single day you blow my mind." I walk over and sit down beside her, giving myself a few minutes to gather my thoughts. "I actually wanted to talk to you about that too."

She squints an eye. "About The Hill Family Charities?"

"No, about your career. What you had to give up for me." I slide my hand across her knee. "I'm sorry."

She looks at me with doe eyes, innocent and curious. "You're not to blame. It was all Delaney. And everyone who believed her lies." She sighs. "I did what I had to do. If the store stayed open, I would've gone bankrupt."

I reach for her, twisting her hair between my fingers. I can't stop touching her, wanting her. "You did more than you should've." I reach into the pocket of my shorts and grab her present. The second she sees the black velvet of the jewelry box her jaw drops and she gasps. But her excitement quickly fades. When I hold the gift in front of me, she frowns. Cocking her head to the side, she studies the elongated shape. She's obviously sad she's not staring at a ring box. That's plain to see. It's written all over her face.

That disappointment actually makes me fucking ecstatic.

Because I still have her engagement ring. It's burning a hole in the top drawer of my nightstand. Just waiting for when I know she's ready...and that day is soon.

"A necklace?" she asks.

I shake my head. "No, not a necklace." I flip the lid, and this time her excitement doesn't wane.

"My bracelet," she whispers. She traces the rubies and diamonds with trembling fingers. "How?" Her syllables are drawn out, slow and stumbling.

"The day you left," I say simply. "When Ella brought over the money, I had a sinking feeling that you sold your bracelet. I called Kyra, and after she unloaded her full vocabulary on me, she told me. She knew the name of the jeweler, so I immediately went there to buy it back. He had already sold it, but I convinced him to have the other party call me. Once I explained everything, the guy was pretty understanding. He let me buy it back." Of course, I had to pay close to double what the guy paid, but I don't dare tell Merit that.

She clears her throat, fighting tears. "I... I can't accept it. I sold it because I needed to. I needed to pay you back for the loan money. Without income from the store, there was no other way."

I examine her, taking my time to etch this memory into my brain. The curve of her neck. The pink glow of her luscious lips. The shine of her eyes glittering underneath the summer moon. I love her so much. So damn much. "I never wanted the money back. Despite what I said when I was... when I was lost and angry and crushed. I never wanted the money. I just wanted a life. With you."

She turns away, her fingers working the hem of her nightgown in worried anxiety. "That doesn't change anything. If I take that bracelet from you, I'll still owe you. I don't wanna owe you. One day—ten years from now, fifteen years from now—something will happen, and you'll think back on this night and think everything I've ever done has been for the money. To get my bracelet back. To get my store loan paid off. To get a free place to live."

I gently tug on her chin, forcing her to look at me. "I'll never think that."

"That's what *she* did, Holt," she continues. "Delaney. She wanted your money. She wanted your attention. Your fame. Your... everything."

"It wasn't too long ago when you said *you* wanted to take everything from me."

"You know what I meant."

"Tell me, Merit."

"I wasn't talking about your money or your fame."

I think back on that night, on our first time together. The first time I felt my body move inside of hers.

"Tell me," I say. Those words taste bittersweet on my tongue. It's what she used to say to me when she wanted to hear *I love you*. Now I say it, and she shies away. Changes the subject. Puts up her walls.

Her voice is broken and scratchy. "I wanted your heart."

I brush her hair from her face. "You've always had it."

She doesn't say anything. For a long time.

Eventually, I sigh and push the bracelet box back into her hand. "Look, this bracelet is a family heirloom. It's part of your history. One day, our son is going to meet a girl. A girl he wants to spend the rest of his life with. A girl he marries and makes babies with. He'll give her this bracelet, and then one day, pass it down to his firstborn son or daughter. It belongs in your family. In *our* family."

Her eyes glisten with unshed tears. Closing the box, she clutches it against her chest. "Thank you, Holt."

Pulling her to her feet, I walk her back to the Children's Wing and then slowly make my way to my side of the house.

Alone.

To my empty bedroom.

Because I'm trying my best to be respectful of Deke and Marie's presence—even though Deke pounded me with the side eye more than once today, giving me the distinct impression that he knows I'm having sex with his daughter. Again.

It takes longer than normal for me to fall asleep. It feels like hours. On top of that, typically, I don't have many dreams. At least, not ones that I can remember. I assume it's because I sleep so hard, passed out to the world. But tonight is different. I keep thinking of her, and I'm caught in between reality and fantasy, between real-world and dream-world. So, when she shakes me, I wake up quicker and easier than normal. I think she only has to whisper my name, instead of scream it.

Squinting in the dark, I lean up on my elbows. "Merit, are you okay? Is the baby okay?"

She doesn't say anything, so I reach out, instinctively needing my hands on her body. When my fingers graze her arm, I notice she's covered in chill bumps. I sit up. "Mer?"

Slowly, my eyes adjust to the moonlight filtering in between the blinds. She grabs the hem of her nightgown and lifts it over her head. She uses the next split second to push her panties down to the floor.

Needless to say, in that split second, I lose my fucking mind.

She's so damn gorgeous.

Her body is changing, and for me, it's all part of the miracle. I mean, I loved her body before pregnancy. And I will love her body after pregnancy—whatever it looks like. But this? This I will only have for another few short months.

Her nipples are hard, just begging for my teeth to scrape against them. Her heavy breasts sway against the force of her staggered breathing, hypnotizing me with every alluring movement. And her hair is wild and carefree, draped around her shoulders like a curtain, demanding I wrap it around my fist.

My dick hardens. Past the point of comfort.

She reaches to pull back the covers. "I need you," she says simply.

Immediately obliging, I push my boxer briefs from my body, freeing my painful erection. "What about your parents?" I ask.

"I didn't really feel like inviting them to this." She giggles with her signature snort.

She's always so proud of herself when she makes a joke.

She pushes my shoulders, forcing me to lie back down on the bed and quickly straddles me. The tip of my dick brushes against her hot and welcoming core, making me growl like a fucking wild and feral animal. She's already soaking wet with desire, and that tiny taste isn't enough. I need more. Now. Her hands splay across my chest, and she slowly lowers herself onto my cock.

She arches her back, stretching her body so her stomach doesn't rub against my pelvis. My hands fly to her waist, pinning her body to mine, and I buck against her, claiming her deepest and darkest depths for myself, making her cry out.

Making her scream into the darkness of *our* bedroom.

Out of all the times, over the past eleven days, that we've made love, had sex, and downright fucked, we've never done it in *our* bedroom.

Oh, how I wanted to.

But I knew this had to be Merit's choice, her decision.

I needed her to want it. Just as badly as I did.

And here she is. Gifting it to me. Even though, it's more than I'll ever deserve.

She whimpers and wiggles, nonverbally telling me not to stop.

And so I don't.

I give it to her. Wholeheartedly and with every ounce of my being. I know she'll probably have bruises. As will I, based off the way her fingertips are digging into my pecs. But that's fine. It's not the first time, and it sure as hell won't be the last.

Because I want her.

Forever.

Forever in my bed. Forever in my heart.

She looks down at me, her eyes heavy with longing and love. "Tell me." Her whisper is soft. So soft I wonder if I imagine it.

"I love you."

She closes her eyes, and a content smile falls on her beautiful face.

And then, I turn my words into a reality.

Chapter 21

Merit

My eyes keep darting to the door, eagerly waiting on them to get here. I tilt my head, wondering if I should just open the sliding glass door so I'll be able to see the second they walk through the living room. After what seems like an eternity, I finally see Ridge's face. Squealing, I jump up from the patio table. It takes Ray by surprise, and he stops talking right in the middle of his story.

I lost track a long time ago. I think he and Jeff are talking about deep sea diving.

Or maybe snorkeling.

Skydiving?

Anyway, who can focus when *this* is about to happen.

Ridge is introducing his new girlfriend to the family. Tonight. At Anna's birthday party.

I race over to the grill where Holt and Crutch are glazing the chicken. "He's here! It's happening!" Of course, their eyes are already trained on them, watching as Ridge ushers his lady across the patio to his parents.

She's definitely not whom I had pictured for Ridge.

She's decked out for a night on the town, and not a night by the swimming pool. I definitely don't think her black leather mini skirt and stiletto heels are appropriate for an eight-year-old's birthday

182

party. Her makeup is impeccable, and her light brown hair has more strategically placed highlights and lowlights than a color wheel.

She's pretty, don't get me wrong, but it's definitely not the natural and effortless beauty that Raylee and Ella have. This girl has to work for hers. And she works it hard. Like a street hooker on two-for-one night.

But there's something else.

Something about her seems really familiar. I cock my head and squint my eyes. "Wait, is that Kimber-Shay Willis."

"Yeah." Crutch's disgruntled growl catches me off guard.

"You know her?" I ask.

"I investigated an auto theft at their dealership a few years ago. She's...persistent."

My brow furrows. "What's that mean?"

Holt rolls his eyes. "Shit, Crutch. Don't tell me you slept with her."

Holy crap.

"Fortunately, no. Not for her lack of trying, though. But even back then I had enough sense not to screw someone involved in the middle of my case." His eyes flicker between mine and Holt's. "Don't tell Lulu. You know how she gets."

"You mean possessive of what's hers," Holt says, with a suggestive wink in my direction.

I ignore him. "Plus, it might hurt Ridge's feelings to know that his girlfriend tried to...well, you know..." my voice trails off.

"Tried to bone one of his best friends," Holt offers.

Not helpful.

Crutch eviscerates him with a glare before turning to me. "How do you know her?"

I can feel the heat of embarrassment scald my cheeks. I know her through Edward, of course. Kimber-Shay's family owns a string of luxury car dealerships all over the Southeast. Their flagship store, the one they started with, is here in town. Edward bought more than one vehicle from her—a Lamborghini, a Maserati, and even a BMW for me. I hated it. It was a really small car. It felt like I was rolling out of bed every time I tried to crawl out of it. "Edward liked expensive cars."

The good humor falls from Holt's face, and he scowls. "Yeah, dickheads usually do," he grumbles underneath his breath. Instinctively, he reaches for me, pulling me closer to his side. His fingertips dig into my hip—the hip that just recently returned back to a normal color. Our lovemaking session the night of Delaney's sentencing was intense, to say the least.

Crutch lifts an eyebrow and smirks. "Yeah, and Lulu's the possessive one, huh?"

Holt shrugs, unapologetic. "Must run in the family."

The clack of Kimber-Shay's heels against the concrete draws our attention. Ever the gentleman, Ridge guides her toward us with his hand on the small of her back. She reaches behind and swats it away. "You're wrinkling my blouse," she snaps.

What the hell?

Is she blind or just stupid?

A good ninety percent of the female population of the world would crawl across a bed of rusted nails and subsequently lick their own bleeding wounds just to have Ridge's hand on the small of their back. He's a damn fine specimen, if I say so myself.

And not only that, but he's kind and funny and honorable.

A woman should never turn that away.

All of a sudden, my own words sink into my heart. I glance up at Holt. Is that what I'm doing? Every time I push him away, who am I punishing more? Him? Or me?

I'm not sure what he sees on my face, but it's obvious he sees something. Softly smiling, he leans down and kisses my temple, giving me flashes of what our lives will be like when we're old and gray and wrinkled.

If only I forgive him.

"Guys, this is Kimber-Shay Willis," Ridge announces. He introduces each of us.

She flashes a brilliant white smile. "Please, call me Kimber," she tells Holt. Her voice is like a kitten's purr. Well, a kitten spawned by the Devil. Her eyes dart to Crutch. She pushes her expensive hair over her shoulder. The movement wafts her perfume in the air. "Crutch, it's good to see you again."

Ridge's eyebrows lift. "Oh, you two know each other?"

"A few years ago, someone broke in and stole a Pur Sang Bugatti. Chip was furious." Her smile thins into a small line. "Crutch was the detective assigned to our case."

What the heck is a Pur Sang Bugatti?

It sounds like the name of a snake, not a car.

"Well, what happened?" Ridge asks.

"Caught the guy, of course." Crutch punches Ridge on the shoulder. "You doubt my abilities?"

He laughs. "Nah. But she did say it was a few years ago. So, that means it was before Marcum retired. I figure you had help."

Chuckling, Crutch swears at Ridge and takes a long drag of his beer.

She turns, focusing her attention on me. "And it's good to see you again, Merit."

"Wait, you two know each other too?" Ridge asks.

"Merit's purchased from us before," Kimber says.

"Not me," I rush to clarify. "Edward."

Ridge nods, knowing I prefer to talk as little as I can about him. "Gotcha."

"How is Edward? How's the Jaguar treating him?"

I guess that means Edward bought a Jaguar.

"Uh, well," I fumble for diplomatic words. "I don't really keep up with him. We divorced several years ago."

She giggles. "Oh, I know that, silly. I just didn't know if y'all were friends. It's so nice when people can stay friends even after a relationship ends. Just look at Chip. My father has been divorced three times, and I'm still very close with both of my stepmothers. We do shopping weekends together."

Why does she call her father by his first name?

"No," Holt steps in. "They're not friends."

Her face falls into one of concern. Well, I think it's concern. She might just be a good actress. "I completely understand. I still have no idea what he ever saw in Delaney Fitts. You know, he bought a Mercedes for her. I tried to talk him out of it, but he just wouldn't listen."

"Kimber," Ridge warns.

"Oh, I'm sorry. I shouldn't have brought it up."

I wanna punch her. But she's Ridge's girlfriend. And I love Ridge. So instead, I plaster a smile on my face and nod. "It's okay. Everything worked out just like it was supposed to. We're all moving on."

"I should say so!" She nods at my stomach. "How far along are you?"

"Thirty weeks."

Her face blanks. She obviously doesn't know what that means. "Coming up on seven months," I add.

"That's great. I know how excited you two must be."

Holt opens his mouth to answer, but he's interrupted.

A little finger pokes Kimber's side. "Excuse me."

She lets out a huff of surprise and jumps. Turning, she stares down at Laura.

Laura stares back. Pushing her glasses up on her nose, she eyes Kimber with suspicion. Her back straightens, and she sticks her little hand in the air. "Hello, my name is Laura Margaret Crutchfield. Pleasure to meet you, ma'am."

Kimber looks at Laura's hand like it's covered in shit. Doing a poor invitation of a welcoming grin, she pats the top of Laura's head. "Nice to meet you too, sweetheart."

If looks could kill, Kimber would be dead. Slaughtered by an eight-year-old. Laura folds her arms across her chest and blows her lips into a pout. "Seriously?" She nods her head at Ridge in accusation. "Are you kidding me?" Turning on her heels, she stomps away.

Kimber, completely unfazed, tugs on Ridge's arm. "How about a drink, babe?"

Anna's finished with her presents, and we're all sitting around eating cake, when Marcum raises his voice and points at the guys standing behind me. "I'm gonna need y'all's help next weekend."

It's a collective *y'all*—Holt, Ridge, Cullen, Crutch, and Will.

"Help with what?" Cullen asks.

"Moving."

"You're moving?" You can immediately hear the worry in Crutch's voice. Marcum is like a father to him. He would be devastated if he weren't around.

"Calm down, son. I know you can't survive if you don't see this balding head of mine at least once a week," he teases. "It's for the kids, Brent and Stephanie." He reaches for Nate and squeezes his shoulder. "They bought a new house. That's why they couldn't come tonight; they're packing." He rattles off the address, telling us where the house is.

"That's just a couple of miles from us," Raylee says. "You're gonna be in our school district," she tells Nate.

He pushes his half-eaten plate of cake in front of Laura. She's already eaten her piece, but Nate always saves part of his cake for her—the parts with the most frosting. She loves frosting. "Yeah. I'll be starting school there. We just went and talked to the front office today."

Laura gasps in excitement, dropping her fork on the plate. "You'll be going to the same school as me?!" She looks at him with pure joy on her face. She has frosting on her nose.

He hands her a napkin. "Wipe your nose," he whispers, before raising his voice for the rest of us to hear. "Different school, L.G. I'm going into high school, remember." He calls her L.G.—short for Little Girl, the nickname Crutch and Ella use.

She rolls her eyes. "How could I forget, Methuselah. You remind us all the time you're older." She draws her words out dramatically, making me snort. She's got such an old soul. "I *meant* you'll be on the same campus as me. I mean, the high school is right next to the middle school, which is right next to my school. It's all one big circle."

"Yeah, you're right," he finally concedes.

She smiles triumphantly. After just a moment, her smile fades, and she watches Nate with discerning eyes. "Don't worry, Nate. Going to a new school and making new friends can be scary. But I'll be there to protect you. I won't let anything bad happen to you." She settles back in her chair and focuses on her cake.

Nate answers the only way he knows how. He checks her water glass and pushes his own in front of her when he sees that hers is empty.

"You can count us in. We'll be there," Will says.

"My shift ends at seven a.m. on Saturday morning," Ridge adds. "I'll be there."

Holt's hands slide around my neck from behind. His fingertips tease my collarbone. "Well, I can't be there. I already have plans."

What? Did he seriously just say that?

After everything Marcum has done for him? And Nate?

I scoot in my chair, straining to turn around and scold him. "Holt," I hiss.

"And you won't be there, either," he says, nodding at Nate.

Nate's forehead creases. "I won't?"

"Nope." He can barely talk because his smile is so big. "That's our first football camp. And as the only freshman on Varsity, I suggest you show up and show out."

Ray slaps the table, laughing. "You took the job back at your old school?"

He nods. "I took the job. I'm going back to coaching football. Not only that, but I pointed out the fact that they never hired an Athletic Director like they were supposed to, expecting all of us to do triple the work—teach in our classroom, coach on the field, and handle the day-to-day planning of our events. So," he holds his arms in the air, "you're looking at the Head Football Coach *and* the Athletic Director. I'll cover the high school and middle school athletics."

Holy crap. He did it.

Pride swells in my chest, nearly crushing my ribs.

After the frenzied chatter settles down, Ella shuffles Hardy on her lap. "How'd you make the decision to go back? I know it couldn't have been easy. Some of those people... some of the things they said..."

Holt looks down into my eyes. His fingers curl in my hair, and he twists the strands back and forth. The movement sends a tickle down the center of my spine. "What about the things I said? No one was more hateful than me."

Sentiment clogs my throat, making it hard to swallow. I feel like I'm suffocating. Suffocating on the truth of his words. But the crazy part is, Holt's the only one who can breathe life back into my lungs. He's the only one who can stop the suffocation that *he's causing*, the only one who can make me whole again.

So, at what point do I forgive him?

At what point do I give in and let us be a family?

He reads my face. He sees everything. He feels everything. I know he does. Because he mimics my own reactions—right down to the painful swallow that bobs against his Adam's apple.

Clearing his throat, he turns back to Ella. "Merit reminded me that a lot of good things happened at that school. Great things, really. Things I shouldn't turn my back on. It gave me a purpose after my injury. And the kids? My team? Man, their support of me never wavered."

Ridge squeezes his shoulder. "Smart move, brother. I'm proud of you."

"You're really gonna be my coach?" The happiness in Nate's voice is palpable.

"Yep."

"And you're really putting me on Varsity? I haven't even tried out."

Holt laughs. "Nate, I've watched every game you've ever played. Even the ones I haven't been to. Why do you think your grandfather carries a video camera with him?" He puts his hands on his hips and sizes Nate up. "You're ready for this."

"And what about you, son?" Teresa asks. "Are you ready for it?"

He winks at me. "We're ready for anything."

Chapter 22

Holt

"It should be illegal to sweat this much. I feel like I've been stuck in an island prison camp for ten years. You know, like those movies where people go to jail in Thailand for smuggling drugs."

I cock an eyebrow. "What classic movie details the life of a Thai prison inmate?"

She pouts. "I watch current movies too."

"When?" I challenge.

She nibbles on her lip, thinking. Finally, she gives up. "That's *so* not the point right now."

I can't help but laugh. "And what *is* the point?"

Just to make her point, she spins to the side, walking like a drunk, and points a finger at me, jabbing the air with every word. "That football should be a winter sport, not a fall sport. The people who first made it a fall sport aren't from Alabama. I can guarantee you that."

Of course, she doesn't see that she's about to walk right into the middle of a wooden power pole. Grabbing her waist, I tuck her against me, shielding her from catastrophe. She wobbles slightly. "Oh, there's a pole," she says absentmindedly.

She's so freakin' funny.

"Well, did you at least have a little bit of fun? Sweat and all?"

She can't hide her grin. "You know I had fun." She tugs on my shirt, forcing me to stop walking.

I shift my duffel bag so it doesn't hit her. For a second, I wish time could just stand still, stop moving, let us live in this moment forever.

Her hair is piled into a messy bun. Long strands stick to the back of her neck, clinging to the beads of sweat. Her cheeks are flushed and tinted pink from the summer sun. She's wearing a yellow tank top that showcases her growing stomach. She started the night with a little white sweater, refusing to show her arms because she thinks her armpits are turning darker and it makes it look like she hasn't shaved. Of course, I can't tell any difference in her armpit skin. Needless to say, that sweater came off before the first quarter was even done. Her short khaki shorts showcase the lean muscles of her legs. Just looking at them gets me horny as hell.

Unable to stop myself, I reach up with my free arm and turn my ballcap around backward.

Her eyes instantly widen in delight, and she takes a step closer to me, pressing our bodies together. "You were on fire tonight. I'm so proud of you. You've handled this like a champion. All the players? Their families? The school? You've brought everyone back together. It's amazing." Her eyes fall to my lips. She licks her own. "Three wins down."

"And what do I get for winning three games in a row?"

She folds her hands across the top of her stomach and looks down, playing Shy Merit. "Why, I just don't know, *sir*."

I put my hand next to hers and press down. "Son, I think Momma is trying to seduce me." Of course, our son immediately answers to my voice, tossing and turning and kicking.

Her head falls back in laughter, and she playfully slaps my hand away. "Don't get him on your side. He's supposed to be on my side."

"It's the same side. We're a family."

Giving me a sheepish smile, she turns and keeps walking to the truck. Racing behind her, I open the door and help her climb in. I get a whiff of her shampoo. Apparently, it's green-tea scented. Whatever the hell that means. I have no idea why girls like to change their smells so often.

On the drive home, she tells me everything that happened in the stands while I was down on the field. Apparently, the mascot fell down the stairs, the couple behind them got into a fight over the cost of a hot dog, and Anna and Laura decided that the other team's coach was a *meanie pants* because he cursed at a player. Eventually, we settle into a comfortable silence. I glimpse at the clock, disappointed with how late it is. Tonight would be a perfect night to surprise her with fried rice takeout from the Japanese steakhouse, but they're already closed.

I glance over at her profile, noticing just how much she's changed in the past few weeks. We have another doctor's appointment next week. Seven-and-a-half months. I can't believe we're already there. She's still on the slender side for her pregnancy, but the doctor says everything is just perfect.

I turn down the volume of the radio. "You know, we really need to start discussing names."

Her eyeballs nearly bug out of her head. "Oh. Yeah. I guess we do." Her voice is fake. Pretend. Completely un-Merit.

I study her. She tries to avoid my stare, but she's too curious not to steal a peek. Laughing, I slap the steering wheel. "Mer! You've already got a name picked out, don't you?"

She shifts in her seat, preparing to defend herself. She's so damn sexy and cute, I can't help but touch her. I slide my hand across the console and caress her upper thigh. When chill bumps break across her smooth skin, I realize I'm about two damn seconds from swerving my truck to the side of the road so I can pull her over on my lap.

"Well, yeah," she starts. "But you may not like it. But... but... I... it just means a lot." She runs her hand along the length of my arm, tracing the vein.

I wait, but she doesn't say anything else. "Well," I prod, "do I get to hear our son's name?"

She takes a fortifying, deep breath. "Daire."

My heart immediately explodes in my chest. "After your brother?"

She nods, dabbing at the sudden wetness in the corner of her eye.

I smile. Nothing has ever felt more right. "It's perfect. Absolutely perfect."

Relief settles on her face. "Good, I think so too." Her brow furrows. "I haven't asked Daddy yet, though. I feel like I need his permission. Like, I'm taking something from him, you know? I mean, Daire was his son."

"Let me ask him."

"Really?"

"It would be my honor." Taking her hand, I gently kiss her wrist and then drag her knuckles across my lips, relishing in the taste of salt on her body. "Let me ask him."

She leans back in her seat, sighing contently and softly rubbing the skin I just kissed—back and forth with the thumb of her other hand, like her fingertips are trying to memorize the invisible map left behind by my mouth.

"Well, now that that's settled, we need a middle name," I say.

She repeats herself. "Oh. Yeah. I guess we do." Once again, her voice is completely fake. But unlike before, this time, her tone actually has me a little worried, a little on edge. The slight tinge of airy hope has been replaced with weighted seriousness.

"Don't tell me, you already have a middle name picked out too?"

She just shakes her head. "No."

She's lying.

And I definitely don't like this lie. Something about it raises my hackles, makes the hair on the back of my neck stand up.

"Don't lie, Merit."

"Mmmm?"

"You obviously have a middle name picked out. It's written all over your face."

She doesn't answer. She just looks out the side window, watching the cars drive past.

"Tell me the truth."

She slowly rolls her head in my direction. All of a sudden, it's like she's too exhausted to even lift her head. "Well." She pauses for so long before continuing, I actually get scared. "I was thinking about... Hill."

What?

"What?" I frown, turning the name over in my head. "Daire Hill Hill?"

"Daire Hill Browning."

What. The. Hell.

"Excuse me?" It's the only thing I can think to say. I'm too damn stunned.

"Holt," she says with a soft yet firm voice, "it's more difficult when mothers have different last names from their children. We get that questioning stare—people wondering if we're divorced. Or if we never changed our last name to that of our husband's. People wondering if we never even married. Or if we adopted and didn't change our child's last name. As the primary caregiver, all the legal stuff will be so much easier if me and the baby have the same last name. You know, school and medical stuff. Please understand."

I should be understanding. I should be compassionate. At a minimum, I should at least be diplomatic.

But I'm not.

My pride is hurt. My sense of belonging is shattered. More importantly, my love for this woman and child blind me. It's an all-consuming solar flare, flashing with a light so bright that it darkens everything else around me. And needless to say, that doesn't exactly make me diplomatic.

"Are you fucking kidding me right now?"

She folds her arms across her chest. "Holt."

"How can you even suggest such a thing? Are you still *that* mad at me? Are you doing this to punish me?" I knock the ballcap off my head and drag my hand through my hair. "He's my son. We shouldn't have different last names. None of us! We're a family. Same name; same family. If you would just marry me, this wouldn't be an issue."

Her mouth drops open. "What?"

Well, shit.

That's not exactly how I imagined myself proposing. I've been biding my time, waiting for the right moment. Waiting for her to truly forgive me. And then, I was gonna propose the shit out of her. You know, with a grand romantic gesture—Merit-style, of course—that shows her just how much she means to me.

Her eyes narrow into slits. "What did you just say?"

"I said we should get married."

Well, shit. That sounds just as bad.

Her face pales, and her eyes darken. I watch the lively colors—the greens and blues and browns—fade to gray. Completely void of life. Her lip quivers for a split second before she crushes her emotions, taking them and burying them deep in her injured soul. The soul that's been battered and bruised by me, more than once.

Her jaw tenses. Sitting forward in her seat, she calmly folds her hands in her lap. "You don't have to marry me just because you're afraid of losing your child. I told you that would never happen." She swallows. "Maybe it's time we circle back around to the custody papers."

I'm suffocating.

Sinking in a hole of quicksand that I'll never be able to crawl out of. My throat tightens, making it hard to breathe. My whisper is strained, barely audible in the quiet of the truck. "You're never gonna forgive me, are you?"

She looks down at her hands. "I never said that."

"You didn't have to."

It goes without saying, we don't share a bedroom tonight. In fact, she didn't even say goodnight to me. She just barreled through the Big

House, hightailing it to the Children's Wing. I walked behind her, trying to search for the right words. Obviously, I never found them because my dumb ass didn't say one damn thing. Not even when she closed the door to the Children's Wing in my face. Even from the hallway, I could hear the lock click on her bedroom door.

That sound shattered me. It took all my willpower not to kick the damn thing down, sweep her into my arms, and beg for forgiveness. I wanted nothing more than to hold her, kiss her, comfort her.

But how could I?

After the things I said.

How could I?

Knowing that she'll never forgive me for what happened *then*. In January. When I threw her out of my life.

That will always be hanging over us.

Delaney's in prison, but *we're* the ones being punished. Still locked within a jail of my own making. Me. Merit. Daire. *We're* the ones suffering.

I need time to figure out what the hell I'm gonna do.

I could never be with anyone else, never love anyone else.

I meant what I said... I will fight for Merit's love and forgiveness until my dying breath.

So, that means this battle may never end for me. And I reckon it's time I come to grips with that harsh, fucking reality.

How do I fight for her without making her miserable in my conquest?

Because if I keep hurting her, *is that really loving her*?

Standing in the shower, I replay the night over and over in my head, until the water turns cold and my skin feels raw. Like a zombie, I crawl into bed, tossing and turning instead of immediately passing out, like normal. I'm not sure how long it takes, but eventually I fall asleep.

But again, it's not normal.

Normally, a freight train couldn't wake me.

But tonight? Tonight, I sit up the second her hand jiggles my shoulder.

"Holt?"

Something's wrong. Her voice is shaky, upset.

"Merit?" I glance at the clock, blinking several times to adjust my eyes. It's just past three in the morning.

"Holt. Something's wrong." Her words confirm my fears.

Cold terror pushes through my body, shooting adrenaline straight into my veins. Jumping out of bed, I turn on the lamp, nearly knocking it over. "What do you mean something's wrong?"

She doesn't even have a chance to say anything. Her hands cradle her stomach, and she doubles over in pain. "Agh!" Her cry is a cross between a grimace and a wail. It's a sound I never want to hear again as long as I live. I'd saw off my damn arm, right now, with a toothpick, if it meant that Merit would never be in that kind of pain to make that kind of sound again.

The fact remains, I've been around Raylee while she was in labor. I've been around Ella while she was in labor. Yes, they made noise. Yes, I know it hurt. But no matter how loud they got, there was this kind of strength behind them. An intense domination. An unspoken force of nature that only women have. Them telling the world, *I can do this. This is supposed to happen. I can handle this, and you can't. I'm in labor. I'm having a baby. I'm in control. And I'm the anchor holding everything in place.*

None of that is behind Merit's scream.

This scream is pure pain and panic.

Grabbing her elbow, I gently set her on the bed. Curling into a fetal position, she rolls back and forth, moaning. I keep whispering to her, trying to get her attention. Tears stream down her face, crushing my heart in my chest. After a minute, the pain seems to ease just enough for her talk. She chokes out my name, gagging on her sobs. "Holt..."

"Just your stomach?" I ask.

She nods.

Gently, I lay my hand on her stomach, willing my son to kick. He doesn't.

"Are you bleeding?"

She closes her eyes and curls tighter.

"Merit, answer me. Are you bleeding?"

She blinks, trying to focus on my words. She looks drunk. "A little."

Racing to the dresser, I throw on shorts and a T-shirt and kick my feet into a pair of old sneakers. Scooping her from the bed and into my arms, I head downstairs, only pausing for a quick second to pocket my cell phone from the table outside the bedroom.

Five missed calls. All from Merit.

Fuck. Me.

I am such an idiot.

After tonight, everything changes. I'm never sleeping without Merit—or without my cell phone—for as long as I have breath in my body.

I can't keep pretending Delaney didn't change anything. Because she did. She changed everything. And I've got to stop fighting it. I have to give into it. It's the only way we're going to heal.

All of us.

She leans into me, the heat from her tears burns my neck. "Oh, it hurts. It hurts. It hurts."

I kiss the top of her head. "I know, baby. We're going to the hospital." I grab the blanket from the back of the couch when I jog past it. Loading her into the truck, I tuck it around her, hoping it gives her a little bit of comfort. She always washes our sheets and blankets in a detergent that smells like lavender. She said it's supposed to be calming.

The drive to the hospital is a blur. My heart is beating a thousand times a minute. And yet, it feels like it's frozen in my chest. My emotions clog my vision making it hard to see. And yet, I'm hyper-focused on everything around me. I even notice one of the light-up letters is still burnt out on the building sign for *Run and Jump and Twirl.*

Despite the tremble in my hand, I have enough control in my muscles to dial the answering service for our doctor. They say they'll get the message to him immediately, but I throw in a couple of curses for good measure. You know, just to emphasize the magnitude of the situation.

Throughout it all, I keep talking to Merit. Encouraging her, consoling her. Holding her hand. Raking my fingers down the side of her beautiful face. Trying to do anything and everything to soothe her fear and worry. Because I sure as hell can't take away her suffering and screams, no matter how much I want to.

If only I could...

I would sacrifice myself—die, right here and right now—if only I could heal her. And our son.

Please God take care of her.

Speeding into the parking lot, I pull Merit from the truck. Before wrapping the blanket around her, I check the leather seat for blood. Relief courses through me when I don't see any. Hopefully, she's not bleeding that badly. If she were bleeding bad, I'd see it, right? No blood is a good thing, right?

By the time I'm ten feet from the door, I'm already hollering. "Hey! Hey! I need a doctor."

The security guard rushes forward, holding his hands up, warning me to slow down. It only takes a second for him to recognize me. His eyes widen in shock, but he quickly recovers. He holds open the entry gate, bypassing the security check point and metal detector. "This way."

I've never been so glad to be famous.

Merit wails in pain. Her body is tense and tight. Brittle and clenched.

No one can ignore her. Every head in the waiting room turns in our direction.

I rush past them and race to the nurses' station. All of a sudden, three people are by my side, thrusting a gurney in front of me, ordering me to put Merit down.

I have no idea where they came from. Normally, I know everything about my surroundings. As a quarterback, you have to be aware of what's happening around you. It's all about perspective and periphery.

And yet, I completely missed these people.

They could've fallen from the sky for all I know.

An older lady seems to take charge. She has frayed gray hair and a pin on her shirt shaped like a guitar that says Nurses Rock. "Tell me what's going on?"

"She's in pain and she's bleeding. It's too early for labor. This can't be it. Something else is going on. Something's wrong."

My voice is calm and steady and firm. A coach's voice.

But inside? I'm anything but calm and steady and firm.

I feel like a dollar bill that's been run through the washing machine.

"How far along is she?" the nurse asks.

I skirt around her, following them into the room, refusing to let go of Merit's hand. "Seven-and-a-half months. She's due October 3rd."

A guy about my age with red hair and glasses steps into the room, quickly putting gloves on his hands. "Merit Browning?"

I nod.

"Dr. Skinner called right before you got here. He's on his way in."

There's a flurry of activity. Question after question. They guide me out of the way, saying I have to give them room to work. They push Merit's nightgown up around her breasts, and when they spread her legs, showing her panties, I nearly collapse on the floor.

Blood.

The center of her white cotton panties is soaked in blood.

I close my eyes so tightly I see spots. Purple and black and yellow. They dance in a line across the back of my eyelids. When I open them, they've draped a cloth over her for modesty, and the doctor is giving her a vaginal exam. Without warning, he pulls his hands from her. "We need to get her to OB Imaging. Now."

Merit's in the middle of another spasm, retching back and forth on the bed, her face contorted in agony.

Lifting the side arms of the gurney, they immediately start pushing her away from the room. I'm already in the hallway, following them to the elevator, when the nurse squeezes my shoulder. "You'll have to wait down here, in the waiting room. I promise we'll come get you as soon as she's done with imaging, as soon as we know more."

"What?" I can't even fathom what she just said. Is she fucking crazy? "She's my wife. I'm not leaving her side."

Wife.

It might be a white lie in words, but it's not a white lie in my heart.

The nurse peers deeply into my eyes, shifting her face to block my view. "You don't have a choice." She nods, letting me know she understands my feelings. "I promise, we'll get you back to her as soon as possible."

The elevator bell rings, and the doors slide open. "Holt!" Merit tosses her head back, frantically looking for me.

Shouldering my way between the people, I grab her face, peppering her with kisses. Her brow is covered in sweat. "I'm here. Everything's gonna be okay."

The doctor nods at the open elevator. "We need to go."

"Everything's gonna be okay," I repeat. "I'll be right here waiting."

Her eyes widen and tears roll down her face. Her cheeks are rosy and chapped. "I forgive you."

I can't fucking breathe.

"What?" My voice sounds fractured and full of disbelief. It doesn't even sound like me.

"I forgive you. And I love you."

Bending down, I kiss her lips. Her tongue grazes mine, and the passion and love that's always been there grows even deeper. Without our permission, the doctor starts pushing the bed into the elevator. Quickly giving her one last kiss, I watch in stunned torture as the doors close.

The nurse guides me back out to the waiting room, telling me I need to fully register with the front desk and fill out patient paperwork. Bypassing that, I walk straight outside. The night air is sticky and hot, plagued with the smell of cleaning fluid and cafeteria food, like it's permanently etched in the bricks of the building. Engraved in the concrete of the sidewalk, in the pine bark around the shrubs.

Folding my hands on top of my head, I pace back and forth, trying to compose myself.

It doesn't help.

Sighing, I pull out my cell phone. My body's shaking so badly I'm surprised I can even punch the numbers.

Deke answers on the second ring, his voice laden with sleep and panic. "Yeah?"

I repeat the words we've had to say too many times tonight.

"Something's wrong."

Chapter 23

Merit

I yawn so wide it hurts my jaw.

I guess I should get used to sleepless nights, we have a baby on the way. But I just hope that the future sleepless nights will be a little less eventful than they were last night.

Instead of walking straight through the living room to get to the Children's Wing, Holt turns and walks up the stairs. I shift my head on his shoulder. Of course, he refused to let me walk and is, once again, carrying me. "Where are we going?"

"To *our* bedroom. After last night, we're never sleeping apart again. Not as long as there is air in my lungs and a heartbeat in my chest." He licks his lips. "Oh, and by the way, starting tonight, I'm sleeping with my cell phone by the bed."

I lift an eyebrow. "But if I'm sleeping with you, I won't be calling you. It'll be a moot point."

"Ah, but one day Daire will be sixteen years old and out driving by himself late at night. What if he gets a flat?" I watch as his forehead crinkles. "In fact, I think I'll surgically attach my cell phone to my hand," he says.

I catch myself smiling, despite the lingering pain and soreness in my side. It's nothing now. Nothing at all compared to what it was. Fortunately, the pain meds and anti-inflammatory have already kicked in.

Round ligament pain.

Evidently, it's a thing. And it's real.

Really real.

Round ligament pain occurs when the ligaments supporting the uterus stretch to accommodate the growing belly. The pain can be sharp and severe, but it usually resolves itself quickly, and the damage to the ligament is mild.

Well, not in my situation.

The doctor said it was one of the worst cases he's seen. He classified it as a Grade II tear.

Most of the time, round ligament pain occurs gradually throughout the second trimester, but since our son decided to save all of his growth spurts for the last trimester, my body is having to adjust at a rapid speed. So, I've been given medicine and a maternity support belt. It's a huge, Velcro garter belt for my stomach. I feel like a complete spaz wearing it, but at least I can wear it underneath my clothes.

Plus, it does help with the pain. And my sore back.

And the bleeding?

The doctor said it looked worse than it actually was. Bloody show. He said my body is just preparing for birth, and that bloody show can happen several weeks before it's time to actually have the baby.

I don't know who was more relieved with the news—me or Holt. If I had to guess, I would say Holt. Apparently, he thought the imaging process was taking too long because he came barreling down the hallway of the OB floor, screaming my name like a lunatic. Fortunately, Dr. Skinner arrived quickly and went right to work, to not only calm our nerves but ease my pain. By the time the Emergency Department gave us the discharge papers, half of the waiting room was filled with a hodgepodge of our family—Ray, Teresa, Raylee, Ella, Ridge, Dana, and Marcum.

Well, technically, I guess they're Holt's family.

But they feel like my family too.

Early morning sunlight creeps into the bedroom from behind the blinds. The bed is rumpled and unmade—just the way we left it. The second my body hits the mattress my eyes start to close.

"I should really take a shower," I say, fighting another yawn. "Wash the hospital off me."

Holt lovingly brushes hair off my forehead. "You can do that when you wake up. Right now, you need to rest."

"And I need to get out of these hospital-issued panties. It feels like I'm wearing papier-mâché lingerie." Exhaustion can't stop my giggle. Or my snort.

Holt rolls his eyes. "You can burn your underwear when you wake up. Sleep," he orders.

Burrowing into the blanket, I watch as he walks away. "Come to bed. Aren't you tired?"

He turns, leaning in the doorway. I love it when he does that. It's so mysterious and sexy.

He smiles softly. "I'll be up soon. Your parents and grandmother should be here in less than an hour. I know we already called to tell them what the doctor said, but I just wanna make sure they know everything is gonna be okay."

I should wait up for them too, but I can't. I'm too damn tired.

I'm already falling asleep when his whisper tickles my ears, the sound low and rumbly like thunder. "Tell me."

Butterflies flutter in my stomach. It was so easy so say those three little words in the hospital, in the middle of our panic. When I was worried something could go wrong and I'd never see him again.

But now?

Now, I'm nervous. Because I'm putting myself out there again. Making myself vulnerable. Opening myself up to heartache.

But none of that is of any significance. Because I never really had a choice in the matter.

My love for Holt will never stop. It's constant and pure and un-equivocal.

I don't have a choice.

If I want my heart to beat, *I have to love Holt Hill.*

So, I answer him. "I love you."

He stares at me, soaking it in. The joy and adoration etched across his face is the most beautiful thing I've ever seen.

He gives me that sexy little wink, teasing me. "I'm glad I won that battle."

Chapter 24

Holt

I open the door as soon as I see the truck pull into the front driveway. Deke and Marie have the new code for the security gate, so I didn't have to buzz them in via the app on my phone. Which is good. Because I'm so freakin' frazzled and exhausted, I can't remember where I left the damn thing.

The kitchen, maybe?

Marie rushes in first, falling into my arms and hugging me tightly. From the corner of my eye, I see Granny edging up to the front steps. There's only three of them, but I don't know how tired she is. The last thing we need, after the night we've all had, is for Merit's grandmother to face-plant on the brick pavers. Tucking Marie against my side, I reach out, offering my forearm. Granny wraps her hand around me and eagerly walks her way into my embrace. By the time Deke makes it past the threshold, I've hugged both women and confirmed ten times that Merit's going to be okay and that she's resting peacefully.

Shutting the door behind him, he holds out his hand, and I give it a shake. Taking one look at the man's face nearly sends me into a spiral. The weight of the world is etched into his features. It's like he's taken every ounce of worry and pain from his daughter, as well as his wife and mother, and shouldered it himself. He's filled every laugh line, every wrinkle, every freckle and mole with their struggles, wanting to ease their burdens and fears, if only by one small fraction.

Talk about fucking strong.

Talk about fucking love.

The patriarch standing before me is a pillar among men.

But despite his stability and sturdiness, despite this façade he's gifting to the world, I can see that deep down, anxiety and concern course through his blood like an artesian well, constantly pumping, constantly flowing.

And that's when it hits me. Like a ton of bricks. Like an eighteen-wheeler…

That's what being a father is.

That's what being a husband is.

That's what being a son is.

It's a thousand different emotions whipping through your soul like a hurricane. All at the same time. And all for the sake of love.

And Merit's worth that. Our son is worth that.

I'll carry their troubles and drown myself in all-consuming worry, if it means they can be happy and healthy.

"And what about your parents?" Marie asks, interrupting my interior revelations.

"They'll come over later this afternoon. Everybody headed home to get some sleep.""Speaking of, I know you said she was asleep, but we'd like to see her. Can we just take a quick peek? We promise not to wake her."

I would never deny entry to Merit's family. They're my family too. "Absolutely. Of course."

Marie and Granny turn and take a step in the direction of the Children's Wing. "She's not in the Children's Wing. She's upstairs. In our bedroom."

My voice is firm and heavy, leaving nothing up for question or debate. I respect the hell out of the people in front of me, but they need to know, Merit is mine. This is *our* house and *our* life, and I will never spend another night sleeping without her by my side.

This is it. This is me being a husband.

This is me being exactly what Deke is.

This is me...standing in front of him the way he's standing in front of me.

Both Marie and Granny glance at him, their gaze darting from my eyes to his.

He simply nods at the stairs behind me. "You wanna show them, Holt? I'm just gonna use the restroom." Without another word, he walks down the hallway, and we hear the soft click of the bathroom door.

Granny grabs the banister with one hand and reaches toward me with her other one, wiggling her fingers, begging me closer. "Hold my hand so I don't fall, Holt." Her eyes narrow as she studies the marble staircase. "This house has more daggum steps than the Great Wall of China."

Once we make it upstairs, I open the bedroom door, and I'm fairly certain all three of us heave an audible sigh of relief just looking at her. With blankets tucked around her body like a cocoon, she's in a deep, steady sleep, treading that thin line between heavy breathing and all-out snoring. It's the best fucking sound I've heard in hours.

Well, besides her voice saying she forgives me and she loves me.

That was definitely the best.

Content with our voyeurism, we head back downstairs, meeting Deke in the living room.

Granny yawns, quickly setting Marie off, and she does the same.

"Why don't y'all head back to the Children's Wing? Get some sleep? Rest for a few hours? I promise I'll come get you as soon as she wakes up."

Marie nods. "That may be a good idea. I think the exhaustion and the worry are finally catching up with us."

"You know where everything is. Please, make yourself at home. Everything here is yours." My words are true. Like I said, we're a family. All of us.

Granny's already halfway down the hall when Marie turns to Deke. "Hon? You wanna get the bags from the car now? Or drive it around to the Children's Wing later?"

He opens his mouth to answer her, but I interject. "I can help you with the bags in a bit, Deke. I was...uh...well, I was hoping we could talk for a minute."

When he lifts a questioning brow, I follow up with something more generic, "Feel like a beer?" Of course, I guess it's a stupid-ass thing to say. I mean, it's nine in the morning.

"Got anything stronger?"

His response catches me by surprise, and I chuckle. "Sure do."

He gives Marie a quick kiss and follows me into the kitchen.

I open the liquor cabinet above the kitchen sink. I guess I could use a different cabinet—something more accessible—but with the kids running around here so often, this seemed like the safest place, especially considering it's so high that even I have to balance on my tiptoes if I want something from the back. Not to mention, I don't drink hard liquor all that much; I've always been more of a beer guy. So, storing it in a barely used cabinet doesn't bother me.

I know I've got some vodka, tequila, and gin—along with a handful of other spirits—floating around in the cabinet somewhere. But as of right now, two whiskey bottles are standing sentry front and center. Well, those and a floppy, plastic drink pouch of a pre-mixed daiquiri with a picture of a half-naked woman on the front of it. She's sitting on a lounge chair next to a palm tree. Call me psychic, but Deke doesn't really strike me as a daiquiri-type of dude.

So, my choices are regular, old Jack Daniel's or Macallan 25... which is over two-thousand bucks a bottle. It was a gift from someone after my second Super Bowl. So, needless, to say, it's now aged well over twenty-five years.

My fingers hover between the two bottles. I'm about to ask him which one he would like when he interrupts my weary, runaway thoughts.

"Hell, Holt, you don't need to woo me. Give me the fucking Jack."

Yanking it from the shelf, I grab two glasses and sit down next to him at the kitchen island. Sliding the bottle in front of him, I figure it's best to let the man pour his own drink. I'm not sure how many fingers he feels like; but if his emotions of worry and panic were as powerful as mine last night, he may very well chuck the glass to the side and gulp straight from the bottle.

He sighs low and deep, before grabbing the Jack and emptying a good four fingers into the crystal tumbler. Taking the bottle, I pour the same amount into my glass even though I only plan to have a small sip or two. I need all my faculties intact if I'm gonna take care of my girl.

My girl and my son.

We sit in stillness for a few minutes, drinking and watching the morning sun dance across the kitchen in slants of white and pale yellow as it filters in through the window blind.

Deke breaks the silence. "So, how scary was it?"

I spin the tumbler around in my hand, watching the brown liquor swish up and down, back and forth. "Fucking terrifying, sir."

He softly clears his throat before taking another sip and then hissing through his teeth at the burn.

"There was blood," I croak.

"Yeah, you said."

"I've never prayed so hard in my life."

Now, it's his turn to chuckle. His laugh is filled with hope and heartbreak. "You say that now. Just wait. Every crisis comes with its own volley of requests to the Man Upstairs. It's called being a father. And it's the fucking scariest thing you'll ever do."

"It can't be. The scariest thing I ever did was toss Merit out of my life."

"I thought that was the worst thing you ever did?" he asks.

"Same thing," I answer honestly.

He just nods, giving me space to say what needs to be said.

"I love your daughter, Deke. I will love her until my bones turn to ash. I don't ever plan to spend another moment of this life without her by my side. I'm gonna make her my wife. We're gonna raise our son and surround him with as many brothers and sisters as Merit will give. She is my lifeblood." I push my drink out of the way and drag my hands though my dirty and wild hair. I have no choice but to be honest with him. "I nearly messed everything up again."

Tension bunches in his shoulders, and he grips the glass tighter. He studies the granite countertop, avoiding my gaze at all costs. "You nearly threw her out again?"

"No sir, of course not."

"You cheat on her?"

What the hell. "Hell, no. Of course not, sir."

"You hit her? Violate her? Make her feel worthless?"

What. The. Ever. Loving. Fuck.

My voice vibrates with anger. My fists clench in fury just thinking of Merit being mistreated. "She's the love of my life. I would never do anything like that. Fucking never."

His body relaxes just a bit, and he spins on his barstool. Looking me dead in the eye, he gives me a little one-shoulder shrug, nonverbally asking what the hell I did.

"I thought about stopping."

He shakes his head in confusion. "Stopping what?"

"I thought about stopping my fight for her. I started thinking that maybe my fight was hurting her instead of healing her. I love her so much, the last thing I ever wanna do is be the cause of her pain. *Again.* So... I thought about stopping."

"So?" This time, he shrugs both of his shoulders. "You thought about it. Thinking and doing are two different things."

"I know that now." I sigh so deeply my chest hurts, sending a scorching pain through my ribs. "I was always so confident, so brazen, so sure of life. And then, everything was upended by my arrest. Ever since that day, I've been second-guessing every decision I make. One minute, I'll feel like my normal self. Secure and assured.

And the very next minute, it's like I'm cowering in a corner. Insecure and uncertain. I've been teetering on the cusp of living and just-surviving." A cynical laugh bellows from my throat, bringing a sting of Jack with it. "Basically, I've been a big ol' pussy. Fuck that shit. I'm ready to live. I'm ready to love."

"And forgive."

My head whips in his direction. My heart thunders violently, bruising my lungs. "What did you just say?"

His lip twitches into a smirk. "You think that girl of mine didn't wanna talk to her momma and daddy when shit was hitting the fan?"

I'm totally confused. "What?"

"When she was in line for OB Imaging, she borrowed a nurse's cell phone and called us. She told us that she forgave you. Said she finally spoke the words to your face."

Holy shit. My swallow is loud, echoing in the kitchen. "She did. She forgave me."

"So, when are you gonna forgive yourself, son?"

I blink, trying to absorb his question into my brain. I say the only syllable I can muster, "What?"

Apparently, that's my favorite word tonight.

"Well, I know I didn't get a college degree, but it seems to me your insecurity and uncertainty has been growing and thriving on one simple thing—your regret." He picks up his tumbler and downs the rest of his drink in one massive swallow, whistling when it sends a fire down his throat and into his stomach. "Don't get me wrong... it's good to *feel* the regret and *acknowledge* it. But you gotta stop letting it consume your identity. Let it be a *part of you*. Don't let it be *the whole*."

I sit for a few minutes, marinating on his words of wisdom.

He's right.

I don't deserve Merit's forgiveness; I acknowledge that.

But I'm gonna accept it.

And I'm gonna return that gift to her every single day. For the rest of forever.

And it starts now.

"Deke, tell me about Daire. Tell me about your boy."

This time the '*what*' flows from his mouth.

"Well, with your permission, I'd like for my son to know every single thing about his namesake. It doesn't matter that his heart only beat for two months and not twenty years. His life and his love matters. It matters to you. It matters to Merit. And it matters to me."

He quiets. For a few seconds, the only noise sailing through the room is that of his gruff, heavy breath. When he turns back to me, unshed tears fill his eyes. "You wanna name my grandson after my son?"

"I do. Yes, sir."

Wiping a rogue tear from underneath his eye, he clears his throat and shifts on his seat. Giving a hearty chuckle, he slaps me on the shoulder. Hard. "Well, I reckon you better pour me another drink then, son. I've got stories for hours."

Chapter 25

Merit

It's late afternoon when I wake. Holt's not next to me, but I know he's been here. The pillow beside me is still indented from the weight of his head. I hear the soft murmur of voices downstairs. Making my way to the bathroom, I turn on the shower and undress, carefully folding my new maternity support belt so the Velcro doesn't stick where it's not supposed to.

I don't even have time to step one toe inside the shower before Holt is coming through the door. "Mer?" His breath hitches in the back of his throat when he sees my naked body.

Despite the stretch marks now dotting my waistline—matching perfectly with the ones on my upper thighs—and the swollen ankles, Holt still looks at me like I'm beautiful. Always with hunger in his eyes and lust on his face.

Clearing his throat, he forces himself to recover. "I thought I heard the shower. Why didn't you come get me? You need help."

Unable to bear the intensity of his gaze, I wrap a towel around me. "It's okay. I can handle a shower on my own."

He folds his arms across his chest. "You did hear the doctor when he told you to take it easy, right?"

I snort. "Well, he wasn't covered in ultrasound lubricant, and he probably didn't smell like he rented a vacation bungalow in a medical waste trash can."

Holt chuckles. "Good point." He pulls his T-shirt over his head. The ripple of his muscles heats every part of me. Watching him feels like taking a walk in the sun on the first warm day of spring. "Don't think of it as *me hovering.* Just think of it as us killing two birds with one stone." He pretends to sniff his armpit. "Because I definitely need a date with a bar of soap myself."

Smiling, I reach into the linen closet and grab him a fresh towel. He strips down and guides me into the shower. The hot water rinses over me, washing away the residual ache and tightness of the previous night. He hands me a shampoo bottle and gently kisses my neck. This isn't our first shower together. In fact, showering with him is actually one of my favorite things to do. We have our own special routine, our own special dance.

After shampooing and conditioning, I prop my leg up on the tile bench and lather it with shaving cream.

"You're shaving?" he asks.

What a stupid question.

I can't help but giggle. "Yeah. Why?"

He shrugs, not sure how to respond. Water falls across his face, chasing the pathways created by his freckles. He loves watching me shave. I know he does. He doesn't have to say anything. The hardening of his erection says it all.

And when I shave my pubic area clean, he turns away, soaping himself for the fifteenth time.

We finish showering, and he helps me dry off. I'm standing in front of the mirror combing my hair when he comes up behind me, planting his body firmly against mine.

He's all hard lines and erotic electricity.

"So, are you still hurting?"

"Not really. The medicine seems to be working."

He nuzzles against me. His hot breath sends a shiver down my spine. "You know, I did some reading online about round ligament pain."

"You did?"

"It says that having an orgasm can actually relax the muscles and ease some of the tension and nerve pain you've been experiencing."

My desire for him is so strong, my own lip quivers. As much as the next sentence hurts to say, I say it. "Holt, I...I just don't think it would be smart. I feel better, but my insides are still pretty sore. And..." I watch myself blush in the mirror, "you're really big, in that department. It may hurt."

He stares at my reflection. "I would never hurt you. Do you trust me?"

I study his eyes, falling deeper and deeper into the color. Intense and mystical, it's the most beautiful shade of blue ever known to exist. "Of course, I trust you."

Looping his finger in the fabric of my towel, he pushes it to the ground. Grabbing my hand, he leads me to the bed and lays me down.

My body throbs with need. I need this so bad. But I'm scared.

"Holt, are you sure?" His cock is huge, and I feel so tender and swollen.

"Baby, I don't need my dick to make you come. I don't even need my fingers. All I need is my tongue. I'm gonna lavish you. I'm gonna lick you slow and sweet. I've got hours."

And with that, he buries his head between my legs.

And he's right.

I do relax.

Three times.

I meander down the stairs, eager to see my parents and Granny. And also eager to dig into the fried rice that Holt said Cullen was bringing for everyone.

I hear everybody outside on the patio, so I decide to detour into the kitchen for some water first. Rounding the stairs, I pause in the doorway, listening to the one-sided conversation.

"Are you kidding me right now, Kimber?" Ridge's tense voice stops me in place. "So, you're telling me your eyelash appointment is more important than this?"

I peek around the corner. He's holding his phone so tightly his knuckles are white. "She doesn't need a gift to feel better. Merit just loves having her family around. That's all she needs. *Us.*"

He's right. That's all I need. All I want.

Well, him. Not necessarily her.

He sucks his bottom lip between his teeth. "No, everyone's already here. Except Cullen, he's on his way with the food."

He inhales. "Kimb—"

He doesn't even get her full name out. I can only assume she cut him off.

After a minute, he sighs. "Okay. I understand." He swallows so loudly his throat makes a noise. "I'll give her your best."

Closing his eyes, he nods. "I love you too."

I wait until he hangs up and then I knock on the doorframe.

Visible relief drowns his face. He breaks into a wide, happy smile. "Hey, you. You're a sight for sore eyes." I cross the distance between us, falling into his all-encompassing hug. He nuzzles against my hair. "I'm surprised Holt let Rapunzel out of the tower."

I lean back, looking into his eyes. "I'm surprised you know who Rapunzel is."

"You have met Anna and Laura, right?"

I giggle, choking on a snort. "Good point."

"You gave us quite the scare."

I shake my head and rub my stomach. "Blame him," I say, talking about Daire.

"Ah, I can't go blaming my godson, can I? I mean, I'm gonna be the one he calls when he wants to escape y'all."

I roll my eyes. Nodding at his phone, I change the subject. "Everything okay?"

He looks down at it, sizing it up like it's a foreign object, new and unfamiliar. "Yeah. She's just not very good at...the hard things, the emotional things." His eyebrow lifts. "Her family is...very professional."

"Sounds like someone I used to know," I say, thinking back on my time as Edward's wife.

He smiles softly. "Yeah, I guess it does, doesn't it?"

"Why are you with her?" I ask honestly, praying I don't offend him.

"She's different once you really get to know her."

I squint, trying to read his face. I don't know him like I know Holt. Ridge is harder to read. "But does she make you happy?"

He freezes, thinking. Eventually, he opens his mouth to answer but the moment is interrupted.

Holt walks into the kitchen, arms filled with takeout bags. As aways, it only takes him a split second to size up the scene in front of him. Years of playing on the field make his eye/brain coordination quicker than most. "I'd think twice before trying to steal my girl, brother," he says. "Don't forget she's used to a real man." Passing us, he gives me a wicked little wink.

Cullen rounds the corner, holding even more bags, and not missing a beat, "You know, if you're picking Conway brothers, all the ladies say I'm better in bed."

My curiosity is immediately piqued. "Y'all sleep with the same women?"

"Of course, not," Ridge scoffs. "But trust me, if we did, they would definitely say I'm the better Conway brother."

Cullen leans against the kitchen island, pinning Ridge with a stare. "Katie Ellis."

Ridge's eyes widen and his head falls back. "Oh, shit," he chuckles. "I forgot about Katie Ellis."

"Yeah, she was a nice girl." Cullen looks over his shoulder, searching for Holt. Pointing a finger at him, he flashes a demented smile. "In fact..."

Gasping, I immediately close my eyes and slap my hands over my ears. "Holy crap! I don't wanna hear it!"

Covering your ears never really does anything, though. I can still hear. "C, if you say another word, I swear I'll kill you," Holt threatens.

Cullen bursts into laughter. "Hey, look, it's the face."

"I don't make a face," I growl, peeking through squinted eyes.

Right then, Granny walks into the kitchen, and her muffled voice sings in my ears. "Sweetheart!" Before wrapping me in a hug, she taps my nose. "What's with the weird face? Are you still hurting?"

Behind her back, I flip the bird to the three jackasses laughing at me.

Holt's arm wraps around me, pulling me against his body. True to his word, his cell phone is right beside him on the nightstand. I know it's weird for him. He keeps picking it up to make sure the volume is turned down as low as possible, but still loud enough for him to hear in the event of an emergency.

Which, as we know, is ridiculous.

For one, I'm right beside him. You couldn't even fit a sheet of paper between the two of us. I'm not going to call him with an emergency.

Two, a foghorn could be blowing in his ear, and he wouldn't wake up. I think having a burglar creep around your house for three months straight is proof of that.

He kisses the shell of my ear, sending a delicious shiver down my spine. "Are you feeling okay?"

"I'm just sore." I think back to last night. "I really hope that doesn't happen again. I don't think I've ever been so scared."

"You and me both."

I yawn, smiling to myself and thinking about the wonderful night we had *tonight*—what a difference just one night can make. All our family, coming together, just to make sure I'm okay. "I wanna go home to the farm."

Holt freezes, not breathing. "What?"

He thinks I'm talking about leaving him. I have to admit, the thought terrifies the shit out of me too. "Just for a few days," I add.

He leans over, searching me for the truth.

He can't see my face in the dark, so I reassure him with my words. "Only for a couple of days, I promise."

Content with my answer, his body relaxes, and he settles back down on the bed. "When?"

"Tomorrow?"

His fingers trace up and down my thigh, from my knee to my hip. "Okay. You can ride back with your parents. I'll drive down Friday night as soon as the game is over. We'll stay the weekend there. Come back home next Sunday evening."

"Are you sure? Why not just drive down on Saturday morning? The game won't get over until late. I hate to think of you driving in the middle of the night."

He nuzzles against me, inhaling the scent of my shampoo. "You do realize tomorrow is Sunday? So, we're talking about you being away from me for five whole nights. I have no intentions of making it six."

"Oh, that *is* a long time, *sir*," I tease. "How on earth do you plan to survive?"

He playfully bites my neck. "Ever had phone sex, Mer?"

Chapter 26

Merit

"Want some company?" Daddy asks, sitting in the rocking chair beside me.

It's a beautiful night, light on mosquitoes and heavy on the songs of cicadas and tree frogs. I kick my feet up on the banister railing of the front porch and use it to rock myself back and forth, inhaling the sweet night air. The smell of Bermuda grass is permanently engraved in the air. It's carved into every molecule.

Daddy reaches over and tugs on my sleeve. "Looks good on you."

I rake my hands across the flannel button-up. I've officially outgrown my normal nightgowns—it felt like I was sleeping in a toddler's leotard last night. And I'm too stingy to spend money on something I may only wear for another month, so I fished some of Papa's old shirts out of the closet. My grandfather was a large man. Larger than life, both physically and in personality. His Triple X button-ups give plenty of room for my still-growing stomach.

Daire rolls over, spinning. I can't imagine *not* feeling this feeling. A thousand words could never describe how amazing it is.

"Do you think this will be his legacy?" I whisper, nodding to my right, where acres of Bermuda grass grow. "That he will wanna do this? Be a sod farmer?"

Daddy chuckles. "It's a little early to tell, don't you think?"

"You know I'll never let it leave the family. I'll move back and take it over myself if I have to. I love it too much to ever let it go."

"True, you love it. But it's not your passion. Your joy is still locked up with that abandoned store." He sighs. "I just want you to be happy."

"I know." We rock, content in the silence for a few minutes. I scrape my fingernail across the arm of the rocking chair. "He said we should get married."

Daddy side glances at me. "Said you should get married? Or asked you to get married?"

I frown. "I'm not really sure. It wasn't exactly the best conversation."

Daddy lifts a questioning eyebrow.

"I had just told him that it would probably be best for the baby to have my last name. Not his. I told him that it would make things easier." I suck my bottom lip between my teeth. "And... I might've brought up the custody papers again."

Daddy bites back an amused smile. "Well, I can definitely see how that talk might've ended poorly."

I shrug, not sure what to say.

"Well, from where I sit, there are three questions you have to answer."

"What?"

"Do you forgive him? Do you love him? And do you wanna marry him?" He bumps against my shoulder, trying to ease the tension of the moment. "Cause the second one needs to stick better than the first one," he jokes, referring to my marriage with Edward.

I roll my eyes. "Haha." Reaching for my water bottle, I kill time, taking slow sips.

"Well," Daddy prods, fishing for answers.

There's no point in doing anything but answering honestly. Daddy can't pick up on my lies the way Holt can, but he's a smart enough guy to know bullshit when he hears it. "I finally forgive him. But you know that already. I told you that on the phone from the hospital."

He lifts his hands in agreement. "I know. I'm just checking to make sure it wasn't something you only said and only felt in the heat of the moment."

"No, not the heat of the moment. I forgive him. Really, I do." Ever since last Friday night, when I thought my life and the life of our child was in danger, I finally let go of the bitterness and hostility and fear. It's lifted a weight from my soul. A weight of chains and locks that I didn't even realize were holding me down and suffocating me.

"And I love him. I never stopped loving him. He's the love of my life. Sometimes, I think my heart is gonna explode because I love him so much."

"And marriage?"

I swallow, and my throat makes a weird gurgling noise. "I wanna marry him. I want him to be my husband. Forever. But I don't want him to marry me simply because we're having a baby." I shake my head. "And that doubt will always be in my mind. That he's just asking me because it's the noble thing to do, because he's scared of losing his son."

Daddy nods, thinking about everything I've said. "I probably shouldn't tell you this..."

He knows just what to say to fire my curiosity. With that one simple half-sentence, he pokes smoldering embers with a firework. My heart immediately starts beating faster. "What?"

"He asked me for your hand in marriage."

"He did?" I furrow my brow thinking back to all the times Holt and I talked this week. "Did he call you? What night did you talk to him?"

"He didn't call. He asked me in person." He stops rocking and levels me with a stare. "Last Thanksgiving."

What? Did he just say last Thanksgiving?

I push a rogue hair from my eyes with trembling fingers. "Did you say last Thanksgiving? As in last November? Like nearly ten months ago? That November?"

He laughs. "Sweetie, there's only one November."

I blink, trying to absorb that information. "Before I was pregnant?"

"Before that little boy was even a twinkle in your eye, yes."

"What!" Unable to control the volume of my voice, I find myself shouting. "Why didn't he ask me?!"

Dad cocks his head. "Well, I could be wrong, but I do believe he went to jail, from what I remember," he says, dipping his words in sarcasm.

Well, I sure as shit remember him going to jail. Clear as day.

He texted me right before coming in the house so I wouldn't get scared. So, I'm only slightly surprised when my door opens and he immediately climbs into bed with me.

"Holt! This is my bedroom. What about my parents?"

"What about them? I'm pretty sure they know how babies are made, so us sleeping in the same bed shouldn't come as any big surprise by now. They know we're back together; they know I'm never leaving your side again. Besides, we slept together at our house last weekend, and they didn't say anything."

Our House.

Back Together.

Never Leaving.

A comforting joy surges in my heart.

"True, but..." my voice trails off.

"But what?"

"It's just different when it's your childhood bedroom." I lift my head off the pillow and nod to the shelf in the corner. "And there's still Barbie dolls watching over you."

He follows my eyes. "Yeah, that's definitely creepy." Framing his body over mine, he slides a leg between my thighs and brushes his lips against my jaw. "Maybe we should give them something to look at." He kisses me. Deeply and passionately. Breathing his air into my lungs, his tongue tangles with mine. He tastes like mouthwash and smells like grass and the night air. My fingers tangle in the blond curls around his neck.

Greedy desire curls low in my stomach. My clit immediately throbs, awakening to life with just his kiss. I wrap a leg around him, grinding my crotch against his thigh, aching for his fingers, his tongue, his cock. And when the edge of my panties catches against the crease of his pocket, I wiggle like a madman, trying my best to work the fabric off my pussy. If I could just get a little more friction....

He chuckles, and I feel the vibration in my own chest. "Mmmm. There's my greedy little baby." When my back arches, pressing my body against his even more, he growls. Low and primal. "I missed you," he whispers.

"I missed you more." I kiss the freckles on his nose, trying my best to be patient and not fuck his leg like a horny dog. "I hear congratulations are in order, Coach. Another win."

"It nearly went into overtime, but I threatened the kids with double sprints every day next week if they made me one minute late for getting down here to you."

I roll my eyes. "Somehow, I doubt that."

"Well, let's just say I thought it."

His mouth finds mine again, and his hand slides over to my breast. My fingers reach for the hem of his shirt, eager to take it off him. He must be sweating because my chest feels wet.

Without warning, his lips pull away from mine. "Why is your shirt wet?"

"From you. You're sweating."

He shakes his head. "I'm not sweating. I had the AC blasting so I wouldn't get sleepy on the drive."

His hand cups my left breast again. "Did you spill something?"

"No." I push my hands between us, feeling both of my boobs. Sure enough, my shirt is soaked. "What is on me?"

I scramble to sit up, and Holt reaches over and turns on the lamp. Together, we both stare at the wetness staining Papa's old shirt.

I gasp. "Oh my gosh. I think I'm leaking milk."

His eyebrows shoot into his hairline. "Shit. Are you serious?" He breaks into a wide, contagious smile. "Let me see." He reaches for my buttons, but my hand slaps over his. He frowns, like a scolded child. "Mer? Are you okay?"

Instantly, my eyes fill with tears. Willing myself not to cry, I lie back down, turning on my side, away from him. "I'm fine." My emotions and pregnancy hormones rage, leaving me fragile and unsure of myself.

He eases his fingertips underneath my shirt and traces the curve of my spine, tattooing his love into me with his calloused touch. "You're obviously not fine."

"I am. Let's just go to sleep." I reach for the lamp, but his hand gently wraps around my arm.

"You forget I can read your face." Bringing my wrist to his mouth, he kisses it. "Talk to me. Tell me what's wrong."

Sighing, I flop onto my back and stare into his eyes. I open my mouth and close it. Amused, he licks his lips and patiently waits. Eventually, I find the words. They may not be the right words, but at least it's something. "My body is completely different. Look at me. I mean, what if you never find me attractive again." I fully expect him to laugh, so I cover my face with my hand so I don't have to experience the humiliation with my own eyes.

"Merit, look at me."

"No."

"You know I'm not gonna accept *no* as the answer, right?"

He's not lying. He won't accept it.

I drag my hands down my face and push myself up. Leaning against the headboard, I study him.

Gorgeous. There's no denying it. He's painfully gorgeous. Definitely one of those guys who's only going to get better looking as he ages. I don't see a balding head and floppy beer gut anywhere in Holt Hill's future.

"You're beautiful," he says.

"Me being beautiful, and *you* finding me attractive are two very different things."

Scooting closer, he reaches out, grabbing a lock of my hair and twisting it between his fingers. "Have I ever told you what your hair reminds me of?"

I'm afraid to move. I don't want him to stop playing with my hair. It tickles.

"The redwood trees in California. Brown with streaks of red and black. Just like your eyes, the color is different every time I look at it. It changes every second of every day."

My whisper is hoarse. "I've never seen the redwoods. I've never been to California."

"I'll take you there one day. Both you and Daire." An idea flashes in his eyes, and he grins. "When he's older, we'll buy an RV. Take off every summer and explore the country."

"You're planning for the future?"

"Always." He leans forward and kisses me. "And I'll always be attracted to you. I wanted you from the very first second I laid eyes on you at the store, and I've wanted you every second since." His soft smile falls, thinking about our past, and he grimaces with a brief flash of shame. "Despite what I said after going to jail, despite how I lied, I always wanted you." Sighing, he drags his nose along the line of my cheekbone, the dip of my jaw, the sensitive column of my neck. "I want my hands on you. And I want my body inside of yours."

My heart beats faster, and my chest heaves with every panted breath racing from my lungs, as he covers my mouth with his.

His kiss takes new meaning. It's deeper and stronger. Just like us.

Drawing back, he pulls his shirt over his head, gifting me with the glory of his body. My fingertips glide across every muscle, every line, every curve. His hands actually shake as they work the buttons of my shirt. He stops kissing me and watches in awe as he pushes the shirt from my shoulders. My wet and sticky skin glistens with moisture. Fondling my swollen and oversized breast, he slowly and seductively squeezes. The pressure sends a shock of desire deep into my core, making me moan.

Sure enough, a small amount of clear-white milk pebbles from my nipple.

I have to admit it's pretty damn shocking. I mean, I'm making milk. I'm a human being, and I'm creating a drink. The thing that will keep our child alive.

Bending his head, he takes my nipple in his mouth, sucking and licking, driving me to the brink of erotic insanity. And just when I think I can't take anymore, his free hand snakes into my panties and his finger plunges deep inside of me. My head falls back. Before my scream can escape, he shifts, playfully biting my bottom lip. "Shhh. Don't forget, baby, you aren't allowed to have boys in your room."

Even my giggle is filled with heat and steam. "Then, you better get out, *sir*."

"Over my dead body." He rubs his freckled nose along my collarbone, smelling my skin. "I just tasted the milk you are making for our son. That's so fucking hot."

"And now?"

He makes quick work of his belt. "And now, I need to be inside of you."

That sounds like a battle I can let him win.

Chapter 27

Holt

I lean against the doorway, watching her.

"I thought you were only gonna work for an hour?"

Looking up from her laptop, she smiles. Stretching her arms high above her head, she flops backward on the bed. "Well, I was. But you should see the number of applicants we have. I can't believe there's so many people." Her eyes widen. "These resumes are crazy. I mean, these people are legit. Like Washington, DC-politician-people legit."

I snort. "I think the last thing The Hill Family Charities needs is a Washington, DC, politician. Half of them were on the news crucifying me a few short months ago."

She blinks, frowning. "I know."

"Well, pick out the ones you like the best and set up interviews with us and Rob," I say, talking about the lawyer we hired a few weeks ago. He'll represent both the Foundation and us, personally.

"Okay."

"But for now," I draw out my words, "take a break and come outside."

She sits up and starts typing on the computer again. "I will in a minute. I just wanna finish this up."

I swear this woman is going to kill me before the end of the night.

Clearing my throat, I wait until she glances up, before lifting my arm and slowly spinning my ballcap around backward.

Her eyes devour me, nibbling on my skin and picking the meat from my bones. She purses her lips in thought. "Are you trying to seduce me?"

"Maybe," I tease.

She pouts. "You realize there's nothing I can do to seduce you back. I'm bigger than an eighteen-wheeler."

I roll my eyes. "First of all, you're not big. In fact, I plan on shoving food in your mouth every chance I get these last few weeks because I don't want a skinny noodle for a child. Second of all, *everything* you do seduces me."

She crosses her eyes and makes buck teeth. "Everything?" she asks with a lisp.

Laughing, I close the lid of her laptop and grab her hand, pulling her off the bed. "Everything. Now, come on."

The September night actually has a small chill in it, which is completely unexpected for this time of year. Hopefully, it will keep the mosquitoes away. Stepping off the porch, she wraps her hands around my bicep and kisses my shoulder. "Where are we going?"

"You'll just have to wait and see." From here, she can't see the far side of the barn. I'm so excited I nearly toss her over my shoulder and sprint. Of course, that would ruin the natural element of the surprise, so I patiently wait—like a good boy. As soon as she sees everything, she gasps. Immediately, she bounces up and down on her toes. "Movie night?"

I repeat her words back to her. "Movie night."

Just like when she was growing up.

The projector is set up, waiting to paint the movie all over the side of the barn. The chairs are draped with blankets and pillows, to make things more comfortable. The pop-up table is covered with snacks and candy.

In fact, Granny is standing there chomping on M&Ms so loudly, she sounds like a horse.

Merit's smile is so wide I worry she might break her jaw. "What movie are we watching?"

Nodding to Deke, he turns on the system, and the home screen of the DVD flashes, coloring the night sky.

"*White Christmas*," she whispers.

I nuzzle against her ear. "Well, it's your favorite, isn't it?"

She nods, not saying anything.

I study her face, instantly knowing what she's thinking. "You haven't watched it, have you? I mean, since I was arrested. We were gonna watch it that day and then... our lives were ripped out from underneath us."

Swallowing, she puts on a brave face. "Don't you ever get tired of reading my mind?" she says with a devoted smile.

I bend down and smell her hair. "Never."

My dad's voice immediately catches Merit off guard. "Is the movie invitation open to anyone?" Right on cue, he, Mom, Raylee, and Ella come into view, walking the worn trail between the house and the barn.

Merit yelps in excitement. "What! Of course!" She races up and wraps my mom in a hug. "What are y'all doing here?"

She shrugs, playing coy. "What can I say? I've always loved this movie."

Merit cranes her neck to see if anyone else is hiding. "Where are the kids?"

"Will and Cullen are working at the bar, so we left four children in the very capable hands of Crutch and Ridge," Raylee says.

"And now that Hardy can stand on his own, he's discovered the joy of throwing everything on the ground. Breakable or not." Ella's stiff shoulders relax, and she bites back a smile. "Ry's already called three times to apologize for broken things."

Eager to get this damn show on the road, I usher everyone to their seats, and we start the movie.

We're only five minutes in before I call it quits.

I'm about to fucking explode.

Nerves fire in my stomach like a Molotov cocktail. My hands are twitching, and my leg keeps bouncing up and down like I'm hooked to an electric fence. This is way worse than the Super Bowl.

Way, way worse.

And so much fucking better. The best. The very best.

"Shit. I'm dying." I growl, falling to my knees in front of Merit.

Her brow furrows. "Holt?"

From my periphery, I can see everyone else stand up. I take a split second to pray that Granny doesn't choke on the Skittles she's now two-fisting. Raylee fumbles with her cell phone, trying to hit the record button without missing anything.

My hands snake up the length of her tanned and toned legs. "Merit, I can't wait any longer. I can't wait another minute, another second without knowing that you're mine. Forever."

She does her best to keep her eyes locked on mine, but her gaze keeps flittering back to the movie playing on the barn.

Like a lot.

I squeeze her thighs. "Uh, Mer, not to interrupt, but I'm kinda in the middle of something."

Her pink lips pout. "You should really pause the movie. The beginning is where you get all the backstory. You'll miss it."

And...that's My Merit.

Laughing, I nod to Deke. "Could someone please stop the movie for my girl?"

Satisfied with the frozen picture, her eyes meander back to me. She immediately blushes and looks down at the ground. "Sorry."

I lift her chin. "No, you're not," I say, teasing her with a wink.

Giggling, she snorts.

In that moment, I'm so overcome with love for her, I don't know how I'll ever be able to function in life. It feels like the only job I should have in this world is loving her. And our son. And keeping them safe.

I slide my hand across her flushed cheek and tangle it in her hair. "Tell me."

"I love you."

"I worried I'd never hear those words again." I shake my head. "I don't deserve your love, Merit. But I promise that I'll do my best every single day of our lives to earn it." I scoot closer, positioning myself between her legs. "I promise to never leave. I'll never walk out. I'll never give up on us. Never again. I promise to love you and provide for you. I'll support you and cherish you. I want all of your dreams to come true. There's not anything in this world you can't do. You're the smartest, kindest, bravest woman I know."

I wipe a tear from her face. "I promise to be the best father. I promise to love our son and give you more babies. I promise to protect this farm and the legacy that your family has built.

"I promise to watch old movies and eat blueberry pancakes." I shrug, "And hopefully lots of steak once you can smell it again without throwing up."

She laughs and more tears fall. "I promise to make fun of you every time you scrunch your nose at another woman. I promise to laugh with you, learn with you, and grow with you. I promise to never change you, never mold you, never break you."

I lean forward, kissing her lips. She tastes like salt and popcorn. "I promise to worship you and make love to you and make you feel like the most beautiful woman on the face of this Earth.

"I wanna build our life and grow old. And when I take my last breath, I want you by my side, holding my hand."

Taking a deep breath, I pull the ring box from my pocket. I flip the lid, presenting her with the diamond and ruby ring. "Merit Eliza Browning, will you marry me?"

Chapter 28

Holt

Glancing down, she spins the ring on her finger again, watching the light bounce off the diamonds and rubies.

"You keep looking down at that thing and you're gonna get a crick in your neck."

Her lips curve into a sly smile. "If you didn't want me looking at it, you wouldn't have gotten it so big."

Propping my hands on my hips, I glance down at my crotch. "Well, if you like looking at big things…"

Laughing, she snorts and tosses the instructions for the crib assembly at me. "*That* doesn't shine as much as this," she says, wiggling her finger at me.

"True," I concede. "And I have to say, it was pretty damn funny when you flashed that big ol' ring to the nurse last night."

Merit immediately scrunches her nose. "She shouldn't have been hitting on you."

She's so freakin' funny.

"She was asking for an autograph and a penny for her little cousin. I don't really think she was trying to get in my pants."

Her eyes widen, and her face grows serious. "Trust me, she was. That look she was giving you? Like she wanted to eat you for breakfast, lunch, and dinner? I know that look."

"You do? And just how do you know that look?"

Bright pink blushes across her cheeks. "Because it's the look I've given you since the day we met."

She's right. And I love it.

I finish tightening the last screw and shake the crib, making sure it's stable. After last weekend and our engagement, Merit finally agreed that we could start buying baby stuff and set up the nursery.

In *our* house. For *our* life. Together.

It's been a whirlwind of a week. Unable to control our excitement, we went to the store Monday night after school and football practice and bought all new furniture and decorations. Even though the bedroom for Anna, Laura, and Ty is bigger, Merit refuses to displace them, so Daire will have the bedroom next to that, right across the hall from our room.

And last night was the first part of our Baby Class at the hospital. Who knew you needed to take a class to have a baby. I mean, really? Would the hospital actually turn us away if we showed up without the proper credentials? The class runs in a two-part session—Friday night and Saturday afternoon. We had to do this weekend because it's my only bye-week; we didn't have a game last night.

Not to mention, tonight is our baby shower.

And so much more. She just doesn't know it yet.

I glance at my watch. "We should get ready. Class starts in an hour."

Her frown is almost comical. "Yeah."

Something's been bothering her since last night, and she hasn't told me what. At first, I thought it was the nurse thing, but this is something different. Something more.

"You plan on telling me what's wrong? What's been bothering you?"

"Nothing's bothering me."

"Don't lie, Merit."

"Mmmm?"

"Something's clearly wrong. It's written all over your face."

She rocks back and forth in the new glider, pretending to pick at something on the fabric.

"Tell me the truth."

Growling under her breath, she slaps the arm of the rocker. "That class made me mad. I don't wanna go back."

Well, this should be interesting.

"Why did the class make you mad?"

"I don't like that instructor. I don't think she knows what's she's talking about."

I try to bite back a smile. "You don't think she knows what she's talking about? She's been a labor and delivery nurse for twenty-five years."

"So?"

I pull the matching foot stool in front of the glider and sit down in front of her. "What did she do? Did she say something to you?"

"Not to me. To the class. Didn't you hear her? She said that when your water breaks it could be a big gush or a slow trickle."

I lift an eyebrow, waiting for more. "Yeah?"

"A slow trickle?" Her voice hitches up in disbelief. And just in case I didn't hear her, she leans forward and points a finger in my face. "A slow trickle." She falls back in her seat. "Can you believe that?"

My hands glide across her black leggings. On Wednesday, she decided her legs were too big to wear shorts anymore. It's ridiculous, really. She's beautiful and gorgeous, and her legs look amazing. Just like always. Especially when they're wrapped around me. Sliding my fingers under the hem of her shirt, I fiddle with the Velcro holding her maternity belt tight around her stomach. "Okay, but what's wrong with that? That's what the books say too."

She folds her arms across her chest. "Well, just how in the world am I supposed to know if my water breaks? A small trickle! I pee on myself all the time. Like all the time. Every freakin' day. What if my water breaks, and I don't even know it. What if Daire comes out while I'm on the toilet peeing? Like one of those women you see on TV."

Oh my gosh. This has to be one of the funniest conversations I've ever had.

And I can't even laugh.

Trust me, I know better than to laugh at my pregnant, soon-to-be-wife who is *this close* to delivering our child.

"Merit, you don't have to worry about that. That's not going to happen. I'm sure you'll be able to tell the difference between a pee trickle and a water-breaking trickle. You'll feel it. You'll know. I promise."

She looks at me with wide eyes. Her green shirt brings out the swirls of green and brown. "You promise?"

I grab her neck and pull her into a kiss. "Yes, I promise. And if you don't believe me, just ask the women. Your mom and granny are downstairs. And everyone else will be at the shower. I'm sure they will all tell you the same thing."

Finally satisfied, she smiles. "Okay."

A strand of hair falls from her ponytail, and I push it back. "Are you excited?" I ask, switching topics.

Her face instantly brightens. "I'm so excited. I wish Kyra was here now. But she should be here by the time we get back. I still can't believe their original flight was canceled."

Little does she know, Kyra and Toby, Kyra's boyfriend, didn't have a canceled flight. They got here on Thursday, just like planned.

And we've been lying to Merit this whole time.

Well, *I* didn't lie to her face. I said I would never lie to her, and I meant it. Kyra, however? Kyra made no such promise and had no problems lying to her best friend. So, every time Merit's said something about it over the past couple of days, I've just smiled and nodded. And quickly changed the subject.

Standing up, I give her a kiss on the forehead. "Go get ready. I'll clean up here and meet you downstairs."

As soon as she's out of the room, I pull out my phone and do a group text to every woman in my life.

Holt: If Merit asks you, you need to tell her that you had a "gush" when your water broke and you immediately knew what happened. Please do not mention the word "trickle." Ever.

"Where are we going?" she asks when I miss the turn.

"Just a quick errand."

"An errand?" She glances at the clock on the dashboard. "But it's nearly time for the shower to start. Kyra should already be there." She looks down at her shirt and grimaces. "Plus, I have to change."

During the delivery room and maternity ward tour, they tried to impart the wisdom of using hand sanitizer frequently. There's a sanitizer machine outside of every room. Merit went to use one, and the whole front of it broke off and squirted sanitizer all over her face, in her eye, and down the front of her shirt. I have no idea how it happened. It was an automatic machine; she didn't even have to touch anything. But in true Merit fashion, it happened. We had to spend the next ten minutes at an eye-washing station with a nurse rinsing Merit's eye.

And Merit thought that nurse was hitting on me too.

And he was a dude.

"It won't take long. And I promise it'll be worth it." When that doesn't convince her, I say the words that Curious Merit can never ignore. "It's a surprise."

She studies my face. Seeing the unbridled excitement I can barely contain, she giggles and snorts. "Okay."

Reaching behind her, I grab an extra T-shirt from the back seat. "Put this over your eyes."

She lifts an eyebrow. "Over my eyes?"

"Yeah, like a blindfold."

"Like a blindfold?" she laughs. "Holt, what's going on?"

I tickle her nose with the shirt. "Come on. Just do it."

She sniffs it, inhaling deeply. "It smells like you." I assume that's a good thing because she twists it into a bandana shape and ties it around her head.

Her fingers tap against her thighs in anticipation. "Where are we going?"

"I told you it's a surprise."

"No hints?"

"No hints," I say.

We drive for the next couple of minutes, and she jabbers the whole time, trying to get me to confess to what's about to happen. The second I park and turn off the engine, she reaches to move her blindfold. "Are you ready?"

I pretend to slap her hand. "No, I'm not ready. I'll tell you when I'm ready. Now, sit there. Don't peek. I'll be back in just a minute." When she doesn't say anything, I warn her. "Merit..."

"Okay. I won't peek. I promise."

Jumping from the truck, I race over, talking to everyone, making sure everything is ready to go. One of the signs is crooked, so Ridge rushes inside to fix it. Jogging back to the truck, I open the door and unbuckle her seat belt. Hauling her into my arms, I walk across the parking lot.

She squirms against my grasp. "Don't carry me. I'm too big."

"You're not too big," I say, adding a tickle to her ass for good measure, "and the last thing I need is for you to fall down because you're trying to walk in a blindfold."

She rubs her nose against my neck, sending her hot breath down my spine. "Then let me take the blindfold off."

Stopping at the right spot, I set her on her feet, making sure she's stable. "Okay. You can take it off."

She doesn't move.

"Mer?" I ask.

Her lip quivers. "I'm nervous. This surprise has me nervous."

"Don't be nervous." I brush my fingers across the small of her back. "What can I do? What do you want?"

She holds out her right hand. "Hold my hand."

I can't help but think back to when I first met her. "You remember when we first met? You didn't want me to hold your hand."

"Of course, I *wanted* you to hold my hand. That's what scared me the most."

Wrapping my fingers with hers, she reaches up and rips off the blindfold.

Merit

Words.

I should be saying words, but I'm not.

I can't even believe what I'm seeing. It very well could be a mirage.

It's my store.

But it's so much *more* than my store.

The setting sun is already behind the building, and the *Run and Jump and Twirl* sign is lit up, bright and brilliant, the bulbs recently replaced. Dangling in the front window is a sign that says, "Grand Re-Opening Coming Soon!"

And it's not only my store; it's the whole shopping complex. The whole front of the strip mall has gotten a face lift—fresh paint, new awnings, and huge flower planters with the most gorgeous flower arrangements known to mankind. Even the empty storefront next door to me shows signs of life, like a new store is coming or something.

Slowly, I glance around. Everyone is here.

And I mean everyone.

My parents. Granny. All of Holt's family. The Conways. The Marcums.

Anna, Laura, and Ty are jumping up and down, screaming and

holding handmade posters covered in so much glitter that I can't even read what they say. Not only that, but strangers have stopped to see what all the fuss is about. People gaze out of the coffee shop, curiosity getting the best of them. Cars driving in the parking lot pull to the side and lower their windows.

Movement from the new storefront catches my eye. A sign like the one hanging from my window falls open. *"The Letterhead.* Coming Soon!"

The Letterhead.

Why does that sound so familiar?

The front door opens, and a little body bounces outside like a rabbit hopping down the lane. A body I love.

"We can always change the name if you want," Kyra says. "We were drinking that night we were playing around with names, and that's the only one I could remember."

"Kyra?" My voice gets strangled in my throat, and it sounds more like a frog ribbit than an actual human voice. In shock, I turn to Holt. "Kyra?" I ask him.

"I know it's been a few months, but surely you didn't forget what she looks like," he says with a devilish wink.

I blink, feeling faint and dizzy. "Wha...what's happening?" I'm completely dumbfounded. On top of that, I feel like a dumbass because I can't even talk straight.

I think my tongue is numb.

He gathers me in his arms. "It's your store. Your dream. You worked so hard for it, and you had to let it go because of me. That should have never happened. But it did. And I will never be able to tell you how sorry I am for that."

"My store?"

"Run and Jump and Twirl is ready for you whenever you're ready for it." He looks over at Kyra and nods to the other sign. "Not only that, but the stationery store too, or whatever you wanna call it. It's yours. Well, yours *and* Kyra's. I tried to split it 50/50, just like you wanted, but Kyra wouldn't hear of it. She said you're the one

who came up with the idea. You're the one who always pushed her and boosted her confidence in her creations, when she wasn't even sure she could make it in graphic design. Kyra insisted you be majority owner. So, you are. In the stationery store, you own 51%, and Kyra owns 49%."

"Are you serious?"

He licks his lips. "Very."

"Kyra's back?"

He nods. "Toby already has a job lined up in town too. This trip isn't just a visit for them; it's a move." His deep blue eyes dance. "And she didn't make me grovel too much. She actually jumped at the idea." He cocks his head, "Well, after she cussed me out for about ten minutes."

Kyra scoffs and folds her arms across her chest. "You deserved way more than ten minutes of foul language."

He laughs, flashing his brilliant white teeth. "Point taken."

I can't find any words in my vocabulary, so I just repeat what I already said, "My store?"

"*Run and Jump and Twirl* is all yours. No loans. No liens. No attachments. There's more than enough money in the business bank accounts for you to get everything set up for both stores. And," his eyes scan the crowd, landing on my parents, "I paid your parents back for every cent they gave you when you handed over the envelope full of cash."

"I can't believe you did this."

"I love you, Merit. I told you I will always support your dreams."

Kyra finally invades our space. "Listen, I don't mean to ruin this beautiful moment," she narrows me with a stare, "but you do realize that I haven't seen you since March, right?" She thins her lips. "By the way, what's all over the front of your shirt?"

Somehow, I snap out of my daze and crush her against me, holding my best friend—and business partner—so tightly I worry I'll suffocate Daire.

That's all it takes. Everyone goes berserk and rushes us. Hug after hug. Excited chatter bursts my eardrums. Laughter vibrates against my ribs. Pushing his way through the throngs of people, Holt hauls me into his arms. My legs wrap around his waist, and my fingers tangle in his blond curls. His lips find mine, and he claims me, marking me as his.

Eventually he pulls his face away, needing a breath and a break to collect himself. Because our make-out session was quickly morphing into something not safe for public viewing. "Are you happy?"

"Oh, Holt, I'm so happy." I lower my forehead to his. "But really, you didn't have to do this. I would've been okay. I could've just gotten a regular job somewhere."

He smiles softly. "I know. And that's just another reason I love you."

I take another look at my store. Well, my *two stores*. The walls are coated with my blood, sweat, and tears. Years and years of hard work.

And I'm so excited to do it all over again.

"It's so beautiful. The whole complex looks great. I can't believe Stan did all of this," I say, talking about the owner and landlord. "And he did it quick too. I just drove past here two days ago." I lock my ankles around his waist, holding him tighter. "He didn't try to swindle you on the leases, did he? I know he let me out of my lease early in March; but normally, he's pretty shrewd."

"How could he? He's not the landlord anymore."

My brow furrows. "He's not? Who is?"

Holt shrugs. "I don't know. I heard it was some good-looking guy."

Holy crap.

"Holt?"

He waggles his eyebrows. "Ever make love to a real estate magnate?"

I toss my head back and laugh. "No, but I think I may tonight."

Chapter 30

Merit

This acid reflux is killer.

Granted, I did eat fried rice for supper. And a hot dog during the first quarter. And a Snickers bar during the second quarter. And I may have had a couple of sips of Anna's slushie. Well, really, half of it.

But still.

It shouldn't be this bad.

I lean forward, inserting myself between Raylee and Ella. "Do y'all have anything for heartburn?"

Ella cocks her head, wafting the smell of her shampoo in my direction. "You're sick?"

I shake my head. "Just too many flavors in my stomach."

"I think I have some Tums out in the car," Raylee says, standing.

Pushing up, I rub my chest. "I'll go with you. I need to stretch my legs."

"Me too," Ella adds. She looks behind her to Teresa, who's holding Hardy on her lap.

Teresa smiles brightly. "We'll watch the kids, sweetie."

I glance one last time at the field, catching the play, before we walk up the bleachers. We're still pretty far from the gate, but that doesn't matter, Crutch immediately knows his wife is in the vicinity.

He's like a hound dog with a nose specifically designed for her. His eyes latch onto her, devouring her, like he's never seen a woman more beautiful. And I have to admit, Ella is gorgeous. But, of course, she's not the only hot one in that relationship.

Crutch is drop-dead sexy tonight. Black polo with the sheriff's department logo. Jeans. Boots. Gun.

He's like a modern-day cowboy.

Of course, I prefer my modern-day football player with blond curls and deep blue eyes and freckles on his nose.

Crutch slides an arm around Ella's back. "And just where are you ladies off to?"

"Merit has indigestion. Raylee's got some medicine in her car."

His brow furrows. "I'm working the gate." He searches the crowd, looking for someone. When he loudly whistles, Ridge immediately appears from down the hill, catching Crutch's eye.

Excusing himself from the group he's talking to, Ridge jogs over to us. "What's up?"

"The girls need to get something from Raylee's car."

Raylee dramatically sighs. "Y'all do realize that three grown women are quite capable of walking across a parking lot by themselves, right?"

Ridge wraps an arm around her shoulder and pushes her forward. "Yeah, but good thing you don't have to."

We're nearly to Raylee's SUV when it happens.

In one way, I guess it's good to know I was wrong.

Very wrong.

It feels like someone just popped an industrial-strength rubber band inside my body. It's an audible snap. I can actually hear it vibrate against my own eardrums.

It feels like I just got kicked by a goat.

Yeah, that happened once, so I know what it feels like.

The second my water breaks, fluid pours down my legs, soaking my panties and leggings. Liquid pools on the pavement. And the very next second, everything inside of me *drops*. Including Daire.

There's a heaviness in my crotch, like a bowling ball is about to fall out of me.

I feel *open.*

Exposed.

I feel like I need to… squat.

So, that's what I do. I squat down, slapping my hands on the pebbled asphalt. A cry falls from my mouth.

Ella's hand circles my shoulder. "Merit?"

Ridge spins on his heels, instantly hearing the worry in her voice.

"What's wrong?" Raylee asks.

"Her water broke," Ella answers.

Her words slowly sink in. I can't believe she just said what I was thinking. That makes it real.

Very real.

"Holy shit!" Raylee bounces up and down.

Racing to my side, Ridge bends down and scoops me into his arms. "Change of plans. We're going to my truck instead."

I can't believe this is happening. Like right now.

"It's too early," I protest. "It's not time. There's still fifteen more days to go."

"Tell that to my godson. He has other plans."

A cramp—well, I guess, it's actually a contraction—overcomes me, making me wince. Fortunately, it only lasts for a few seconds. After that, I'm extremely cognizant of the fact that Ridge's hands are near my ass and sliding all over my drenched clothes. Even his shirt is wet. "Oh no. You're getting…my stuff…all over you."

He glances down, checking his shirt. It doesn't faze him. "It's okay. I'm used to it."

"You're used to it?"

He lifts an eyebrow. "Merit, I'm a paramedic. I've delivered babies before."

Holy crap. "Are you gonna deliver my baby?"

Gifting me a gentle smile, he chuckles. "No, the doctor's gonna delivery your baby. At the hospital. We have plenty of time."

Raylee opens the front passenger door to his truck.

"No." He shakes his head. "Open the back. She'll be more comfortable back there." He then tells Raylee to get in first and sets me down beside her.

Crutch calls out in the distance, racing over to us. "What's wrong? Did Merit fall?"

"Her water just broke." Ella breaks into a wide smile.

"Holy shit," he says.

That seems to be the consensus.

"We need to go get everyone," Ella grabs his arm, pulling him.

Ridge is about to shut the door when I kick it with my foot. "Wait! Don't tell Holt!"

Ella lifts an eyebrow. "Excuse me?"

"He's down by a touchdown. Wait until the game's over. Don't tell him now."

Crutch turns to his wife, lowering his voice. "Is she crazy? He'll kill us."

"Merit, we need to go. Now." Ridge slams the door.

I pound on the window, yelling behind the glass. "I mean it! Don't tell him yet. He needs to focus on the win."

Jumping behind the wheel, Ridge pulls out of the parking lot. Raylee's like a cat on a hot tin roof, hopping all over. And as for me, things are starting to get pretty damn uncomfortable down there—well, everywhere, really. My back is tight, and it feels like someone is rolling over it with a bicycle.

Yeah, that happened once too.

Ridge hits the button for his flashers and drives at a speed usually reserved for ambulances. I don't have my seat belt on, so I'm flopping around like a wet fish. Raylee's phone rings, and I hear her talking, but I can't even focus long enough to decipher who's on the other end of the line.

Ridge's voice catches me off guard. I look up to see he's on the phone too. "Deke? It's Ridge." After a pause he says two simple words. "It's time."

I can't believe it's time.

"Daddy?" I lean on the console, wondering if he can hear me.

"Merit, you need to sit back. You don't have a seat belt on," Ridge orders, before turning back to the phone. "We're on our way to the hospital. She's in labor." When I don't sit back, he calls for Raylee and she gently pulls me against her lap.

Ridge watches us in the rearview mirror before he responds to whatever my dad asked. "He'll be right behind us. They're having to pull him from the game."

I look at Raylee, pouting. "I told them not to."

She just laughs, "Yeah, he'll probably be mad about that."

A super-fierce contraction sends my body into a spasm, making me hold my breath.

"Merit, you can't do that. You have to breathe," he says.

I do my best to follow Ridge's instructions, but it's hard. Not only because of the pain, but because of the emotions swirling through my body like a firestorm. As soon as the contraction ends, I burst into tears.

Raylee squeezes my arm. "Oh honey, don't worry. You can do this. Everything's gonna be fine." She tosses her hand in the air. "I read something that said eight babies are born every second in the world. Hell, if I can do it—twice—you are more than capable. I'm a wimp."

I rub my eyes. "It's not that."

And surprisingly, it's not. There's a strange sense of calm flooding my body. Like a fine mist settling over a lake in the early morning. I'm not sure what all will happen, but I *know* we will be okay. Daire and me. Me and Daire. We're going to be fine and healthy.

"Then what's wrong?" she asks.

A loud sob wails from my body like a siren. "I can't believe I'm not married."

"Huh?" The look on her face is priceless. If I were in a better frame of mind, I'd laugh.

"I can't believe I'm gonna be an unwed mother."

"You're engaged." She points out the obvious, nodding to the ring on my finger.

"Engaged isn't the same as married." I attempt to wipe the snot from my nose, but I only succeed in spreading it all over my face. "What will my grandfather think?"

Raylee's eyes widen, and she leans forward, grabbing the back of Ridge's headrest, whispering into his ear. "I thought her grandfather passed away?"

I nod and hiccup, angry that my face is now sticky and itchy from the tears and snot. "He did. He's dead," I say bluntly. Falling back in the seat, I wiggle around through another contraction. "But can you imagine what he'd say? In the Old West, I'd be labeled as *ruined.*"

Raylee just stares at me. Eventually, she plasters a big smile on her face. "Well, hey, it's the twenty-first century. Times change." She shrugs, "Besides, he'd probably be more upset by the thought of you using a big, hot pink dildo."

"Fucking shoot me now," Ridge mumbles from the front seat.

At the hospital, everything is a rush. A whirlwind. It's obvious they do this kind of stuff every day, but I don't. It's quite overwhelming. By the time Holt races into the delivery room, I'm already in a gown and hooked up to monitors.

He told me the vision he'll have of me on his death bed will be that time at the farm—the moment he was able to fully soak in my pregnancy. White sundress. Rubber boots. Setting sun.

And this? This is the vision I'll have of him on my death bed. The look he gives me when he comes into the room? I've never seen that look before. Never. It's more than adoration. More than worship. More than awe. We own each other. In this very moment, I know we will own each other forever.

Not to mention, he looks delicious. That coach's polo hugs his sweaty body in all the right places. His rippled arms are still carrying sunburn across every corded muscle. His jeans are slung low on his hips, and his sweaty blond curls peek from beneath his ballcap. There's even a piece of grass stuck to his cheek.

And then he kisses me.

"Hey."

"Hey," I say back.

"Can I make a request for the birth of our next child?"

"Next child?" I snort. "Can we make it through the birth of this child first?"

He completely ignores that comment. "Promise you'll never put football ahead of our family. You do that, and I'll do the same."

I nibble on my lip. "But you were down by a touchdown. I figured we had time."

"It's just a game." He kisses me again, sucking my bottom lip between his. "You're my life."

I wish I could soak up more of the moment, but a contraction hits. Hard.

Shit. This hurts.

Holt grabs my hand, holding it tight. As soon as it passes, Raylee jumps up, offering me ice chips. By now, everyone else is filtering in, and my delivery room has more people in it than a discoteque.

"What's going on? What'd the doctor say?"

Ridge speaks up from the corner of the room. He's already changed shirts. One of the nurses gave him a scrub top. Really, I think she just wanted to watch him take his shirt off. "She's already at seven centimeters. It happened really fast. Doc's surprised since this is her first."

Holt lifts an eyebrow in good humor. "Something you're not telling me?"

I scowl. "Yeah, you and your super sperm are taking a long hiatus after this."

He just laughs. "Epidural?"

Raylee nods. "She requested it. We're just waiting on the anesthesiologist to come in to administer it."

I reach out for Holt's arm, but my IV catches in the bedsheets, pulling the needle at a weird angle. "Ouch."

He gently untangles the cords. "What do you need, baby? Tell me what to do."

"You need to give Ridge some money," I whisper.

His nose scrunches, making his freckles jump. "I do?"

By the time I got out of the truck, Ridge's tan leather seats were tinged pink, covered in fluid and blood and mucous. I point to my crotch, safely hidden under the stiff hospital sheets. "*Stuff* got all over his seats. We need to pay to have it cleaned."

He just smiles and nods. "Don't worry about it. I'll take care of it."

Knowing Holt, he'll probably try to buy his best friend a whole new truck.

"Mom and Daddy? Granny?"

"I've talked to them. Their bags were already packed, so they just tossed them in and got on the road. They're driving as fast as they can."

"Holt," Crutch peeks into the room, interrupting us, "he's here."

"Who's here?"

Holt ignores me again. "We're ready for him. Bring him in."

"We're ready for who?" I ask.

When Pastor Clark walks into my hospital room, I'm completely shocked. Why on earth is the football team chaplain here?

Holy crap. Am I dying? What if something is wrong, and they aren't telling me because they're afraid I'll flip out.

My voice catches in my throat, suffocating me. Sweat breaks out on my brow. "Pastor Clark? Am I dying?"

He holds the Bible in front of his chest and gifts me a comforting smile. "Of course, not." His grin shifts, and his eyes dance. "Now, who's ready to get married?"

What a stupid question.

Chapter 31

Holt

It's a good thing Merit is asleep. Otherwise, she'd get on to me. I'm supposed to let Daire sleep in his crib. Everyone says we need to get him into a routine, including Merit. But how am I supposed to just let him lie there when he's so freakin' cute?

My son.

My perfect little man.

Keeping any focus on the game tonight was almost impossible. But I did what I had to do. We won again. And I rushed home, eager to see my family.

I can't believe it's been two weeks. Two weeks of me being a father. Two weeks of me being a husband. Granted, we just went to the courthouse yesterday to get the marriage license; but we were married by a preacher. It doesn't get more real than that in my book.

Daire Browning Hill was born at 3:50 a.m., weighing six pounds five ounces, and measuring twenty-one inches. He's long and lean. He has a mass of wild, light brown hair—which I hope darkens just like his mother's. Why? Because I can tell his eyes are going to be just like hers. They're light now, but the swirls of brown and green and blue are already forming. He sleeps like a champ. Eats like a champ. And only cries when he's hungry or wet or curious he's missing out on something fun.

My mom said I should soak this up because it just means our second child will be a holy terror. Which isn't very comforting because *I* was *her* second child. I think she's trying to tell me something about my time as a baby.

Merit has taken to motherhood like a fish in water. I knew she'd be perfect, but she's even more spectacular than I imagined. In fact, watching her is my favorite thing to do. I especially love watching when she holds him, humming off-tune songs from her old movies.

Deke, Marie, and Granny all stayed for the first week. Then, Deke and Granny went home so Deke could return to work on the farm. He drove back up today, and he'll be taking Marie home on Sunday. And of course, my parents have been here every day. Along with everyone else. It's been nice to see everyone fawn all over Daire and cater to Merit. But they've also been very respectful of our time as new parents, giving us space to bond as a family.

I've only had one real 'oh shit' moment, and it didn't even involve Daire. It happened two days after we came home from the hospital. I found Merit crying in the bedroom, and she refused to tell me what was wrong. She even lied, straight to my face, telling me she was fine. The fact that she lied to me and refused to come clean, after my prodding—like normal—scared the shit out of me. After thirty minutes of the back and forth, I tucked my tail between my legs and sent for reinforcements. Otherwise known as my mom and Marie. And like any good husband, I eavesdropped on the conversation.

"Honey, I really wish you would tell us what's wrong. What you're thinking, what you're feeling," Marie says. "I can guarantee we've been through the same thing."

Merit sniffles. "No, you haven't."

Her mom gently laughs. "I promise we have. Motherhood changes so much, and you may feel like you're on an island, isolated and alone, but I promise you're not."

"Merit, we can help you. You just have to let us in," Mom adds.

Merit struggles to get her words out. "Oh no, I can't say anything. Especially not to you."

"Me?" Shock laces my mom's voice. "You're my daughter now, a part of my family forever. You can tell me anything."

Merit's sob nearly pierces my eardrums. "Your son will never wanna have sex with me again!" I hear her flop on the bed, and it sounds like she's crying into a pillow.

What the hell is she talking about? Why wouldn't I wanna have sex with her. I always wanna have sex with her.

"What?" Marie raises her voice so Merit can hear over the sounds of her own cries. "Merit, what are you talking about?"

She blows her nose. "My crotch looks like Quasimodo! It's a disaster... a complete shit-show of a disaster. I'm swollen and disfigured." It sounds like she's back to talking into the pillow. "I'll never be the same again."

I don't have to see Mom and Marie's faces to know what their long pause means. It's pretty obvious, they're trying to hold back their laughter. Marie clears her throat. "You just gave birth four days ago. Your body endured a trauma. It just made a human being. You have to give yourself time to heal."

She hiccups and sniffles again. "No. I'll never be normal again. I think something went wrong. Like really, really wrong. Like, maybe, I need reconstructive surgery or something. My outside is puffy and angry, like some kind of deformed marshmallow. And my insides feel like a deflated balloon. I feel like an eighty-year-old hooker." She bursts into tears again. "My husband will never wanna touch me again."

Bullshit. I will always want her. I want her for the rest of my life. I'll prove it, right here and right now if I need to. Anything to stop my wife's tears. My dick is as ready as it's ever been.

They spend the next fifteen minutes comforting her, telling Merit that her body will return to normal—in fact, it will be even better than it was before. They tell her that her hormones are raging, and those little bastards are giving her an unrealistic vision of her own body.

"He'll want me?"

The brokenness in her voice absolutely shatters me. I wish I could kiss her right now. Kiss away all her worries, all her concern.

"Yes," Mom assures her. "My son is completely and totally in love with you."

"Trust me, as soon as you get clearance from the doctor, he'll wanna make love to you all the time," Marie says.

And when my mom starts talking about Kegel exercises and my dad's penis, I throw up a little bit in my mouth and decide that eavesdropping is highly overrated.

"He calmed down?" Her voice takes me by surprise.

Spinning around, I catch her leaning against the doorframe. She's back to wearing her simple and sexy-as-hell, white cotton nightgown. Her redwood hair is a wild mess, and her swollen breasts are calling to me, like a siren in the middle of the ocean.

Holy hell.

"What?" I ask, swallowing against my dry throat.

She pushes off the doorway and pads across the room. "Well, I can only assume he was crying. Because my husband knows better than to take him out of his crib when he's peacefully sleeping." She mocks me with sing-song words.

"Oh, absolutely," I say, giving her a little wink.

Wrapping an arm around my waist, she leans forward and kisses Daire's forehead, pausing to inhale his scent. "Mmm. I wonder when he will stop smelling so good?"

"Well, he definitely didn't smell good when he shit all over me this morning."

And it's true, he did.

When he gave a little cry at four this morning, letting us know he needed something, I woke up first and rushed to get him so Merit could sleep. Believe it or not, I heard him. Even my sleep habits have done a complete one-eighty since Daire came along. The slightest noise on the baby monitor makes me jump. There's no more sleeping through the noise of a freight train.

Or I guess I should say, no more sleeping through some crazy bitch breaking into my house and framing me for seducing a student.

It's like my actual body chemistry has changed.

Merit giggles. "Yeah, that was pretty gross." She snorts. "And funny."

"I'm glad you enjoyed it." I lean forward, capturing her mouth with mine. Her breath is hot and sweet, and she takes an extra second to deepen our kiss.

"Congratulations, Coach," she says, changing the subject.

"Ahh, so you already heard?"

"Another win. Who would have ever thought you'd be on track to win another State title? After everything you went through this year."

"After everything *we* went through."

She rubs her nose against Daire and pats my ass. "Come to bed. You need to sleep while you can. You never know when he'll wanna wake you up so he can poop on you again."

She walks out of the room, laughing at her own joke.

I gently lie my son back in the crib, making sure his Smart Sock is snug on his foot.

This is it.

This is life.

How'd I get so damn lucky?

Chapter 32

Merit

I pull back the fabric on the baby wrap carrier and look at Daire. He looks like an angel when he sleeps.

Who am I kidding... he looks like an angel all the time. My baby. My son. My perfect little boy.

And I can't get enough of him.

I decided to get us out of the house today. We both needed fresh air and sunshine, but I thought he would get too hot with us just sitting by the pool. So I decided we should take a walk through one of the parks in town. There's a mile-long walking trail that winds through a wooded area, so the temperature is naturally several degrees cooler.

I'm about halfway into the walk when I hear something. It sounds like someone walking through the woods. Like feet crunching on leaves and sticks.

Who the heck would be walking through the woods when there's a path right here?

I slow my stride and meander closer to the edge of the concrete, trying to see what's out there. If there's a damn bear or bobcat in these woods, I'm gonna be shitting a golden brick. And fighting like one of those MMA guys to keep Daire safe. I wrap my arms around him, hugging his little body close to mine. The hairs on my arms stand straight, and it feels like ants are crawling across my skin.

What the heck?

I hold my breath. Do I hear someone breathing?

Is someone out there?

Watching me? Following me?

Following *us*?

Another stick cracks in the woods, right in front of me.

All of a sudden, Holt's voice catches me by surprise. "I would run up there, but I don't wanna scare you."

I yelp. And a little pee comes out.

I spin around, catching him standing about ten feet behind me. "Holt Hill! You gave me a freakin' heart attack. What are you doing here?"

He eyes me up and down, studying my body like he can see right through my clothes, and then his mouth turns up into that sexy, confident, signature smirk. "You peed a little bit, didn't you?"

Bastard.

I snort, looking down to see if my scream woke Daire. Nope. Out like a light.

"Mer?" Holt draws out my name in a teasing voice.

I scoff. "Well, what do you expect? You scared me."

His laugh is breathless and perfect. As always. He trots up to me, wrapping an arm around my waist and stealing a peek at Daire. Lovingly, he rubs his fingertips across the crown of our son's head, brushing the soft hair away from his closed eyes. And then... he looks at me. I mean, he *looks* at me. Lifting his arms, he grabs his ballcap, and turns it around backward.

Slowly and methodically.

His right arm finds its way back to my waist and slides down to my ass, squeezing it. When I open my mouth to protest that someone may come along the path and see us, he uses that as an opportunity to kiss me. His mouth slants over mine, and his tongue pushes into me, licking and lapping, tasting and tangling.

There's a thousand different ways for Holt Hill to kiss me. And just when I think I've had the best he has to offer... he surprises me. Each and every time.

My breasts grow heavy and throb, pulsing with passion...and milk.

Desire and longing pool low in my stomach, making my core vibrate with an ache for more. So much more than the quick 'clit job' he gave me last night. We played nice, and he kept his tongue and fingers all in *exterior territory*, if you will. I was more than happy to return the favor with a blow job, but both of us are definitely excited—and nervous—to get the clearance from the doctor for intercourse.

Eventually, he pulls away, peppering my lips and jaw and neck with sweet, tender kisses. "Four more days," he whispers.

The countdown is officially on. I go to the doctor on Monday for my six-week follow-up, and we pray he will wave the white flag, giving us permission to do what we want.

What we need.

And if I'm truthful... the need is real. I need sex. I need his physical touch. My body is different than it was. Thoughts of inadequacy have plagued me off and on since Daire's birth. Sometimes, the feelings come out of nowhere, so sharp and so fast, it's like a knife to the chest. And Holt's the only one who can stop the bleeding. He's the only one who can stitch me and make me whole. I need him to love me and cherish me and make me feel beautiful.

And there's nothing that makes me feel more beautiful than when Holt stares into my eyes while making love to me.

"Think you can make it four more days?" I tease.

His gaze drops to my lips. "If you wrap those pouty and perfect lips around my cock and drain me like you did last night, I can probably make it."

Shit. My nipples are hard.

"And what about me?"

His head lowers, and his breath whispers across the shell of my ear, sending shivers down my spine, one slow inch at a time. "There's my girl. Greedy and ready for more? I can fuck that clit with my tongue. I watched the cum pour out of you last night, that beautiful little pussy of yours begging for more. And I can give it to you, baby. If you want my tongue and fingers on you for the next four days, you can bet that fine ass I'll give it to you."

And… Daire starts to cry.

We both frown and look down at our wriggling son, our feverish and lust-fueled trance broken.

"Maybe he doesn't like it when we talk dirty," I say, thinking about what we just exposed his ears to.

Holt just laughs and reaches into the baby wrap so he can wrangle Daire into his arms. I hold back the fabric, giving him easy access. "I bet he doesn't mind. He's probably thinking how incredibly lucky he is to have a Momma and a Daddy who love each other so much. A Daddy who wants to do nothing but worship the ground Momma walks on." He leans over and gives me a peck on my kiss-swollen lips.

In his arms, Daire settles down, eyes open, peacefully looking left and right to see what's happening in this new and unfamiliar surrounding. Falling in step together, we continue my late afternoon walk. "What are you doing here?" I ask him again, curious considering he never answered me the first time.

"It's Thursday. Remember…short practice today."

"Oh, that's right." I shake the baby fog from my brain. "My days are still so messed up and jumbled."

"I got your text saying that you were coming here, and I wanted to see you, of course." He looks around, studying the trees, bushes, and flowers lining both sides of the trail. "I've never been here. It's nice." He nods over to his left. "What were you doing when I got here? You were looking in the woods. Did you see something?"

"It was probably a squirrel or a chipmunk." I giggle, snorting on my laugh. "I was plotting in my head how I would attack if it were a bear or a bobcat."

Holt bounces with laughter, making Daire grin sideways. Yeah… he started smiling last week. He's a genius. And if anyone tells me it's just gas, I'm gonna throat punch them. "And just how would you fight if a bobcat pounced out of the woods?"

I shrug and thread my arm through his, taking care not to tug too hard so he doesn't lose his grip on Daire. (Like that would ever happen.) "I'd have to be scrappy. I've gotta protect what's mine."

He leans over and kisses my head, giving a soft and loving sigh when he breathes in the scent of my shampoo. "That's right. You do."

We're getting close to the end of the trail, looping back around to the parking lot, when a woman jogs past us. She's a perky little thing—perky boobs, perky ass, perky ponytail. And a perky little eyebrow that lifts and then winks at my husband.

My. Husband.

Red hot anger flares in my body.

How dare she? The man is holding his infant son in his arms.

And he's obviously not a single dad. I'm right freakin' here. Unless I somehow obtained the superhero power of invisibility without even knowing it.

Once again, Holt catches me off guard when he bends down and kisses my nose. "And there's my girl, protecting what's hers...right down to the scrunched-up nose."

My jaw slacks open. "I don't scrunch my nose."

Holt turns around. Walking backward, he pumps Daire's tiny fist in the air, like Daire's the one talking to me. "Oh baby, that's not a battle you're gonna win."

Chapter 33

Holt

I'm not surprised when I wake up and she's not here.

I was waiting for it. I've been waiting for it all day. But she didn't say anything, so I didn't want too either. I was putting the ball in her court, wanting to follow her lead, wanting to support her in any way I can.

Yanking the comforter off the bed, I silently trudge across the hallway, dragging it behind me. She's right where I knew she'd be, standing over his crib, watching him.

Daire is two months old today.

The same age as his namesake was when he passed away.

I don't have to say anything for her to know I'm here. The intensity of our love hammers through the darkness, chipping away at the fear. She knows I'm watching her.

Just like she's watching our son.

"How can people survive something like that?" she asks, not turning around.

"I have no idea," I answer honestly.

"My parents. Crutch and Ella. They've all lost a child. How do you go on living after that? If something happened to him…" her voice trails off, choking with emotion.

I wrap my arms around her and kiss her neck. "You don't have to worry about that. Nothing's gonna happen."

"You don't know that."

"You're right, I don't. But I have faith. That's all we can have as parents. Faith that everything will be all right. Faith that God will keep our son safe and healthy. That he'll grow up, become a strong and honorable man, and give us a slew of grandchildren."

Daire opens his eyes and blinks. We instantly do that thing all parents do—where you freeze and stop breathing, eagerly praying that your baby doesn't cry. Deciding our conversation isn't too important, he yawns and goes back to sleep.

Merit sniffles. "He's perfect."

I spin her around and wipe her silent tears. "You're perfect." Pulling her over to the loveseat tucked in the corner of the nursery, I settle her body next to mine and cover us with the comforter.

"We're gonna sleep in here?"

I lift an eyebrow. "You plan on leaving him tonight?"

She shakes her head. "No."

I drag my fingers through her hair, draping it over my arm so it doesn't get caught underneath us and yank her neck. "Yeah, me neither."

It doesn't take me long to doze off, comforted by the fact that we're both in the same room with Daire and he is safely snuggled in his crib with all the technology that's monitoring his breathing and heart rate. How did the fucking pioneers do this shit without smart phones and baby monitors and cameras? I'm a damn nervous wreck twenty-four-seven, and I *have* all of those things...

Anyway, I doze off, but for some reason, it's not a peaceful sleep. And since I'm in my new era of no longer sleeping through the end of the world, restless nights bother me. It's like my body knows when something is about to happen, when something's not right.

Leaning up on an elbow, I wipe the sleep from my eyes and check on Daire. He's still slumbering; I can hear his steady little baby snore. So, shit, why can't I sleep?

Merit's tucked against my body with her back against my front, but when I gently push the hair away from her eyes, I can feel the hitch in her breath. She stiffens, waiting to see if I'm going to say something or lie back down. "Mer? What's wrong? Are you still worried about him?"

Grabbing my hand, she kisses my wrist, mimicking the action I've become so fond of. "Everything's fine. I'm just having trouble sleeping. Don't worry about me."

Don't worry about her? That's like telling a starving man not to think about a steak dinner.

Even ignoring that flippant comment, it's pretty obvious to see that this has nothing to do with normal insomnia. It's something more. I don't even have to see her face to know that 'everything's fine' is a lie.

"Don't lie, Merit."

"Mmmm?"

"Something's wrong. Something's really bothering you. What is it?"

Instead of immediately answering, she grabs my arm, forcing me to hold her tighter. The act alone fills me with love and terror, all at the same time.

"Tell me the truth."

She inhales so deeply, her back shudders against my chest. "Do you ever feel like we cheated fate?"

"Cheated fate? What are you talking about?"

"Like... we weren't meant to be together, weren't meant to be happy? Like the universe ordered we should stay apart—stay broken up—and never heal, never forgive." Her voice lowers to a whisper, and I can hear the thick emotion, nearly preventing her from speaking. "Like the universe determined we shouldn't be a family. And then we broke those rules and did our own thing."

What. The. Hell.

I spring into a sitting position, bringing Merit with me. Manhandling her, I spin her around and haul her onto my lap. Cradling her cheeks, I wipe the runaway tears that are streaming down her face and fucking breaking my heart in the process. "What are you talking about? Where is this coming from?"

She glances over, immediately worried about waking Daire. "I... I don't know," she stutters. "It's just sometimes... I feel so happy, so loved, and so *in* love with you and Daire, that it almost feels like I'm doing something wrong. Something bad. Because what did I do to deserve this much joy?"

"Look at me." I force her wandering gaze back to my steady one. "We are right where we are supposed to be, right where we're meant to be. Together. Nothing tore us apart but my own stupidity. I won't even blame Delaney for it because that was all me. You are my everything. You and Daire are the reason I breathe, the reason my heart beats, the light to every dark thing in a bad world. Fate wants us together. It *needs* us together. Because if we aren't? The universe will cease to exist. Every single thing and every single person around us will implode. Our love? It's the one thing keeping the Earth in orbit."

I watch as my words calm her. Slowly, a peace settles on her face, bringing me a happiness that I'm going to hold onto forever. I dare the fates to rip it away from me. Fucking let them try; they won't get far. Nothing can pry this bliss from my steadfast grip. This joy is a prisoner of my heart—captive for all eternity—and I'm never letting it go.

"How'd I get so lucky? How could God make you just for me?" she asks.

I kiss her lips, relishing how soft and full they feel against my own. "The same way He made *you* for *me*."

Nodding, she buries herself against my chest. "You're right."

"Of course, I'm right. Aren't I always," I joke. She chuckles, blowing her hot breath across my bare skin. I give her a few more minutes to calm down before I press her for more details about her feelings. "Where in the world did all of that come from, Mer? Have you been feeling that way for a while?"

She shakes her head and furrows her brow. The moonlight slanting in through the blinds shades everything in streaks of black and blue. "I don't know. I've just felt... *off* the past couple of days. I guess it could be some delayed postpartum depression or something." She looks up at me and drags her finger across the stubble on my jaw. "You think that's it?"

I shrug. "It could be."

"And I've been a little paranoid too."

"Paranoid?"

"I thought someone was following me and Daire at the grocery store the other day. Some guy. And I had the same feeling that day at the park when you showed up."

What. The. Ever. Living. Fuck.

The hairs on my arms stand at attention, and a protective fury clenches my heart in its fist, squeezing it in a death grip. "What the hell? Are you serious?"

Well, that was a stupid question.

I have no idea why I asked it. Of course, she's serious.

"When I tried to look, I didn't actually see anybody," she says. Like those words alone will appease me.

"Are you sure?"

"Yeah. Do you think some of the other paparazzi are back? Do you think they are trying to get pictures of Daire?"

I drag my hand down my face, scratching my chin in thought and praying those vultures aren't chasing my son down grocery store aisles. I mean, he's only two months old; they're not going to see anything but maybe the occasional spit-up. This is exactly why we did posed photos last month, sold them, and donated all the proceeds to The Hill Family Charities. "I don't know. I can reach out to Chloe and see if she can ask around?" Lifting her chin, I rub my nose against hers. "But if anything like that happens again—if you get that feeling, no matter how minor—call me immediately. I'll drop everything and come to you. And if for some crazy reason, I don't answer, call Ridge or Crutch. Got me?"

She nods, exhaling all of the tension and feelings of powerlessness from her body. "Okay, *sir*."

Despite the serious nature of the moment, a smile tugs against my lips.

Her arms snag around my neck, drawing me back to her. Our kiss is slow and languid. I work my tongue around hers, sucking and nipping, showing her that we have all the time in the world to be happy. Our pain has come and gone. We weathered it; we survived it.

We have nothing to worry about.

Merit

I wrap my legs tighter around his waist.

My hands chart the muscles of his back, wishing moments like this would never end. Sliding my fingers through his hair, I tug on the blond curls, just the way he likes.

Just the way *I* like.

His hot breath skates across my neck, and his facial scruff scrapes against my cheek. "Tell me," he commands, playfully nibbling on my ear.

"Your cock is so big," I jokingly tease. My raspy giggle strangles in my throat.

Lifting on his forearms, he pumps into me harder, making my back arch. I bite back a scream. "The other thing," he growls.

My eyes find his. It's still dark outside, so the deep blue of his irises is black. "I love you."

He gives me a winning smirk. "There's my girl." Rising to his knees, he lifts my ass in the air and feeds his body into mine. Over and over and over. "So fucking wet. So fucking perfect. So fucking mine." His calloused fingers play across my heated skin, setting it ablaze, scorching every part of me.

I'd be lying if I said it wasn't different. If I said it didn't *feel* different.

Because it does.

I mean, it's just science.

Holt? His body is the same. Long and lean. Hard and muscular.

But mine is different. And it always will be. I grew a tiny human, and that same tiny human came out of my body.

Yes, the sex is different, but I actually think it's better. My orgasms last longer. They're more intense, which I didn't even know was possible. More than that, our emotional connection is stronger. He's my husband. Forever. And we made a family. Together. It might not have been the most conventional approach, but we arrived at the same place, nonetheless.

And trust me, we are counting down the days until we can get rid of the condoms. I only started taking birth control pills last week, so we've been having to play it safe with Holt's self-proclaimed super sperm. Much to his chagrin. Apparently, he made a promise to himself while I was pregnant that he would never again—in his life—wear another condom.

Seeing as how I am the one in control of my pussy and can withhold it from him if I so choose, he quickly modified his promise. I told him that if he wanted to stick it in this momma, he had to wrap it up until the birth control pills take effect.

"Merit." My name is a whisper on his lips, letting me know he's close.

I reach for him, only able to grab his thighs because of the angle. "More," I beg.

That's another thing. My orgasms may be better, but it takes me longer to get there, simply because I spend the first five minutes of each romp thinking I hear Daire cry.

My plea spurs him. Holt never wants to leave me unsatisfied. And because of that...I stay truly satisfied.

All the time.

He shifts his position. Bracing one hand on the headboard, he lowers his body onto mine, careful not to crush me, but using his pelvis to create the perfect amount of burning friction against my clit. "Rub against me, baby. Give that greedy little clit what it needs." His other hand grabs my hip, digging into my soft skin with a bruising force, determined to mark me with his love for days to come.

Holy crap.

It hits me like a freight train. Bliss. Wonderful and pure bliss. Unable to help myself, I cry out. Holt captures my scream in his own mouth, kissing the holy hell out of me, not even caring we both have rancid morning breath.

And then he stops kissing me. Stops even breathing.

His own orgasm is so intense, I worry his heart might stop beating. I put my hand on his chest to reassure myself.

Thump. Thump. Thump.

It hammers in a fast rhythm, soothing my nerves.

Eventually, he chuckles and slowly rolls off me. Pulling me against him, he kisses the top of my head. "You afraid I'm having a heart attack?"

"Well, you did kiss my morning breath. That's enough to send anyone into cardiac arrest." I giggle, snorting.

"Good thing I was caught up in other stuff besides your breath." He grabs a tissue from the nightstand and rolls the used condom in it. "I'll be so damn glad when we can stop using these."

"For someone who never went without a condom before me, you sure are fond of riding bareback now," I say, teasing him.

"That's because your body is made for mine. My wife. Forever." He lifts up on an elbow. "Besides, you basically just said I'm hung like a horse. Bareback should make you happy," he says, giving me his sexy little wink before crawling out of bed. Hitting the alarm clock, he turns it off before it actually starts buzzing.

I stare at his naked body as he slinks across the bedroom. "Why are you still meeting the kids for morning workout? It's the week before Christmas break. Aren't they ready for some time off?"

He pauses at the bathroom door, gifting me more time to ogle him. "You'd think so, but I think they're still dealing with the disappointment of the loss. I mean, they fought hard as hell, and there's not one thing about our playtime that I would've changed." He shrugs. "The title just wasn't in the cards for us this year. But I can't help but think they all wanted some *triumphant return* for me," he says, using finger quotes. "Like something in an inspirational movie or something." He sighs. "I think they feel like they let me down. Anyway, they keep showing up every morning. As long as they show up, I'll show up."

He's right. It was a hard-fought game. It's hard to even fathom that they made it to the State Championship for the second year in a row. But then, to lose by only one field goal? A field goal earned by a field position from a questionable penalty? It was hard on everyone. Especially Nate. Holt actually played him in over half the games. He even started in three of them. It's clear to see he's got a future in this.

But something about him reminds me of Holt.

Something tells me Nate's view of football is just like Holt's.

It's not my life. It's just a really fun game that I happen to be really good at. It's fun. That's why I love playing.

And that approach is good. It'll help keep a level head on his shoulders.

"What about you?" he asks with a smile. "You and my son headed off to work today?"

"Yep. There's a ton of deliveries scheduled. For both stores." I can't help but smile myself. Things are coming along great. We didn't really hit the ground running until a couple of weeks ago. I needed time to bond with Daire and heal from giving birth, and Kyra still had to make a couple of trips back to Minnesota to finalize everything for her and Toby's permanent move back here. I think Toby was more excited about the move than Kyra, considering they'd been living with her parents the past several months. But we've been hitting it like gangbusters the last few weeks. Yesterday, the contractors finally finished the interior door between the two stores. It's an open archway, connecting everything so we can move back and forth as needed.

And I'm more than glad that work is done now. Because the noise was too much for Daire, so everyone's been watching him for the past week while I was at work—Ridge, Ella, Cullen, Teresa, Dana, and Nancy. It's been a revolving door of love. But I missed him. Like, a lot.

We agreed that Daire would come to work with me until it becomes impractical. I know that interaction with other children is important, and when the time comes, we'll put him in the same preschool as Hardy and Ty.

He flips the light switch in the bathroom. "Well, I've got that meeting at the central office this afternoon. It should be done about two. I don't have to go back to school after that. I'll stop by and help." Before he shuts the door, he stares at me. Deeply. Intently.

Quickly growing self-conscious, I cover my bare chest with the sheet and try to calm the wild strands of my bedhead.

Chuckling under his breath, he just shakes his head. "I love you, Merit. Get some more sleep."

Snuggling back in bed, content and happy, I'm about to drift off to sleep when I hear Daire babbling through the baby monitor. That means he's had enough rest. I've got about three minutes before he gets bored and starts crying. Tugging my nightgown over my head, I count my blessings with every step down the hall.

"How many more boxes?" Holt asks Craig.

"A bunch. I could barely fit anybody else's stuff on the truck."

"Hey, I'm trying to fill up two stores," I protest.

Holt twists back and forth, stretching his back. When he catches me watching him, he winks. "You sure? Maybe you just like watching me flex my muscles." Just to prove his point, he lifts his arms and slowly spins his ballcap around backward.

He likes to play dirty.

"My muscles too," Craig jokes, rubbing his beer belly.

"That's it," I laugh. "Definitely." Reaching into one of the boxes, I pull out a set of cardigans with butterflies on them. "Anyway, if you wanna blame someone, Craig, blame my husband. He's the one who put me *back* in business."

"Well, my wife deserves it." Holt's voice holds a delicious sweetness, a real honesty.

Craig wipes the sweat from his brow. "Congratulations, by the way. On the wedding, I mean."

I'm about to thank him, but I'm interrupted by the front door chime. "That must be Raylee," I tell Holt. She said she was going to stop by and check out the progress. The truth is, she needs her Daire fix. She can't go too long without getting cuddles from her nephew. Tossing the unfolded sweaters to the side, I head out of the back room.

When I turn the corner, my life ends.

Literally.

One second, I'm fine. I'm happy.

The very next second, I die. My heart stops beating, and my soul drains from my body, slithering out of my pores and coiling on the floor around me like a snake.

A strange man is standing over my son as he peacefully slumbers in his playpen. In fact, the man's not just standing over Daire, he's picking him up.

The stranger glances at me, and our eyes meet.

I'm in shock, so I'm not exactly sure how long it takes my brain to process what I see. But at some point, it does, and I realize he's not a stranger at all. He's a man I know.

Trenton Trevors.

Heidi's uncle. Denise's brother. Delaney's former boyfriend—the only person to speak on her behalf at the sentencing hearing.

I open my mouth, prepared to scream, ready to tell him to get the hell away from my child. But nothing happens. Just a small growl comes out, not the bloodcurdling scream that I want. My eyes blur, and my body feels like it's weighted down in quicksand.

The first step is the hardest.

It feels like it takes me ten years to make that one small step. In reality, it's probably the fastest I've ever moved.

Trenton scoops him into his arms, and Daire wakes up, gasping from the sudden movement. Racing forward, I reach for my baby, ready to punch and claw and pry this bastard's eyeballs right out of their sockets. But he's prepared for me. He sidesteps and slams me into the side of a metal rack that we haven't finished putting together. I topple on top of it, slamming my right temple into a sharp edge. The pain seers through me, sending a sizzling ache down my spine. A bright white light flashes across my vision, blinding me for a second.

And in that second, I die again.

Because when my blurry vision returns, I watch that man walk right out the door with my son.

Chapter 35

Merit

The good humor in Holt's voice jars me. It's completely out of place and completely foreign for the moment. He just doesn't know it yet. "Mer? What'd you break now?"

I flop around on the ground, stumbling to get up. Blood is already dripping down my face, pooling on my oversized T-shirt.

There's a dizziness making me sick, making me unstable.

Walking from the back, Holt's eyes widen when he sees me. Concern and worry etch into his face, marring its beauty. Darting to my side, he wraps an arm around my waist and easily lifts me to my feet. "What happened? Are you okay?" He tugs my chin, trying to look at the side of my head. "Let me see."

"Daire." My croaked whisper sounds like a wounded animal.

Holt stops breathing.

Glancing at the playpen, he turns back to me when he doesn't see our baby. I'm already taking a step in the direction of the front door, willing one foot in front of the other.

That's all he needs.

He takes off in a mad sprint. I've never seen someone run so fast. Ever.

And I never will again. It's inhuman.

It's superhuman.

By the time I make it out the front door, all hell has broken loose. Holt's halfway hanging out of the driver's side door of an old SUV. It's clear he's trying to pull Trenton out of the car, but it's not working. Trenton starts to drive—erratically weaving left and right, stopping and going. He finally gets traction and steps on the gas. That doesn't stop Holt. He tries to run along with the car. Eventually, his feet start dragging, and he's thrown. Slamming into the asphalt, he rolls a couple of times before stopping.

I'm so torn on what to look at.

Do I watch my injured husband roll across the parking lot?

Do I watch the man drive away, kidnapping my son?

Kyra's voice echoes in the background. "What's going on?"

Jumping up, Holt races back over. His knees look like they've been through a paper shredder. They're drenched in blood and decorated with rocks. His shirt is torn, and his arms are covered in scratches and road burn. "Call the cops!" he screams, shocking the-ever-living-shit out of Kyra.

Hauling me into his arms, he races to his truck. Shoving me over the console, I tumble into the passenger seat. I'm still trying to right myself when he puts the truck in drive and yanks around the line of cars waiting for the front parking spaces at the coffee shop. He drives across the median, kicking up grass and dirt all around us. We bounce violently across the curb and push our way onto the street. Brakes squeal. Horns honk. I brace my hand against the window. Blood smears everywhere.

The SUV is two cars in front of us. Holt speeds up, not slowing down.

"Put your seat belt on," he yells. Tugging his cell phone from his pocket, he tosses it on my lap. "Call the police."

I have no idea how I have the coordination to call 911. But I do.

It doesn't even feel like my fingers are connected to my body. It's like I'm a marionette and someone else is pulling my strings, operating me, and making me move.

I don't even let them answer before I shout into the phone. "Our son's been kidnapped! Our son's been kidnapped!"

Holt weaves around the traffic, trying to keep up with Trenton's car. With a shaky hand, I buckle my seat belt while trying my best to explain what's happening to the 911 operator. We're running red lights and creating absolute fucking havoc. Things are happening at a speed which my brain can't even comprehend. It's like I'm processing the scene before me through flashes of a dream. Like short, vibrant fireworks are popping and bursting behind my eyelids every time I blink.

When a cement truck nearly plows into the side of Trenton's SUV, I scream. I can barely hear the piercing shriek above the ringing in my own ears.

It doesn't take long for the 911 operator to tell us to stop chasing them.

She wants us to stop chasing after our son?

Stop? Is she out of her fucking mind? That's my son.

"Over my fucking dead body. I'm not stopping," Holt says, leaving nothing up for debate.

The double talking is making my throbbing head split wide open. I plop the cell phone down in the cup holder. It's on speaker, and she keeps talking; but I can't pay any attention to what she's saying. Not her.

I need to focus on Holt. And Daire.

He looks over at me, wild-eyed and crazed. "I'm not stopping."

I nod. "I know."

He takes a sharp turn, following Trenton down a service road and back onto Main Street. It doesn't take a genius to see he's about to hit the rural highway. It's one of the backroads that eventually leads to a web of interstates going all over the Southeast.

"If he gets away, we will never see our son again."

Tears stream down my face. Licking my lips, I taste salt and blood.

"Merit! Did you hear me?"

I nod, unable to speak.

"I'm not letting him out of my sight. If he gets away, we will never see Daire again. I need you to understand what that means. Do you understand? I'll fucking wreck him into the side of a tree if I have to. Tell me you understand."

All I can think is *Daire's not in a car seat.*

Where is my baby? Is he bouncing around in there? Is he already hurt? Already dead?

"Merit!!"

"Yes! I understand!"

All of a sudden, we side swipe a car, sending it plowing into a metal guardrail separating the northbound lanes from the southbound lanes. "Shit!" Holt spins the wheel, quickly recovering. Stepping on the gas, he refuses to backdown. "I'm sorry. I'm sorry. I'm sorry." He mumbles under his breath, apologizing to the lives we might've just hurt.

Turning in my seat, I watch steam pour from the crumpled hood of the little black car. I don't see anyone moving.

Holy shit. What if we just killed someone?

A pickup truck tries to block our path, obviously thinking we're a menace to society and trying to play Good Samaritan.

Holt cuts to the side, avoiding him and choosing to drive into oncoming traffic, instead. I close my eyes and grab the hanging door handle above me. A jumble of profanities vomit from Holt's mouth. And still, I keep my eyes closed. Once I feel the jostle and dips of us passing back over the median, I open my eyes.

On the rural road, the traffic dies down, but that doesn't stop the chase. I'm too scared to even look at the speedometer. The houses and trees lining the road are flying by me so fast, that alone tells me all I need to know.

We are reckless.

And fucking determined.

In the background, the 911 operator is still talking. Yelling, really. But I don't have time for that.

We lose sight of Trenton's SUV as it goes over a small hill. "Speed up!" I scream at Holt. My voice is scratchy, and it feels like my head is about to explode. My vision starts to blacken around the edges.

The nose of the truck catches up with the horizon, and before we know it, we're right on him. Giving the gas one last punch, Holt rams into the back of Trenton's car.

Hard. Really hard.

I slam forward in my seat. Fortunately, I'm strapped into my seat belt. That's the only thing that stops my head from blasting against the windshield. Holt's not so lucky. He never put his seat belt on. His head smacks against the steering wheel right as the air bags deploy. The loud pop hurts my ears.

Peeking above the pillowed device and puff of powder, I watch as Trenton's car spins around and around, eventually coming to a stop after slamming into a concrete pillar at the threshold of a small bridge.

Fifty feet below, a swampy pile of marshlands glisten under the already-setting winter sun.

The pain of the wreck doesn't slow Holt down. He jumps from the truck, like he doesn't feel a thing.

The blood on his air bag tells a different story.

I fumble with my seat belt. It takes a couple of attempts before it finally releases. Stumbling from the truck, my bleeding head flings blood all over the door.

I can't even see straight. It feels like my brain is a balloon, ready to burst. My entire face feels numb. I blink, forcing myself to focus. Trenton is already running toward Holt, with a baseball bat in his hand. He's covered in his own blood and dragging his right leg behind him in a weird limp. Right when he swings, Holt lifts his left arm, shielding his face. The sound of the wood on Holt's arm makes my stomach turn. I can hear his bones breaking.

I know the sound of broken arms quite well.

Holt howls in pain.

Trenton repositions himself, dragging the bat high above his head. Holt takes that split second of freedom to tackle him. Burying his shoulders into Trenton's waist, he pushes with the force of his legs, treating Trenton like a tackle dummy, pushing him backward and backward and backward.

Refusing to drop the bat, Trenton's hurt leg causes him to stumble over the lift of the foot curb of the bridge guardrail, throwing him off balance. Holt uses that to his advantage. Dipping low, he grabs the back of Trenton's thighs. Screaming through the pain of a broken arm—and who knows what other damage—he flips Trenton over the side of the bridge.

My hands fly to my mouth, covering my scream.

Holt doesn't even bother looking over the side to see where Trenton fell. Turning on his heels, he runs over to the car. Yanking open the passenger door with enough force to tear it from its hinges, he calls to our son, like Daire's old enough to actually answer. "Daire! Daire!" If I weren't about to die again, I'd find it funny.

The last thing I see before my world fades to black is my husband pulling the limp body of our baby from the mangled wreckage of the car.

Chapter 36

Holt

I lean forward, looking at her sleeping body. For the five-thousandth time.

"When is she gonna wake up?" I grumble, dragging my good hand through my still bloody and dirty hair.

Plopping back down in the chair, I accidentally hit my temporary cast and wince in pain. Motherfucker, that hurts.

Deke shakes his head. "Son, you may be the most impatient man I've ever met."

I lift an amused eyebrow and nod to the leg he's bouncing up and down. "You realize that leg's been shaking nonstop for the past hour? If you were holding a glass of milk, it'd be butter by now."

He snorts. "Eh, that's just the farmer in me." He shrugs. "Always needing to move."

Marie reaches over and holds his hand, too nervous to join the teasing. But who can blame her, she only stopped crying a couple of hours ago.

Holding hands—it's a sweet gesture, and it makes me miss my own wife. She's only two feet away, but it feels like a million miles. She's been off the anesthesia for hours now. She should be awake.

A small little moan comes from the hospital bed. My body instantly reacts, jumping to be by her side. Pain sears through me, pulsing through every nerve-ending. But it doesn't matter. Nothing matters now. Because that little moan is the sweetest sound I've ever heard.

Her eyes flutter beneath her closed lids, and she moans again. Finally, she blinks. One. Two. Three times. It takes a minute for her eyes to focus, but eventually they find mine.

"There's my girl," I whisper.

Her swollen face clouds with foggy confusion. When she opens her mouth, nothing but a groggy whimper comes out. I'm not supposed to give her anything to drink when she wakes up—not until the doctors clear her—but I know she has to be thirsty. I dip my fingers in my cup full of melted ice chips and rub them across her lips. Her tongue immediately darts out, licking the droplets. Knowing my good hand still has crusty, dried blood on my fingernails doesn't stop me. It probably should, but it doesn't. Slowly, she works her lips back and forth, easing the dryness.

She looks over at Deke and Marie. "Hey, sweetie," Deke's voice immediately cracks with emotion. Marie's started crying again, but this time her smile overshadows the worry.

I know the second it hits her. The memory. The reality of what happened.

Just like always, I can read her face.

Why?

Because Merit was built for me. And only me.

Her eyes widen in fear, and she immediately flinches from the pain in her tender skin.

"He's fine. He's safe," I assure her.

Worried I don't know what she's thinking, she drags our son's name from her scratchy throat. "Daire."

"He's fine. I promise. Not a scratch on him. He's safe. Mom and Dad took him home to sleep. You'll see him soon."

There's so much more to say, but the doctors and nurses come in to check her. Pushing me out of the way, they spend the next several minutes checking her stitches and reading monitors. The activity completely works her into a frenzy. The only thing that calms her down is listening to my voice and holding my hand. My good hand, that is. By the time they leave the room, her eyes are already starting to fall. She's completely exhausted, but because she's curious, she keeps trying to talk, keeps trying to ask questions. But her words come out jumbled and sleepy.

"Mer, get some rest. I promise we'll be right here when you wake up. We'll talk about everything." I lean forward and kiss her forehead. "I'll be right here. I swear."

The second she's back asleep, the orthopedic surgeon, Dr. Cain, steps into the room. "I heard she woke up. Everything looks good?"

Ridge leans against the door, hands shoved in his pockets.

Marie nods. "So far so good. The doctor says she's gonna be just fine."

He pins me with a stare. "Does this mean I can finally take you into surgery?"

"No. She fell back asleep before I could really talk to her. I need to speak to her first. What if she wakes back up and doesn't remember that I told her Daire is all right."

"Then, we'll tell her," Deke says.

Dr. Cain frowns and shakes his head. "I have to advise against waiting any longer, Holt. The longer we wait, the more damage there could be."

"Holt." Ridge's stern voice, pierces my ears. "You need surgery. Now."

"I can't. I promised her I would be here when she wakes up." I look at my best friend—my brother—knowing he'll understand. "You know what that means."

Sighing, Ridge clamps down on Dr. Cain's shoulder. "C'mon, Doc. We need to give him more time. He made a promise. He can't break it. That would make him a liar. And he doesn't lie. Not to Merit, he doesn't."

I'm crunching on some fresh ice chips, dreaming of the tallest glass of ice water known to mankind. Since I'm still in line for immediate surgery, I'm not allowed to eat or drink anything.

And that just plain sucks.

It's been three hours since Merit fell back asleep, and I needed to stretch my legs for a minute. The soreness of every bump and bruise and cut is starting to settle in my body with a vengeance. My two black eyes make me look like a rabid racoon. My shredded knees—which still need stitches from where the asphalt tore at the waxy scars from my previous surgery—are staining the bandages with fresh blood. And my broken arm? Well, let's not even go there.

When I round the corner of the hospital room and see Merit sitting up, awake and talking, I nearly shit my pants.

Well, not literally. But I do drop the ice chips.

"What the hell?" I say, laughing. "How long has she been awake?" I ask Deke and Marie.

"About fifteen, twenty minutes. We told her you'd be right back."

"Did you tell her anything?" I ask them.

Marie shakes her head. "No, that's your place." She smiles genuinely. "She's your wife."

"You know, *she* is right here," Merit says. Her voice is scratchy and shaky, but perfect nonetheless. "I'm not sure what all is wrong with me," she frowns, studying my war-torn body, "or you, for that matter. But I'm pretty sure I'm not deaf."

I can't help myself. Bending forward, I kiss her, pouring my love into her. Her dry lips grate against mine like sandpaper, and her breath smells like she's been eating a shit sandwich.

All in all, it's the best kiss I've ever had.

Because she's okay. And Daire's okay. And we're still a family.

She doesn't waste any time, immediately bombarding me with questions. "He's okay? Really?"

"Really," I nod. "He was on the floorboard of the SUV. There wasn't much damage there. There was one small scratch on his leg, but nothing worse than what he does with his own little fingernails."

Baby fingernails are sharp.

"You're sure? You had the doctors check him? What about internal injuries? Damage we can't see?"

"We're sure," Deke answers for me, biting back a smile. "Your husband might have gone a little overboard. I think *'berserk'* is what I heard from one of the nurses."

Her forehead creases in question. "What's that mean?"

I shrug. "I might not have been satisfied with just the two pediatricians on staff."

"You got them fired?"

She's so freakin' funny.

"No, but..." I draw out my words. "I might've flown in a couple of doctors from Atlanta."

"What? What doctors? Was he acting sick or hurt? What had you so worried about Daire?"

"Not just Daire. You too." I gently hold her hand, careful to avoid the IV sticking out. "I had some connections from playing—some really great doctors I met before. There's a traumatic injury pediatric specialist, and a micro-neurosurgeon who's also certified in facial reconstruction and plastics."

She gasps in horror. "He needed facial reconstruction?"

"Not him. You."

Her eyes widen. Untangling her hand from mine, she gasps when she feels the bandage on the side of her face. "I needed facial reconstruction?"

I shake my head. "No, Mer, that's a poor choice of words," I explain. "But that cut to the side of your head was really bad. It actually severed your superficial temporal artery. That's why you bled so much. Not to mention, blood was getting trapped between your scalp and skull, creating swelling."

She feels the edge of the bandage again. Pressing a little harder, she winces. "Am I gonna be okay?" She bites down on her lip. "My face feels a little numb."

"That should all go away," I assure her. "The cut was pretty jagged, but he did an excellent job. He wants you to heal for a couple of weeks, and then he'll do another surgery. After that? He says you won't notice anything at all. You'll never even know you got cut."

"How did you even get him here?" She looks around the room, searching for something. "Wait, how long have I been out of it. How many days have I missed?"

I can't help but laugh. I could play a joke on her and tell her it's been a week.

She immediately cocks her head. "Holt Hill, this is not the time for jokes."

"I thought *I* was the one who could read *your* mind? Have you been holding out on me?" I tease with a wink.

She's not amused.

"It's Saturday afternoon. It's not even been a full twenty-four hours."

"And you had time to fly doctors in? How?"

Crutch's voice booms from the doorway. "I might know some state troopers in the Atlanta area."

Her eyes flicker back and forth between the two of us. "Holy crap. You had the doctors arrested?"

Crutch chuckles. "I don't have *that* kind of pull. But they may have had police escorts to the Atlanta airport after they agreed to come." He clears his throat. "I guess your husband can be pretty persuasive when he wants to be."

Please. Those doctors jumped at the opportunity. To be the ones to save the redeemed football hero, his injured wife, and kidnapped baby? The doctors may be great, but trust me, they know a dollar sign when they see one. They can ride this for the rest of their careers.

Crutch dramatically sighs. "Not to mention the private planes to our local, podunk airport."

Merit's gulp is audible. "Private planes? Do we have enough money for that?"

I take a moment to soak in her innocence. Just another one of the many reasons I love my wife.

"Can you please stop spilling all of my overprotective secrets to my woman?"

Crutch just gives me a shit-eating grin. "And can I please tell everyone she's awake?" Switching eye contact, he looks to Deke and Marie for their approval as well.

"Yeah, make sure Mom and Dad head this way with Daire. She wants to see him."

Tears fill her eyes, and she nods. "Yes. Definitely."

I hand her a tissue with my good hand. "Don't rub, just dab," I tell her. "You have to be careful with the stitches."

"But I'm gonna be okay?"

"You're already okay." Emotion catches in my throat, making it hard to speak.

I can't believe how close I came to losing it all. It still feels like a nightmare. Like something that didn't really happen. I've just been going through the motions—focusing on the health of my wife and son. I haven't given myself a chance to fully digest what happened.

And that includes killing someone.

Her voice trembles. "What about you?" Her finger reaches out and traces my facial scruff. "Your face is black and blue."

"The steering wheel won that battle."

"Did you break anything?"

"Not in my face."

"Your arm." Horror streaks across her face. "I heard it. When he hit you with the baseball bat, I heard it break."

Marie sniffles, wiping away more tears. "Oh, my goodness."

I snort. "Yeah, that didn't feel too good."

"That's it?" she asks, nodding to the cast. "It looks kinda flimsy. How long do you have to wear it?"

I glance at Deke and Marie, pausing before answering. "Well... I... I actually need some surgery myself."

"You do? When?"

Ridge strolls into the room, smiling brightly at Merit. "Look at you. You're a sight for sore eyes."

"Ridge, Holt needs surgery." Merit thinks she's the first person to deliver this news.

He cocks an eyebrow in my direction. "Yeah, I know. I'm the one who's been trying to calm his orthopedic surgeon down since last night."

"Since last night?"

I skirt the subject. "I flew in Dr. Cain too. You heard me talk about him. He did my surgeries last time—my fusion and my knee work."

"Yeah, but what is Ridge talking about? Calming him down?"

I scowl at Ridge. "Nothing," I say, trying to downplay it. "He just wanted to do surgery last night, as soon as he got here. And... I wanted to wait."

"You mean you wanted to wait until my surgery was done and you knew I was okay."

"There was no way in hell I was gonna let you wake up without me by your side. No damn way."

"But waiting may've caused more damage," she says with a sniffle. "Is your arm hurting?"

Yeah. It feels like I'm being pummeled by a hailstorm. And the ice balls are stuffed with razor blades.

Since I don't lie to her, I just shrug with a smile. "It'll be fine. It's not my throwing arm."

Not satisfied with my answer, she defers to the firefighting paramedic. "Ridge?"

"Broken in six places. He needs two rods and more screws than a Home Depot. There could be permanent nerve damage from waiting, and limitations to his mobility."

I roll my eyes. "Well, thanks for sugarcoating it, dumbass. Why don't you go tell Dr. Cain I'll be ready as soon as I reunite my wife with my son."

"Holt, how could you wait? This could affect your career, the way you coach."

"Hey, I told you. Nothing comes before our family. Not even football." Wrapping my good arm around her, I hold her close to me. Her hair smells like blood and antiseptic.

After a couple of minutes, her haunted whisper cuts through the room. "What happened to him? Is he dead?"

I clear my throat, trying to find the words. I repeated them ten times over for the authorities, but it's different saying them to Merit. Because I never want her to be scared of me.

And frankly, I'm a little scared of myself.

What if this makes me different?

What if this changes me?

It was different before, with the arrest. Because I didn't do that. I didn't do what I was accused of.

But this?

I did it.

There's no denying I did it.

"He's dead. I killed him."

Merit

Passing by the hallway mirror, I check my face.

Holt was right. The surgeon was good. Excellent, really.

Fifteen days later, and my scar is healing into a thin pink line. It's somewhat noticeable, but not glaring. And you can't even see it when looking at my face head-on.

One more surgery and it will be gone forever.

And that's what I've spent the past few days thinking about. This scar—it's the pinnacle of the worst fucking twelve months that any human could ever have.

Yet, it's also been the best twelve months that any human could ever have.

A battle between good and evil. Right and wrong. Forever and never.

And we are...the war has finally been won. And we are the victors.

Me. My husband. My son.

Holt smiles the second I walk in the living room. He's laid across the couch, holding his cell phone in his right hand while his casted left arm is propped on a pillow. My eyes are instantly drawn to his taut, tan skin. He just finished working out, and he's shirtless.

I assume my husband is the only man in the world who willingly chooses to work out while recovering from a near-death experience.

He said his arm may be broken, but the rest of him is perfectly capable of moving.

I straighten a sagging ornament on the Christmas tree and plop down next to him.

"And everything's taken care of?" he asks the person on the other end of the line. After a second, he rolls his eyes. "Yes, Rob, I know they haven't even talked about kids yet. But one day, they'll have kids, and they'll know what we went through. I mean, I know they say they understand now, but it'll make more sense to them once they have their own children. And if they never have kids, we'll just open the trust to them. I just wanna make sure they're taken care of." He lowers his voice and shakes his head. "I could've hurt them."

He's talking about the people in the other car we hit. Turns out, it was a couple of newlyweds. They just married the summer before and were in town visiting friends. Fortunately, they weren't even injured when we hit them. It's a miracle really. It could've been bad. Holt's already given them money for a new vehicle, but he didn't feel like that was enough. Especially after he found out that they turned down interviews and paydays from every major TV news program, newspaper, and magazine in the country. Everybody wanted to talk to the young husband and wife whom Holt Hill *'nearly killed'* in the wild chase to save his kidnapped son. But they refused to talk. They said it wouldn't be right to exploit our tragedy. So, Holt decided to establish a trust for their future children—education expense, medical expense, things like that. So, they don't have to worry.

Rob, the new attorney for the Foundation—who's also acting as our personal attorney—thought the idea was crazy. But he's slowly learning the man my husband is.

Honorable and loyal. The epitome of a family man.

The complete opposite of Trenton Trevors.

For a while, we were worried the police would charge us with something, despite the assurances from Crutch and Marcum. If not murder, then public endangerment or something like that because of the way we drove through town. But we did what we had to do. That became more evident with everything the police found.

His trunk told a story that would make anyone sick. He packed all of his belongings with no intention of ever coming back. Money, passport, guns, computer. Even an old baseball trophy. His laptop confirmed his plans for our son.

He was going to sell him.

Holt was right; we never would've seen Daire again.

There was already a buyer lined up in Mexico.

There was no plan for ransom, even though Holt would've given every single penny he had to get Daire back safely. No, Trenton wanted us to wallow in pain. He wanted us to feel loneliness and despair. Just like him.

How do we know?

Also, in the trunk was a handwritten letter already stuffed in an envelope and addressed to Holt and me. It was even stamped. He was just waiting to mail it.

And now he's dead. And I never thought I would say I was happy to see someone dead, but I am.

Holt's struggled with it more, knowing that his hands physically killed someone. But at least he's had people to talk to. Our family. Both Crutch and Marcum were in the military before joining the sheriff's department. They've never come right out and said they've killed people—but it's pretty plain to see. There's an empathy there that the *normal* person just doesn't have.

He hangs up the phone and pretends to make a big show of looking behind my shoulder, down the hall. "Letting our son wander the house by himself? Might I suggest playing with the breakables in the trophy room? Perhaps watching a porno in the theater room?"

Snorting, I toss a pillow at him. He easily catches it with his good hand. "I put him down for his nap early. I swear he understood me when I told him we're having Christmas Eve supper at Ella's, so he needed to rest. He immediately yawned and scrunched his butt like he does when he's ready to snuggle."

It's true. Daire's a genius.

Smartest baby ever.

I lift an eyebrow. "Besides, I better never catch him watching a porno."

Holt flashes me his sexy grin. The blinking Christmas tree lights shine across his face, highlighting his freckles. "You realize our son will be seventeen one day, right? He'll be a dirty, filthy-minded little seventeen-year-old. Who watches porno and hides it from his parents."

I cover my ears with my hands and hum. "You're lying to me. You promised never to do that."

Laughing, he pulls my hand down and lovingly kisses my wrist. "You're right. It's a horrible lie." His hand traces my thigh. I can feel his callouses through the thin fabric of my tights. "The doctor's office called while I was working out. They're shutting down until after New Year's and wanted to know if you decided when to have the last surgery?"

I nibble on the corner of my lip. "I'm not gonna have the surgery."

Confusion shrouds his features. "Huh?"

"You can barely see it. It's healing so much better than I thought it would. But... he's right. The doctor, I mean. If he does another surgery, he'll make the scar disappear forever. I don't think I want it to disappear forever. I think I want it. To remind me of what we nearly lost. To remind me of what we have to fight for. Me and you."

He quietly sits, not saying anything.

Nerves fire in my stomach like flaming acid.

"Unless you want me to have the surgery? Unless you find it hard to be attracted to me..." My voice trails off as I reach up and trace the thin line with my finger.

Roughly wrapping his hand around my arm, he tugs me onto his lap, carefully holding his cast out of the way so I don't bump it. His breath scatters across my face. He smells like mint and sweat and shampoo. "Hey, that's not possible. You're the most beautiful woman I've ever seen. Scar or no scar, that doesn't matter to me. I want you." His deep blue eyes stare into mine, boring a hole into my soul. His mouth parts, and his tongue grazes across my lips. His whisper is a growl. A command. A domination. "I fucking want you."

Desire pours into me, like a waterfall flowing into a river, constantly running, more and more, and never filling up.

Scrambling from his lap, I quickly take off my clothes. His eyes widen, and his cock jumps with every piece of clothing I toss to the side. Looping my fingers in his waistband, he lifts his hips, making easy work of his flimsy workout shorts and boxer briefs.

Every nerve-ending in my body tingles. I want him too. I want him so badly I can't even think straight.

We've only made love once since Daire was taken. And that was just two nights ago. Before then, we were too busy nursing our injuries. Not to mention, my birth control pill should be in full effect now. Two nights ago, we still used a condom. Right now? Hell, no.

I want *all* of Holt Hill.

Everything he has to give.

"Don't let me hurt your arm," I say, mindful of it as I straddle him.

His right hand drags across my breast and down my waist, settling on my hip, pinning me to him with a possessive and protective hold. "I'd let you break the damn thing again just to be inside of you." He bites the side of my neck, sucking away the pain, intent on branding me. "To feel you. I want *all* of you. Everything you have to give."

And once again, he reads my mind. Reads my face. Reads my heart.

Slowly, I lower myself onto him.

And I make love to the famous Holt Hill.

The football player who walked into my store that fateful day in July to buy a pair of purple tennis shoes.

Epilogue

Holt

Ninety.

I'm damn old.

Getting old sucks. My skin is thin now. The kids all joke that we keep the house hotter than the hot tub. I finally had to get hearing aids a couple of years ago. Merit said the neighbors could hear every football game I watched. And I had to install an elevator in the house because I was worried one of us would fall down the stairs. Merit said it made more sense for us to just move into one of the first-floor bedrooms, but I couldn't bring myself to leave *our* room. Too many good things happened there.

Like making love to my wife.

Sleeping with the kids on stormy nights when they got scared.

Having late-night conversations, worried about whoever might be missing curfew and forgot to call.

A lifetime of memories.

And many of them rehashed tonight.

It was a good party. A great birthday, surrounded by family and friends. Not all of our friends, though. Some have already left us. But what do you expect? Like I said, we're old.

Our kids were there. And the grandkids and the great-grand-kids. We even have two great-great grandbabies now—twins. They're two months old.

I'm not sure what I did to earn such blessings in life. But I have them. Blessings in abundance.

I have to say, I sure was right about one thing, though. I have super sperm.

Merit stopped taking her birth control on Daire's second birthday. Exactly nine months to the day, Vera was born. My mom was right; that little girl kept us on our toes, not letting us sleep for one year straight. Merit stopped taking her pills again on Daire's fourth birthday. Exactly nine months to the day, Gracie was born. Unfortunately, God had other plans, and we joined the club that no parent wants to be a part of—the same as Merit's parents and Crutch and Ella.

Gracie was born with a rare and complex heart defect called Ebstein's anomaly. It was discovered within hours of her birth. She survived her first heart surgery but needed another at three weeks. Her little body just couldn't recover after that. It was the best and worst three weeks of my life. I'm not sure how Merit and I survived, but we did. We leaned on each other, fighting for each other. Fighting for our other two children. We refused to let go. And somehow, we made it out the other side, even stronger than before.

After that, Merit wasn't sure if she wanted any more children. I left that decision in her hands, telling her I would support her, whatever she decided. Secretly, I wanted another. I wanted to bring that joy back into our lives. No one is a better mother than Merit, and she had so much love to give.

On Daire's sixth birthday, she stopped taking her birth control pills. Without telling me. Sure enough, she got pregnant immediately. A little over a month later, she surprised me with her sonogram picture on my birthday. And with Adam, everything felt complete. That little nagging feeling telling me we needed *more* was finally satisfied. For some reason, it almost felt like Daire's happiness rested in Adam's hands. Come to find out, it kind of did.

I coached high school football until the time I retired at sixty. But I still had plenty to keep me busy—Merit's stores, the Foundation, the sod farm, our other businesses. All are in the very capable hands of our family now. They have been for years. And everyone and everything is thriving.

Rolling over in bed, I kiss Merit's cheek and wrap my arm around her. The sad truth is, today was a busy day. We'll be tired tomorrow. That happens now. At our age.

"Tell me," I demand.

She pats my hand, giving me a bone-tired, little chuckle. "I love you."

Closing my eyes, I breathe deeply, inhaling her scent, as the pull of sleep tugs at me. I'm back to sleeping how I did before we had kids. There could be a fireworks show in the bedroom, and I still wouldn't wake up. And I don't dream anymore. Or if I do, I don't remember them.

But tonight is different.

Tonight, I dream.

Of Merit. Of my wife. Of the love of my life.

She's standing on the back deck, the one that's connected to the barn at the sod farm. It's the middle of summer, and the setting sun is pouring light over her. She's wearing a short white sundress and yellow and green rubber boots. Her redwood hair is piled high on her head. And when she stretches her back, she gifts me a glorious view of her round and growing belly. The belly growing our first-born son.

And I realize I never was a skeptic. I thought I was, but I was wrong.

I was just the believer waiting for Merit Eliza Browning Hill.

I was the football player who walked into her store that fateful July, looking for a pair of purple tennis shoes.

Bonus Content: Want more Holt and Merit?
Visit to download Merit's Epilogue
https://BookHip.com/MNTXMBW.

Can't get enough of The Hill Family Universe?
That's good. Because more is headed your way.
Our Lower Alabama sod farmer, Daire, has his own
romance story to tell. Did you pick up on that?
But for now, he's just a little boy. And it wouldn't
be right to skip over Ridge, Cullen, and Laura.
They deserve some happy-ever-after. Don't you think?

Gratitude

It happened again.

I wrote words.

I dreamed about them, obsessed over them, and then put them on paper.

I pray from the depths of my soul that everyone loves every page, every paragraph, every sentence, every freakin' syllable.

This world that I've built feels tangible—first with Crutch and Ella, and now, with Holt and Merit. I want the Hill Family Universe to grow and thrive and prosper. And... I'm terrified that it won't. I think it's my life's biggest fear (to date).

So, I need to extend my utmost appreciation to every single person who bought, downloaded, read, loved, rated, and reviewed The Reality Duet. I'm a super small fish in a really big pond, and the words and affirmations of encouragement from those who reached out to me after reading The Reality Duet made all the difference... in my heart and in my psyche.

Thank you. I love you.

I hope I never let you down.

A super big thank you, peppered with hugs and kisses to those who offered to be a part of the Halcie Dawn Permanent ARC Team. I'm blessed beyond measure that you want to support me during this crazy dream-quest of me becoming a writer. The fact that y'all are willing to take time out of your lives and schedules to read my books and help me shape them into the very best versions they can be is nothing short of spectacular. Thank you for your friendship, hard work, eagerness to promote my novels on social media, and all-around awesomeness! Thank you... Heather S.S., Jenney M, Ashley R, Erica A, Ali S, Amber W, Jennifer S, Jessica V, Jessica A,Kandi S., and Sambora C.

Thank you to everyone on social media who has posted about The Reality Duet and/or The Skeptic's Duet. So far, everyone has been so very nice. Let's hope that continues. Haha! Seriously, for indie authors, word of mouth is everything; and I'm so honored and thankful for every post, repost, tag, and mention.

Thank you so very much to Erica Anderson with Get Lit Author Services. You have been so kind and supportive. I'm so glad Instagram brought us together! Your content creation is perfection, and a huge weight (aka burden) was lifted from my heart when we started collaborating. Your work on my graphics, reels, and ARC Team set-up has given me the gift of time and allowed me to better focus on writing and editing. Thank you!

Thank you to my friend, mentor, and super-amazing author, Kelly Elliott. You always take time out of your busy day to answer any question I may have. I'm so grateful that Elaine put me in contact with you. I pray every day for your continued growth, success, and happiness.

Thank you to Stacey Blake with Champagne Book Design for designing the most gorgeous covers ever for The Skeptic's Duet. You are an absolute dream to work with—so responsive and attentive. Even when you knew something probably wouldn't look good, you still changed it just so I could look at it and say... "Umm, yeah, no." I'm so grateful that Elaine put me in contact with you. (Elaine for the "win" again!) Lord willing, I'll be able to keep writing and publishing, and we'll be able to work together five hundred more times!

Thank you to Elaine York with Allusion Publishing for being YOU—my editor and my friend. I'm so blessed that you agreed to accept me as a client. Can you believe we've been through four books together now?! Thank you for your continued work and support on The Reality Duet (aka my obsessive need and compulsion to make post-publication edits). And thank you so much for working, reviewing, editing, and formatting The Skeptic's Duet. The entire Hill Family is floating around in my brain, just begging for their stories to be told, and I can't wait for you to read them. I value your opinion—oh, so much—and I want nothing more than to make you proud of me. I hope I do...

To Dandy and Big, the most amazing parents ever...I love you. Thank you for supporting me, always giving me hope, and pumping me with confidence when I start to doubt my abilities. I am so lucky to have you in my life, and my love for you both knows no bounds. And to Dandy, thank you for being the Ultimate Permanent ARC Team Member! You read, read, read until your eyes are blurry just to help me.

To my Boo Boo Bear... I can't believe you are eighteen, and I refuse to acknowledge any other birthdays that you will have in the future. Don't grow up on me! Just kidding, of course. I am so honored to be your mother, and I am excited to watch you grow in the next steps of your life—graduating high school and attending college. You are so intelligent, kind, loving, funny, and empathetic. You make every day better. You make every day worth living.

To Kuntry, my husband and my best friend, thank you for your unwavering love and support. This past year was unprecedented for us. I never thought I would lose a job and be unemployed at the age of forty-three, completely starting over in my career. Not once during these past fourteen months (as I'm typing this), did you ever make me feel like a burden or anything less than your equal. Every morning, you kissed me goodbye and headed out to your beyond-stressful job, working hard for every single cent you brought home to our family. No matter the day, the hour, or the minute, you love me like the world is ending. You're mine. And I'm never letting you go.

To the Lord my God, my Almighty Savior Jesus Christ... Thank you. Your blessings pour over me. I am loved and worthy by Your Grace.

About the Author

HALCIE DAWN is a happy and blessed wife and mother. She attended the University of Alabama where she graduated with a bachelor's degree in Business Management. A lifelong avid reader, her love affair with books started with the original *The Babysitter's Club* series when she was in the third grade and morphed into a love of all things romantic. After years of thought, she finally placed finger to keyboard and penned her first contemporary romance. *The Reality Duet—Escaping Our Reality* (Book One) and *Finding Our Reality* (Book Two) released in November 2024. When not writing or reading by the swimming pool, she can be found watching true crime documentaries or *Psych* (for the millionth time). Halcie lives in Alabama with her amazingly wonderful, funny, kind, and handsome husband and son. And she lives next door to her parents, whose antics often have her laughing so hard she pees her pants. But without a doubt, the star of the home is the family morkiepoo, Princess Doodle Fluffybutt.

Connect with me:
Website: www.halciedawn.com
Instagram: halciedawnromance
Facebook: www.facebook.com/halciedawn
Facebook Reader Group: www.facebook.com/groups/
halciedawndaydreamers
TikTok: www.tiktok.com/@halciedawnromance